BOUND
for SIN

———— ❖ ————

Tess LeSue

JOVE
New York

A JOVE BOOK
Published by Berkley
An imprint of Penguin Random House LLC
375 Hudson Street, New York, New York 10014

Copyright © 2018 by Tess LeSue
Excerpt from *Bound for Temptation* copyright © 2018 by Tess LeSue
Penguin Random House supports copyright. Copyright fuels creativity, encourages
diverse voices, promotes free speech, and creates a vibrant culture. Thank you for buying
an authorized edition of this book and for complying with copyright laws by not
reproducing, scanning, or distributing any part of it in any form without permission.
You are supporting writers and allowing Penguin Random House to continue to
publish books for every reader.

A JOVE BOOK and BERKLEY are registered trademarks and the B colophon
is a trademark of Penguin Random House LLC.

ISBN: 9780451492593

First Edition: September 2018

Printed in the United States of America
1   3   5   7   9   10   8   6   4   2

Cowboy by Claudio Marinesco/Ninestock
Cover design by Alana Colucci

Praise for *Bound for Eden*

"Western aficionados will welcome a refreshing new voice in the sub-genre."
—RT Book Reviews

"I look forward to the next book by Tess LeSue."
—The Reading Cafe

"Lots of humor, engaging and completely lovable characters, *Bound for Eden* was just what I was looking for in a book escape."
—Tome Tender

"I adored Tess LeSue's *Bound for Eden*! Her voice is brilliant, funny, and immediately draws you into the book. The hero is sexy and protective, the heroine is fierce and independent, and I couldn't stop turning pages."
—Jessica Clare, *New York Times* bestselling author

"Tess LeSue has written a great Western romance with all the sass, fun, and riveting action a reader could want. This novel is a rollicking ride with more twists and turns than a bronco with a burr under his saddle . . . You can't finish *Bound for Eden* without a smile on your face."
—May McGoldrick, *USA Today* bestselling author

"I was blown away by the sparkling brilliance of [Tess's] writing. She has a real gift for historical atmosphere, compelling characters, sexual tension and witty dialogue."
—Anna Campbell

"[Tess's] writing is lively and taut and generates emotion. Her characters spring to life and her stories move at a fast pace."
—Anne Gracie

"An accomplished mix of comedy and suspense, I found myself cheering with the heroine as she boldly navigates the journey to Oregon and eventually, her freedom. I absolutely loved it."
—Victoria Purman

For Isla Susana,

my glorious daughter.

ACKNOWLEDGMENTS

Life is busy and challenging and difficult and tiring and taxing—but it's also exhilarating and exciting and inspiring and filled with love (both the sparkly kind and the less glamorous but more muscular kind). I'd like to thank everyone who sparkles and/or flexes their muscles to hold me up.

The people who are at the center of it all: my kids (who are the *best*); my parents (who would think I was ace whether I was a writer or a window washer); my brother (who was my first audience); my cat Lucy (who would be an Insta star if she wasn't so sensible); my BFFs and fellow writers Lynn (the ultimate warrior cheerleader), Chelsea (my fellow Poseur), and Dan (who looks good sculpted in cheese and who has the best wife ever: love you too, Clare). And then there's Jonny: thanks for everything except drawing on me with indelible ink, hiding my coffee, tricking my kids into thinking I'm older than I am, and telling people I don't know who Thor is (for the record: I know who Thor is).

Thanks to my extra family: Dean and Dot, Anna and Sam and the girls, and to Nick (who I wished lived closer because he loves food as much as I do).

Thanks to Victoria Purman, Bronwyn Stuart, Trish Morey, Anne Oliver, Elizabeth Rolls, Anne Gracie, and Anna Campbell, and to the sensational writers of Romance Writers of Australia and the South Australian Romance Authors. And thank you to Sarah Tooth and to Writers SA. I have been embraced, supported, encouraged, cheered on and inspired by y'all.

Thank you to Flinders University—this book was written while I was on study leave and I thank them for the opportunity and support. Thanks also to Patrick Allington for his help last year (freeing up a little bit of my time made *all* the difference—thank you) and to my colleagues up on the hill.

And now to the people who make my dreams come true: thank you to Clare Forster and Benjamin Stevenson at Curtis Brown Australia, and to Kristine Swartz and the whole team at Berkley—thank you especially for embracing such a looooooong book.

Last but not least, the most important people: the readers. To each and every person who picks up a book and steps through into another world and embraces another way of being. You're my heroes.

A respectable widow of means seeks resourceful frontiersman for the purpose of matrimony. The lady seeks passage west to land owned in Mokelumne Hill, California. The advertiser presumes her manner and appearance will recommend her and expects applications from responsible parties only. Interviews are scheduled for the 6th of next month, beginning at nine o'clock in the morning, in the front parlor of the Grand Hotel. Please be prompt.

Independence, Missouri, 1849

NOW *THAT* WAS how a man should look. Suffocating in the stuffy hotel parlor, Georgiana Bee Blunt looked longingly out of the window, where she could see a backwoodsman tethering his animal to the hitching rail outside Cavil's Mercantile. The fellow was a *brute*. He had a wild head of bristling black hair and a stiff beard, and his arms were the size of smokehouse hams. And if that wasn't enough to make him look like a character from one of her dime novels, he was also clad head to toe in buckskin. And the *size* of him! My, but he looked like he could rip an oak from the earth bare-handed. That was exactly the kind of man she needed, and exactly the kind of man she had advertised for.

It was also exactly the kind of man who had *not* answered her advertisement. Georgiana sighed and looked over at the candidate sitting opposite her. He was a dapper, charming, handsome man, with very white teeth and very shiny hair. His fingernails were perfect ovals. And his shoes . . . They were spit polished until they gleamed. How did he do it? She couldn't set foot outside without the bottom inch of her dress getting covered in dust. Had he shined them in the foyer before he'd come in for his interview?

She couldn't imagine the brute outside doing that, she thought, stealing another glance. He was reaching over to unbuckle his saddlebags, and the buckskin stretched tight over the broadest back Georgiana had ever seen. She sighed again. It was probably too much to hope that he'd come to answer her advertisement.

"Mrs. Smith?"

It took Georgiana a moment to remember that *she* was Mrs. Smith. She'd adopted the name to hide from that horrid Hec Boehm and his henchmen, but she kept forgetting to answer to it.

"Yes?" She gave the man her full attention and tried her best to look as she imagined a Mrs. Smith should.

"As you can see, Mrs. Smith, I have a pedigree that would please even the most discerning mother." Mr. Dugard beamed at her with his white teeth.

Oh no. He wouldn't do at all.

"Thank you so much for your time, Mr. Dugard." Georgiana tried to smile back. "But as you can see, I still have so many people to interview, and the hour is growing late . . . " She stood and, because he was a gentleman, he stood too.

"If I could ask you to leave your details, I'll be in touch as soon as my decision is made," she assured him.

"As luck would have it, I'm staying right here in the hotel," he said.

Of course he was. Most of them were. She resolved not to use the dining room tonight; she had no intention of talking to any of them again, let alone marrying one of them. They were all so sociable and polite and courteous and *civilized*. It was enough to make a woman scream. Her ad had clearly specified *frontiersman*. She didn't want a well-bred man, or a good-looking man, or a charming man, or a clever man. She'd had quite enough of that with her first husband (God rest his sordid soul). All she was looking for was a simple, hardworking and reliable *brute*. Like the one outside.

The one who was *not* walking toward the hotel to answer her ad. She watched glumly as he headed in the exact opposite direction. He'd been joined by another rough-looking man and was heading for the saloon.

Perhaps she should have scheduled her interviews for the saloon, she thought with a sigh. The men there were probably far more likely candidates than the ones she was meeting here.

"May I say, Mrs. Smith," Mr. Dugard was saying in his low, suave voice, "I hadn't expected to find you so young, or so beautiful."

She flinched. God save her from men with silver tongues. She wouldn't be in this situation if it hadn't been for Leonard and his pretty words. She had no interest in listening to any more pretty words in her lifetime.

Mr. Dugard took her gloved hand and raised it to his lips. His dark eyes were moist with admiration. It took all of Georgiana's willpower not to yank her hand away. She suffered through the press of his lips on the back of her glove.

There was a disapproving cough from the doorway. The hotelier, Mrs. Bulfinch, was glowering at them. "I hate to break up your tête-à-tête," she said in her clanging voice, "but there are still *men* in my foyer." She said it like they were an infestation of mice. "You promised me, Mrs. Smith, that this affair would be done by midafternoon. It's now almost five." She gave a sniff and drew herself up to her full height of four foot nothing. "I've dismissed them all and told them to come back tomorrow. This is a respectable hotel, and I shan't have men clogging up my foyer at all hours."

Oh, thank heavens for ghastly old Mrs. Bulfinch! Now Georgiana wouldn't have to interview another pale, clean, nice man! At least not until tomorrow . . .

And maybe before then she could hunt the brute down and she wouldn't need to face tomorrow at all, she thought hopefully. She stole a glance at the saloon. It was a shame ladies weren't allowed in there, or she would have headed straight across the road and through the doors.

"May I escort you into supper?" Mr. Dugard asked hopefully.

Lord, no!

"I'm sorry," Georgiana said, skipping out of his reach before he could take her arm, "but I really must collect the children." If she could get through the knot of hopefuls on the porch, that was. They were milling about, just waiting for a chance to speak to her; each and every one of them was holding his hat politely in his plump, clean hand and giving her an earnest smile. They were a horrific sight.

She'd never moved so fast in her life. She grabbed her bonnet and purse, and was out the front door and off the porch before anyone could so much as make a move in her direction.

She took a deep, grateful breath of dusty air as she plunged down the street. She'd been cooped up in that parlor all day, with its smell of desiccated rose petals and burned coffee. Mrs. Bulfinch didn't hold with open windows: too much dust. After today, Georgiana was sure she would forever associate the smell of mummified roses with disappointment.

She'd met at least two dozen men today, and not a single one of them was suitable. They'd be eaten alive out west! Just imagine if they met rogues and gunslingers like Kid Cupid or the Plague of the West! They'd probably faint dead away. No, she needed someone who could get her safely to her son . . .

The thought of Leo took any trace of sunshine out of the day. Her son, her eldest . . . all alone out there with those horrible men . . .

Don't think about it. You can't afford to think about it. You have to keep moving.

He was safe so long as they needed her signature on that deed. And she was on her way. Soon, she thought desperately, soon I'll be there. She felt the two thousand miles between them like a searing pain. Goddamn Leonard for taking the boy with him. And double damn him for dying and leaving her baby stranded on the other side of the country, twelve years old and all alone, held hostage . . .

Don't. Don't think about it.

Georgiana was sweating but felt icy cold, even though she caught the full flood of afternoon sun as she headed to Mrs. Tilly's to get the other children. Leo was tough, she reminded herself. Of all the children, he was the most resilient. He'd had to be; he'd been the man of the house since he was knee-high. His father would swan out of their lives for years at a time, telling Leo to look after his mother, and it was something the boy had taken to heart. He wasn't one to cry or feel sorry for himself. She used to watch the way he kept his head high and his expression brave every time his father left, and the way he'd comforted her and the younger children, and her heart would break for him. Her eyes welled with tears. Her poor boy.

It was just one more disaster in Leonard's long line of disasters, and he wasn't even here for her to rage at. This was precisely why she would be choosing her next husband with her head rather than with her heart. Her next husband would protect her children and not abandon them (or kidnap them and take them two thousand miles away from her); he would be frugal and sensible and not sell the rug out from under her; he would be predictable and reliable and not flit from place to place with no thought of building a home for his family. If she had to give up her hopes of marrying a man she was attracted to, she would . . . After all, what real use was attraction? And she was certainly happy to give up any idea of a love match. Love had caused her nothing but pain.

"DID YOU FIND your prince then?" Mrs. Tilly asked her hopefully when Georgiana stepped through the front door of the tearooms. "I saw that nice Mr. Dugard heading over to the hotel. He's a handsome-looking man."

"Yes, he is." Georgiana pulled a face as she let Mrs. Tilly usher her to a table by the window and pour them cups of tea. The older woman also put out a plate of strawberry tarts and immediately popped one in her mouth.

"And he's a capable man," she said as she brushed crumbs from her lip. "He used to run a furniture store in St. Louis."

"He might be capable enough for St. Louis, Mrs. Tilly," Georgiana sighed, "but he didn't look anywhere near capable enough for the *wilds*. I can't imagine him fording a river or shoeing a horse."

Georgiana flushed as Mrs. Tilly looked pointedly at Georgiana's silk skirts and heeled slippers.

"It's a wonder you want to go at all, if it's so fearsome," Mrs. Tilly clucked as she sipped her tea. "You'd be better off keeping the little 'uns here. We have a school and lots of nice men."

Ugh. *Nice* wasn't what she was looking for.

"I'm committed to going to California, Mrs. Tilly," Georgiana said firmly. "That's where our land is. Leonard built us a house in the lovely little town of Mokelumne Hill." Or so he said. "It has rocking chairs on the porch and enough bedrooms for the children to have one each." She'd believe it when she saw it. But that's certainly what he'd written in his letters. "And my son is there." Oh no, there went the tears again. Georgiana fumbled for her handkerchief. She hated crying in front of people, but these days the tears just erupted. She could be perfectly serene and then, bang, she'd be crying. She had to stop thinking about Leo. She couldn't afford to be crying all the time; there'd be time for crying once he was safe.

"Oh, you darling love." Mrs. Tilly was welling up in sympathy. "How insensitive of me! I'm sure your people are looking after the lad, but I know how a mother feels."

Georgiana just wanted the whole moment to end. She didn't want comfort or fuss—it didn't do any good. She just wanted to get on with the whole ordeal: get the husband, pack the wagon, and get on the trail. The sooner she got on the trail, the sooner she could reach her son. Crying solved nothing at all.

"How were the children today?" she asked, desperately trying to change the subject as she blotted her eyes.

"Energetic." Mrs. Tilly didn't quite meet Georgiana's gaze.

Georgiana stood. "I should get them out of your way. It's getting late."

"Oh no!" Mrs. Tilly looked a touch panicked. "Finish your tea first. And have one of the tarts; the children helped make them. They're with Becky; they're fine, no need to worry."

"I really should feed them."

"They had some tarts less than an hour ago." When Georgiana didn't sit, Mrs. Tilly got to her feet too. She was looking a trifle anxious, Georgiana thought. Her stomach sank. Oh dear. What had the children done *now*?

There was a clanging sound from the back of the house. Georgiana saw Mrs. Tilly flinch.

"Now, don't be too mad at them!" Mrs. Tilly cautioned. There was the sound of something breaking, and Georgiana turned on her heel and made for the kitchen. "They're high-spirited boys!"

The devils looked up with wide-eyed innocence as she threw open the door to the kitchen. Their faces were white with flour. Even her daughter, Susannah, the sensible one, was covered in powder from head to foot.

"Mama!" two-year-old Wilby shouted, holding out his pudgy hand. Pasty white sludge oozed between his fingers. "Glue!"

"Oh my."

The white sludge was everywhere: dripping from the wall sconces, blobbed on the bench tops, splattered across the windows.

"Well," she said, aiming for calmness, "aren't you all very clever, discovering the recipe for glue."

"Glue!" Wilby shouted again, before shoving his hand in his mouth.

"William Bee! Don't eat that!" Georgiana pulled his hand from his mouth and got glue and slobber all over her glove. She eyed it distastefully. Mothering really was a messy business. This was only her second month without a nanny, and she had to admit, she was struggling.

"He can eat it," one of the twins (Phineas?) said impatiently. "It's just flour and water."

Georgiana cleared her throat.

"It's really Becky's fault," Mrs. Tilly said quickly in defense of the children.

"My fault!" The girl was outraged. She popped up from in front of the stove, which she'd clearly been scrubbing vigorously. She was a mix of soot and glue. "How is this *my fault*?"

"I told you to watch them," Mrs. Tilly scolded. "You know what they're like."

Georgiana blanched. If she'd been a better mother, this never would have happened. *You know what they're like.* Wild. And running wilder every day. They certainly hadn't been like this when Mrs. Wyndham, the nanny, was still around.

Georgiana bit her lip. What would Mrs. Wyndham do in this situation?

"How was I to know they'd make *glue* while my back was turned?" Becky complained.

This never would have *happened* if Mrs. Wyndham had been here, that was the whole problem.

"Well, your back shouldn't have been turned. Don't think I

don't know where you were. I saw Fancy Pat's horse tethered up outside. And I don't know how many times I have to tell you that you're throwing good after bad, consorting with the likes of him. Your poor parents must be rolling over in their graves."

"His name's *Pierre*," Becky said, sounding more outraged by the minute. "It's *French*."

"Now, now," Georgiana interrupted, still striving for calmness as she surreptitiously looked around for something to wipe her slobbery glove on. "It's hardly Becky's fault." She turned a stern look on her children. Only Susannah had the good grace to look shamefaced.

"They promised me they'd clean it up before you came in, Mrs. Smith," Mrs. Tilly said hurriedly. "And really, there's no harm done."

"See," the other twin said. (Was it Philip? Surely, a good mother would be able to tell them apart?) "She doesn't mind."

Georgiana shot him a black look. "My dear Mrs. Tilly . . . and Becky . . . " It was proving difficult to keep her voice even. "The children and I would like to take you to supper to make this up to you. Please. If you'd like to go and freshen up . . . " She cleared her throat dubiously as she took in Becky's filthy face. "The children and I will get your kitchen in order. And then we'll all go out for a nice meal." Georgiana peeled off her slobbery glove.

"Oh no!" Mrs. Tilly sounded scandalized. "I can't let a lady like you scrub my kitchen."

"Oh, don't worry," Georgiana said grimly, "*I* won't be the one doing the scrubbing."

"You don't need to. Becky can—"

"Becky can get scrubbed up for tea in no time," Becky said quickly, cutting Mrs. Tilly off mid-sentence. She wriggled out of her apron and hung it on the back of the kitchen door on her way out.

"Please, Mrs. Tilly." Georgiana tried to smile at her. "It would be our pleasure."

Mrs. Tilly looked dubious but nodded and retreated. She paused at the door. "They were perfect angels for most of the day," she said weakly.

"Were you?" Georgiana asked once the door swung closed.

"We're perfect angels *now*," Phin said, rolling his eyes. "We're only *not* angels if you don't like glue."

"Indeed." Georgiana felt ill as she looked at the paste smeared in lumps all over the kitchen. "How does one clean glue?"

"Vinegar," came a muffled voice from behind the kitchen door.

"Thank you, Mrs. Tilly! We'll see you in an hour for supper!"

There was a pause, and then they heard footsteps retreating down the hall.

"We could let Wilby lick it all up," Philip suggested.

To Georgiana's dismay, Wilby didn't look entirely unhappy at the prospect.

"Listen," she said, thinking fast, "if you can get this place clean by the time they come downstairs for supper, I'll buy you rock candy from Cavil's Mercantile in the morning."

"How much rock candy?"

"More than you deserve. And if you *don't* get it clean, I'll tell Mrs. Bulfinch that you'll help her wash her unmentionables tomorrow. It's laundry day at the hotel."

"You wouldn't!"

Of course she wouldn't. And of course Mrs. Bulfinch wouldn't either. But the twins didn't need to know that. "Just test me."

Maybe parenting wasn't so hard. She watched as they hurried to grabs mops and buckets. The children were the only good things Leonard had ever done in his life, she thought fondly, as she watched the curly dark heads bent over the concoction of vinegar and water they were brewing in the sink. They were working the water pump madly. With any luck, they could clean up the mess without destroying Mrs. Tilly's kitchen. Georgiana tugged off her other glove and set to work helping them. She didn't have much experience scrubbing kitchens or . . . well, anything. But now that her trust fund was exhausted and they had no more money for servants, she guessed she'd just have to learn.

❧ 2 ❧

"**D**ID YOU GET a room?" Matt asked when Deathrider joined him out the front of Cavil's Mercantile.

Deathrider looked like his name personified. His skin was waxy, and his eyes had the unfocused stare of someone who was using up all his energy just staying upright. He still hadn't recovered from the gunshot wound he'd sustained back in Kearney. "No beds," he grunted.

"What do you mean, no beds?"

"The man at the saloon said there are no beds."

Matt felt like punching something. This was because Deathrider was an Indian. He knew it. This last month had been the most hellish month of his life. He'd been holding on to the idea that things would get easier once they got to Independence, but so far that just wasn't the case.

Matt unbuckled his saddlebags. His old gray donkey, Fernando, gave a cranky *hee-haw*. Matt pulled his ears absently and then hefted the saddlebags over his shoulder. He was bone-tired from the trail, and the last thing he needed was trouble finding a bed. "C'mon," he growled.

"Sam!" he bellowed as he pushed into the dark saloon. "What's this I hear about you not having a bed for me?"

"Well, look who it is," the bartender said. He spat tobacco juice at a spittoon so full it made a wet sloshing sound as the stream hit. "You're late. You said you'd be here by the end of March."

Matt always stayed at the Lucky Star when he was in town. Mostly because it was the only place that didn't run whores. Matt didn't like whores. They made him uncomfortable. And he didn't want to stay in a bunkhouse; he wanted his own room, away from other people. Matt didn't care much for people.

"I had a room for you at the end of March," Sam told him.

"We got held up."

Matt saw the way Sam's eyes slid over Deathrider.

"We?" There was another slosh as Sam spat his juice.

"This is my . . . brother." Matt was still getting used to the lie. "He said you don't have room for us."

Sam shrugged. "I don't. I ain't in the business of keeping rooms empty when there's money to be made. I don't know if you've heard, but there's a gold rush on."

Matt grunted. He'd more than heard; he'd had a busy few months at the end of last year finding the fools lost on the Siskiyou Trail from Oregon down to California.

"They're piled four deep up there," Sam told him, jerking his head at his rooms upstairs. "And you'll find it's the same everywhere. Town's bursting at the seams. On the upside, you should do a roaring trade putting together your train this year."

This would be the fifth year in a row Matt was taking a train on the trail. As always, he was dreading it. He didn't know why he did it to himself, except he was good at it and he couldn't think of much else he would rather be doing. It paid well, but Matt didn't really need or want the money. He'd sort of just fallen into it when his brother Luke had given it up; it was either stay home and be a third wheel in the house with his brother and his new wife, or find something else to do. He'd tried running cattle with his brother Tom for a while, but he found he hated cows even more than he hated people, if such a thing was possible. At least with the wagon trains he got to ride out by himself. The people tended to stay in a neat clump and not have to be herded the way cows did. But they complained a lot more than cows did.

"Are you telling me there ain't a single bed in town?" Matt felt more than ever like punching something. He didn't fancy another night sleeping out rough.

"'Fraid so. I can sell you a drink though."

"I bet you could," Matt said sourly. But there wasn't much daylight left, and they needed to find a room.

"The Grand Hotel probably still has space," Sam said grudgingly. "That woman charges a fortune, and people get mighty pinchy about their pennies when they're heading west.

It's an expensive business as it is, without paying through the nose for a bed."

Matt grunted his thanks, and they headed back out into the street. He didn't want to spend a fortune on a goddamn room. But he also didn't want to sleep another night on the ground. He'd been looking forward to cleaning up and enjoying a decent mattress. Damn it. He could wring Sam's neck.

You're just tired. It's what he told the emigrants on the trail when they got low, and there were many points on the trail when people got low. *It's nothing a decent feed and a good night's sleep won't improve.* It was good advice, advice Matt's father used to give them when they were boys. Matt had been pretty young when his father had died, but he'd never forgotten those words. It was true. When life got to you, it was always best to put your worries aside until you'd eaten and slept. Problems had a way of looking bigger when you were tired and hungry. Especially when you had to pay a goddamn ransom for somewhere to rest.

"Looks like we're headed for the Grand Hotel," he grunted. It was a mark of how low Deathrider was feeling himself that he didn't protest.

"You wait here," he told Deathrider shortly, pointing at their animals, which were still tethered across the street from the hotel. "Let me deal with this. You give people the terrors."

Deathrider didn't protest. It was true.

It had been a hell of a month. Matt rubbed his face as he headed for the fancy hotel. A hell of a year so far. At some point, Deathrider's notoriety had snowballed, and it had become a sport to hunt him. They'd run into a mess of trouble back in Fort Kearny, and Deathrider had taken a bullet. They'd laid low until he was well enough to travel again, and by then word was getting around that Deathrider, aka the Plague of the West, had been killed. Matt had bullied his friend into using the gossip to his advantage; they'd dressed him as a white man and passed him off as Matt's brother Tom. Everywhere they stopped, Matt had spread the gossip about the Plague of the West's demise. He only hoped the story would get picked up by one of those wretched dime novelists. A book about Deathrider's death would set them both free.

* * *

THE GRAND HOTEL was a three-story brick slab with pretensions of grandeur. There were white columns all along the length of the porch and wicker furniture for people to take their ease. A couple of scrappy hickory trees grew out the front, and there were dusty-looking rosebushes by the stairs. Lanterns were burning along the brick wall of the porch, and light fell through the windows in warm pools. But for all its grand pretensions, the rawness of the town clung to the hotel too; it looked hastily built, and the stairs were slightly askew. They creaked under Matt's boots as he climbed them. The place was busy. Matt hadn't seen so many freshly scrubbed and suited men outside of a church. They were sprawled in the wicker furniture and clumped along the railing, talking in low voices. They all looked as though they were waiting for something. Or someone.

Matt hoped it wasn't him.

"Best wipe your boots." The advice came from a scrawny-looking fellow who was sitting in the rocker closest to the door. He had an elaborate waxed mustache, which barely seemed to move when he spoke. It sat as stiff as a pencil. He peered at Matt over a pair of pince-nez. "Mrs. Bulfinch is rather particular about her floors. She *hates* dust."

"She's living in the wrong place, then." Matt wasn't much for conversation at the best of times, and now certainly wasn't the best of times. He wiped his boots on the mat. It didn't seem to do much good. The dirt was baked on.

"By the look of you, I'd hazard a guess you're fresh in from the frontier!"

Matt grunted.

"My girls and I are headed west ourselves."

"That so?" Matt ducked through the front door before the man could continue. The fellow didn't seem daunted; in fact, he followed Matt inside.

Into what could only be described as a man's worst nightmare. Matt had never seen anything like it. The place was too pink to be believed. The wallpaper was flocked pink on pink, the rugs were pink, and the lampshades were frosted pink glass. All of it a dusty, grayish pink that made Matt think of faded roses. Even the air smelled pink.

He didn't like it.

There was a small brass bell on a doily-shrouded desk and a prissily lettered sign: "Please ring for attention." He rang it, trying to breathe through his mouth so he wouldn't have to take in the smell. It was like a graveyard for roses.

"Where are you from, Mr. . . . ?"

Matt rang the bell harder.

"My name is Pierre LeFoy," the man said brightly, holding out his hand for Matt to shake. Matt didn't shake it. He just kept ringing the bell. The sign was clearly inaccurate—no attention was forthcoming. Unless you counted the attention he was getting from the skinny little man with the French name.

When Matt didn't shake his hand, LeFoy awkwardly let it drop. "Are you here to answer Mrs. Smith's advertisement?"

"No," Matt said shortly. He gave up on the bell and instead bellowed up the stairs, "Is anyone in?"

"Me neither. But I think we may be the only ones. It's been quite a parade today."

"Listen," Matt sighed, "I don't mean to be rude, Mr. . . . LeFoy, was it?"

The man nodded.

"My brother and I have been in the saddle for eleven days straight. I haven't had a hot meal in almost a week, and I haven't slept in a bed in God knows how long. I ain't had a good day, and I ain't in a good temper. So I'm not the best person to be talking to right now."

Mr. LeFoy looked taken aback. But only for a moment. Then he took the bell from Matt's hand and put it back on the desk. "Our landlady is hard of hearing. You'd need to be clanging that right next to her ear for her to hear it. Why don't you have a seat and I'll see if I can find her for you; she's probably in the kitchen preparing for the evening meal. Which is served promptly at seven. I recommend avoiding it at all costs, as she is a terrible cook." LeFoy gave him a sympathetic smile. "If you fancy a hot meal, I can recommend Gillette's cookhouse. I'll be taking my girls there for supper in about half an hour and would be more than happy to show you the way."

"Uh . . . thanks." Matt watched as the dapper little man disappeared through a door under the stairs.

He braced his arms on the desk and closed his eyes. He wanted this day to be over.

"Well, why didn't he ring the bell?" A strident female voice broke the silence.

LeFoy was back, trailing a woman no bigger than a gnat. She wore a lacy white cap and a faded pink dress. A bunch of giant fabric roses was pinned to her narrow chest. She didn't look big enough to produce a voice that size, but she fairly crackled with energy.

"Why didn't you ring the bell?" she snapped at Matt, and then she continued without giving him room to draw breath, let alone reply. "We're full except for the Palatial Suite."

"The Palatial Suite?"

"I'm afraid the widow and her little 'uns have taken the Imperial, which is our blue-ribbon suite on the third floor. But the Palatial is the next best we have, and it's directly opposite." She shot LeFoy a withering look. "Ideally, it's suited for a family party. But it's all I have."

LeFoy's attention seemed to be riveted by a glass bowl full of dried rose petals. He was running his fingers through them. At least he was until the old woman gave his knuckles a rap. "That's not for touching. You'll get your finger oils in there and mess it up." She turned her snapping gray eyes back to Matt. "This one and his three hellions are crammed into a Gold Standard room." She sniffed. "I've had to levy an extra charge, as the rooms are clearly designed for two people and not an entire tribe."

"They're small girls," LeFoy told Matt, giving his sore knuckles a surreptitious suck.

"I used to be a schoolmistress, Mr. LeFoy, and I know very well how much space three girls occupy. And let me just say, *your* girls occupy more space than most." She shook her head disapprovingly. "They're circus performers," she told Matt.

"*Entertainers*, Mrs. Bulfinch," LeFoy corrected, sounding a touch wounded.

"They have a traveling show." She made it sound like a traveling brothel.

"My girls sing," LeFoy explained to Matt.

Matt didn't care a fig if they sang or danced naked down the main street of Independence; he just wanted a room.

"How much is it, and how much to stable the animals?"

Mrs. Bulfinch named a ridiculous sum, made even more ridiculous by the fact that she doubled it when she found out his brother would be joining him, but Matt was too tired to argue. He slapped his money down and signed the register.

"Supper costs extra."

Matt glanced at LeFoy, who shook his head and pulled faces behind her back.

"Thanks, but I think I'll try my luck at a cookhouse."

"I don't hold with drunkenness in my establishment," Mrs. Bulfinch snapped, closing the register so sharply it almost caught Matt's fingers. "So if it's a saloon you'll be visiting, you'd best plan to spend the night there, rather than bringing your degeneracy back here with you. And," she said ominously, leaning forward and dropping her voice to a fierce whisper, "I hope you know it goes without saying: no women."

"He's not going to a saloon; he and his brother are coming to the cookhouse with me and the girls, Mrs. Bulfinch," LeFoy jumped in to defend him.

"Friends, are you? I should have known. You look like the type to hang around with circus folk."

"We're not a circus!" LeFoy couldn't keep the frustration out of his voice.

"Come now and I'll show you to your room. I don't have time to stand about yapping or supper will burn. You can stable your animals after I show you upstairs. Or I can have my stable hand do it, for a fee."

"We'll do it ourselves," he said shortly.

"Is that mutt yours?" Mrs. Bulfinch peered out the window, to where Dog was pacing around the horses.

"My brother's."

"You're to tie him up in the stable, you hear? I won't have him bothering my guests."

Matt was beginning to wonder if the bed was worth it. Maybe it would have been easier to sleep rough.

"Is your brother coming in?" she snapped. "I'll be wanting to show you to your room now. I have supper on; I can't be standing here waiting for you to sort your animals."

If Matt felt out of place in the pink hotel, Deathrider sure looked it. He came in like a dusty shadow, silent, seething with exhaustion.

"You'll take your hat off indoors," Mrs. Bulfinch ordered him. Deathrider looked her up and down.

"Just do it," Matt sighed.

He did, and his long black hair tumbled down his back. If possible, Mrs. Bulfinch looked even more disapproving.

"You'll get that cut if you're wanting to stay here."

Deathrider went to leave. Matt blocked his way. "Don't be an ass," he said under his breath. Then he turned to the hotelier. "We've been traveling for near on two weeks without rest. If we could just get a feed and a night's sleep, we'll make sure we clean ourselves up proper tomorrow."

Mrs. Bulfinch sniffed, but she liked their money too much to cause more fuss. Matt bet she'd kick up again tomorrow though, if they still looked like trail hounds then.

"This way," Mrs. Bulfinch said sharply, taking a lamp and heading for the stairs, which were, of course, carpeted in pink.

"The girls and I will wait on the porch for you," LeFoy called after them.

"Don't go hollering up my stairs," Mrs. Bulfinch hollered down at him. "This is a respectable establishment."

"I don't suppose you provide a bath?" Matt asked tiredly as they passed first one landing, then another.

"Not for the likes of you. There's a washbasin in your room. And there's a bathhouse in town you can make use of."

Matt sighed. He wasn't up to a bathhouse tonight. It was no skin off his nose if he dirtied up Mrs. Bulfinch's sheets; he wasn't the one who'd have to wash them.

"This is your room," Mrs. Bulfinch said when they reached the top floor. "There's only the two suites up here, yours and the Imperial." She fixed them with a gimlet stare. "Mrs. Smith is a lady of quality, you mind. From New York. You watch your manners, and don't bother her or her children. If I hear you've been improper in any way, I shall be sending for the sheriff!"

"We ain't planning on bothering anyone," Matt told her, struggling to keep his temper. "We're just looking for a bed."

"Well, the Palatial has the biggest bed in the house," she announced as she unlocked the door and threw it open. "There's two rooms: this one and the one through there. This one has the double bed, and the other has two singles. As I said, it's meant for a family."

It was a nice clean room, which, thankfully, wasn't pink. It had pale blue wallpaper and a big brass bed next to the fireplace.

"You have that," he told Deathrider. He poked his head into the second room. It was smaller but perfectly serviceable, with matching single brass beds. Matt could sleep in here. It was better than he was used to.

When he turned back around, he found Deathrider had fixed Mrs. Bulfinch with his unblinking pale stare. She might be an old dragon, but even she wasn't immune to the sense of danger he emanated. Deathrider held out his hand, and she gave him the key with obvious reluctance.

The minute the door closed behind her, Deathrider sat down heavily on the bed.

Matt eyed his own bed longingly through the open door. But as nice as it would be to lie straight down and sleep, his stomach was rumbling, and he knew if he didn't eat now, he'd wake up in the middle of the night, ravenous, and there wouldn't be anything to eat but the hardtack in his saddlebags, and he was sick to death of hardtack.

"You up for going out for food?"

Deathrider answered by unbuttoning his shirt. Matt winced. The flesh above and below the bandage was swollen and red.

"I'll ask Doc Barry to come see to you," Matt said. "I'll bring you some food too. Just rest up. I'll see to your animals."

Deathrider nodded and collapsed back on the bed.

Matt didn't envy him the wound, but he did envy him the rest. He dragged himself to the washbasin. The reflection in the shaving mirror was daunting. His beard and hair were a wiry, matted mess; the grime from the plains had worked its way deep into the creases beside his eyes; and his nose and lips were flaking from the sunburn he'd got a few days ago. He gave the neatly folded linen washcloth and the porcelain washbowl a doubtful look. He couldn't imagine being able to shift even one tenth of the grime with those.

Why even bother?

He jammed his hat over his filthy hair and headed for the door. He'd face it tomorrow. After all, who did he have to impress?

Nobody, that was who.

❧ 3 ❧

IT WAS *HIM*! The brute! The brute was here, in the cook-house! Oh my, and here she was, looking a fright! Georgiana tugged at the bodice of her dress, which had great oily stains from the glue. She cursed herself for not going back to the hotel to change. She'd meant to, but halfway there, Wilby had thrown a colossal tantrum, and Susannah had been dragging her feet, and they'd all been hungry and tired, and the thought of going back to the hotel and out again was too much. There'd also been the deterrent of the men she'd interviewed today, most of whom were back at the hotel, hanging around, just waiting to catch her alone. The last thing she felt like was running that gauntlet. Who could have imagined there were so many men looking to be husbands? Especially to a woman with so many children.

They thought she had money, obviously. She should never have put "widow of means" in the advertisement. It made her sound wealthier than she was. These days she had enough money to get them to California and set up a store, and that was about it. What she'd meant by "widow of means" was that she wasn't a burden. She had land. She had money to get them west. She had a plan for the future. But it had been clear from their careful questions today that they'd all read it differently. Especially because she'd made the mistake of saying the land was in Mokelumne Hill. *And how big is your claim? Was your husband mining it?* They all had the shine of gold fever in their eyes. She'd been sure to tell them that there was no claim and there was no gold; there was just the house in the town and her hopes of setting up a mercantile business. She didn't have gold—not anymore. She had to sign *that* land over to Hec

Boehm, or who knew what would happen to her son. But she couldn't tell anyone about that.

At the thought of facing the men at the hotel, she'd given up on any idea of dressing for dinner and gone into the first cookhouse they passed. The place was a revelation after Mrs. Bulfinch's stuffy dining room. Georgiana loved it. It was like something out of a novel. It was a big, rough-hewn hall with raw pine tables and benches, pewter dishes, tin mugs and sawdust on the floor. There was only one thing on the menu, which was beef and beans. And there was only one thing to drink, which was coffee. It was exactly how she'd imagined the frontier to be. Much more so than Mrs. Bulfinch's airless Grand Hotel, which was a bit like a maiden aunt's house.

The children loved it too, and Becky seemed happy enough. It was only Mrs. Tilly who was dubious. But the food was actually very good and seemed to pacify her. And the patrons were mostly emigrant families, so it wasn't too rough. Although it was very loud.

Too loud for the brute by the look of it. For a minute, Georgiana thought he would bolt, and her heart plummeted. But then the tide of people behind him seemed to sweep him along to the serving hatch, and he surrendered and went with the flow. He really did look like a character from a dime novel come to life, Georgiana thought admiringly as she watched him take off his hat and have a good look around the room. He was even bigger and rougher than he'd looked from a distance. He was *precisely* what she'd been picturing when she'd come up with the whole mail-order husband idea. He didn't look like anything—or anyone—would intimidate him.

"Oh!" A breathless noise from Becky dragged Georgiana's attention back to the table. The children had already bolted from their food and run off to play. Their toys were strewn everywhere, discarded where they'd fallen. But that wasn't what Becky was making noises about.

"It's *him*," she sighed. Georgiana followed her gaze and felt a stab of jealousy. Becky was looking straight at the brute.

"Him who?" Mrs. Tilly craned her neck. And then her expression turned very cranky indeed. "Oh, for heaven's sake! Did you tell him we'd be here?"

Becky gave her a disdainful look. "And how could I do a

thing like that when I didn't even know we'd be coming here?" Before Mrs. Tilly could stop her, she was on her feet and skipping through the crowds. To Georgiana's brute!

"I'm afraid I'll rue the day I ever took her in," Mrs. Tilly despaired.

Georgiana was already ruing the day.

"He's about as French as my French hen," Mrs. Tilly muttered.

And then, miracle of miracles, Becky walked straight past the brute, who didn't so much as blink at the sight of her, he was so busy paying for not one, not two, but three bowls full of beef and beans. And they weren't small bowls.

Georgiana gave herself a shake. Of course Becky wasn't interested in him. Look at him. He was a beast.

"That girl is a perfect fool if she believes a word he says," Mrs. Tilly was saying. Georgiana wasn't really listening; she was searching the room, trying to see if there were empty seats. How could she get the brute to sit at their table? There was a big gap right next to them, where the children had vacated the benches, but why would he sit here and not somewhere else?

"He has some sort of traveling show." Mrs. Tilly was sighing. "Those are his three girls there. Sweet little moppets, but really, who drags their children around the country like that?" There was an awkward pause. "Oh. I didn't mean any offense . . ."

Georgiana craned her neck to see what the brute was doing. He seemed to have paused and was speaking to someone out of Georgiana's line of sight. "Believe me, Mrs. Tilly, I wouldn't be moving if I didn't have to." Which wasn't entirely true. She'd always longed to travel. That had been one of the ways Leonard had wooed her, with promises of adventure. None of which had ever eventuated.

But she was here now, wasn't she, finally having an adventure. Without him. And, she had to admit, even if it was trying and frightening and she was worried sick about Leo, she'd never felt so alive in her entire life.

"And of course she's bringing him over," Mrs. Tilly said, throwing her hands in the air. "Her mother would be rolling over in her grave."

Becky came back into view, trailing a man Georgiana vaguely recognized. He was slender and neat, with a very carefully styled mustache. He really did look very familiar. Lord, she hoped he wasn't one of the men she'd interviewed today. That would be embarrassing.

Behind the slender man came three little girls, in descending order of height. They were dressed identically, in green gingham, and they had riotous golden curls that burst out of some very badly done braids. To Georgiana's shock, bringing up the rear like the last duckling waddling after the mother duck, came the brute.

He was coming to her table! Her heart started pounding. Hard.

She ran a hand over her hair. Her chignon was in complete disarray. She looked terrible. But then he got closer, and she had a clearer view of the state of him, and her hand dropped from her hair. At least she was clean, which was more than she could say for him. His buckskin shirt may have never been washed in its lifetime, and his hair was a thick mat of knots. Most of his face was obscured by beard. And look at his *hands*. They were the size of anvils, enormous muscular paws. But the really notable thing was how deeply ingrained the dirt was; his fingernails were black with it.

"See, we have plenty of room," Becky was chattering as she brought the party to their table.

If the brute looked big from a distance, he was enormous up close. Enormous and not particularly friendly. He had the look of a bear that had been woken from hibernation.

"Pierre, you remember Mrs. Tilly, the lady I work for?" Becky shoved Wilby's wooden sword off the table. Georgiana caught it and then removed the rest of the toys before Becky could sweep them aside, which she seemed in a hurry to do.

Mrs. Tilly gave the neat little man a look that should have reduced him to ashes. He adjusted his collar nervously.

"And this is Mrs. Smith," Becky said offhandedly. She was clearly not very enthusiastic about her beau meeting Georgiana.

"We've already had the pleasure," the man with the mustache gushed.

Becky's face blackened, and Georgiana flinched. Oh no. *Had* she interviewed him today?

"My girls and I are staying in the Grand Hotel," the man told Georgiana, oozing charm. Georgiana wasn't charmed. "We spoke briefly at breakfast. Over the coddled egg."

Georgiana smiled politely. She had absolutely no memory of it. But she'd spoken to so many men today.

"The hotel is bursting at the seams with Mrs. Smith's suitors," the little man told Becky with a twinkle. "It's impossible to take a step without bumping into one of them."

Georgiana still couldn't tell if he included himself in their number, so she just kept smiling politely.

"Are we going to sit?" the brute asked bluntly. "My beans are getting cold."

"Matthew?" Mrs. Tilly sounded shocked. She seemed to have just noticed him. "Matthew Slater, is that you? Look at the state of you!"

Mrs. Tilly *knew* him. Georgiana couldn't believe her good fortune as she watched Mrs. Tilly cluck over the brute, settling him on the bench next to her.

"I was expecting you in March," the widow was scolding him. She had completely turned her back on Pierre LeFoy. Becky took advantage of her rudeness and sat Pierre next to her. Georgiana found herself surrounded by the little girls. At least Mrs. Tilly and the brute were sitting directly opposite her, so she could eavesdrop, and hopefully when Mrs. Tilly had stopped fussing over him, she might remember to introduce him to Georgiana.

"You're Philip's mother," one of the little girls said as she bent low over her bowl and began shoveling beans in.

"Yes," Georgiana said absently.

The brute was suffering graciously under Mrs. Tilly's motherly attentions, but he clearly wanted to be left alone to eat. He was eyeing the way the little girl was shoveling beans with no small amount of envy.

"I hope you're getting a haircut first thing in the morning," Mrs. Tilly was saying. "It's a disgrace." She patted his arm. "Eat. We've finished already."

"I only just got in from the trail." His voice was a pleasant surprise, low and smooth. He didn't sound half as rough as he looked. Somehow that was reassuring. Georgiana might be looking for a frontiersman, but she didn't exactly want a ruffian. She watched as he fell to his food in relief, finishing one of the bowls in three huge spoonfuls. He mopped it out methodically with a hunk of corn bread. His manners weren't too terrible. Nothing she couldn't live with.

"There's always time for a haircut," Mrs. Tilly disagreed. "And a shave." She paused. "And a bath."

"Mrs. Bulfinch doesn't have baths. Not for the likes of me, she says."

He was staying in her hotel! Georgiana squeaked.

They both looked over at her. Oh. Oh. Oh *my*. He had the most beautiful eyes she'd ever seen. They were the warmest, most hypnotic golden-brown. They had flecks of light that put Georgiana in mind of dust motes floating in sunshine . . .

"Is that true, Mrs. Smith?" Mrs. Tilly asked. "Matthew, this is Mrs. Smith. She's from New York."

He gave her a polite nod. Georgiana tore her gaze from his. It took some effort.

"I would have thought a fine hotel would furnish a bath," Mrs. Tilly said, frowning. "She certainly charges exorbitant prices."

"We have a bath," Georgiana said, struggling to think straight.

He was in her hotel. That was marvelous. It would give her time to examine his suitability. It was a relief to think that there was at least *one* possibility for a husband, if the rest of her interviews came to nothing. "Our suite has a washroom."

"We don't have a bath in our room," LeFoy interrupted, leaning over Becky to try and join the conversation. "But we can get a tub sent up when we want to bathe."

The brute didn't look surprised. He gave an imperceptible shrug and went back to his food.

"She honestly refused you a bath?" Mrs. Tilly sounded outraged on his behalf.

"I can go to a bathhouse tomorrow. I was lucky to get a room, I guess, looking like this. Sam said everywhere is full."

"Yes," Mrs. Tilly sighed, "it gets busier every year."

"I can't complain," the brute said, stacking the second

empty bowl inside the first and dragging the third one toward him. "It's good for business."

"Well, I must say you're leaving it very late this year. The captains have been out in the town square for weeks already, signing people up. If you're not careful, you'll be left with the dregs. Did you know Slumpback Joe's group is already at more than 150 parties? Can you *imagine*?"

The brute grunted. "The trains have been getting bigger every year. Last year Andy Sawyer had close to three thousand people in his party. It was chaos. You could see 'em on the horizon, just a big cloud of dust, like a storm coming."

"What's this?" LeFoy was still struggling to join the conversation. "What's this you're saying about wagon trains? Did I hear someone say Slumpback Joe? We were thinking about employing him. Should we not?"

"I thought you said you might stay here," Becky said, sounding hurt.

LeFoy smiled nervously. "We might." He cleared his throat. "But we might not."

"Papa says there's a market for theater out west," one of the girls told Becky.

"Does he now?" Becky didn't sound too happy about it.

"And we can perform along the way."

"Matt here's the best wagon train pilot in the country," Mrs. Tilly said proudly. "Better even than his brother."

"That wouldn't be hard," the brute said dryly. "Luke gave it up before the trail even got busy."

"We're heading for California," LeFoy said. "If you can take us on, I'd be glad to hear your price."

"We haven't signed up for a train yet either," Georgiana said quickly.

"Best wait to see what the new husband wants to do," Mrs. Tilly advised, giving her hand a pat, "whoever he might be."

Georgiana had to bite her tongue. She had no intention of letting her husband decide anything on her behalf. She'd do the deciding about her life, thank you very much. She'd had quite enough of being at the mercy of a husband's whims.

"I don't go to California," the brute said, swiping out his final bowl with the corn bread.

Georgiana's heart sank.

"But it's the same trail till we get to Fort Hall. I often join up with Josiah Sampson and then we split at Fort Hall: he goes to California; I go on to Oregon. If you find Josiah in the square, tell him I sent you. He's the one I'd recommend. He's sensible. Not like some of them others. Slumpback Joe's liable to get you lost before you even find Courthouse Rock."

Oh. Well, that was disappointing.

Georgiana wondered how firm he was about not going to California. If she decided he was suitable husband material, she wondered if he and this Josiah fellow could swap trails . . .

"Do you have a wife in Oregon?" she asked. One might as well be blunt. That was the big question, wasn't it? There was no point in thinking about him further if he was already married.

"Nope." He finished his final mouthful and pushed his tray away. And then, to Georgiana's dismay, he got to his feet.

"You come by tomorrow," Mrs. Tilly told him, "and I'll feed you up. But you get a bath and a haircut first, mind, or I won't let you in the door."

"I ain't going yet," he said, picking up his tray. "I'm just getting more food."

"Lord, but that man can eat," Mrs. Tilly said as they watched him walk away. "Becky, we'd best do some extra baking in the morning."

"How long have you known him?" Georgiana asked, as she admired the way his shoulders stretched out the buckskin of his shirt.

"Oh, years and years. Ever since his brother gave up the trail. Matt came out a year or two after that to pick up his business. He's a sweet boy."

Georgiana could think of many ways to describe the brute, but "sweet boy" wasn't one of them.

❧ 4 ❧

GEORGIANA WILTED AT the disastrous sight of her off-spring. She was already out of sorts, as the brute had left the cookhouse without so much as a backward glance, and this was all she needed to round off the day. The children were playing by the water pump out the back of the cookhouse with a mob of other wildlings, including Mr. LeFoy's girls, and they were coated in mud.

"Oh, for the love of . . . !" Mr. LeFoy sounded as frustrated as she felt. "Ginger! Flower! Honey! Get here this minute!" His refined accent had slipped a little, Georgiana noticed. There was a bit of southern twang in there.

"You'll be glad of that bathtub tonight," Mrs. Tilly said dryly once they'd rounded all the children up.

"I would understand if you don't want to mind the children tomorrow," Georgiana said regretfully, "after the performance they've put on today."

"Oh, don't be silly. I love children." She laughed and took a step back as Wilby drifted too close. "But I'd prefer them cleaned up."

Georgiana could see a long night stretching ahead of her. She found herself longing for the luxurious bathroom in the New York house, and the armies of servants she'd grown up with.

"Come on, Becky," Mrs. Tilly said, "we'll leave them to their scrubbing."

"Oh, I could come and help . . ."

"No, you couldn't," Mrs. Tilly said firmly, taking her arm. "We've got to be up early to do the baking. Now, say good night and we'll be on our way."

Becky turned a dewy gaze on LeFoy, who was too distracted by his children to do more than wish her a brief good night. She looked crestfallen as Mrs. Tilly led her away, and she shot a resentful glare at Georgiana, who got to walk home with him.

By the time they all got back to the hotel, the mud had started to dry and the children were looking like clay sculptures. Thankfully, there was no one out on the porch to see them.

"I suppose we should go in the back door," Georgiana sighed, grabbing Wilby's pudgy hand as he lunged toward the porch. "I dread to think what Mrs. Bulfinch will charge us if the children get mud in her foyer. Boys!" she called after the twins as they tore off around the back of the house. "Don't you go in the house until I get there!" Then she realized she had no hope of them obeying her and darted after them, hauling Wilby with her. He squealed with joy. "Susannah, you come too!"

"Horsey ride!" Wilby yelled.

"Stop right there!" Georgiana ordered as she rounded the corner in time to see the twins belting up the back step. She felt a stab of panic at the thought of the twins ruining Mrs. Bulfinch's carpets. Her cash reserves were getting low, and she couldn't afford any more cleaning charges.

To her surprise, the twins heeded her. She was tired and her temper was frayed, and she guessed they could tell. She let Wilby go and advanced on them. "You are not stepping so much as a toe on that woman's floor until you get some of that mud off you."

The twins looked down at their filthy bodies.

"How do you suppose we do that?" Phin (Philip? Lord, would she *ever* be able to tell them apart?) asked.

"Start by scraping your shoes on the mat," Georgiana suggested.

Philip snorted as he looked down at the rush mat. His twin gave the soles of his feet an exploratory rub against the rough surface. The other one shrugged in quick defeat and reached for the door handle. "We'll have a bath upstairs," he said.

"Don't you dare go in the house!"

Vaguely, she heard Wilby squealing with delight, but she couldn't look away from the twins. She knew the minute she did they'd bolt inside. It was like staring down a pair of wild dogs. Show no fear.

Then she heard a splash.

"Wilby!"

The toddler had found the horse trough.

"*Wilbeeeeee.*" Georgiana dashed over to haul him out of the water.

He was fine. More than fine, he was grinning from ear to ear. The filth on his skin had become a sludgy slime, and he slipped through her fingers, landing with a slosh that splattered on her skirts. It went nicely with the glue stains. She shot LeFoy a helpless look as he rounded the back of the house with Susannah and his girls.

"Brilliant!" Phin punched the air.

"Good work, Wilby!" The twins tumbled down the back step and over to the trough.

"What are you talking about? Look at him!" Georgiana was at her wit's end. It had been such a long day. All she wanted was to curl up in bed, alone, with a book. But that seemed a very distant possibility as she took in her filthy, irrepressible little monsters.

Why did everything have to be so *hard*?

"Bath!" Wilby yelled, throwing his hands in the air and splashing the twins.

Before Georgiana could draw breath to protest, the twins had joined him in the "bath." Then, with a shower of giggles, two of the LeFoy girls had leapt into the horse trough too.

"C'mon, Sooky, get in!" Phin stripped off his sodden shirt and whirled it around his head, sending it flying in the direction of his sister.

Susannah was speckled with mud, like a freckled egg, but was nowhere near as filthy as her brothers. She was holding her skirts primly in her bunched fists and jumped backward, squealing, as Phin's shirt slopped at her feet. The older LeFoy girl looked similarly offended. LeFoy himself didn't seem to know whether to laugh or to join the fray.

Georgiana pressed a hand to her head. Her children were in a horse trough, slick with mud, their clothes a ruin, splashing one another and cackling. *Where* was Mrs. Wyndham when you needed her?

"That's full of *horse spit*," Susannah yelled at her brothers. "You're bathing in *horse spit*!"

Oh my, she was right! They'd all catch some horrid equine disease, and then Georgiana would be *worse* than the worst mother of all time. "Out!" she shrieked. "Get out of there before you catch your deaths!"

LeFoy cleared his throat. "Flower! Honey! You heed Mrs. Smith and get out." He gave Georgiana a sympathetic look. "Why don't I have Mrs. Bulfinch set up a couple of tubs in the laundry room?" He gestured to the lean-to at the back of the hotel.

Georgiana could have kissed him. Or wept. Or both. "Oh yes, please, Mr. LeFoy. Would you mind?"

"Not at all." He disappeared into the house.

"I told you to get out!" Georgiana snapped at the twins. She no longer cared a fig that her dress was getting ruined; she reached over and plucked Wilby's writhing, slimy body from the trough.

"Don't pop an eyeball," Philip scoffed. "A little horse spit never hurt anyone, and we're much cleaner than we were." He held out a bare arm for her to inspect.

"Except that you'll drip horse spit all over Mrs. Bulfinch's floor!" Susannah shrieked. "It's disgusting."

"You're not to go back in the water," Georgiana told Wilby as she dropped him to the ground. "Now, get out!" she told the twins.

"If we get out, Flower and Honey have to get out too," Phin said obstinately.

The girls had already started climbing out.

"Dog!" Wilby shrieked with joy and pointed at the mouth of the stable.

Georgiana groaned as he plunged off toward the stable. There was a dog tied up at the entrance, watching them closely. It was a smudgy gray and black color and had piercing predatory eyes. It looked too much like a wolf for Georgiana to be comfortable. She scooped Wilby up before he reached it. The wolf-dog looked like it might eat Wilby if she let him get close enough.

"I think it's wrong to keep dogs tied up," one of the dripping-wet LeFoy girls complained. "Especially a dog like that. You should untie it."

Over her dead body. "Everyone stay away from it," Georgiana instructed. "One doesn't go about untying strange dogs. For all you know, it might bite you."

"I think it looks sad."

"Everyone in the laundry room," she snapped, sounding more like Mrs. Wyndham by the minute. "Now!"

LEFOY TOOK THE boys to one tub and left Georgiana with the four girls. If Georgiana thought the girls would be easier to wash than the boys, she was mistaken. Susannah and Ginger went first, as they were marginally cleaner, and they were no trouble at all. But Flower and Honey could have given the twins a run for their money in terms of boisterousness. Mrs. Bulfinch had strung up a sheet between the two tubs, "For the sake of decency," she said primly, and Georgiana could hear Mr. LeFoy fighting to keep the twins under control, but she still envied him. Flower and Honey made the twins seem like saints.

By the time everyone was clean and dressed in their nightclothes, Georgiana was soaking wet. She sat by the stove while she combed out the girls' knots and braided their hair, and soon her dress was steaming. By that time, the boys were long dressed and Wilby had fallen asleep, curled up like a puppy in one of the wicker laundry baskets.

Mrs. Bulfinch had taken to hovering in the doorway, watching them disapprovingly. As soon as the boys were clean, she made LeFoy get in the tub behind the makeshift curtain and get himself clean too.

"You're not going anywhere looking like that!" she had snapped at him, eyeing his muddy, wet clothes with distaste. The boys had soaked him through with their splashing.

She had Ginger go and fetch him some fresh clothes. And then once he was bathed, she supervised him emptying the filthy water from the tubs, all the time clanging in her loud voice about the role of discipline in children's lives.

"You'll be needing to bathe too," Mrs. Bulfinch told Georgiana sternly once the final braid was tied, taking in her stained and sodden clothes and the mud splatters on her face and neck.

Georgiana sighed. A bath sounded like a nice idea. She could shut herself away in the small bathing closet upstairs, and maybe she could read and take a nip of sherry as she relaxed. She was only afraid she might fall asleep. "Thank you, Mrs. Bulfinch, if you could have the water sent up, I would love a bath."

"Oh, there's no one to be fetching water at this time of night. You'll have to take your bath down here."

Georgiana was scandalized. The laundry room didn't even have a door!

"I'm not prepared to discuss it," Mrs. Bulfinch said when Georgiana opened her mouth to protest. "You'll certainly not be tracking muck through my hotel. Look at the state of you. You're drenched through. I'll put your young 'uns to bed for you and bring you down some fresh clothes."

The children looked horrified by the idea.

"But anyone could walk in!" Georgiana protested. Was she *insane*? The laundry was open to the yard! There was only a wooden screen across the entrance.

"Not in *here*." Mrs. Bulfinch looked at her like she was a half-wit. "You can bathe in the scullery; the door has a latch. No one uses the kitchen this time of night anyway, and you can use the back stairs to get up to your room, so you don't run into anyone afterward."

Georgiana wished she could just click her fingers and be clean and tucked up in bed. This didn't sound relaxing at all.

"Come on, children."

"We can wait for her here," Phin said quickly. "We don't mind."

"Nonsense. It's well past a respectable hour for children to be in bed." Mrs. Bulfinch clapped her hands at them, rounding them up like they were chickens.

"I can carry the little one," Mr. LeFoy volunteered.

Georgiana thanked him as he scooped Wilby up and followed Mrs. Bulfinch and the children out of the laundry.

"You might as well get their clothes in the copper pot to wash while you wait for me to bring yours down," Mrs. Bulfinch said over her shoulder as she left, "and heat some more water for your bath while you're at it."

Georgiana had never realized how much *work* there was in organizing a bath. She was so tired; it was an effort to work the water pump and carry jugs to the two big copper pots that sat on the stove. She'd also had no idea how much work the laundry was, or how much work it took to get the children through the hazards of an ordinary day. She thought longingly of Mrs. Creed the housekeeper and Mrs. Wyndham the nanny, and of the unseen troops of scullery maids and laundry maids and housemaids who had kept her life clean and neat and effortless.

Not anymore.

This was life now, she realized as she used the wooden paddle to stir the clothes in the copper. Perhaps it was just tiredness, but Georgiana couldn't quite suppress a few self-pitying tears. They rolled into the bubbling water and dissolved. No one was coming to help her. She was all alone. If she wanted a bath, she had to draw it; if she wanted well-mannered children, she had to discipline them; if she wanted *anything*, she had to make it happen . . .

She gave in and had a good cry as she wrestled the bathtub into the scullery and carried endless jugs of warm water from the copper pots to the tub. She kept moving because she had no other choice. Someone had to wash the clothes. Someone had to fill the tub. And that someone was now her.

"You make sure you empty that tub when you're done," Mrs. Bulfinch ordered when she delivered Georgiana's nightgown and robe. "I'll sit with the children. Don't be long."

Georgiana was glad to latch the door behind her. She fought her way out of her gown, which had buttons designed for a lady's maid to undo and required contortions for her to unfasten. She kicked the gown across the floor and wriggled out of her undergarments. The warm water was heaven. She wished nothing more than to close her eyes and relax into it, but she was torturously aware that Mrs. Bulfinch was waiting upstairs for her, probably tapping her witchy black boot and giving the children nightmares. So it was a short and unrelaxing bath. She scrubbed her face and washed her hair, and once she was dressed, she had the thankless task of emptying the tub one jug at a time. By the time she eventually trudged up to bed, her back was aching. It was the least relaxing bath she'd ever taken.

❧ 5 ❧

M ATT DIDN'T CARE if the moon had barely risen and it was his first night of civilization in months; he didn't feel the need to visit a saloon or a whorehouse or to seek the company of other people; he just wanted to be alone in his own room and to sleep in a comfortable bed. You'd think a wish that simple could be granted, wouldn't you? But that was never the way his luck ran.

For a start, he'd forgotten to feed his animals. And then there was Dog, who came whining out of the stable the minute he saw Matt coming and needed to be settled.

But none of that would have bothered him overmuch. What bothered him was that he had company.

"What kind of horse is that?"

"Is that an Indian pony?"

And not just any company. Children.

"I bet it is. I've never seen one in real life, but I've seen pictures, and they're always speckled like that."

"What's its name?"

Loud children.

The two boys were already in the stable when he got there. They were climbing around the hayloft and had straw sticking up in their dark curls.

Matt didn't have much experience with children, but it didn't seem right that they were climbing around a hayloft well after dark. It also didn't seem right that they were so forward in approaching strangers. Was it normal for children to talk this much? He had nieces back home in Oregon, but they were too young to do much talking. Not like these two boys, who never seemed to *stop* talking.

"Shouldn't you be in bed?" he asked, scowling.

"We don't have horses anymore." They ignored him and just kept chattering.

"My horse was called Goliath and his was called Apollo."

He didn't know how old they were. They were however old up-to-his-belt-buckle was. Old enough to talk, that was for sure.

"Apollo's a grand name for a horse," Matt said as he rustled up some oats for the animals.

"No grander than Goliath," one of them replied.

They looked the same. Exactly the same, right down to the moles next to their right eyebrows. The only thing different about them was the color of their shoes. One wore black boots and one wore brown.

"Why do you have so many horses?"

"They ain't all mine." Matt didn't know why he was talking to them, except that it was easier than *not* talking to them. When he didn't speak, they barraged him with questions until his head hurt. Not that the questions stopped when he *did* answer them.

"Did you steal them?"

"What?" Matt gave them a disgruntled look. "No."

"Well, whose are they?"

"You ask a lot of questions."

"Curiosity is a virtue. That's what they used to say at school. When we went to school."

"Mrs. Wyndham used to say curiosity killed the cat though," his brother said.

"I don't see how it could be both," the first kid complained.

His brother shrugged, clearly used to the contradictory nature of adults.

"Here." Matt thrust empty pails at the boys. "Make yourselves useful and fill these up. There." He pointed them in the direction of the oat bin. "And then take the oats over *there*." He pointed at the feed troughs. "And don't drop any, or that old witch will charge me for it," he muttered under his breath.

"I'm Phineas Fairchild Bee Blunt," one of them introduced himself, sounding very pompous and formal. "And this is my brother Philip."

"Just Philip?" Matt asked dryly. "Didn't you leave any names for him?"

"Philip Leavington Bee Blunt," the other one said. "The Leavington is from my maternal grandmother's side of the family."

"As is the Fairchild in mine," his brother interrupted, an edge of competition in his voice. "Fairchild was Grandmother's maiden name."

"The Leavingtons are a much more prestigious strain of the family."

"The Fairchilds have more senators."

"The Leavingtons have an earl in their lineage."

"The Fair—"

"Whoa!" Matt interrupted, holding up a hand to still the barrage of name-dropping. "Just a word of advice, Your Majesties: around here people don't much care about things like lineage."

"Of course they do." Phineas rolled his eyes. "*Everyone* cares about lineage."

"Now you sound like my brother talking about his horses." He pulled a face. "Speaking of which, get to and feed these ones before they get so hungry they decide to eat you."

"Horses don't eat people."

"These ain't like your fancy eastern horses," he told them with a straight face. "They like the taste of people."

They got moving at that.

"You didn't tell us your name," Philip prodded him. He knew it was Philip because of the brown boots.

"Just plain old Matt Slater." Matt threw blankets over the horses, taking particular care with Luke's fillies, which were headed to market before Matt left town. "Not so much as an earl in my lineage." He needed to get the fillies rested up and glossy again before he showed them to Jackson. It was a long way to bring them to sell and in no way worth it for the money, Matt thought grumpily. Luke was just doing it to show off to the old man. Matt's brother was smug as smug could be about his breeding stock. As far as Matt was concerned, one animal was as good as another, provided it was healthy and could do the job you put it to.

"Well, clearly, you're *not* plain old Matt," Phineas disagreed. "Clearly, your full name is Matthew."

"Nobody calls me that, so I don't bother with it." Matt ushered Dog into the stall with Fernando and his own horse, Pablo, and closed the door.

"But it's your legal name."

"I guess so." He put the pails back on their hooks. "Thanks for your help. Now, you'd best get back where you came from. I assume you're from the hotel? Your mother's probably worried sick about you."

"She's asleep. She fell asleep trying to get our sister down for the night."

"She's a bit hopeless that way," Phineas agreed. "You should see her. She can't make it halfway through a lullaby without getting sleepy."

"And then Susannah just sits there playing with her dolls while Mother sleeps."

"She's probably tired." Matt would be, if he had to listen to these boys all day. He was tired after half an hour with them. "I'm going to bed myself, so I'll take you in."

They protested mightily, but Matt herded them like recalcitrant cattle, and they were upstairs before they knew what was happening.

"Which room are you in?" he asked as they rounded the second landing.

"The Imperial. Right at the top."

The Imperial. That was the room that the impossibly pretty blue-eyed woman was in, the wealthy one from New York. Which meant these two chatterboxes were hers. Which meant he was sharing a floor with them all. He didn't know which was worse: the thought of running into these talkers every day, or having to see their mother. He didn't like the way she made him feel. Like he was walking along a cliff edge.

"Well, off you go, then."

They stared at him, obviously burning with more questions.

"Get in there or I'll wake your mother."

That did it.

"See you in the morning, Mr. Slater."

He earnestly hoped not.

❧ 6 ❧

GEORGIANA TOOK EXTRA care dressing the next morning. She was still in mourning for Leonard, so she had to wear black, but she used her mother of pearl hair combs to decorate her simple chignon, and she pinned her moonstone brooch at her throat. It was one of her few remaining pieces of jewelry. She was hoping Matt Slater would be at breakfast so she could further their acquaintance.

"How many more interviews do you have to do today?" one of the twins asked. He was swinging on the back of a chair like a monkey.

"Too many." Georgiana pulled a face.

"They're all a bit rubbish, aren't they? None of them look like they could wrestle a raccoon, let alone a bear." He sounded thoroughly disgruntled.

"I don't see why you need another husband," his brother said. For some reason he was under the bed and only the tips of his boots were visible. "Your last one didn't work out so well. I don't really see the point of them."

"Don't talk about your father that way, Philip."

"I'm Phin."

"No, you're not." Susannah kicked at his protruding boot. "Stop confusing her. She just works out which one's which and you go *confusing* her. That's Philip, Mother."

"I know," Georgiana lied. "And the *point*, Philip, is that the frontier isn't a safe place for unescorted women and children."

"Would our father have been any good at 'escorting' us?" Phin asked curiously.

"Of course he would." Susannah sounded outraged that he would even ask.

"How would you know, Sooky? You don't even remember him," Phin scoffed.

"Neither do you!"

"I do . . . a bit. He smelled like brandy."

"I remember that," Susannah insisted.

Phin scoffed again. "No, you don't."

"Stop it," Georgiana snapped. "Now, we're going to go down to breakfast, and I shan't hear any more bickering!"

"Fine with me. Look at this!" To Georgiana's horror, Phin stood on the writing desk.

"For the love of all that's holy, get down from there!" Georgiana lunged at him, but before she reached him he did a neat backward somersault off the table. "Phineas! This is not a circus!"

"Isn't it great? Honey taught me!"

"Honey?"

"Honey LeFoy. Honestly, Mother, you never pay attention."

"I have a lot on my mind at the moment," Georgiana defended herself. "Now, go and get your little brother, and never do that trick again. At least not inside," she relented. Because it really was rather a good trick.

"Now," she said once they were clumped by the door, ready to go down to eat, "you're to be on your best behavior, do you understand me?" She gave them her sternest look. None of them seemed the least intimidated by it. "The longer we take to find me a husband, the longer it will take us to get on the trail and the longer you have to be cooped up at Mrs. Tilly's."

"I like Mrs. Tilly's," Susannah said, surprised. "She gives us strawberry tarts."

Georgiana couldn't think what else to threaten them with. And they knew it. "Humph." She bent down and scooped Wilby up. "Come on, then."

They were relatively well-behaved for a flight of stairs or two. There was no bickering and no sliding down the banisters. But then the twins caught sight of the dining room and perked up, like bloodhounds getting a sniff of a trail, and went pelting down the stairs, taking them two at a time.

"Phineas! Philip! Walk, don't run!"

"Can *I* still go to Mrs. Tilly's?" Susannah asked.

Georgiana took her little hand and pulled her along, wanting to catch the twins before they wreaked havoc.

Oh my. She entered the stuffy dining room to find Matt Slater was already there. And that her boys had taken the liberty of joining him at his breakfast table, even though there weren't actually any seats available. They'd dragged two chairs over to where he sat at the head of the table, and sat at the corners of the table, on either side of him. She could tell it was Mr. Slater, even though he had his back to her and his wild hair had been cut, because there weren't many men with backs that broad. His buckskins were gone, replaced by a clean white shirt and black trousers, but it was very clearly him. She would have known him anywhere.

She took a deep breath and approached.

The three men sitting with Mr. Slater looked taken aback at the twins' intrusion. Georgiana sighed. That did seem to be the usual reaction to her children.

"I'm very sorry," Georgiana apologized, as she swooped down on them. Two of the gentlemen at the table leapt politely to their feet. The third, a scruffy bearded man, slowly took the hint and also rose. Matt Slater, she noticed, didn't. But he did glance up at her.

Georgiana just about dropped Wilby in shock. He'd shaved. And he was scrubbed clean. He practically shone he was so clean. And . . . oh my. Oh my, my, my.

He was . . . *beautiful*. There was just no other word for it. He had an aquiline nose and a sharply bowed mouth. His jaw could have been carved from marble. No, not marble. Nothing so cold. *Amber*. He had high, sharp cheekbones, and there was a dimple in one cheek, a deep groove that made her long to see him smile. And then there were those eyes, of course, thickly fringed with black lashes, flashing with golden lights.

Who could have *known*? Who could have known *that* was under all those whiskers?

Georgiana felt like she'd caught sunstroke. She was hot and fuzzy-headed and her pulse was erratic. Oh my. A fluttery, pulsing warmth uncurled inside her, something she hadn't felt in many cold and lonely years. It was a wonderful feeling. It made her feel seventeen again.

But then reality crashed in. Oh. *Oh*. She didn't know if she could keep the disappointment from her face. Because the sight of him, and that feeling in her belly, meant only one thing.

She couldn't marry him.

He was too beautiful. She couldn't marry a man who looked like that; she couldn't give in to those wonderful sparkling feelings. Not after Leonard. It wasn't safe. *She* wasn't safe.

Why couldn't he have just kept the damn beard? Now she was back to where she'd started!

"It's fine, Mother," Phin said. "We'll sit here, and you can go over there." He gestured at a table halfway across the room. "You can watch us from there."

"What?" Georgiana tore her gaze away from the beautiful brute and frowned, confused. What was he talking about?

"We're fine here," Phin said. "We'll stay here and see you after."

Oh, that's right. She was dealing with the twins.

Georgiana smiled stiffly at the gentlemen. There was no way she was leaving them at this table. She leaned close to her son, dropped her voice and tried to sound threatening, all without losing her smile. "Get up," she hissed.

They didn't get up. Or even look like they were thinking about it.

"Mrs. Smith! Good morning," a jovial voice interrupted. "It's such a pleasure to see you again!"

Oh no. It was Mr. Dugard. He was seated at the table right beside them. He gave her a little wave and stood.

"Mrs. Smith!" The gentleman standing opposite her started blushing and fussing. *"You're* Mrs. Smith? I have an appointment with you this morning. Arthur Conroy." He held out his hand for her to shake.

"I do too," one of the other gentlemen said, sounding vaguely surprised by the fact. If possible, he looked paler and limper than both Dugard and Conroy combined.

"I don't," the scruffy man said, a bit bewildered. He had the white napkin tucked into his shirt. It was splotched with egg yolk. "I'm with him." He pointed at Matt.

"I have three seats at my table," Mr. Dugard said brightly. "You can sit here with me. It will be close enough to your charming sons for you to keep an eye on them."

Georgiana didn't want to sit with Mr. Dugard.

"Why don't we pull the tables together?" Conroy suggested, giving Dugard an irritated look.

"Yes," the pale man agreed. "It would be our pleasure."

"Why don't Doyle and I just move and make things easier," Matt Slater sighed.

"No!" the twins exclaimed simultaneously.

His eyebrows went up at their vehemence, as did Georgiana's.

"I'm sure they don't want to displace anyone," Georgiana said hastily. What on earth had gotten into her boys? Why were they so keen to sit with Matt Slater?

Oh dear, she made the mistake of looking at him again. That *mouth*. She'd never seen such a pointed bow or such a full lower lip on a man. In fact, she didn't think she'd ever even noticed a man's mouth before. She couldn't for the life of her think what Leonard's mouth had looked like . . .

"If you're moving tables, we're going with you," Phin told the brute cheerfully.

"Why would you go with him?" Georgiana asked, exasperated. In fact, why were they sitting here with him in the first place?

"He's our friend."

If possible, the brute's eyebrows shot even higher, until they all but disappeared under the dark hair that flopped over his forehead.

"What do you mean, 'he's our friend'?" Georgiana looked back and forth between the twins and the brute. Wilby was squirming in her arms.

"Matthew is our friend," Philip said patiently, speaking to her like she was a half-wit.

"It's Matt," the brute growled, "and one conversation doesn't make us friends."

"Of course it does. We introduced ourselves. That's how these things work."

"It's settled, then," Mr. Dugard said, interrupting. "We'll join the tables together."

Oh no. She was in trouble. Her pulse had jumped at the thought of sitting with the brute. She didn't *want* her pulse jumping.

"Biscuit!" Wilby said, reaching out a chubby hand for the brute's biscuit. His fingers opened and closed impatiently.

"Get your own, Wilby," Phin told him.

"Good idea." Georgiana plonked her youngest son in Phin's lap. "Why don't you take him over to the sideboard and get him a plate. Philip, you can take your little sister."

The twins opened their mouths to protest.

"Don't," she said sharply. "You're on thin ice already. Off you go and get some breakfast." She watched them like a hawk as they took their younger siblings in hand. "And don't you dare torture her," she warned Philip.

He gave her a look of wide-eyed innocence.

"Don't worry, Mother," Susannah said primly. "If he does, I shall scream."

"Please don't," Georgiana pleaded. "We're in public."

"It looks like you have your hands full there, Mrs. Smith," Conroy said. He sounded a touch nervous.

"It's nothing a father's firm hand wouldn't solve," Dugard reassured her. It didn't reassure her. It only made her put another mental strike through his name.

"So . . . " the third gentleman said, watching the children as they piled their plates high with biscuits and bacon, "you have *four* children?"

"Five."

If possible, the pale man went even paler.

"Are you joining the tables together or not?" the brute asked impatiently. He was looking increasingly irritable. "My food is getting cold."

Georgiana saw Dugard's distaste for Matt, but the men obediently pulled the two tables together. She also saw Mrs. Bulfinch giving them the evil eye as she delivered a fresh plate of scrambled eggs to the sideboard. She didn't approve of her tables being moved. Or of the men flocking around Georgiana. If she'd said it once, she'd said it a thousand times: it wasn't decent.

"Shall I get us a pot of coffee?" Dugard was solicitous. "Or would you prefer tea?"

"Coffee, thank you." Georgiana slid into the chair next to Matt Slater. At least here she wouldn't have to look at his face. That seemed safer.

"We'll take coffee too, won't we, Seb?" Slater said, without looking up. Georgiana thought she detected a thread of humor in his voice.

"Tea for me," the pale man said, and he quickly took the seat opposite Georgiana.

"Me too." Conroy sat on her other side.

Dugard found himself fetching pots of tea and coffee for the table, and by the time he got back all the seats were taken and he was stranded down the far end of the table with the children. He looked none too pleased about it.

Georgiana downed her first cup of coffee quickly. She needed it. Conroy and the other man, who said his name was Peterson or Patterson or something she couldn't be bothered to remember, assailed her with questions. Nothing very interesting, just the same questions she'd fielded all day yesterday: how much land did she own in Mokelumne Hill, had her husband been mining it, was there any gold, how much capital did she have to get herself established in California? Not a single man so far had asked her anything about herself or the children. They didn't ask how old she was or what her favorite color was; they didn't want to know how recently she'd been widowed; they didn't ask her what she was hoping for in a husband; they didn't even ask the children's ages. All they cared about was land and gold.

Beside her, Matt Slater's chewing slowed as he listened to their barrage of questions and to her careful answers. His attention made her nervous. From the corner of her eye she saw his cutlery pause in midair.

Eventually, she heard him clear his throat. "You gentlemen might want to let the lady eat," he rumbled.

Georgiana risked looking at him. His golden-lit gaze was sympathetic. Oh no. No, no, no. That was even worse.

"I'm sure Mr. Dugard is happy to watch the kids while you go grab some food, Mrs. Smith," he said dryly. "He seems keen to volunteer—what was it again, Dugard?—'a father's firm hand'? Might be a good chance to practice."

"Absolutely." Dugard forced a smile, but his eyes shot daggers at Matt Slater.

"Thank you." Georgiana was up like a shot. He was thoughtful too. It just got worse and worse.

To her dismay, the other two gentlemen followed her to the sideboard.

"The food here is simply deplorable," the milky one confided, as he trailed her down the buffet. "You're probably safest with the biscuits and apricot conserve."

Feeling contrary, Georgiana scooped a spoonful of eggs on her plate. He wrinkled his nose. She added a second scoop.

"The bacon's hot," Mrs. Bulfinch said from behind them. The man jumped a mile. He was clearly scared of her.

"Wonderful," Georgiana said grimly, adding the blackened bacon to her watery scrambled eggs.

"You know what's wonderful?" Conroy leaned over Patterson to talk to her. "Seeing a woman with appetite! Are you a good cook, Mrs. Smith?"

"I don't know," Georgiana answered honestly. "Are you?"

"Pardon?"

She left them prodding at the biscuits and went back to the table.

"You seem to have a lot of friends in town," Slater observed when she sat down.

"They're not her friends," Phin objected.

"Consider us *new* friends," Dugard said.

"I'd rather not." Phin didn't even look at him as he dismissed him.

"They're all trying to marry her," Philip told Matt. He barely looked up from his syrup-drenched griddle cakes. Georgiana wished she'd seen those on the buffet. You couldn't really get griddle cakes wrong. Especially with that much syrup on them.

"So I gathered." Matt was giving Georgiana a calculating look. She wished he wouldn't. That was a face you could fall in love with, and she had no intention of ever falling in love again. It led to no good.

"Have any of you gentlemen been to California before?" Matt asked them.

They shook their heads. Slater's companion Doyle smirked into his coffee.

"Going for the gold, I assume?"

Conroy and Peterson/Patterson nodded.

"Not just for the gold. For a chance at a new life, Mr. Slater," Mr. Dugard said somewhat piously. "For the *freedom*."

"I wouldn't be going to California, then. Oregon's where I'd head for freedom. California's full of ruffians."

"Really?" Phin and Philip perked up.

"I said *full*," Matt told them. "They don't need to be adding you two; they've got enough already."

The boys laughed.

He was good with the children too. Georgiana swallowed hard. She was getting a headache. It only got worse when she realized what he was doing. He was distracting the table, asking about their travel plans, and what they knew about the goldfields, so that she had the chance to eat her breakfast in peace. And it worked. Except for the interruption of Wilby, who climbed into her lap and started eating her eggs, everyone left her in peace. Georgiana was able to eat what she could, and have a second cup of coffee, without having to answer a single question about her land in California.

It was a surprisingly gallant gesture. She hadn't expected it from a man as rough as he was. She found herself darting sideways glances at him, wondering what other surprises he held.

No. Stop it. It was best not to know.

"You planning on using oxen or mules?" he was asking the men.

None of them knew.

"You hired a captain yet? Or joined a group?"

They hadn't.

"Bought a wagon?"

Of course not.

It was crystal clear that none of them had the slightest idea what they were doing, and they were all woefully unprepared for the journey ahead. It was another timely reminder that they were exactly what she *wasn't* looking for in a husband.

She sighed. Please let today bring her a man who knew what he was doing. A man as capable and strong and brave and kind as the brute, as *brutish* as the brute, but without that face. Someone like he'd been yesterday. Scruffy and stained and rough and utterly without charm. She only had a handful of weeks until the wagon trains rolled out. She had to get this settled and her travel plans fixed before the spring rains came and went. According to her guidebook, the parties would roll out after the rains. She didn't have a moment to lose.

"Hurry up, children, we have to get you to Mrs. Tilly's for

the day." She pushed her plate away and cleaned Wilby's face up with her napkin.

"Huh," Doyle said, brushing crumbs from his beard, "that's exactly where we're headed too."

Of course they were. Now that she'd decided he was unsuitable, he was going to be everywhere she turned, just like these other men, dogging every minute of her day.

"Excellent, we can go together," the twins declared, dropping their cutlery with a clatter.

"I ain't going yet," Matt told them. "I've got to take some food up to my brother."

"We'll wait for you."

"Phineas! Philip! You don't go imposing yourself on perfect strangers," Georgiana scolded.

"He's not a stranger."

"We need to have a talk about who is and isn't a stranger," she snapped, once she'd dragged them away from the table and the brute. "You don't know him from Adam! You can't go about trusting everyone you meet."

"Why not? You're going to *marry* a perfect stranger."

Georgiana silently counted to ten so she wouldn't lose her temper. "I'm interviewing them first."

"Well, *we* interviewed *him*."

"When?"

"Oh look!" Philip pointed at the front window of Cavil's Mercantile. "You promised us rock candy yesterday if we cleaned Mrs. Tilly's kitchen . . . "

"And we did!" his twin finished.

They took her by the arms and dragged her across the road. Georgiana gave in. She *had* promised. And perhaps with their mouths full of candy they wouldn't be able to talk.

BY LUNCHTIME, GEORGIANA was wishing she'd bought herself some candy too. It would have cheered up a very dreary day. And the worst part was that *more* men kept arriving. Word seemed to have spread. It was utterly ridiculous. She was a near-destitute woman with five children, but by some warp of Chinese whispers through the saloons and stores of Independence, men were flocking to the hotel, thinking they had a chance to marry a gold claim.

She could see the greed in their eyes.

"Do you want your lunch in here again, while you keep going with this lot?" Mrs. Bulfinch asked at noon on the dot, her voice clanging over the chimes of her grandfather clock.

"Heavens, no!" Georgiana couldn't keep the horror from her voice.

Mrs. Bulfinch pursed her thin lips. "I can't say I approve of advertising for a husband," she said, and Georgiana braced for another lecture. "But . . . "—the landlady smoothed a doily on the side table—"your endeavors are proving very good for business."

Georgiana imagined so. Every room in the hotel was booked solid, and the dining room was bursting at the seams. She imagined the widow was doing a brisk business in tea and coffee too, considering the number of men loitering around the hotel all day.

"I'm having to do two sittings for lunch," Mrs. Bulfinch confided, "so I'd best be off. Will you be wanting a table at this sitting or the next?"

"Neither," Georgiana said hastily. "I think I'll take a walk and get some fresh air. Perhaps visit the children at Mrs. Tilly's."

"I'll tell the men you'll be back in an hour, shall I?"

Georgiana pursed her lips. "Make it two. I need to make some inquiries about our emigration."

Thank goodness Mrs. Bulfinch enjoyed bossing these men around so much. It meant Georgiana didn't have to go out there and face them. She took her guidebook and her parasol and slipped out the back door and through the kitchen, leaving her suitors to the formidable hotelier.

The guidebook said people gathered in the town square to find wagon train captains. Georgiana hadn't gone to see for herself yet, so she decided to detour past the square on her way to Mrs. Tilly's. She wrapped her shawl tighter, as there was a brisk breeze up, which took some of the warmth out of the day. But, oh, it was nice being out in the world, and not cooped up in the dusty rose smell of the parlor anymore. Georgiana felt herself relaxing as she walked off the torpor of the morning. Or at least she *was* relaxing, until she noticed the way people were staring at her. Every second man she passed tipped his hat at her. Some of them she recognized from her interviews, and some she didn't. She dropped her parasol to her shoulder to shield herself from their stares.

She heard the crowd in the town square from a distance: a wave of noise rose above the rooftops. She turned the corner, and suddenly, she was in a sea of humanity. It wasn't just wagon train captains who were lining the square: there were also wagonmakers and livestock traders, merchants and blacksmiths, all loudly hawking their services to a stream of emigrants. The place resembled a makeshift marketplace. Georgiana let the crowd carry her along like a current.

"Wagons!" one man was yelling, his voice hoarse. "Prairie schooners! Conestogas! Handcarts! Made to order! Some frames in stock, ready to go sooner!"

"*Our* wagons are guaranteed waterproof!" his nearby competitor was barking.

While she'd already ordered her wagons, she hadn't yet bought animals to pull them or supplies to fill them. She stopped and listened to a man explaining why oxen were better than mules, and then she moved on to the next person, to hear why mules were better than oxen. One woman was crying out about the importance of taking a milk cow on the trail, while right next to her a man insisted goats traveled better than cows and gave milk more reliably. Then there were the blacksmiths, shouting about the quality of their kettles and pots, and the grocers pointing people in the direction of their stores, with recommendations of how much flour, bacon, coffee, sugar and salt they should be buying.

It was head spinning. Georgiana felt a vague sense of panic. She didn't even own a kettle, let alone a milk cow! She had so much to do . . .

She wriggled through the crowd in search of the captains. That's where she should start. She should find a group to join, or she and the children would be stranded. And, despite what Mrs. Tilly had suggested last night, she had no intention of leaving such important matters to a husband . . . particularly as the quality of husband was proving to be of concern.

She could worry about kettles and cows once they were booked in with a group. Maybe the captain could give her advice on what kind of kettle she'd need, because the Lord knew she had no idea.

Matt Slater was a captain. He'd know about kettles. *Stop thinking about him.* He wasn't even going to California. He was going to Oregon.

He said he didn't have a wife there, but maybe he had a fiancée, or a sweetheart?

Stop it.

She was going to California. It didn't matter what Matt Slater was doing.

She needed to join a train—that was the *only* thing she should be thinking about right now. Matt Slater had mentioned someone who led parties on the California branch of the trail. She couldn't remember his name; it was something biblical. He and Matt Slater shared the trail until Fort Hall, she remembered. She bit her lip. Maybe Mr. Slater was here somewhere and she could ask him what the man's name was again . . .

Georgiana craned her neck to see over the crowds. Sure enough, there he was, under a sycamore. He was speaking quietly to a small group, and his friend Doyle was next to him, holding a ledger and scratching down names. The group in front of Matt included no small number of women, Georgiana noticed. The one in the blue bonnet said something, and he laughed politely. She couldn't see from her vantage point whether his dimple flashed or not when he laughed. Blue Bonnet would have been able to see. She felt a stab of jealousy and crept closer, straining to hear what they were saying. Another group had moved in behind Blue Bonnet and her companions, and Georgiana had to step sideways to get a clearer view of Matt. He caught the movement and looked over. Without thinking, she waved at him. She saw a faint frown pass over his face, and he turned back to Blue Bonnet. Georgiana wanted to *die* from embarrassment. Why had she waved like that? Like some kind of ninny schoolgirl.

"Well, look who we have here." As she was shriveling with mortification, a horribly familiar voice slid out of the crowd behind her. "If it isn't Mrs. Blunt . . . or is it *Mrs. Smith* now?"

Georgiana jumped out of her skin and snapped around. How had they found her? They were supposed to be waiting for her in the town of St. Joseph's. They weren't supposed to realize she wasn't coming to meet them until she was well on the trail, out of their reach!

Wendell Todd and Kipp Koerner slunk into view. The weeks since she'd seen them hadn't been kind to them. They were travel stained and gaunt.

"You look overwhelmed by the crowds, missus," Wendell said, his lip curling into a sneer. He was older and bigger than Kipp, and clearly furious with her. "Why don't we escort you somewhere quieter?"

"No, thank you." Georgiana took a step back, hastily taking stock of her escape routes. There weren't any easy ones. She was hemmed in by people.

Wendell grabbed her arm and she gasped. He wasn't gentle. "That wasn't really a question," he hissed. "Move."

"No." She didn't know where her bravery came from, except she felt reasonably safe, surrounded by so many people. "Get your hands off me or I'll scream."

Wendell's gaze was feral with anger. "You seem to be forgetting that we have your son."

"You seem to be forgetting that you need my signature on that deed." She yanked her arm away.

The air whistled through Wendell's teeth as he drew a sharp breath. "You see Kipp here, missus? I can send him on ahead, you know. We won't kill the boy, but we can make him suffer. Is that what you want?"

Of course that wasn't what she wanted! Georgiana felt shaky and on the verge of tears. God damn it! She'd nearly got ahead of them! She hadn't wanted them standing over her for the next few months, dogging her every step, scaring the life out of her children. She was going to California, just like they wanted; she was giving them the land, just like they wanted. She wished they'd just leave her alone and let her do it.

But of course they wouldn't. They wanted to make sure she didn't hire men to come after them, or alert the marshals. If she'd still had money, she *would* have hired someone, someone *lethal*. And the only reason she hadn't told the law about the kidnapping was that she'd read enough dime novels to know that lawmen could be as bloodthirsty as the criminals out west, and she didn't want Leo caught up in a gunfight . . .

"And," Wendell said, his voice dropping and getting more vicious by the moment, "don't forget we can take one of the others. How many do you have again? Four here in town? I reckon we can get a lot of cooperation out of you with four little 'uns to play with."

Georgiana wilted.

"There's a girl." Wendell had her arm again. "Now, let's go somewhere private and talk about what 'Mrs. Smith' has been up to, shall we?"

"I don't think the lady wants to go with you."

Oh my. Georgiana watched in shock as Matt Slater's giant paw closed around Wendell's wrist. Where had he come from? She looked up. He towered over them, and even without his bristling beard and wild hair, he looked like he'd just wrestled a bear. And won.

*D*ON'T GET CAUGHT *up in it.* Matt didn't want drama and difficulty. And yet, what was a man supposed to do, when he saw a slip of a woman being terrorized by thugs? Especially *this* woman, who looked like she should be packed in cotton wool. Was he supposed to stand by and let it happen?

Why not? She's not your responsibility.

She wasn't anyone's responsibility; that was the problem. The damn fool woman was running amok, placing ads for husbands and wandering around a half-wild town unescorted. Didn't she know that she stood out a mile, with her fancy dress and fancy ways? Didn't she know what a temptation she was? She was the female version of gold dust. One look and men got fever-struck. They just didn't have women like her in Independence. Hell, they didn't have women like her anywhere he'd ever been.

She was breathtaking. Who'd ever seen eyes that blue on a person? They were the color of a June sky. The color of prairie flax in summer. They made a man daft with how pretty they were. And then there was her curvy little figure. He'd seen the way men looked her up and down as she passed them by. Like this morning at breakfast. She walked through the room and every head turned.

And now here she was, wandering about the town square on her own, when it was packed full of all kind of rough sorts, who were just passing through on their way to the shimmer of gold over the horizon. Gold most of them would never see, the idiots. And each and every one of them turned their covetous gazes on this woman the minute they saw her. And then, when they learned she had a gold claim and was advertising for a husband, that covetousness turned to pure greed.

Didn't she see that?

No. He could tell she didn't. There was a palpable naïveté about her. She acted like the town was one big cotillion that she could waltz through until she found a partner to stick with. But things just didn't work like that. These weren't eligible gentlemen, waiting to fill out her dance card and fetch her lemonade; they weren't bound by the social mores she was used to. If she went into the saloons and whorehouses on the backstreets, she would be able to see for herself. These men saw, they wanted, they took. Someone needed to tell her so, before she got herself and those young 'uns tangled up with the wrong sort.

The sort like these two right here. They were scrawny, underfed-looking types, greasy and travel stained. One was so young he barely counted as a man, but he had a crafty rat weasel look, and Matt wasn't prepared to underestimate him.

Matt had seen Mrs. Smith the minute she sailed into the square. She was impossible to miss: her skirts were the size of a church bell, twice the size of any other woman's, and her dress had glittery black things all over it, which sparkled in the sun. No one else around here sparkled like that. The women around here all wore homespun and gingham. They had straw hats. Mrs. Smith didn't have a straw hat; she had a tiny, decorative black excuse of a bonnet and a black parasol made of lace; its fluttery edges caught the breeze as it bobbed above the crowd, loudly proclaiming her whereabouts. Everything about her was eye-catching, and no matter how hard he tried to ignore her and concentrate on his business, he was painfully aware of where she was as she paraded about. And then she'd neared his group, and he'd broken out in a prickly sweat. He felt those prairie flax blue eyes sweep him from head to toe, and it was an effort to concentrate on what the lady in front of him was saying. And then the two thugs had appeared behind her, and whatever they'd said had seemed to shock the hell out of her. He'd clenched his teeth and tried to resist the urge to get involved. Because it was *none of his business.* But then the idiot had gone and grabbed her.

Matt bent the man's wrist back until he let go of Mrs. Smith's arm. When the idiot finally did let go, Matt stepped slightly in front of her, to shield her.

"You've got no place in this," the stranger warned. His gaze flicked about, trying to gauge if anyone else was going to step in too. It didn't look it. The square was insanely busy and too chaotic for anyone to take notice of a low-key altercation like this one.

"Tell me about it," Matt snapped. "You think I want to be interrupting my transaction to deal with you two? But you got no call to be manhandling a respectable woman in plain day."

"Stay out of it, mister. You got no idea what you're getting into."

Something was off here. Matt stole a glance at Mrs. Smith. Her face had drained of color, and those big blue eyes were haunted . . . but she didn't look surprised. Or affronted. She looked watchful, like she was waiting for something inevitable . . .

Damn it. It was clear as day: she *knew* them.

What the hell *was* he getting himself into?

"She's with us," the young one told Matt. He had a wicked-looking scar down one side of his face and another one on his upper lip that made his mouth lopsided. They weren't good signs. He might be young, but he'd clearly survived a few bloody brawls.

"That true?" Matt searched her face, trying to work out what to do.

"In a manner of speaking," she admitted, her voice not entirely steady. Her June blue eyes had a suspicious shine. Was she about to cry? Hell.

"Look," he said, adopting as reasonable a tone as he was able, "Mrs. Smith has an appointment with *me* right this minute. Why don't you wait for her back at the hotel, like all the others? She'll talk to you when she returns." Buying her some time seemed the least that he could do. Hopefully, it was *all* that he'd have to do.

The older one snorted. "And who do you think you are to be telling us what to do? We don't need an *appointment* to talk to her."

"I'm afraid you do," Matt said. "Ain't you seen the line?"

"And what's *your* appointment about?" The young one's gaze slid back and forth between Matt and Mrs. Smith. "You answering that advertisement?"

Matt felt, rather than saw, Mrs. Smith flinch. The parasol jerked at the edge of his vision. So she was surprised that they knew about the advertisement, was she?

But *everyone* knew about it; it was the talk of the town. Why shouldn't they know?

Except, of course, her name wasn't really Smith, was it? It was Fairchild or Leavington or Bee or Blunt, or some arrangement of all of them, at least judging by her boys' names. And these two might be well aware of that. The "Smith" might even be *because* of them.

She was plainly scared to death.

"If you want to know, Mrs. Smith is thinking of joining my wagon train," he told the two thugs. He didn't know why he was lying for her, except it seemed the decent thing to do.

"No, she ain't," the older one said.

"She's coming in ours," the young one told Matt forcefully.

"Yours?" Matt couldn't keep the disbelief out of his voice. "You captain wagon trains?"

"No," the young one sneered, "but we've already signed up for one."

"You have, have you?" Matt had never liked bullies. And these two were bullies, plain and simple. "But has *she*?" Matt turned to Mrs. Smith.

She seemed uncertain.

"She has," the older thug said firmly.

"Who's your captain, then?"

"None of your business!"

"I think it *is* my business, since the lady already has a verbal contract with *me*," he continued to lie, silently cursing himself for a fool. What was he doing? He wasn't even going to California. But these idiots didn't know that. He hoped Mrs. Smith didn't look too shocked by his storytelling. If she could go along with him, perhaps he could extract her from this. Even if only for the afternoon.

"I'm getting mighty sick of you, mister," the older one growled. "Why don't you move along now."

"Slater! Matthew Slater! Don't move a muscle! I need to talk to you!" Someone's arm waved above the crowd, trying to catch Matt's attention.

"Well, look at that," Matt said, peering over their heads at the beefy man cutting through square toward them. "If it isn't the sheriff."

They got all rodenty at that, twitching like rats in the henhouse. He thought they might scamper off, but they didn't. If anything, they only grew more threatening, fixing their hateful stares firmly on Mrs. Smith. She made a small breathless noise, and without thinking, Matt found himself taking her hand. She flinched, and then he felt her fingers curl around his, clamping onto him. She was trembling.

Goddamn it all to hell and back.

She was terrified. Matt didn't know what to do about it, except to hold her hand a bit tighter and to keep brazening his way through it.

"Slater!" Sheriff Keeley was puffing as he reached them. "I need your help with a matter. Fill me in on that mess in Kearney."

"Always happy to help," Matt said, relieved. He'd dug himself a pretty hole here, and he was glad someone was offering him a ladder out of it. He kept tight hold of Mrs. Smith as he pulled her away from the rodents. "Come on, Mrs. Smith."

"She needs to talk to us." The young one was clearly furious. "We got business together."

The older one held her gaze. Something awful passed silently between them.

Matt wasn't about to leave her with them. If she had to talk to them, she could do it somewhere safe, where people would know if something happened to her.

Not that it was his business.

Except, idiot that he was, he seemed to have made it so.

"We should be back at the hotel in a couple of hours," he told them, "should you wish to continue this conversation. Does that suit you?" He turned to Mrs. Smith. Her eyes were shinier than ever, and she was white with tension.

She nodded and tried to find her voice. It cracked when she spoke. "Yes. Yes, thank you."

"There you go." He didn't give the rodents time to protest. "We'll see you at the hotel, gentlemen. Shall we say 4 P.M.? I'm sure Mrs. Smith will be finished with her day's business by then. Don't be late."

The older thug gave her a look of pure poison. "We'll bring

the children with us, shall we? Save you having to collect them from the teahouse."

Damn it all to hell. They were using the children to threaten her? What kind of mess was she tangled up in?

He saw the sheriff giving them a look over. Keeley was no fool. Maybe Matt should take Mrs. Smith along with him, so Keeley could have a chat with her. Then Matt could wash his hands of the whole affair.

"The children are fine where they are," Matt said, and it was impossible to keep the anger out of his voice.

"What children?" the sheriff asked.

"*My* children," Mrs. Smith said, and Matt could hear that she was angry too. Angry, but also intimidated. "They're staying with Mrs. Tilly, and I'm quite happy for them to remain there until suppertime. I'd *prefer* it." Her voice grew firmer and steadier.

"And you're meeting these gentlemen at four?" The sheriff rested his hand on his holster.

She nodded nervously.

"Seems like it's all arranged, then." The sheriff's tone brooked no argument. "The lady will see you at the Grand Hotel at four. And I'll be over at Mrs. Tilly's this afternoon," he said, an undercurrent of warning in his voice, "and I'll be sure to check on the little 'uns while I have my afternoon teacake."

The rodents were silent, but their eyes glittered with fury and frustration.

"Four o'clock, then," the older one agreed, his lip still curled in that feral sneer. If looks could have killed, Mrs. Smith would have fallen stone-cold dead as they slunk away.

"Oh my," Mrs. Smith said, her fingers abruptly going limp in his. "Do you think they'll go after the children now?"

"I'll send Freeman over to the teahouse," the sheriff reassured her, gesturing to his deputy. "Off you go. And don't stop anywhere on the way, you hear? Go and drink some tea until I get there this afternoon."

"You just want me to sit at Mrs. Tilly's all day?" The deputy didn't sound happy about it.

"Until this lady here or I come and tell you otherwise."

The deputy grumbled under his breath but went along. As he left, Mrs. Smith pulled her hand away from Matt's.

"I have to get him out of the jailhouse anyway," the sheriff confided after he'd ambled off. "At least while that whore is locked up. He don't do nothing but moon over her, so I might as well have him being useless over there at Mrs. Tilly's as useless back at the jailhouse with Seline." The sheriff gave Mrs. Smith a long look. "I think you'd best come along with us, Mrs. Smith. Give us an idea of who those two are and what they're up to. But you might have to wait with the whore while I take care of my business with Mr. Slater."

She looked horrified at the idea. But she didn't protest.

"Let me just tell Doyle where I'm going." Matt excused himself and headed over to where Seb was standing, juggling the ledger and trying to answer questions from the party Matt had abandoned.

"I'll try and get back this afternoon, but if I don't, just take as many bookings as you can," he told Seb. "But you make sure they're capable and not too dumb, you hear? No more disasters like the year we had the McCappins. I ain't going through that again."

"You want me to organize a meeting time at the Saturday dance again, like last year?"

"Yeah, we'll do it every Saturday till we leave. Good chance for them all to get to know one another." He clapped his hand on Seb's shoulder and headed off.

By the time he got back, Mrs. Smith was looking edgier than an unbroken filly, like she might bolt at any moment. It'd be easier for Matt if she did. But, sandwiched between Matt and the sheriff, she came along, edgy or not.

As IF IT wasn't bad enough being left to wait in a jailhouse, Georgiana had been left to wait with a whore. The woman was caged up in a small cell in the corner of the sheriff's office, and she'd eavesdropped on every word of Georgiana's brief conversation with the sheriff. It had made it seem even tawdrier to have a whore witness the lies Georgiana heard coming out of her own mouth.

"They're my cousins," she'd heard herself say when the

sheriff questioned her about the scene in the town square. The lie was patently ridiculous, as Wendell and Kipp barely looked the same species as Georgiana, let alone as though they were closely related.

The whore had leaned against the bars, her enormous breasts bulging over her corset, and had smirked at every word Georgiana said.

"You're a terrible liar," the whore drawled once the sheriff had gone.

Georgiana felt rude ignoring her, as it was such a small room, but she'd never even seen a whore before (at least as far as she knew), and she didn't know where to look, let alone what to say. The woman certainly fit the image Georgiana had of soiled doves. She was in her unmentionables, for a start. In public. She had a Chinese robe thrown on, but she let it fall open, and most of her body was on clear display. Georgiana had noticed how the sheriff couldn't keep his gaze away from her, try as he might. Her breasts looked like they might just burst out of her corset at any moment. But even if she had been fully dressed, her unnaturally bright red hair and rouged cheeks would have given her away. As would the smudgy black kohl around her tawny green eyes.

"But you're a smart girl, honey," the whore continued in a thick Tennessee drawl. "There ain't no point in accusing a man of rape, not to another man at least. They stick together."

"No one tried to rape me," Georgiana said, aghast.

The whore shrugged. "Whatever you say."

"I had an altercation with my cousins. It's just a misunderstanding." She'd spent the whole walk to the jailhouse trying to work out a story to explain her run-in with Wendell and Kipp, and this was the best she could come up with. It wasn't a good story, but at least it was a story. The sheriff had seemed dubious, but he hadn't outright called her a liar the way the whore did.

"Where you from, honey?" the whore asked. She was obviously bored in the cell and wanted to make the most of the company. Georgiana wasn't sure which was worse, having to lie to the sheriff, or having to talk to the whore. The sheriff was probably worse, but not by much.

"I'm from New York," Georgiana said, keeping her eyes fixed over the whore's right shoulder. All that bare flesh was too much for her constitution.

"Oh, I'd love to see New York! I ain't been farther east than Louisville, Kentucky." The whore's face turned dreamy. "I once had a man who wanted to take me to New York." She sighed. "But then he got married and all that talk stopped. They do that, you know; tell you stories and paint you a picture about the places they'll take you and the things you'll see. They tell you you'll be a princess and they'll carry you off on their white horse. But they're always just stories. They get up in the morning, put their boots on and never once even get their horse out of the stable to take you for a ride."

"I know," Georgiana said grimly, thinking of her husband.

The whore gave her a curious look.

"I mean, I imagine," Georgiana said, lifting her chin. She had her pride.

"I'm Seline." The whore stuck her hand through the cell bars for Georgiana to shake.

Georgiana wished she hadn't. She took it gingerly between her fingers and shook it once, dropping it as fast as she could.

The whore laughed. "You ladies are all the same. You think you're so much better than me, but you're as much a whore as I am. You just call it marriage. And those men answering your advertisement, they're whores too."

"You know about my advertisement?" Georgiana felt uncomfortable at the idea.

"Honey, *everyone* knows." She cocked her head. "Did it work? Did you find a husband yet?"

"Not yet," Georgiana said stiffly.

"Well, when you have a candidate, you should come ask me about him. Chances are I'd know him. They all come to the Bunkhouse sooner or later; it's the best cathouse in town. And I'm the best cat in the cathouse," she said smugly.

Georgiana blushed.

"Seriously," the whore said, "you come and ask. I can tell you which ones are mean. It's always worth knowing that. You don't want to be marrying a man who's mean. Trust me, I should know."

Thankfully, they were interrupted at that point.

The whore gave a shriek when she saw who was coming through the door.

"Matt Slater, is that you? Honey hush! You shaved again. You know I *love* it when you shave."

The brute stood dumbstruck. Georgiana felt a stab of pure jealousy as she saw the way his eyes were fixed on the whore's chest. And was he *blushing*?

"Did you come to rescue me?" the whore asked, fluttering her eyelashes.

"I came for Mrs. Smith," he mumbled.

He *was*. He was blushing. Georgiana's jealousy turned to anger. She had no right to be angry at him, but that didn't stop the fact that she was.

"Lucky Mrs. Smith," the whore hooted.

Matt Slater flinched. "Let's go," he muttered.

"You come and visit me when I'm back at the Bunkhouse, you hear," Seline called after him as they left, "and I'll give you a special welcome!"

So he visited whores. She didn't know why that disappointed her so much. He was a frontiersman, and she supposed that's what they did for company on the frontier. He wasn't married. A man had needs.

That made her think of Leonard. Married men had needs too. He had been away for years at a time, and she'd always had a sick certainty, which sat like a lump in her stomach, that he found other women on his travels. Women who weren't her.

This was why she should choose a husband she wasn't attracted to, one she wouldn't love, because of this horrible feeling of shame and hate and rage and . . . failure. She needed a man she didn't care about, so that raw part of her wouldn't die a small death every time he found comfort in the arms of another woman.

❊ 8 ❊

WENDELL AND KIPP were back at the hotel when Georgiana and Matt returned, and they'd made short work of annoying the men waiting for their afternoon interviews.

"You can't cut in!" one particularly irate New Englander protested loudly.

"We just did."

Georgiana stepped in just as Kipp pulled a knife on the poor man. "Wait!" She gingerly touched Kipp's hand and turned the knife away from the clueless New Englander. "I'm so sorry, but I just need to speak to these men for ten minutes," she apologized to the crowd.

"I've been waiting since yesterday, and they only just turned up!" The knife hadn't discouraged the New Englander. If anything, it only seemed to have fueled his irritation. His voice got prissier the more irritated he grew.

"They're not here for the interviews," she told him, striving for calm. It wasn't easy. Not only were her nerves shredded by Wendell and Kipp's presence, but she was wrung out by her lunchtime adventures with the jailhouse and the whore. Her lunchtime adventures that had meant she'd completely missed lunch and was cranky with hunger.

"They're my cousins," she told the men in the foyer as she facilitated Wendell and Kipp jumping the queue. Or perhaps it was the brooding bulk of Matt Slater standing behind her that convinced them.

"Your cousins?" The New Englander was clearly dubious. And why shouldn't he be? It was the most bald-faced lie Georgiana had ever told. Almost.

"If you could just be patient for another few minutes," she asked, "we're making arrangements for the trip to California."

"I should think you'd want to wait to hear your husband's opinion on those matters," the New Englander said, disgruntled. Georgiana mentally crossed him off the list, even as she gave him a sugary smile.

"What are *you* doing?" Wendell Todd snapped when Matt moved to join them in the parlor.

"It's a public room," he said.

No one was more surprised than Georgiana that Matt had continued to shadow her. He could have left her at the jailhouse; he could have left her on the front steps of the hotel; he could have left her in the parlor with Wendell and Kipp. But he didn't. He just kept coming along. Like a guard dog.

Georgiana couldn't deny that she was relieved to have him there. He took up residence in one of the salmon pink velvet chairs by the window.

"What *are* you doing?" Georgiana whispered as she sank into the chair beside him.

"Witnessing," he told her, not bothering to lower his voice. He'd left the door ajar, she noticed.

"Close it," Wendell ordered.

"You close it." Matt slouched back in the chair, legs spread. His expression was unreadable.

"*I'll* close it," Kipp snapped, kicking it closed with a slam.

"No one asked you to be here." Wendell was too highly strung to sit. He stood by the fireplace, jiggling his leg. His spurs chimed every time he jiggled.

"*She* did." Matt jerked his head at Georgiana.

Georgiana felt like someone was sitting on her chest. She needed to keep this under control. These men had her son. She couldn't afford to antagonize them more than she had already.

"What have you told him?" Wendell demanded.

"Sit down, Mr. Todd, and we can talk in a civilized fashion," she implored.

"Not until you tell us what you've told him."

"She ain't told me anything, except that you're her cousins," Matt sighed. He didn't sound like he believed a word of it.

"That's right," Kipp said, thrusting his chin out, "we're her cousins."

"Look. I'm only here to see that you talk civil to the lady. I don't care *what* you talk about, so long as you keep it nice. I don't give a fig if you're her cousins, her stableboys or her great-aunts. Just keep a civil tongue in your heads." He reclined and rested his head on the back of his chair. "Don't mind me. I'll just take a doze while y'all talk." His eyes closed.

No one believed for a minute that he wasn't listening to every word they said.

"That's really all you told him?" Wendell was still jiggling with nerves.

Georgiana met his eye and nodded. "It is."

"Why wasn't you in St. Joseph's, like we arranged?" He flicked a glance at Matt. "We were waiting for you . . . cuz."

Georgiana steeled herself and actually told the truth. "I wanted to get a husband first."

Wendell put his hands on his hips and shook his head. He looked frustrated. "We *said* we'd take you there. What do you need a husband for?"

"I've got the children to think of."

"*We're* taking you to California!" Kipp's narrow face was pinched with anger. Of the two of them, he was the one who scared Georgiana more. "You think you can get around us with a husband?"

"We'll protect you," Wendell insisted, glaring at Kipp. "That's what we're here for: to get you and your little 'uns there safe."

Ha. Except for the fact that just a few hours ago they were threatening to hurt the children to keep her cooperative.

"And then?" Georgiana asked. She was sweating. She didn't know how to control this conversation. "And then what? We get to California . . ."—she paused as Wendell pointed to Matt and gave her a warning look—"and you help me . . ." she finished by mouthing the words *get my son back*. "And then what? I'm in California, with a pack of children and no money." Saying it so baldly made tears prick her eyes.

"Don't do that," Wendell said tightly. "Don't go using your tears against us."

She thought Matt's eyelids opened a crack at that.

"I have to think of our future."

"You can get a husband in California once our business is done," Kipp said dismissively. "So you can go right out there

and tell those fancy boys to get. You ain't going to be marrying anyone. Not yet."

"Wait a minute, Kipp." Wendell grabbed his companion by
the arm and tried to silence him. "You got that land on the
main street of Mokelumne Hill, don'tcha? As well as the gold
claim?" he asked Georgiana.

She nodded stiffly. "My new husband and I will be setting
up a mercantile business."

"There's good money to be made doing that," he said.

"I'm sure there is. But I can't do it alone. I *won't* do it
alone." She wasn't backing down on this one. She was getting
a husband, and they could just accept it. They needed her, and
she needed *this*. What if something happened to her? What if
the deal with Hec Boehm went wrong and the children were
left alone? She was going to ensure they had someone to look
after them.

"I see," Wendell said slowly. "You're that determined?"

"I am." There was steel in Georgiana's voice.

Wendell nodded.

Georgiana fidgeted. The silence dragged on. What was he
thinking? What were they going to *do*?

"Kipp. Come here, I want to talk to you." Wendell gestured
him to the door. "You wait here," he told Georgiana.

"What do you think they need to talk about, in secret like
that?" Matt asked, without opening his eyes.

"I don't know," Georgiana said anxiously. "But it's probably not good."

"They're your cousins, huh?" He shifted in his chair.

She didn't answer.

"None of my business," he muttered.

It *was* none of his business. So why was he here?

She jumped as the door opened and hurriedly looked away
from Matt before they caught her mooning over him.

"We told 'em all to go," Kipp announced.

"You what?" Georgiana couldn't believe it. Of all the high-
handed . . . She hadn't found a husband yet!

"We told 'em you don't need them anymore." Wendell
looked pleased with himself.

"What gives you the right?" She was *sick* of these men telling her what to do. Leonard. These two. They all treated her

like she was some half-wit child. Well, they had another thing coming if they thought she was going to stand for that!

"You don't need 'em anymore," Wendell told her. He was frighteningly smug. "We found you a husband."

Her mouth fell open.

Beside her, Matt sat up. The news of their matchmaking seemed to have shattered any pretense of sleep.

"You *what*?" Georgiana's stomach sank.

"*I'll* marry you," Wendell said. He looked proud of himself.

Georgiana struggled to comprehend what he was saying. "*You?*"

"Me."

"It's perfect," Kipp told her. "You want a husband, Wendell ain't married and he fancies the idea of running a store."

"And you ain't a bad-looking woman," Wendell added.

Georgiana's head was swimming. Oh no. No, no, no, no, no, no. She met Matt's gaze. He was poised, waiting for her to say something. She knew if she asked, he would step in.

"I think it would make your *kids* mighty happy," Kipp said. There was malice in his eyes. He meant Leo.

She broke out in chills. Was that a threat?

Of course it was. Of course these rat-faced cowards were threatening her child. The kind of men who could hold a child hostage clearly wouldn't blink at using him to force his mother into marriage.

"So that's settled, then," Wendell said. "We'll get married. We'll do it as soon as possible."

"No!" She wouldn't marry a man like him in a blue fit.

She heard Matt sigh as he got to his feet. Wendell and Kipp's hands leapt to their weapons. They kept them there, frozen, waiting to see what Matt would do.

He didn't do anything. He just stood there, a mountainous presence in the dusky pink room, watching them.

Wendell's expression darkened. "You said you wanted a husband."

"I can't marry you," she said desperately, casting around for a way out of the trap.

"Sit back down," Kipp warned Matt.

"Why cain't you marry me?" Wendell demanded.

"I just can't," Georgiana repeated. She inched in front of

Matt. She was scared they'd shoot him, or stab him; Kipp looked like he was just waiting for the opportunity. But Matt took her by the shoulders and set her firmly aside.

Damn them all! She wasn't a sack of wheat!

"Why not?" Wendell asked forcefully.

"Because I'm already married!" she blurted.

"What?" He was looking really murderous now, and Kipp had drawn his weapon. "No, you ain't."

"I am! I got married!" She heard the edge of hysteria in her voice.

"Oh yeah?" He clearly didn't believe her. "Who to?"

Who to? Georgiana felt faint.

"Who to?" Wendell demanded.

"To . . . to . . . *him*!" Georgiana panicked and did the only thing she could think of.

She pointed straight at Matt Slater.

❦ 9 ❦

"WHAT THE HELL was that?" Matt bellowed when he finally had her alone. He'd dragged her upstairs to her rooms. The door slamming behind them actually seemed to shake the hotel, he slammed it with such force.

"You don't actually have to marry me," she said quickly, trying to appease him.

"You're damn straight I don't!"

"Keep your voice down." She couldn't take any more shouting. Her ears were still ringing from the scene in the parlor.

He made a huffing sound and ran his hands through his hair until it just about stood on end.

"I'm sorry for dragging you into this." She really was. She'd well and truly painted herself into a corner this time.

He gave her a filthy look. "You didn't seem so sorry when you were telling them about our wedding."

Georgiana blushed. She had rather blathered on. What could she say? She'd panicked.

"Jesus," he said, sitting down hard on one of the wingback chairs. He rubbed his face. "You want to tell me what just happened down there?"

Georgiana struggled to find the words to explain it. It was all such a *mess*. And it wasn't like she could tell him the *truth* . . .

"I don't know what kind of trouble you're in, lady, but that was a *dumb* move."

She knew it was. It didn't even save her from Wendell's plan to marry her, because once they found out her story was a big fat lie, she'd be right back where she started.

Matt Slater looked up at her, his golden-lit eyes utterly exasperated. "Give me one good reason why I shouldn't go down there right now and tell them we ain't married."

Georgiana's heart was pounding as she sized Matt up. Was there a chance he *wouldn't* go down there and tell them? It hadn't occurred to her that he might *keep* playing along. He'd clearly been too bamboozled to protest downstairs, and then too concerned for her immediate safety afterward. But she hadn't considered that he'd continue to lie for her, that he might help her fake a marriage . . .

Was that even possible?

Could they get away with it?

Her mind whirled as she sorted through the possibilities. What was the benefit of pretending to be married to him?

It kept Wendell and Kipp at bay.

Was that all?

Well, there was *him* . . .

Her gaze swept his long legs and wide shoulders. He caught her looking and she blushed. He was far too gorgeous for comfort . . .

That was a negative, not a positive, she reminded herself firmly. It would be risky to spend time in his company. There were other negatives too, such as the fact that pretending to be his wife meant she couldn't choose an *actual* husband, which meant she was stuck with her original problem: taking the children on a two-thousand-mile journey without anyone to care for them if something happened to her.

But it wasn't like a better husband had presented himself, was it? The candidates so far had been utterly useless, or she wouldn't even *be* in this situation.

Say she and Matt Slater *did* pretend to be married . . .

He would be able to help her get provisioned; he knew the trail; he would certainly be able to keep the children safe until they reached Fort Hall. He would discourage men who might take liberties with her. But what would happen then, when they reached Fort Hall and the California Trail split from the Oregon Trail? They certainly couldn't continue the lie of their marriage after that, if he went one way and she went another. She and the children would be very much alone, travel-worn and at the mercy of Wendell and Kipp, but this time deep in the wilderness, way beyond the reach of the law.

It wasn't a good plan. There were just too many holes.

But if they admitted they weren't married now, Wendell would try to force her to marry *him*. Georgiana shuddered. No. The fake marriage was far better than that.

She was overwhelmed by the way her mind raced to and fro, hitting dead ends at every turn.

Was Matt Slater even a man she could trust? She examined him. He had his head in his hands, so she couldn't see his face. He was as big as a grizzly bear and seemed more capable than anyone she'd ever met. And he was without a doubt the best-looking man she'd ever seen, even with his face covered.

But that wasn't really a positive, was it? In her experience, good-looking men were vain and prone to peacocking. They thrived on the attention of women, and that wasn't something she wanted in her life again. In her experience, it led to jealousy and hurt and piercing loneliness.

What *did* she actually know about him? She couldn't really base her children's safety on a gut response to seeing him for the first time, in his buckskins with his bristling black beard, looking like a wild frontiersman. That didn't tell her anything except that he looked fine in buckskins and hadn't shaved in a while. She needed to consider his qualities. Beyond buckskins and beautiful brown eyes.

What *qualities* did he have?

Well, he'd been kind to her, for a start. He didn't always look happy about it, but he had been kind. He'd stepped in when Wendell and Kipp had surprised her in the square today. And when Mrs. Bulfinch had interrupted that horrible scene in the parlor just now, he had defended her then too. And then he'd whisked her safely through the crowd of impatient men, who were sick of waiting to be interviewed. At every step he'd been protective—in an irritable sort of way.

And then there was the way he'd been nice to the boys at breakfast this morning. He'd even made them laugh. They hadn't had much in the way of fatherly attention in their lives, and it had pinched Georgiana's heart to watch it.

He'd also thoughtfully deflected the hopeful "husbands," so she could eat. That had been kind too.

So he was kind, considerate, a protector . . .

You're being hasty. Her mother's voice sounded in her

head. That was exactly what her mother had said all those years ago, when Georgiana had set her heart on marrying Leonard. And this was exactly the same mistake she'd made with Leonard: forming a character judgment after only a couple of meetings. She should know better by now. It took time to really know someone. A pretty face and a pretty manner could only hide a rotten heart for so long.

I am being hasty, Mother. But I don't have time to be anything else . . . Sometimes needs must. And this was one of those times. A fake marriage to Matt Slater was better than a real marriage to Wendell Todd. Even without knowing Mr. Slater well, she knew that much. At the very least he wasn't holding her son to ransom, as Mr. Todd was. It was a low bar to set, but she hadn't been the one to set it.

"They don't want you marrying," Matt said, breaking into her thoughts, "that was perfectly clear. Unless it's to one of them."

Georgiana nodded absently. How could she convince him to keep up the charade? Or better yet, make the marriage real . . . She wasn't really safe from Wendell and Kipp until she was married for real.

"They've got something on you, don't they?" he asked shrewdly.

"Not exactly." She paused, trying to choose her words carefully. "They've got something of mine I need to get back." She took a deep breath. There was no harm in trying, was there? "Mr. Slater, I appreciate everything you've done for me . . ."

He looked suspicious.

She couldn't really blame him for that. She tried to think of how to broach the subject, and in the end opted for bluntness. "I need a husband," she said.

He blanched.

"And I'd like that husband to be you." Oh my. It was like stepping off a ledge and dropping into empty space. Her stomach was headed for her toes as she waited for his response.

"Oh no." He was on his feet in a heartbeat, towering over her until her neck was sore from looking up. "I told you: I ain't actually going to marry you."

"You probably heard just now in the parlor, I have a piece of land on the main street of a gold mining town," she said quickly. "It's not much, but it should be a perfect place to build a mercantile store."

"That's nice for you." He was looking at her like she was a rabid dog. She half expected him to start backing toward the door.

"I have enough funds put aside to set up the business." She nervously smoothed her skirts. "I'm young enough, and obviously fertile. And I hope I'm not too displeasing to look at."

"No." His fierce black eyebrows drew together, and he started shaking his head. "No. No way in hell."

"I *need* a husband, Mr. Slater. You must see that. I can't be traveling alone, not with children."

"So pick one! There's dozens of them crawling around down there. And dozens more out there in town." He flung a hand at the window. "The place is seething with them!"

"Trust me, I *would* choose one of them . . . if even *one* of them was so much as halfway suitable."

He gave a short laugh. "That ain't much of a compliment to me, is it?"

"You said you weren't married," she continued.

"You can stop right there, missy. I ain't married and I ain't *looking to be married*. So you can get all these ideas out of your head."

Georgiana pulled a face. No. He wasn't open to the idea at all. Oh well. It had been worth a shot. She'd try another tack.

"If you can't marry me," she suggested, "can you at least *pretend* to be married to me?"

"Lady, you're unhinged."

"No," she sighed, "just desperate."

"Again, that ain't much of a compliment to me."

"Were you looking for compliments?" She looked up at him. "I can do compliments if it would help?"

"No!" He was startled. Then horrified. "Don't."

"You said you join up with a California train for the journey? That you travel together?" She kept her voice calm and reasonable as she prepared to explain why a pretend marriage wasn't a completely insane idea.

He nodded, still looking at her like she was rabid.

"Couldn't we simply pretend to be married until the wagon trains separate? That should keep me safe from Wendell, at least for a while . . . and then you can go on your way to Oregon. With no harm done."

"You want me to pretend to be married to you for the next few months?" Disbelief wasn't a strong enough word to describe his reaction.

"Yes, please," she said meekly.

"And what are you going to do then?" He seemed astounded by her stupidity. "I don't see what good this does."

Georgiana flushed. She knew it sounded ridiculous. But she couldn't think of anything that wasn't; the whole situation was ridiculous. "I don't know," she admitted, "but it gives me time to think of something."

Matt sighed and rubbed at his face. He wasn't saying no, she thought hopefully.

"I just need some time," she pleaded. "Otherwise, Wendell will drag me to the altar first thing tomorrow."

"If he does, you can always say no," he told her. "There's a whole bit in the wedding where they give you the chance to do that."

"No, I can't." She clutched her stomach at the stabbing fear, which was all too constant since she'd learned of Leo's kidnapping. "I can't tell you why . . . but I can't say no."

"What in hell do they have against you?"

She couldn't tell him. It was too risky.

He made a disgusted noise. "Lady, it won't work."

"It doesn't have to work for long!" But the longer the better, as she didn't have a clue what to do next.

He had a patient look on his face, and when he spoke it was like he was talking to a small child. One who was slow on the uptake. "And if they don't want you getting married, what's to stop them getting rid of me?"

Georgiana frowned, not following.

Matt sighed and drew a finger across his throat. "You know, *getting rid of me*."

"They wouldn't!"

"You sure of that, lady? They seem to have some mighty strong incentive to keep a tight rein on you, even if you won't tell me what it is. And that—Wendell is it?—he seems set on you for himself. Wouldn't it be a damn sight easier for them to get rid of me than to put up with me?"

Oh my. He was right. What *was* to stop them killing him? He was in their way. Georgiana wasn't used to dealing with men like this. Her knees went weak under her, and she sank to the desk chair, her skirts ballooning around her.

"What's your real name, lady?" he asked, a touch of concern in his voice.

"Georgiana Smith."

"Ha. You might want to tell those boys of yours. They introduced themselves by some fancier names than that."

Georgiana winced. All four children were finding it difficult to remember to use the pseudonym.

"So is it Leavington Bee Fairchild? Or Blunt Fairchild Leavington?"

They really had given their full names, she thought dryly. "My name is Georgiana Bee Blunt," she admitted.

"Suits you better than Smith."

She didn't know if he meant it as a compliment or not. It was difficult to tell. "Please don't say anything tonight," she begged. "That's all I ask. Just give me tonight to work out what to do."

Matt promised, but that was all he was going to promise. He planned to stay well out of it from here on in.

❧ 10 ❧

"I KNOW YOU AIN'T married."

Matt kicked himself for answering the door. He should have known it would only bring trouble. He'd just got back to his room, and he was out of temper. Time was getting away from him. He still had to get his whole train provisioned and staffed, and sign up paying customers, and he was weeks behind schedule. He hadn't managed to get free of Mrs. Blunt until late afternoon, and all he'd achieved so far today was meeting a few potential scouts. Hopefully, Seb had signed up some more customers, or the day would be a total loss.

He'd just come back to the hotel to feed his animals and check on Deathrider before heading out again to find Seb. Doc Barry had been by and seen to Deathrider's wound. He'd agreed to keep quiet about the gunshot and instead to tell people Tom Slater had been snakebit—for a price. The doc and his wife were coming along with Matt's train, at a whoppingly discounted rate. That was another one Deathrider owed him.

Matt thought for sure he'd had his fill of trouble for the day, especially since he'd been lucky enough to avoid running into Mrs. Blunt on his way up to the room. It had been a close call, as not five minutes after he'd closed his door, he heard her tribe emerge onto the landing. They made enough noise to wake the dead.

They certainly woke Deathrider, who was in the filthiest mood Matt had ever seen. The Indian was usually implacable. Matt had seen him face down grizzlies, plow through blizzards and withstand white people slinging insults at him without so much as twitching. But now, the mere fact that the sheets were scratchy was enough to send him into a fit. He was clearly in pain, but stubborn as ever, he thrashed at the sheets until they pulled free, and then he flung them across the room. Which was stupid, as it only pulled at his stitches and caused more pain.

He was getting ready to hurl the pillows after the sheets when the knocking sounded at the door.

"Well, get it," Deathrider snapped.

Matt moved at a snail's pace, just to annoy him. It was good to see he was well enough to annoy.

"Don't be a horse's ass."

Matt slowed down even further. He heard Deathrider growl. He turned his back on him and opened the door.

"I know you ain't married." Wendell Todd was standing on the landing, his expression an oily mix of smugness, irritation and triumph. He spat the words at Matt before the door was even all the way open, and his rodent eyes gleamed with pleasure.

Matt didn't invite him in. He had a half a mind to simply close the door in his face.

"You know what I did today, while you were closeted away with her?" Wendell's rat face grew crafty. "I went out hunting. I'm a good hunter, Slater."

"That so?" Matt felt nothing but boredom. He was utterly sick of the whole stupid situation. He shouldn't have come back to the hotel. He should have left Deathrider to his thirst and his scratchy sheets. If he had, he wouldn't be talking to this rat-faced fool.

"I spoke to the judge and went around to all the churches in town. There weren't no wedding today between you and the lady." Wendell's triumph was clear.

Sorry, Mrs. Blunt, Matt thought, glancing at her closed door. Looks like the lie won't even last the night. Matt felt a pang for her, but not enough to protest. It had been a dumb lie in the first place and was never going to hold up for long.

"Who in hell is that?" Deathrider complained from the bed. "Tell them to go and get me some water."

Wendell's gaze darted over Matt's shoulder, and his eyes sprang wide as he saw Deathrider. "I know you!" he blurted.

Hell. Matt grabbed Wendell by the shirt and yanked him into the room, kicking the door closed behind him.

"I know you!" Wendell repeated, looking awestruck.

Matt rammed Wendell against the wall. "No, you don't," he snapped.

"You're that Indian," Wendell blathered, his gaze still fixed on Deathrider, who was naked except for a pair of long underwear, his chest tattoos and the bandage over his wound clearly visible. "You're the Plague of the West!"

Goddamn this town and its nosy people!

"We was there at the trading post when Saltbush Pete tried to shoot you!" Wendell was excited. "We *saw* it!"

Matt shoved him hard. "No, you didn't."

"We did." Wendell looked confused.

"You're mistaken. This is my brother Tom."

"You were there too! I didn't recognize you without the beard." He clearly wasn't that bright. "Are you an Indian too?"

"Clearly not." Matt sensed Deathrider rising from the bed behind him. "And he ain't either. He's plain old Tom Slater from Oregon."

Wendell was transfixed by the sight of Deathrider. "Saltbush Pete tried to shoot you in the back, and you moved just in time. I saw it. It was like some magic Indian trick."

"Kill him," Deathrider said flatly.

Wendell flinched. "You cain't kill me."

"Get back to bed and let me deal with this," Matt snapped at Deathrider. "You'll only rip your stitches and bleed all over the place."

"Get off me," Wendell said.

Matt felt something hard press into his gut. He knew it was the muzzle of a gun before he looked. So Wendell wasn't that stupid, then.

"See what you've done," Matt complained to Deathrider as he backed away from the pistol.

"I wasn't the one who let him in."

"If you'd left your damn sheets alone, he wouldn't have seen your wound and got all excited. You'da just been a sick man in bed."

"Shut up," Wendell ordered, waving the pistol to get Matt to back up. He looked more triumphant than he had when he'd shown up, if such a thing was possible. There was even more of a weasel gleam in his eye than before. "I got you," he said. "I got you now."

"I don't know what you think you've 'got,'" Matt sighed, "but it probably ain't something you want."

"Sit down." Wendell gestured at the bed.

"I'd rather not."

"Put your gun away," Deathrider ordered.

Wendell laughed. "How dumb do you think I am?"

"Pretty dumb."

"See, this is why people shoot at you," Matt complained. "You go around provoking everyone."

"I got a deal for you, Slater," Wendell announced. He had his gun trained on Deathrider now. Matt didn't fancy his chances, even with Deathrider unarmed. "Sit down, the both of you, and I'll tell you about it."

"How about I stand here and you tell me about it?"

"How about you act like a man and take that gun off him?" Deathrider snapped at Matt. He was looking off-color. Getting out of bed clearly wasn't agreeing with him.

"You should probably sit down," Matt told him.

"I *will* shoot you!" Wendell sounded plenty frustrated.

Deathrider held up his arms, exposing the swollen flesh above and below his bandage. "Go ahead. Put me out of my misery."

"He crazy?" Wendell asked Matt.

"No more than usual. He's sick. So hurry the hell up and tell us about your deal so I can get him back to bed." Matt put a restraining hand on Deathrider's arm. "Go on, we ain't going to attack you. Say your piece."

"I might attack you," Deathrider said sourly.

"I ain't scared! *I'm* the one with the gun."

"For now."

"Hurry up and get this done before you don't have it anymore," Matt told him shortly.

Wendell was looking nervous. Matt didn't like it. Nervous men got itchy trigger fingers.

"You were saying that I ain't married," Matt prompted.

"No, you ain't!"

"No," Matt agreed, "I ain't."

Wendell seemed surprised he admitted it so readily. "So why'd you say you were?"

Matt felt Deathrider's curious inspection. "It seemed rude

to call the lady a liar," he said gruffly. "And you were terrorizing her."

"Hold on a minute," Deathrider interrupted. "What lady are we talking about?"

"What does it matter to you? You ain't left your bed since we got here," Matt said tersely, "so you ain't even met her."

"So you didn't answer her advertisement?" Wendell asked, ignoring their bickering.

"Hell, no."

"Well, what were you doing, then, getting involved today?"

"He can't help it," Deathrider said. "Getting involved is what he does."

"Would you keep out of this? It's got nothing to do with you," Matt complained.

"Since he's pointing a gun at me, I think it has everything to do with me."

"Shut up!" Wendell ordered. "You tell me how well you know the lady and how long you've been involved! What do you *know*?"

"I don't even know which lady we're talking about," Deathrider said.

"Not you! *Him*."

"I only met her yesterday," Matt told him calmly. "I stepped in because you were bullying her."

"What business was it of yours?"

"None," Deathrider said, at the exact same moment Matt said: "Anyone would have stepped in. You can't go around harassing women like that."

They gave each other disgruntled looks.

"You woulda stepped in too," Matt told his friend grumpily. Then he turned back to Wendell. "Look," he said, "I didn't know the woman until recently. I did the gentlemanly thing, that's all. And boy, do I regret it now. I escorted her back to the hotel, and I was only keeping an eye on her in the parlor so you wouldn't threaten her. She was clearly intimidated."

"I can't imagine why," Deathrider said, glancing at the gun.

"So even though she said you were married, you ain't?" Wendell frowned.

"I already told you we ain't."

"And what are your intentions?"

"What?"

"Don't play dumb," Wendell growled. "Are you planning on marrying her tomorrow? Or the day after?"

"Of course not!"

Wendell looked perplexed.

"You got married?" Deathrider seemed perplexed too.

"No!" Matt took a deep breath to steady his temper. "No. I didn't get married. How many times do I have to say it? The fool woman told a lie, that's all."

"What woman?" Deathrider shook his head. "You never talk to women."

"And this is why!" Matt snapped.

Deathrider snorted. "This is why? Because if you talk to them, you'll end up married?"

"I ain't married!"

"Stop!" Wendell shouted. "You two are giving me a headache."

"That's all him," Matt said. "He could give a saint a headache. You should try being out on the trail with him."

"Shut up! Just shut the hell up, the both of you!"

They fell silent.

"So the lady was lying?" Wendell asked, trying to get clarity.

"Yeah."

"Why'd you go along with it if it ain't true?"

Matt shrugged. "I told you why."

"How long were you planning on keeping it up?"

He sighed. "I wasn't."

Wendell was thinking hard. "Was *she*? Was she wanting to keep it up?"

"Yeah," Matt admitted, "she was." He felt a rush of sympathy for the woman. It seemed like she'd be dealing with Wendell again mighty soon.

An odd look came over Wendell's face. He cleared his throat awkwardly. "She . . . she, uh, said it because she didn't want to marry *me*, didn't she?"

Matt and Deathrider exchanged looks. Was the man *upset*? He looked upset. He sounded it too. His voice had got all thick and shaky sounding.

"It's just . . . " Wendell cleared his throat again. "I thought she *wanted* a husband."

"She seems to," Matt said carefully, "judging by the fact she placed an ad for one."

"She what?" Deathrider butted in.

"She advertised for a husband," Matt told him.

"Why'd she do that?"

"Because she wanted one?" Matt shrugged at his friend. Who could explain women?

"The woman who runs the hotel said she hadn't found one yet," Wendell said, still sounding hurt. "She said dozens of men had come through, and Mrs. Blunt didn't like any of them. Too citified, she said. Well, I ain't citified." Wendell was as down in the mouth as a kid who'd dropped his candy in the mud. "So I don't see why she don't want to marry *me*."

"Women generally don't want to marry men who threaten them," Matt said.

"What do you know about that?" The gun was back on Matt.

"Nothin'," he said quickly. "Only that you and the lady have a past. I don't know the details."

"After you left the parlor, what did she say to you? You were up here a long time."

Matt sighed. "Listen, pal, I don't really want to be mixed up in all this."

"Bit late for that," Deathrider said under his breath.

"What did she *tell* you?" Wendell snarled.

"Nothing!" Matt half shouted back. "She didn't tell me *anything*! And I don't want to know anything! You hear me? I don't *care*. I just want to go about my business."

Wendell gave him a sullen look. Then his gaze slid to Deathrider. "You know what's interesting about seeing you here, fella?" he said softly.

Matt had a bad feeling.

"What's *interesting* is I heard you was dead."

"Would you just kill him and get this over with?" Deathrider asked Matt.

"I've got a deal for you," Wendell said.

"If you don't kill him, I will."

"We ain't killing anyone," Matt snapped at Deathrider. "Get on with your deal, you mule-faced idiot," he told Wendell, "before he loses his patience."

Wendell flushed.

"You said you had a deal?" Matt prodded. "Well, out with it. Tom here ain't as nice as me; he's already done with you, but I'll give you one more chance to put your deal to me, and then I'm done with you too."

"I want you to keep pretending you're married to her," Wendell blurted.

"What?" He'd misheard. He must have misheard.

"I want you to do what she wants: pretend you're married." He scowled suddenly. "But don't actually marry her."

Matt was speechless.

"That's insane," Deathrider said.

"If you don't do it, I'll squeal about this one." Wendell waved the gun at Deathrider. "I'm sure a lot of people would like to know where the Plague of the West is, if he ain't dead."

"Is it me or is *everyone* in this town crazy?" Matt asked his friend.

"Maybe there's something in the water," Deathrider said.

"If you go along with the pretend marriage," Wendell said, continuing as though neither of them had spoken, "I'll keep quiet about the Indian."

Matt pressed the heels of his hands into his eyes. "This can't be happening."

"If you keep pretending, then she ain't going to marry any-one else," Wendell said. "We can come along with your wagon party, and it'll give me time to woo her."

Matt groaned. "That's the worst plan I ever heard."

"No, it ain't." Wendell sounded offended.

"It is," Deathrider told him.

"You ain't heard it all yet."

"There's more?" Matt asked in horror.

"Listen," Wendell said angrily, "I *like* her."

Matt groaned again.

"She's a damn fine woman. Finer than any I seen from here to California."

"That wouldn't be difficult," Deathrider said dryly. "There aren't many women between here and California."

"You ain't got any idea what I'm talking about," Wendell scoffed. "You haven't met her."

Deathrider gave Matt an inquisitive look.

"She is a fine-looking woman," Matt admitted.

Deathrider's eyebrows rose. Matt wasn't usually one to notice women.

"She needs a husband, and I can *be* that husband," Wendell insisted. "She just don't realize it yet."

"I don't see why you need me," Matt said tiredly. "Just court her, like a regular person."

"This ain't a regular situation! If she ain't pretending to be married to you, she'll marry someone else. Someone *not me*."

"Seems like she has every right to do that."

"If you stay married," Wendell talked right over the top of Matt, "she won't be marrying anyone else. We can travel together, and she can get to know me. I can show her what a good husband I'd make, see?"

The idiot had no idea. Matt took in Wendell's scraggy beard and baggy travel-worn clothes, his hollow cheeks and hungry eyes. Even aside from his constant threats of violence, he was hardly a woman's dream husband. Especially for a woman like Mrs. Blunt, who glittered and shone and had skin as smooth and pale as cream; who spoke with a voice like crystal chiming, in an accent so clear and proper she might as well be the queen of England.

"I hate to ruin your grand plan, but I ain't going to California," Matt told him. That should settle it. "So you cain't be coming along with me."

Wendell got that weasel gleam again. "No. But I looked into your travel plans. You travel along with that Sampson fella, and *he* goes to California. We can travel with you till he splits off. By then, I'll have wooed Mrs. Blunt, and you can go on your way."

The idiot was serious. Worse than serious, he was convinced his stupid plan would actually work. He was savoring his triumph already.

"Or we can just kill him now," Deathrider told Matt conversationally.

"You really do think I'm dumb." Wendell shook his head in astonishment.

"We really do," Deathrider agreed.

"Let me get this straight," Matt said tersely, cutting through their bickering. "You want me to pretend to be married to Mrs.

Blunt until we get to Fort Hall, which should take us a good few months. You want me to lie to her children, deceive a whole party of emigrants, mislead my employees, and then at Fort Hall to just say, 'Sorry, folks, none of that was true, we ain't actually married'?" He couldn't contain how stupid he thought the whole idea was. "And what do you think that will do to her reputation?"

"It won't matter, because then she'll marry me."

"Oh, it'll matter," Matt snorted. "It'll matter plenty. You got any idea what small communities are like? How the other women will treat her for being with a man out of wedlock?"

"I expect you'll want Matt to keep out of her bed on the journey to Fort Hall as well?" Deathrider drawled. "Even if you aren't concerned with her reputation, that don't seem fair. If he has to suffer a pretend marriage, it seems to me the least reward he could have is getting to lay with her."

Matt could have thumped him. He was just stirring up trouble for the sake of stirring up trouble. Knowing him, he was half hoping Wendell would do something stupid, just so he could have an excuse to smack him.

"People will get suspicious if they don't share a tent," Deathrider goaded. "They'd expect a man to sleep with his wife. Especially when they're only just married. Newlyweds generally go at it like rabbits."

"You're not to touch her!" Wendell was looking trigger-happy again.

"Look, it just won't work," Matt said, stepping slightly in front of Deathrider. "I said the same thing to Mrs. Blunt today. There are too many holes. No one's going to believe a word of it, and it will do more harm than good."

Wendell was frowning so hard he looked like he might pop an eyeball. "Wait!" he said abruptly. "What if . . . " he paused. Thinking looked painful for him. "What if you *don't* marry her?"

Matt was about ready to start throwing furniture. He'd had about all he could take of dumb folks today. If the idiot didn't get out of here soon, Matt was of half a mind to let Deathrider kill him after all.

"Yeah," the idiot continued, still painfully thinking his idiot plan through, "you could *not* marry her."

"Good plan." Matt rolled his eyes at Deathrider, who seemed captivated by Wendell's thought contortions.

"It's a *great* plan!" Wendell insisted.

"For me to *not* marry her?"

"Yeah!" Wendell beamed at him.

"Fine," Matt sighed. "It's a great plan. I heartily agree to not marry the woman. Now, if that's settled, can you get out of here and let us go on about our lives?"

"Shake on it?" Wendell thrust his hand out.

Matt stared at it. Something wasn't quite right here. "You want me to shake on *not* marrying Mrs. Blunt?"

"Yeah!"

Matt couldn't see a problem with that, no matter how he turned it over. "Fine. I promise not to marry Mrs. Blunt." He shook the idiot's hand. "And," he added, still shaking, "you promise not to tell anyone you mistook my brother for a certain Indian."

"Agreed. But only so long as you keep your side of the bargain."

"Of not marrying her?"

"Of not marrying her all the way to Fort Hall!"

Matt stopped shaking. He felt there was a catch here somewhere. "Not marrying her all the way to Fort Hall?"

"Yeah!" Wendell was so proud of himself he was practically hopping from foot to foot. "You can break off your engagement when you get there!"

"My . . . engagement?" Matt's stomach sank. He dropped Wendell's sweaty hand like it was a hot coal. "What in hell are you talking about?"

"I can still kill him if you want," Deathrider said, but he was sounding bored now. He sat down on the edge of his bed. "Just yell out if you need me."

"I mean you can be *engaged* to be married!" Wendell beamed at him.

"I can . . . "

"You can! You and Mrs. Blunt can say you're waiting to be married until you get to the end of the trail. Because Mrs. Blunt's a lady and wants to be married proper-like."

"And why can't she be married proper-like here in Independence?" Matt felt like he was going mad. He had half a mind to walk out of here and just keep going. He could saddle Pablo and just ride off on his own, and keep riding all the way home to Oregon. Away from all these crazy people.

"Maybe she wants time to get to know you!" Wendell crowed. "Any way you look at it, it works!"

"You hear that?" Deathrider tapped Matt on the leg. "It works."

Matt resisted the urge to kick him.

"And while we travel, I can win her and the children over, you see."

"I don't see," Matt said grimly.

"You'll have to grow back your beard and act more surly," Wendell instructed.

"He can *get* more surly?" Deathrider sounded surprised.

"Just watch," Matt said under his breath.

"It's perfect!" Wendell said.

"No. It ain't."

Wendell pointed the pistol straight at Deathrider and squinted one eye. "There's an awful lot of people who'd like to know your friend here ain't dead," he said in a singsong voice. "And I cain't see that it's a huge inconvenience to you to go along with my plan. Especially to save his life."

"I hate to admit it, my friend," Deathrider said regretfully, "but he's right."

"*What?*"

Deathrider had a malicious twinkle in his eye. "Surely *not* getting married is the least you can do to save my life?" he said.

"You won't even have to do anything!" Wendell assured him. "Just go about your business and let the lady think you're acting as a shield. She won't know I know. It'll give her time to relax and get to know the real me."

"I bet the real you is a delight," Deathrider said.

Wendell didn't seem to register his sarcasm. "And once we get to Fort Hall, you get to go off like you never even met us."

"And what if the lady doesn't like you by Fort Hall?"

Wendell shrugged. "What's it matter to you? You can still call off the engagement, and I'll escort her to California."

Matt felt a stirring of unease. He felt like they were playing with the lady's life. It didn't seem right. But it gave the lady what she wanted. And it kept the idiot quiet about Deathrider. All things considered, it was the path of least resistance.

"Go on," Deathrider said. "Shake on it."

"What in hell was that?" Matt raged at him when they'd ironed out the details and the idiot had finally left.

Deathrider shrugged. "You didn't want me to kill him."

"There's a middle ground between not killing him and going along with his insane plan!"

"It's not so insane. Stupid, yes, but not insane. There's a dumb logic to it."

"Is there?"

Deathrider had the ghost of a smile. "At the very least, it will give us some entertainment on the trail."

"Us? You planning to come along after all?"

Deathrider shrugged again. "Until I get bored."

"At which point you'll leave me tangled up in this mess."

"Looks like it." He winced as he lay back on the bed. He was chalkier than ever and shaking from the effort of staying upright as long as he had. "Where are you going?" he asked as Matt headed for the door.

Matt didn't answer.

"Can you get some water sent up?"

Matt slammed the door on him. The meddling, no-good horse's ass.

❧ 11 ❧

"**Y**OU LOOK LIKE you're celebrating," a honeyed voice crooned as a warm hand slid across the back of Matt's neck.

"Oh no," Matt tried to say, but he was drunk and it came out as nonsense. No whores. Especially not this one. How had they ended up at a whorehouse? The last thing he'd known, they'd been at the saloon.

He was only there to see Seb. They'd gone through their bookings and made lists for the next day. Then they'd had a few drinks. Josiah Sampson had found them sometime around the third or fourth drink, and then there'd been some more drinks. Matt wasn't usually a big drinker, but he'd had a hell of a day.

And now, somehow, he was at a whorehouse.

"I knew you'd come find me eventually," Seline purred as she lowered herself into his lap.

"Matt's getting married," Seb told her cheerfully.

"Not you too!" Seline pouted as she threaded her fingers through the hair at the base of his neck. She pulled on it just enough to direct his line of sight to her cleavage. It was magnificent cleavage, and it made Matt mighty uneasy. He could see the dark thrust of her nipples through the thin white cotton of her chemise.

Matt felt a surge of panic and reached up to pull her fingers off him.

"Yep, him too," a third party chimed in. It was that idiot Wendell, who'd joined them at some point earlier in the evening and had started congratulating Matt loudly on his impending nuptials. Only he kept calling them *nutshells*. Because he was an idiot.

Before Matt had been able to stop it, a group had gathered, and soon everyone was buying him drinks and congratulating him on "landing a big fish," "roping a fresh-looking filly" and "bringing down the doe." They all made it sound like he'd been out hunting.

"Who are you marrying, honey?" Seline's hands seemed to be everywhere now that he'd managed to unwind them from his hair.

"That widow in the advertisement!" Joe Sampson crowed. "Can you believe it?"

The group cheered again and made another toast.

Matt winced. He couldn't believe he was lying to Joe. He and Joe went way back.

"The one from the jailhouse today?" Seline tilted her head. "Well, good for her."

"You mean good for *him*!" Pierre LeFoy slurred. "You hear she has a gold claim?"

"Lucky boy." She rubbed the flat of her hand over Matt's nipple, and he felt a bolt of lightning run straight to his crotch. "You boys ought to buy him a send-off," Seline suggested with a sly look. She jiggled in Matt's lap and they all hooted.

"That's a great idea!" Seb yelled and started going through his pockets. "C'mon boys, let's all chip in. How much do you cost, Seline?"

"No." Matt caught her hands, which were too close to his swelling crotch for comfort. "Not for me, thanks."

The crowd hooted again.

"Don't want to spoil your appetite, eh, Slater?"

"Who can blame him! Have you *seen* her?" Some guy Matt didn't know cupped his hands in front of his chest like he was cupping enormous breasts.

Mrs. Smith. Blunt. Whatever her name was, she did have enormous breasts, Matt thought thickly, through the haze of booze. Incredible, round, high enormous breasts.

He bit back a pained moan as Seline rubbed against him. He had to get out of here *now*.

He lifted her up and set her aside. "Thanks for the offer, but I can't take you up on it," he mumbled.

"Aw, honey, why not?" Seline cozied up to him and rested a hand on his chest. "Might be your last chance . . . and I have been *longing* to have a taste of you." She lunged and was kissing him before he could sidestep her. Her tongue poked wetly at his closed lips. He turned his head away. "You sure, honey?" she whispered, disappointed. "Your brother was the best I ever had, and from the look of you, I reckon you'd be even better."

Matt winced. He didn't want to think about his brother.

"I'm going back to the hotel," he said, trying to find his hat. He seemed to have lost it somewhere, in one of the saloons.

"She waiting for you?" someone cackled.

"I'd be rushing back too if a woman like that was waiting for *me*."

Screw his hat. He'd find it tomorrow.

"Don't wear her out before the wedding," some fool called after him as Matt waved them off.

Vaguely, Matt registered Wendell's black look. Good. Let him stew in his jealousy. It was a hell of his own making.

HE COULDN'T GO in the front door, Matt realized as he stumbled toward the hotel. Mrs. Bulfinch didn't hold with drunkenness, and he was well and truly drunk. Drunker than he'd been in a good long time. Drunk enough to still be thinking about the way Seline had felt in his lap.

The thought sent a bolt of shame through him. There was something wrong with him. He should *want* to take her up on her offer. His body was certainly keen to. Most men would have no compunction about slapping their money down on the table and following Seline upstairs. But Matt couldn't think of anything worse.

He'd tried it once. It hadn't gone well.

No. He wasn't going to think about that. It didn't do any good to go dwelling on it. It was what it was, and he was fine going back to an empty bed. More than fine. He was *glad* of it.

It was well into the early hours, but there were still men sitting around on the hotel porch, the tips of their cigars glowing orange in the night. Matt veered around the side of the building, feeling low as a bug. He fought his way through the hackberry bushes and round to the yard. He cursed when he saw there was a lamp burning in the lean-to around back of the building. Didn't that Bulfinch woman ever sleep?

He steadied himself against the wall of the building and momentarily considered sleeping in the stable.

But it annoyed him to think that he'd be paying through the nose for a brass bed that he wasn't using. Irritated, he ran his hands through his hair and brushed down the front of his shirt. He could probably get past her, if he was careful. He'd just have to try and look sober.

Matt wasn't too steady on his feet as he approached the lean-to. A wooden screen blocked his view into it, but he could see the back door, which was open. He kept his eye on the door as he tried to walk as quietly as possible. As he got closer, he could hear the sound of water sloshing and wood crackling in the stove. Someone was doing laundry. In the middle of the night.

Of course Mrs. Bulfinch was the type to keep a laundry maid chained to the coppers day and night. That woman had an intense aversion to dirt, at least judging by all the extra cleaning fees she tried to charge. And she'd be too cheap to pay for the laundry service in town when she could have some girl slave for the cost of her room and board. Poor girl.

Matt peered around the screen.

Hell. It wasn't a laundry girl. And it wasn't Mrs. Bulfinch. Instead, standing over the steaming coppers, her face flushed and her dark curls damp against her neck, was Georgiana Bee Blunt. Her simple dark dress was unbuttoned at the throat, and she was pink with heat from the stove and from the exertion as she struggled to stir the clothes in the copper with a big wooden paddle. She wasn't a tall woman, and she had to stand on tiptoe to manage. It made her movements awkward and slow.

As Matt watched, she used the paddle to slop some of the clothes into the washtub, so she could swap wrestling with the paddle to wrestling with the washboard. Matt's gaze lingered on the swell of her breasts as she bent over the tub. She was unbuttoned far enough to give him a tantalizing view of plump and creamy skin.

She was even prettier without the sparkling dress and fussy hat. Matt hadn't thought it could be possible for her to be prettier, but she was. Her cheeks were pink, her skin glistened, and her hair was tumbling from its pins in wayward curls. Without

the enormous hoops of her silly dresses, her figure was revealed, in all its neat curves. Hypnotized, Matt leaned his head
against the wooden screen. Still unsteady on his feet, he wob-
bled as his weight shifted, and he knocked the screen. It tee-
tered alarmingly, and Georgiana looked up, startled. Matt
struggled to keep the screen upright, swearing under his breath.

Vaguely, he realized she'd been crying. She quickly swiped
at her face with the backs of her hands. He felt like a heel. He'd
been ogling her and here she was crying. Seriously crying.
Now that he'd torn his gaze away from her figure and up to her
face, he could see she was puffy eyed and red nosed.

"Sorry," he mumbled. "I didn't mean to interrupt you."

She kept her face averted, and he heard her try to sniff surreptitiously.

"Go ahead," he said, "sniff if you want to sniff. I don't
mind." He hadn't spent much time around women in his life,
not until his sister-in-law had moved into the house. And Alex
wasn't as ladylike as Georgiana. She would have just had a
big, loud cry and sniff. And then she would have railed at him
for barging in on her.

Watching Georgiana's embarrassment, he guessed proper
ladies didn't sniff in front of people. And, from the way she
wasn't meeting his eye, he guessed they didn't cry in front of
people either.

In that way, it seemed proper ladies might be like men.

"You must really hate doing laundry," he said, trying to
lighten the mood.

It didn't work.

She looked up at him, and her gaze was full of mute misery. In the lamplight, her eyes were the color of ink. And then,
as he watched, she seemed to pull herself together. He saw her
give herself an imperceptible shake, purse her pretty lips and
take a deep breath.

"I beg your pardon, Mr. Slater," she apologized, pressing
the back of her hand to her forehead and brushing away a stray
curl. "I didn't realize anyone would be about at this time of
night."

He flushed as she gave him a once-over. He knew what
conclusions she must be drawing. He kept a hand on the
screen, mostly to keep himself from swaying, but no matter

how sober he strove to look, he was sure he looked exactly like what he was: a drunk.

"Well, I think you'll find there are a lot of people about this time of night," he said, concentrating on speaking clearly. "Just not anyone you'd care to associate with." He pulled a face at the sound of his own slurring. It was too hard to talk. He didn't think he'd do it again.

"Is that so?" The misery was melting from her, replaced with wryness.

He nodded, sticking to his no-talking resolution.

"I couldn't sleep," she said, shrugging, "and I had all of this to do . . . " She sighed and went back to the washboard. "It seemed a better idea to come down and do it, than lie there and fret."

Matt had a sudden image of her lying in bed. He wondered if her nightclothes looked anything like that getup Seline had been wearing. Filmy thin white cotton not-much-of-anything that showed the warmth of skin beneath.

His gaze ran over her body as she bent over the washboard. She was standing side-on to him now, and he could see the curve of her breast every time she moved her arm. He had an urge to reach out and cup it. He wondered if it would feel firm or soft, if it would give beneath his hand or press back.

Hell. What was wrong with him? He hadn't been this randy in a long time. He was half-swollen and itchy-achy with lust.

He was just drunk. And still all wound up from Seline pawing at him. That was all. And his mind kept drifting back to the idea that he was supposed to play Georgiana's husband-to-be for the next few months. He'd be spending a lot of time with this woman and her blue, blue eyes. Not that she knew it yet.

He needed to sober up. *Food.* That would help. He wondered what Mrs. Bulfinch had lying about. Abruptly, he headed for the kitchen.

"What are you doing?" Georgiana called anxiously, when she heard the bang of him walking into the kitchen table. It wasn't his fault. It was dark.

"Getting some food. Want any?" He stood and waited for his eyes to adjust to the darkness.

"It must be two in the morning!"

"No wonder I'm hungry." He tried to find the icebox and kicked something over. It made a loud clatter.

He heard a sigh. "Do you need a light?" She appeared at the back door with the lamp. God, she was pretty.

"Thanks. I won't take a minute." Mostly because just looking at her made him itchy as hell. The sooner she went back to her wash, the better.

Matt poured himself a glass of milk and fetched the fixings for sandwiches. He cut the bread as thick as planks of timber and piled on leftover boiled mutton, salted butter, mustard, cheese and tomatoes. The mutton was probably stringy as an old boot, judging by his previous experience of Mrs. Bulfinch's cooking, so he lathered on the butter and mustard extra thick.

He caught Georgiana's look of astonishment. "What?"

"Are all of those for you?"

He looked down at the six sandwiches. "Why? Did you want one?"

"No, thank you." She watched him clamp one down, so the filling didn't fall out. "But perhaps a glass of milk . . . " She left the lamp on the table and went to the icebox. Matt found his gaze following her. He couldn't seem to look away. She moved like a waterbird gliding across a river.

He stood at the table and ate, watching her heat the milk in a saucepan. After a couple of sandwiches, he felt a little steadier.

"Warm milk is supposed to help you sleep, ain't it?" he said helpfully. "That's what my ma said when I was little."

"I'm afraid I won't be able to sleep until I finish the laundry." She directed a rueful look at the laundry room. "I made the mistake of leaving some clothes in the copper overnight last night, and Mrs. Bulfinch blistered my ear. I have to get them done and hanging on the line before I go up."

"You'll be up all night," Matt said. "Laundry work ain't quick."

"So I'm discovering," she sighed. "I thought it would be quicker than this."

"You must have done laundry before." How did she make stirring milk so damn sexy? It was something about the way she tilted her head as she did it. It drew attention to the line of her jaw, the long, vulnerable length of her neck, the slope of her breastbone as it led down to the curve of her . . .

For the love of God. Stop looking at her.

"No," she admitted. "Not really. I had to dismiss the servants in January, but there was always a laundry service I could call on."

"There's a laundry in town."

"I'm conserving money," she said quietly. "And I suppose I thought that I should learn. I'll have to do it on the trail."

"It won't be like this," he warned her. "There won't be no warm water. You'll be doing it in the stream."

She looked startled. "Oh. Of course." She poured her milk into a teacup and joined him at the table. "I suppose there's much I haven't thought of." She sat down.

He felt obligated to sit too. It felt wrong standing over her.

But now he was stuck with her, sitting at the table. The lamplight caught the planes of her face and made her eyes big pools. Matt turned himself to the task of finishing his last sandwiches as quickly as possible.

He was quickly sobering up. They'd lapsed into a charged silence. It dragged on so long, Matt had no idea how to break it. He could feel himself starting to sweat. Women made him so damned uncomfortable. Every time he moved, she looked at him like he was about to speak. He resolutely kept his mouth full so he wouldn't have to. Because what did one say to a lady?

What he *should* say was that he had a solution to her problem. What he *should* tell her was that speech Wendell had worked out for him. But Matt had planned to have that little talk in the morning, in the cold light of day, somewhere formal and stuffy like the public parlor. Not in the middle of the night, in the intimacy of a circle of lamplight, when he was drunk and she was flushed and damp and looking as sexy as all hell.

"Well," she said awkwardly, once she'd finished her cup of milk, "I should get back to work."

He nodded and crammed another bite in, so he wouldn't have to talk. She fetched him a candle from the mantelpiece and took the lamp with her. Matt breathed a sigh of relief when she left. He slumped in his chair. It didn't matter how many miles he traveled, how many people he brought safely through the wilderness, how many disasters he averted, how many violent men he faced down, he still found himself unsettled by women. It wasn't likely to ever change, he thought glumly. He was too old now.

It was all right if he was in a business situation, or if there were other men around. It was being alone with them that was the problem. Particularly when he was attracted to them.

Hell. Why couldn't he be like his brother Luke? Luke thrived on being around women, much to his wife's disgust. He could talk a woman into a swoon within all of half a minute. Matt didn't have that knack.

It was probably because he'd spent so much of his childhood without them. His mother had died when he was no bigger than a gnat, followed not long afterward by his father. Once his brother Luke had managed to get them set up in Oregon, it had just been the three of them for the rest of Matt's childhood. Three boys in a leaky, smoky hut in the middle of nowhere. Luke had taken to scouting and eventually being a guide on the trails, so he was often gone for months at a time, and when Tom got old enough, he'd headed out too, running cattle. Matt knew he mostly used it as an excuse to head down to Mexico. Tom had never got over leaving. He would have moved back to their old home in Arizpe, where their mother was from, if Luke and Matt had come with him. But Luke liked Utopia and their land in the foothills of the Cascades, so they all stayed in Oregon. Or rather, Matt stayed. They wandered.

Most of his life had been spent by himself, keeping the homestead running while his brothers flitted about; he only ventured into town when he absolutely had to. He used to find social interactions painful beyond belief. When his brothers were home to look after the place, he took himself off trapping and hunting, avoiding other people wherever possible. His life was a solitary one. And he guessed he liked it that way.

Although, it had been pretty nice when Alex and her family had moved into the big new house. The fires had always been lit, and the rooms were warm; the smell of coffee and biscuits drifted through the house at all hours of the day, and wherever you were you could hear the sound of other people. It had been odd and unsettling but also kind of . . . pleasant. Only it wasn't Matt's home anymore. It was Alex and Luke's. And day by day, he'd felt more alone, even though he'd been surrounded by other people.

He could hear the slap and slop of water in the tub as Georgiana scrubbed her clothes, and he saw her shadow leap on the wall opposite. After a minute, he fancied he could hear a soft sniffle or two. Then a hitching breath. He knew why she was crying. It was because she had to face up to Wendell and Kipp tomorrow, because she was alone with all those young 'uns, without a husband, and facing a two-thousand-mile journey across some pretty hard land, and all without servants.

Matt shook his head. He couldn't imagine what her life must have been like until now. Imagine never having washed a shirt. The trail was going to be mighty rough on her. He sighed. He guessed the least he could do was put her out of her misery tonight. Maybe then she could get some sleep.

He brushed the crumbs off his hands and went out to the laundry room, feeling much steadier than he had before the sandwiches. Sure enough, she was crying.

"Here," he said gruffly, taking the sodden clothes from the tub. "I'll work the wringer."

"No," she protested. Her hands flew up to her face again, clearing away evidence of her tears. Not that she really could. She was all pink and watery looking.

"You'll be here into next week if no one helps you." He fed the first shirt into the mangle. "Besides, you don't look tall enough to reach the handle."

Even that didn't raise a smile.

"Thank you for your help." She sounded tired. Deeply, thoroughly exhausted.

They lapsed into silence as they worked. There was the sound of water running out of the clothes as Matt winched them through the mangle, and the rub of the washboard as she worked the grime out of the children's clothes. The lean-to was steamy and Matt was sweating. It wasn't pleasant. He could smell the booze coming off him. He hoped she couldn't.

"Look," he said abruptly, not knowing a gentle way to break it to her, "I had an idea." It wasn't his idea, of course; it was Wendell's, but he couldn't tell her that. "An idea about us not being married . . ." he continued.

The washboard fell silent. Matt didn't look at her. He kept

his gaze fixed on the mangle. "I ain't going to marry you," he said firmly, "so put that idea out of your head right now. And I ain't of a mind to pretend to be married to you neither."

"I know." There was another little sniffle.

Matt let out a gusty sigh. Hell. He really was going to go through with this. Against all of his better judgment. "But I was thinking . . . there probably wouldn't be any harm in pretending to be *engaged* to be married . . ."

He heard a sudden intake of breath.

He risked a look. She was frozen, her eyes all huge and inky again.

"Only until Fort Hall, mind," he said firmly. "No more 'n that. That's what you asked for today. I can get you safely to Fort Hall all right. You can tell everyone we're planning to marry, but we're waiting till we get to my family in Oregon. That should keep the wolves at bay. But we're breaking off our 'engagement' at Fort Hall, you hear? And then I'm going home. Alone."

"Engaged . . . ?" she breathed. She said it like it was some kind of miracle.

He scowled. It sounded even dafter now he'd said it aloud to her. "You know what?" he said, feeling contrary as all get out. "I reckon I can try and take on a bunch of eligible bachelors when I put the train together. Since you still need a husband. You can spend the trip evaluating them, and then you can propose once we end our arrangement." He felt a jab of pleasure at the thought of irritating Wendell Todd. Imagine his face if she announced her intention to marry someone else at Fort Hall. Especially after the way the bastard had spent the night squawking about Matt's "engagement" to every saloon in Independence. "It's a darn sight more sensible than picking one after a single interview."

"But today you said . . ."

"I said I wouldn't marry you, and I *won't*. I won't *pretend* to marry you either. I ain't the marrying kind. But I reckon it won't do no harm to pretend an engagement. It shouldn't bind us—not in any way we cain't get out of."

"But we told Wendell and Kipp we were married . . ."

"*We* didn't," Matt said grumpily. "*You* did. And don't worry about them. I already spoke to Wendell."

"You did?" The look on her face was indescribable. It was kind of like the sun coming out from behind a cloud. She had no call to look that delighted. Like he'd just proposed to her for real.

"And what did he say?" she asked anxiously.

Matt shrugged. He didn't know what to say to that. *He put his gun away.* "We parted with an understanding."

"You mean he accepts our engagement?" She pressed a hand to her chest.

Matt wished she wouldn't. It was hard not to look at the way her breasts swelled over her hand. He grunted. "He seemed happier to think of us engaged than to think of us married," he said honestly.

"Oh, Mr. Slater!" She kind of erupted with happiness, and to Matt's horror, she flung herself at him. Her arms wrapped around his waist, and her cheek pressed hard against his chest.

He held his hands in the air and stood stock-still.

"Thank you!" She was crying again. He could feel her hot breath on his shirt. It was alarming. His nipples tightened in response.

He could feel the press of her breasts, the weight of her skirts brushing his legs, the heat of her hands against his back. He would have jumped out of her arms if she hadn't been holding on so tight, and crying so hard.

He gave her a tentative pat on the back.

"I can't tell you what a relief this is," she hiccupped. "I've been beside myself all evening. I couldn't see any way out of this mess."

As far as Matt could see, this wasn't a way out of the mess either. It was just a different mess.

Oh hell. She looked up at him. Her eyes were shining. Her mouth was swollen, all red and plump. The feel of her body was beyond intoxicating. He wanted to kiss her, he realized stupidly. More than he'd ever wanted anything in his life. Every thought fled his head. All he could see was lips. All he could feel was the steamy heat of the room and the damp press of her against him. He was swollen and aching and crawling out of his skin with lust.

Maybe he could have kept it under control, if her gaze hadn't dropped to his mouth, if her hand hadn't given his lower back a slow circular stroke, if her red lips hadn't parted and if she hadn't uttered the sexiest little moan he'd ever heard.

"Oh," she breathed.

And then he didn't think anymore. He just gave in and kissed her.

She melted into him. She tasted like salt and honey. When his tongue touched her mouth, she opened for him, and the sensation, the heat, the wet, drove him wild. He hauled her harder against him, one hand plunging into her curls, the other spread against her lower back. He felt her hands sliding up his back. He was rock-hard. He pulled her against him, and the feel of her pressing against his cock was a pleasure so intense he groaned. And then her tongue touched his and he lost all power to even groan.

He didn't know how long they stood there, lost in the steam, their mouths locked together, their tongues sliding, their hands slipping. He only surfaced when her hand settled on his hip and her thumb brushed the tip of his cock through his pants.

"Jesus." He shoved her away from him. "No. Just no. We ain't doing this."

She swayed on her feet, looking more than a little drugged.

"No," he said again, firmly, talking to her like he would to Dog. "This ain't part of the deal."

She tilted her head, clearly confused.

"We're *pretend* engaged."

She frowned. "*You* kissed *me*," she reminded him.

"You shouldn't have kissed me back," he said defensively. "You took advantage of my drunkenness."

"Took advantage . . ." Her mouth fell open in astonishment. "I beg your pardon?"

"No!" Matt couldn't stay here. Not with the way she was standing there, looking all rumpled and kissed and delectable. "No! No. No. *No*." He couldn't seem to stop saying "no." He shook his head. "This was a mistake."

"It was," she agreed. And now she was frowning in earnest.

"If we're going to be pretend engaged, you're not to do that again," he warned. "I won't have it."

"Have what?" she asked waspishly. "Have you kiss me? I'm not sure that's entirely in my control."

He felt like kicking something. Hell. He *had* been the one to do the kissing. He cleared his throat. "Yes. Fine. It was the drink. And that whore got me all riled up."

"Whore!" Her eyes narrowed.

That probably hadn't been the right thing to say. Matt's head hurt. "Let's forget this happened." He caught himself. "Except for our conversation about the engagement. Pretend engagement," he corrected. "That happened, but nothing else did." He didn't want to have that conversation again. "You're happy to still have the pretend engagement, I guess?" Maybe she wouldn't be. After he'd kissed her like that.

She *had* kissed him back though. Hadn't she? What if she'd been trying to wriggle out from under him and he'd mistaken it for her kissing him back? He flushed, feeling ill. He might have made a colossal fool of himself.

"Of course," she said tightly. "Thank you for agreeing to the pretense."

She didn't look happy anymore.

Goddamn it.

"You go to bed," he growled. "I'll finish all of this." He gestured to the laundry. It was the least he could do. He felt lower than a bug.

"It's *my* laundry," she protested. She sounded a bit angry now. "*You* go to bed and *I'll* finish all this."

"No."

"What do you mean *no*?"

"I mean *no*." Obstinately, he went back to working the mangle. He heard her mutter under her breath. The word "impossible" was in there a couple of times.

Stubbornly, she went back to the washboard. He wished she wouldn't. It was supposed to be a gesture, him staying to finish the chore for her. It wasn't much of a gesture if she stayed and did it too.

The early signs of a hangover started setting in as he cranked the mangle in the seething silence. He felt vaguely poisonous. Waves of nausea washed over him. A cold bath. That would help. There was a tub propped against the wall. Maybe once all these clothes were on the line and he'd packed her off, he could fill it up and sink into it. It was the thought of the tub that kept him going through the next hour as he cranked load after load, and then pegged them out on the line in the yard.

She didn't look at him once. But he couldn't help looking at her. Much as he tried not to, his gaze kept slipping back to her. She wasn't crying anymore, but she looked lower than she had when she'd been crying.

This. This was why he should keep away from women.

It only led to misery. Theirs as much as his.

❧ 12 ❧

OH NO. GEORGIANA'S heart sank when she realized she'd left the key down in the laundry. She was painfully tired. So tired it was hard to move. The thought of going back down all those flights of stairs was enough to set her off weeping again. She'd never been so tired in her whole life. It must be nearly dawn.

It had been the most endless, godforsaken day. She rested her forehead against the door and tried to summon the energy to go back downstairs. Oh God. She'd have to face Matt Slater again.

She cringed at the thought. *How* could she have kissed him like that? Shamelessly, wantonly. A man she barely knew.

Well, you are engaged to him.

Pretend engaged.

She remembered the disgust in his voice when he kept saying "no." No, no, no, no, no. He'd been flat-out horrified. And he was right, she *had* taken advantage of him. He'd been glassy-eyed and wobbly on his feet, a man clearly not in control of all his faculties.

But what was a girl to do when a man kissed her like that? And not any man . . . *Him.*

When she was at her lowest ebb, he'd appeared in the doorway, rumpled and boyish, his dark hair tousled, his mouth soft. It was the most relaxed she'd ever seen him. The dimple flashed when he spoke. The lamplight cast the angles of his face into sharp relief. He was an enormous presence in the lean-to, smelling of sweat and whiskey. And the way he *looked* at her. Georgiana hadn't seen a look like that in years. Intimate and full of desire, his gaze followed her every move, his golden-brown eyes intense. It ignited a slow pulse in her that she'd half thought she'd never feel again. The air was charged with desire. Georgiana could feel every inch of her skin, and her heart seemed to slow and skip a beat.

It was glorious.

She felt young again. Not like a tired mother doing laundry, but like a debutante on the dance floor, in the arms of an attentive beau. It was a feeling she'd always associated with summer nights and champagne and being sixteen. It was a revelation to be feeling it in a dim and sweaty lean-to, over a washboard and a pile of wet clothes. It was a feeling she'd thought she'd never have again, and yet here it was, fluttering into her life like a butterfly out of season.

So when he'd kissed her, of course she'd kissed him back. She hadn't been kissed in years, and she'd never been kissed like *that*.

It was nothing like kissing Leonard. Leonard had been slow and careful—*prissy*. That was unkind. But true. She'd had a few clumsy kisses with boys in her youth, but they weren't like this either.

Matt Slater's kiss was elemental. There was nothing practiced about it. He fell into the kiss without thought, moving against her as though he felt her smallest response. He was firm but tentative, gentle but insistent, hungry and wild, tender and slow. It made Georgiana's legs turn to water, and she had to hold on to him to stay upright. It was without a doubt the best kiss of her life.

But, even so, he'd been right. She had taken advantage. She'd half known what she was doing when she'd flung herself at him. She'd been so overcome with relief at his plan that she'd given in to the urge to hug him, but she'd also known the risk. She wasn't actually a young girl, after all. She knew about men and lust.

She knew about herself and lust.

Georgiana straightened up and turned back around to get her key. At least she knew she wasn't dead, she thought, trying to look on the bright side. At least she knew she was still capable of desire and excitement and arousal.

Although, it was going to make their trip to Fort Hall torturous. How on earth was she going to spend that much time with him and not kiss him again?

The hotel was silent as she crept down the back stairs. She knew Matt hadn't gone up to bed yet, as his room was opposite hers, but maybe he'd headed for the main stairs by now and they wouldn't cross paths. She turned the lamp as low as it would go as she reached the kitchen.

He was still down here. She could hear the soft splash of water. What was he doing? There was a louder splash and the sound of tin creaking. Oh my. Was he having a *bath*?

But her key was in there!

Georgiana held her breath and tried to put the lamp down silently on the bench. She took careful steps across the kitchen floor, desperate not to make any noise. Maybe she could get to her key without being seen?

No. As soon as she got close enough to the door to peer through, she could see that wasn't going to be possible. He had his back to her, but she could see the key: it was right on the sill next to his bath.

Damn it. She'd have to wait.

He'd been low in the tub, scrubbing his face, but as she watched, he sat up, splashing. Her eyes widened. His broad, naked, glistening shoulders rose into view. The muscles of his back flexed and danced in the candlelight. Oh *my*.

Go. Go now. Wait upstairs. Hide in the scullery. Go anywhere else but here.

The little voice in her head was shrieking at her to get away from the laundry as quickly as possible. If being near him when he was fully clothed was risky, this was downright dangerous.

But, unable to help herself, she crept closer, keeping to the darkest shadows, trying to get a better view.

She pressed her lips together, to keep from making a noise, as he suddenly stood. Water ran off him, shining in the candlelight, making him look like he was wrought of copper and gold.

Oh *my*.

He was another species altogether from Leonard. Where Leonard had been lean, Matt was solid. He looked like he'd been carved from the bole of a tree. His legs were thickly muscled, as was his back. His buttocks were round and firm, and they flexed as he reached for the towel he'd hung over the mangle.

And then he turned.

Georgiana had to lean against the wall. Her knees seemed to have given out.

His chest was broad and lightly furred with black hair, which speared down over a stomach as hard as stone, down to . . .

Oh *my*.

Georgiana felt a wave of desire so strong it made her tremble. Her legs were quivering and her stomach clenched as she watched him swipe the water from his body with the towel. Her gaze lingered on his hairy calves as he rubbed them. Everything about him was strong and masculine and . . . hard.

Oh, she was in more trouble than she'd realized. Much more. She had a near uncontrollable urge to go in there, to step forward into the circle of candlelight and take the towel from him. To reach up and run the cloth over his collarbone, where droplets clung like diamonds. To rub it down his chest in slow circles, over those small dusky nipples, over the hard pack of his stomach, over those thrusting hip bones . . .

She backed away, trying to regain control of her senses. She was shaking. She could feel her body moistening, loosening, longing for . . . No. Don't think about it.

Georgiana fled to the scullery and locked herself in, as much to keep herself from following her urges as to hide from him.

Remember Leonard, she thought fiercely as she sat on the stool in the dark. She could see a line of candlelight under the door. *Remember the pain and the humiliation. The loneliness.* These feelings she was having for Matt Slater were powerful, but they weren't worth the aftermath.

Even if they felt *so* good.

Georgiana pressed her face into her hands and scrunched her eyes closed. It would pass. If she could just wait it out, the lust would pass. She had years of experience with frustration, and she could get through another night of it.

Oh, this was going to be hell.

IT *WAS* HELL. But somehow, she survived it. Her first meeting with Matt afterward was an awkward conversation outside the dining room at breakfast. He was leaving as she and the children were going in. Georgiana started blushing the moment she saw him and didn't stop for about a good hour after he left.

He, for his part, could barely seem to look at her.

"There's a meeting at Mrs. Tilly's today," he'd growled, keeping his eyes fixed on Mrs. Bulfinch's ugly carpet. "Joe Sampson and I meet our new customers every Thursday morning to run through the provisioning. Wendell Todd is going to meet you there at ten." He scratched at his beard, which was already growing back in. The dark stubble made him look dangerous. "I forgot to tell you last night."

Georgiana nodded. "Thank you," she said stiffly. So they'd made even more arrangements without her. The engagement— *pretend* engagement—had been organized; her travel plans were organized; it was all done for her.

It should have been a relief to have the big decisions taken care of, but Georgiana felt a piercing resentment. It was unsettling to have so many important decisions made without her input. Not that she would have decided differently, but they could have at least *spoken* to her.

"I'll see you at ten," Matt grunted at her. And then he was gone and Georgiana was left blushing, unsettled, and more than a little irritated.

"Can we take our swords to Mrs. Tilly's?" one of the twins asked as he piled his plate high with hotcakes.

Georgiana joined him. She could do with something sweet today. It might improve her mood. "You're not going to Mrs. Tilly's today," she told him. "Well, except for that meeting Mr. Slater told us about, and you won't be needing swords for that."

"Can we still have tarts?" Susannah sounded disappointed to hear they wouldn't be spending the day at the tearooms.

"Why aren't we going to Mrs. Tilly's for the whole day?" Phin demanded. "It's not because of the glue, is it? Because she said again yesterday that she didn't mind."

"*I* mind," Georgiana told him sternly. "But no, that's not why. It's because I concluded the interviews."

"You did?"

The children exchanged anxious glances. Georgiana felt a pang. Perhaps she should have asked for their input? Shouldn't they have a say in who their next father would be?

But no, surely that was too much pressure. She didn't want them bearing any responsibility for who her husband was, for good or ill.

Did she?

Georgiana sighed. Why couldn't parenting come with a guidebook? Every day she felt on the precipice of making some disastrous decision that would prove ruinous to the children. Even when it was something as small as forgetting to clean their teeth in the morning. *Once.*

"So, who is it?" Phin asked curiously.

Oh my, she was about to lie to her children. That was surely a parenting disaster in the making.

"Well," she hedged, pouring syrup on her hotcakes. A lot of syrup. "I've decided *not* to get married yet." She led them back to the table. Wilby crawled in her lap and waited for her to feed him some of her hotcakes. She obliged.

"It was because they were so rubbish, wasn't it?" Phin said.

"Keep your voice down." The room was full of the men she'd interviewed, all of whom were giving her angry looks.

"Well, they were," Phin defended himself. "That one yesterday was the worst."

Georgiana's heart sank. "Which one yesterday?"

"The one we had breakfast with."

"He was out there in the foyer just now," Susannah said, wrinkling her nose.

Oh no. Really? Georgiana felt a bit ill. They weren't going to like what she had to say next, then.

"Look, there he is." Susannah pointed.

Oh thank God. They meant Alistair Dugard.

"Not him," she said quickly.

She saw their palpable relief. She swallowed hard and hugged Wilby a little tighter. She reminded herself she wasn't telling them about her *real* choice for husband, which was far from decided. This was just pretend.

But looking at their expectant faces, it didn't feel particularly pretend. Nor did it feel good to lie to them.

It was better than the alternative though. She shuddered at the thought of Alistair Dugard being their stepfather. Or Wendell Todd.

No, this would be better.

"Instead of getting married right away," Georgiana said carefully, "I've decided to wait until we get to the end of the trail. The gentleman and I are engaged to be married . . . but that's all for now."

"What's the difference? Between that and getting married?" Philip looked confused.

"Engaged means we'll get married eventually, but not yet."

"What's the point of that?"

"The point is, it gives us time to decide whether or not we're suitable for each other."

Phin frowned. "But you said you needed a husband now, so we could be safe on the trail."

"I know I did." Georgiana forced a bright smile. "But this is a better plan. The man I'm engaged to be married to will look after us on the trail, just like a husband would, but—"

"But you have an escape if you don't like him," Philip interrupted. He nodded. "Smart."

"But what if he doesn't like *you*?" his brother asked.

That would make life simpler, Georgiana thought ruefully. Unfortunately, the opposite seemed to be the case. The memory of the kiss came flooding back: the smell of him, the taste of him, the hardness of him against her.

"Why are you all red?" Phin asked. "You were red before, but now you're *red* red."

"It's hot in here," Georgiana lied.

"No, it's not."

"Be quiet and eat your hotcakes."

"You still haven't told us who it is."

Georgiana took a sip of water. It *was* suddenly terribly hot. "It's Matt Slater," she said. Then she braced for the reaction.

"Who?" Susannah screwed up her face.

"Brilliant!"

"But that's fantastic!"

The twins seemed happy, at least.

"He was that man we spoke to just now," Georgiana told Susannah, "the one we bumped into as we came in to breakfast."

"Oh."

"He's great," Phin told his sister. "He has all these horses out there in the stable."

"And a donkey and a dog," Philip chipped in.

Phin gave his brother a scornful look. "Who cares about the donkey and the dog? The horses are top quality." He glanced sideways at Georgiana. "Maybe he'll let us ride them."

"Flip!" Wilby banged his fork against the china until Georgiana took it away from him "Flip! I want to ride horse too!"

"That's Phin, Wilbs," Philip said, leaning across his brother. "I'm Philip. But don't worry, I'll make sure you can ride the horse too."

Their talk turned to the history of riding horses and then progressed to knights and how heavy a suit of armor might be. Matt Slater had been thoroughly dismissed from their minds.

Perhaps the children weren't going to be as concerned with who their stepfather would be as she had thought.

To GEORGIANA'S DISMAY, Wendell Todd was waiting for her on the front porch.

"Mornin'," he said, jumping up from the rocker and running a hand over his hair. He'd done something funny to it.

"You've had a haircut," Georgiana observed.

He beamed and ran his hands over it again. "Do you like it?"

She smiled tightly. It looked terrible. Like someone had taken to it with a blunt instrument. The hair on the back of his crown stood up in feathery spikes, too short to lie down flat on his head.

He'd bought new clothes too, she noticed. And shaved. That seemed to be something people did once they'd settled into town, she mused, thinking of Matt Slater's clean-shaven face, with the lean hollows under his cheekbones and the dimple in his cheek.

Wendell didn't have a dimple. Or a strong jaw. In fact, shaving the beard only served to draw attention to his wobbly little chin.

"I hope you had a good night's sleep," he said, sounding stilted. "And you too, little 'uns."

The children ignored him.

He looked anxious, which was odd. Odder still was how suddenly solicitous he was. The Wendell Todd she knew was a threatening thug. This man was nervous, polite and carefully spoken. What on earth had happened?

Matt, Georgiana thought suddenly. Matt had happened. *I already spoke to Wendell.* That's what he'd said last night. Oh my. What had he done? Had he threatened him?

It certainly seemed so, Georgiana thought as Wendell offered to escort her to Mrs. Tilly's. Wendell had his hat in hand and was giving her a nervous smile.

"I think the children and I are fine on our own, thank you," she said, sidestepping him.

"It's a rough town, missus," Wendell told her. "It's probably best if you have an escort." He gave her a shy look. "I'm sure your new fiancé would agree."

Matt Slater must have put the absolute fear of God into him. Georgiana paused. "Did Mr. Slater ask you to escort me today?"

Wendell looked confused for a split second and then blurted an assent. "That's right, missus, he thought it would be best."

She frowned. She didn't particularly like Matt organizing her life for her like this. She didn't *want* to spend the day with Wendell Todd. But she supposed she would be seeing him at the meeting at Mrs. Tilly's anyway, and she could always get rid of him after that. Earlier, if he reverted to his old repulsive self.

But, to Georgiana's surprise, Wendell didn't show the slightest sign of being anything but courteous. He remained solicitous all morning, following them to the wagonmaker's as Georgiana dropped by to check on the progress of their wagons, and then around the square as she considered the wares on display. He was like a faithful dog. Whenever Wilby dropped his sword, Wendell was there to pick it up, and he even gave the boy a piggyback when he threw a tantrum and refused to walk.

To Georgiana's relief, he also gave up trying to make small talk with her after she discouraged him with monosyllabic answers, and they lapsed into an oddly comfortable silence. Somehow, Matt Slater had wrought a miracle and not only brought the man into line, but altered his entire personality. Georgiana would have to remember to thank him.

Her mind lingered on some very pleasant ways she could do so before she managed to wrest it away.

By the time they arrived at Mrs. Tilly's for the meeting, there was already a crowd. Becky was standing at the front door, directing people. "If you're with Mr. Slater's party, turn left into the blue room," she was calling. "If you're with Mr. Sampson, please go into the yellow room on the right."

Her face darkened when she saw Georgiana. She clearly still hadn't forgiven Georgiana for walking home with Mr. Le-Foy the other night. Mr. LeFoy also happened to be here, Georgiana noticed, with all his girls.

"You're late," Becky said sourly, "and we're very busy. Leave the children in the kitchen. And you're not to touch anything," she told the children fiercely. "I don't have time to be cleaning glue today."

"I won't be needing to leave them today," Georgiana apologized. "I'm sorry I didn't let you know sooner."

"Fine." Becky was clearly not intending to warm to Georgiana ever again. "I don't really have time to talk," she sniffed. "We're expecting a full house, as you can see. We have two parties of emigrants holding meetings."

"We're joining one of those parties," Georgiana told her, feeling sheepish. She didn't know why she felt so sheepish, except that Becky was so obviously displeased with her. Poor love. She was so smitten with Pierre LeFoy that she thought every other woman must be too.

"Which party?" Becky demanded.

"We're going to California!" Phin said. He was clearly champing at the bit to set off. The twins had loved the whole adventure from the first.

Becky scowled. "Yellow room," she snapped, turning her back on them.

Georgiana saw why she was so annoyed: LeFoy was in the yellow room. As were another dozen or so men, all clumped around a big, bluff, blond fellow in buttery buckskins. Georgiana assumed he was the guide. As far as she could see, she was the only woman in the room.

"I think you're in the wrong room," LeFoy said heartily when he saw her. "Mr. Slater is in the blue room." He winked at her.

"We were told this room is for people going to California," Georgiana said by way of explanation.

"Exactly." LeFoy gave her a puzzled look. "And you're going to Oregon."

"No, we're not," Phin said, flopping on the couch between Ginger and Honey. "We're going to the goldfields. I'm going to find a nugget the size of my head. That's what my father told me in his last letter."

"You haven't told them yet?" LeFoy leaned in close and whispered so the children couldn't hear.

"Told them?" Georgiana had no idea what he was talking about.

"About your engagement."

"My . . ." she trailed off, astonished. "You know about the engagement?"

He nodded, smiling at her. "We were celebrating with Mr. Slater last night. And may I offer my heartfelt congratulations." Georgiana turned her head as he tried to kiss her on the cheek, and he caught her ear. She could see Becky scowling from where she lurked by the door.

"You were celebrating last night?" She had a flash of Matt leaning drunkenly against the screen.

"Indeed we were. Wendell here was with us too."

Georgiana couldn't quite disguise her shock. Wendell flushed. She felt a stab of suspicion. Were they *friends* now? She felt a familiar old fear stir. It was the same feeling Leonard had given her. A sense that secrets were slithering beneath the surface . . . and she had no idea what they might be.

"What are you planning on doing with the land in California," LeFoy asked curiously, "since you're going to Oregon with Mr. Slater?"

Georgiana rubbed her forehead. She couldn't for the life of her remember which lie was which. Matt had said something about Oregon last night, but all she'd been able to focus on was the bit about the pretend engagement . . . and his golden gaze and full lower lip . . . and his long, hard body . . . Stop. Stop there.

Of course she wasn't *actually* going to Oregon with Matt Slater, but she hadn't thought about the fact she had to *pretend* she was going. At least until Fort Hall. She frowned. That meant . . . what?

That she needed to be in the blue room with Matt's party, for a start.

She excused herself, without quite answering LeFoy's question, and gathered the children; Wendell followed behind, his arms full of discarded toys.

"But we're going to California," Phin complained.

"We'll discuss it later," Georgiana said firmly. "We're all traveling the same trail together, so don't fret."

She felt a wave of nerves as she approached the blue room. Unconsciously, she found herself smoothing her skirts and checking her hairpins.

She heard him before she saw him; his honey-warm voice was unmistakable, although it sounded slightly rougher this morning. The aftereffects of drink, she supposed. He looked completely incongruous in Mrs. Tilly's elegant tearoom. While the yellow room was set up like a drawing room, this one had tables and chairs, arranged in clusters. Most were already filled with people. Matt Slater towered over them, awkwardly holding one of Mrs. Tilly's delicate floral teacups and answering questions about the trail. His associate Mr. Doyle stood at the sideboard, with the cashbox and ledger.

"Oh, Mrs. Smith!" Mrs. Tilly had emerged from the kitchen with her hands full of fancy cake tiers laden with freshly baked pastries and cupcakes and tarts. "I'm afraid I'm very busy right now!"

Georgiana reassured her that she wasn't expecting her to mind the children; she was here in her capacity as an emigrant.

"You've joined Matt's party?" Mrs. Tilly beamed. "Oh, that's wonderful news." Then her face clouded. "But you really should wait and see what your husband wants, you know. Men do like to have a say in these things."

"I don't think that will be a problem." Georgiana started blushing again.

Mrs. Tilly's gaze flicked to Wendell, who still had his arms full of children's toys. "Oh! Is this the lucky man?"

Georgiana turned redder still. Thankfully, no!

"Not me," Wendell said gruffly. He nodded in Matt's direction. "Him."

Mrs. Tilly followed his gaze and smiled. She clearly thought he meant one of the two men currently talking to Matt. "How lovely," she said vaguely. "You must introduce me later. Now, I'd best get these out before the meeting starts. Why don't you snaffle that last table before someone else does?"

Georgiana's nerves surged as she saw that the only table left was right next to Matt. And that the children had already started for it.

He looked up as she crossed the room. She couldn't meet his eye but felt the weight of his gaze as it followed her. Georgiana kept her attention on the children as they took their chairs and Mrs. Tilly fetched them tea, lemonade and a plate of cakes. Wendell stood by the wall and was soon joined by Kipp, who oozed into the room, looking sullen. He didn't acknowledge Georgiana or the children, or speak to Wendell. He looked like he was in a serious sulk. She devoted herself to keeping the children under control and trying to police their manners as they devoured the cakes. Wilby climbed under the long, lacy tablecloth with his sword and a cupcake, and she left him there, not having the courage to do battle with him in front of a room full of people.

And there were an awful lot of people. More filed in by the minute, taking up places around the walls. Blue Bonnet was here, Georgiana noticed sourly, feeling a silly bolt of jealousy. She was with a large party who came in late and had to stand in the doorway. Mrs. Tilly flapped about, trying to give them cups of tea and dragging a table into the hall so she could fill it with treats for them.

"We don't want you missing out," she clucked. She was pink cheeked with the exertion.

Georgiana could hear a mix of accents and languages; there were Scandinavians and Germans, Frenchmen and a couple of Russians. Behind Georgiana was a slightly ragged-looking family with thick southern accents; they had a swarm of children who sat silently under the father's stern gaze. He was standing, with a swaddled baby in his arms, jiggling to keep it asleep. The mother was in her Sunday best and wrestling with a toddler who refused to sit still. Georgiana noticed the child was reaching for something; she followed its gaze and saw Wilby poking out from beneath the tablecloth, making faces.

"Wilby," she hissed, "stop it."

He gave her an angelic look.

"If you want to stay down there, you behave," she warned. "If you make the slightest noise, or keep bothering that child, you'll have to get up."

He disappeared back under the tablecloth.

There was a squeal, and the next thing she knew the toddler had wrested free of his mother's arms and dived under the tablecloth too.

"Oh!" The mother was out of her chair with alarm. "I'm so sorry, ma'am." She was turning bright red.

"Frank!" the father growled, sounding so fierce that even Georgiana was afraid. "Get out from there!"

There was the sound of giggles from under the table. Georgiana blushed. This was one of those moments when she felt keenly her limitations as a mother.

"I don't mind," she said, giving the couple her own apologetic look. "It's my fault—Wilby was clearly setting a bad example. If your son wants to stay under there with him, it's fine with me. It might keep them out of the way."

"Oh no." The woman looked shocked. "I couldn't . . ."

"They're not doing any harm," Georgiana insisted. "And, really, I don't mind." And she knew if she tried to get Wilby up from under the table, there would be screaming of an order to deafen the whole room. Then she really would be publicly humiliated as a bad mother, because once Wilby got started, nothing could stop him. This was a much easier way to handle things.

"Sarah," the man said stiffly.

"She says she doesn't mind," the woman, Sarah, told her husband, giving Georgiana a deeply grateful look. Georgiana could see why. She thought she had a hard time with her children, and this woman had *twice* as many. Now that her lap was free of the toddler, another one climbed on as soon as she sat back down.

"If you can get yourselves settled, we'll get started in a minute." Matt's voice, rising over the chatter of the crowd, sent a shiver through Georgiana.

He was a natural leader, Georgiana thought as she watched him put his china cup down and take his place at the head of the room. It was more than his stature, although that helped, as he dominated the room with his size; it was something about the way he carried himself, a confidence, a sense that if he made a decision, he would be immovable. All he had to do was stand there and people fell to attention. The murmur of the crowd dropped until there was silence.

"Welcome," he said. His gaze swept the room, and he nodded in greeting as he met people's eyes. "If you're here, it's because you're headed for Oregon. If you're headed for California"—here his eyes darted to Georgiana, and she broke out in a prickly sweat—"you're in the wrong place." He cleared his throat. "Mr. Sampson is through there, in the other room, and he's headed for California. We'll be traveling together for much of the way, but if you're California bound, you need to be in there with him, as the provisioning is different, and you'll need to hear about the California Trail, which you'll be on after we break into separate parties at Fort Hall. So, if you're in the wrong room, now's the chance to head in there." He waited.

A couple of young men left. Georgiana saw Wendell and Kipp exchange a glance. Wendell gave Kipp a nod, and the younger man slid out of the room, headed for the talk on the California Trail. Georgiana was relieved, as she'd felt a momentary panic at the thought of being wrongly provisioned. She needed to get to her son in California. If Kipp hadn't gone to take note, she might have gone herself.

Although, she doubted Matt Slater would let her be underprovisioned, she realized as she listened to him instruct them on preparing for the journey. The man was a stickler for preparation.

"You're not to buy one ounce less than I tell you to," he said sternly, and Georgiana doubted anyone would dare to cross him, as he looked so fearsome. "Seb here has a list for each party, which includes all you'll be needing for the journey. I expect you to buy every last thing on it."

Sebastian Doyle came forward with a sheaf of papers, which he began handing out. Georgiana took one. It was meticulous, outlining everything from the kinds of wagons and animals to buy, down to how much salt to take. It must have taken them hours to write out all these copies.

"Let me look," Phin whispered. The twins loomed over her shoulder, reading along with her: *150 pounds of bacon, 200 pounds of flour, 10 pounds of coffee; pins and needles; brooms and brushes; ox shoes and horseshoes . . .* the list was enormous. And it was going to prove very expensive. Georgiana did some rough figures in her head. All up it was probably going to cost at least one thousand dollars. She swallowed hard. She had the money, but it wouldn't leave much for their start in California . . .

She could hear other people murmuring too.

"You might be tempted to skimp," Matt Slater said, reading their minds. "You might think you can make do on a bit less." He fixed them with a hard look. "You can't."

"How's all this even going to fit in our wagon?" someone said quietly.

"Ideally, your wagon should hold up to two thousand pounds. Twenty-five hundred if you can manage it. That's something you need to stress with your wagonmakers, if you've already ordered your wagon."

Georgiana bit her lip. Oh my. She'd need to go back to the wagonmaker *again* and ask about the volume of her wagons. At least she'd ordered two, as they had a lot of baggage and the wagonmaker had insisted that she would need the room. He'd told her she could hire people to drive them. But now, as she listened to Matt go through the specifications for wagons (the need for waterproofing for river crossings, for example), she realized that she didn't know the first thing about wagons and was naïve to trust that the wagonmaker would do right by her.

"All of these things need to be checked and double-checked," Matt told them. "The wainwrights are under pressure to produce a lot of wagons very quickly for you folks, and they'll cut corners if they can. But those corners can cost you dearly on the trail."

Oh my. She didn't like the sound of that.

"But where do we sleep if the wagon is that full?" someone asked. It was Blue Bonnet, Georgiana saw.

"Tents," Matt said. "They're on the list too."

That was something else Georgiana hadn't considered. Tents. She had a lot of shopping to do . . .

"Tents!" Philip sounded excited. "Can Phin and I have one just for us?"

Georgiana shushed him. She didn't want to miss a word.

After admonishing them to follow his list to the letter (increasing the amounts where needed for bigger parties), he moved on to the types of animals to buy and who the most reputable dealers were. "For a fee, Seb or I can come and help you choose and negotiate prices for the animals," he said. Georgiana took note.

After an hour of answering questions about provisioning, Matt took a break for Mrs. Tilly to refill the teapots. During the break, Georgiana checked on the toddlers under the table, only to find they'd gone to sleep, curled around each other like puppies. That was a relief. She held the tablecloth up so the boy's mother could see. The woman smiled gratefully. Her other little one had also fallen asleep, but the baby was fussing, so she and her husband swapped children. Georgiana watched the ease with which they interacted. It was like a dance. He took one child, she took another, and they exchanged affectionate glances as they did so. She saw how he gave her a tender look as she fussed over the baby. Georgiana's throat felt tight. She felt envy, yes, but more than that she was gripped with longing. What must it be like to have a husband like that? One who could be a helpmate and partner, one who looked at you as though you were his own secret treasure?

Her gaze wandered to Matt.

He was unfolding a large map. A lock of hair had tumbled into his eyes, and he tossed his head to get it out of the way. He glanced over at her table and her heart clenched.

"Boys," he called to the twins. "Come here, I have a job for you to do."

They didn't need asking twice. They leapt to his side. Wendell took the opportunity to sit in one of their empty seats, at Georgiana's elbow. She gave the twins her full attention, so she wouldn't have to speak to him.

"Hold this," Matt instructed them. He gave them a corner each. "Hold it up high."

They did as they were asked. Georgiana had never seen them so obedient.

Matt made a thoughtful noise. He didn't look happy. He came over to the table and took the empty chair. "Get up on that," he said to Philip, placing it behind him. Then he clicked his fingers at Wendell. "Bring me that one too."

"What one?" Wendell asked, bewildered. There were no more empty chairs at the table.

"The one you're sitting on," Matt said shortly.

Disgruntled, Wendell did as he was told, and then, dethroned, he went back to standing against the wall.

Once the boys were up on the chairs, Matt instructed them to hold the map up so everyone could see it. Georgiana watched them bristling with pride over being trusted with such an important job.

"All right folks, not much longer now," Matt called for attention again, and everyone settled back into their seats. The next hour was spent with Matt walking them through the steps of the trail. Georgiana's stomach was in knots by the time he was done. The distances were daunting. As his finger traced over plains and rivers and mountain ranges, Georgiana saw the year stretching out ahead: June crossing the Platte, July passing through Fort Laramie, and there, where his finger paused at Fort Hall, was where her real trials would begin. Because after Fort Hall, she wouldn't be following him. As his finger slid into Oregon, her gaze drifted southwest to California. She would be alone with the children, and with Wendell and Kipp. For a good couple of months in the deepest wilderness . . .

She wished she could duck into the other room at that point, to have some idea of what lay ahead of her. She would have to see the map up close after this, to see the other trail. She needed to know. Was it more or less dangerous than the trail into Oregon that Matt was describing?

Her hands shook as she took a sip of tea, and her china cup chimed against its saucer as she struggled to put it down quietly.

"And by mid to late fall, we'll be here, in Oregon City," Matt said, jabbing his finger at the map. "And that's where your new lives will begin."

People had been firing questions at him throughout his

talk, and there were more now, but Georgiana couldn't take
them in. She was too busy wondering what would happen to
her in California. How savage would Hec Boehm be? Would
he let her see Leo before she signed the deed? Was Leo safe?

Every time she thought of her son, her stomach turned sour
and she grew light-headed with terror.

"Are you cold, Mama?" Susannah whispered, leaning over
the table. "You're shivering. Do you want my shawl?"

Startled, Georgiana saw how closely her daughter was
watching her. She was such a quiet child. She so often got lost
in the chaos when her brothers were around, but she was a per-
ceptive child. When Georgiana forgot to guard her expression,
Susannah invariably noticed. Right now her blue eyes were as
round as saucers, and she was chewing at her lower lip with
anxiety.

"Thank you, darling, that's a very kind offer," Georgiana
whispered back, gesturing for Susannah to join her. She pulled
the little girl into her lap and lowered her face into the curve
of Susannah's shoulder. "You're warmer than any shawl," she
told her. She felt Susannah relax against her.

"Will they be much longer?" Susannah whispered.

"I don't know, darling. I hope not."

But the emigrants in the room seemed to have an endless
flow of questions. Georgiana hugged her daughter tightly as
she heard about scouts and Indian tribes and buffalo hunting
and early winters and trading posts. The questions were inex-
haustible.

Eventually, Matt cut them off. He held up both his hands
and quieted the room. "There's plenty of time to answer all of
your questions," he soothed them. "I'll be here at Mrs. Tilly's
every afternoon between three and five, in her back drawing
room, down the corridor out there. If you have questions, you
can come see me any day, bar Sundays. You can also find me
and Seb in the town square every day except Thursday morn-
ings, when we run these sessions for people newly signed."

"You mean there's more than just us?" someone asked,
shocked, looking at the overstuffed room.

Matt nodded. "There will be. We're looking at a medium-
sized party, which is still going to be in the hundreds of people, folks."

There was a murmur.

"When the parties start heading out in a few weeks, go and watch them leaving. Some are so big they take all day to roll out. It will give you a good idea of what to expect."

"But how do you manage a group that big?" It was Blue Bonnet again, this time sounding disapproving.

"We have scouts, ma'am. And we expect you to manage your own group. We'll lead the way, form a small governing council, run a court if discipline is needed, lead hunting expeditions and do all the planning and trail blazing. But this is a hard journey, and we expect you all to be self-sufficient."

Georgiana took a shaky breath. She didn't feel at all self-sufficient . . .

She hadn't realized the scale of his job. She couldn't quite comprehend the numbers of people he was talking about, let alone picture them all traveling in one big group.

"Now, every Saturday night, Independence holds a dance in the town square. We have a spot under the sycamore, where you signed up with us, where our group settles for the dance. Come meet us there this Saturday and every Saturday until we leave, so you can get introduced to the others in the party. It's a great chance to get to know people and work out who you'd like to travel alongside." He gave them a reassuring smile. "We sure hope to see you there this Saturday."

And that quickly, the meeting concluded. Matt thanked the twins and took his map back, and then he was swamped with people. It seemed there were still more questions to be asked. The twins stayed close, listening attentively.

Georgiana gently nudged Susannah off her lap and stood up. She was feeling quite overwhelmed.

"I'd be happy to take you to buy some things from the list," Wendell said, creeping in beside her.

That was the last thing Georgiana wanted.

"Perhaps," she hedged. "Actually, I was wondering if you could find out from Mr. Koerner about the California Trail? Maybe you could familiarize yourselves thoroughly with the route? Then we could meet later and you could talk me through it? I'd love to see a map."

That might keep him out of her way for a while. She found his presence oppressive, even if he was trying to be courteous.

Wendell leapt at her request like a dog at a bone and disappeared, off to find Kipp.

Once he was gone, Georgiana tried to gather her thoughts. What to do first?

Talk to Matt Slater. That was *all* she wanted to do.

Well, not all. But she couldn't entertain those thoughts. Particularly not here, in public. She fanned herself with her napkin. *Think about something else.*

The trail. How could she check the wagons, provision them, buy animals and do the dozens of other things she needed to do, all while dragging four young children along after her? She needed help. And not help from the likes of Wendell Todd.

Matt said he charged to help get people set up. She didn't have much money left, but she was willing to pay for that. She trusted him.

She just needed a chance to speak to him. Which might take a while, she realized, as she saw the queue forming in front of him.

Matt took the coward's way out and left Georgiana to Seb.

"Can you tell her I'll see her later at the hotel?" he asked his friend.

"You sure? She looks pretty set on speaking to you." Seb was smirking. He obviously thought Matt was being shy with his new fiancée. Which didn't surprise him; he'd known Matt long enough to have some experience with his nerves around women. "You are going to have to talk to her eventually, you know," Seb told him.

Matt scowled. "Tell her I'll be at the hotel tonight."

"Whatever you want, boss."

Matt had agreed to take the Tasker family to order wagons and was glad to slip out with them while Seb was talking to Georgiana. He wasn't ready to see her again yet. Not alone. Not after the dreams he'd had last night. Dreams about that row of little black buttons down the front of her dress and how he could unbutton them one by one by one. Running into her at the hotel this morning had been excruciating. Her big blue eyes, her ridiculously small corseted waist, those damn little buttons running over the luscious swell of her chest. It all made him break out in a cold sweat.

He was sweating again now, just from being in the same room with her all morning. It had been near impossible to concentrate with her sitting at the closest table, those sky blue eyes fixed on him, watching his every move. A couple of times he'd lost his train of thought and had to pause and try to remember what he was talking about. It helped to have the map. When he lost track, he could just go back to talking about the route.

It was a relief to be out of there, away from her, and back to simple business, he thought as he took the Taskers to Archie's. They were a nice family, the Taskers. The kind of family he envied. The old man was a widower and was taking his pack to Oregon for a better life. There were four grown children, three with spouses and children of their own, and a fourth, the youngest, Lydia, who looked after her father in the wake of his wife's death. The lot of them were easy with one another, teasing their father, Herb, about how he might find a new wife in the new land. Matt was jealous of their ease, and of the fact that they still had their father.

He couldn't imagine having his own father still a part of his life. He wondered what it would be like. It looked pretty nice.

He enjoyed spending the afternoon with them at Archie's, looking at near-finished examples of wagons and helping them order what they'd need. And they needed a lot, as there were so many of them.

"I can't do it quickly," Archie apologized to Matt once the family had ordered their wagons and departed, in a flurry of excited chatter. They were off to buy some of the things from Matt's list, and they were full of praise for his organizational skills. Matt liked his clients happy before they started on the trail; they needed to feel safe at the start, as they were always anxious about the road ahead. He wanted them to know they could trust him. A little trust early on went a long way toward running a smooth train. He'd learned that lesson the hard way.

"I'm busy night and day already," Archie complained. "I would have told them I was booked up, except I'd never say no to you."

"I appreciate it," Matt said.

Archie shrugged. "You've given me a lot of business over the years. And the people you bring always pay up front, like I ask."

"I bring them to you because you're always ready on time," Matt said. "I'll be back again tomorrow. I might have a couple more for you."

"I don't have time," Archie complained. "I just told you that."

"We'll just swing by and see how you feel tomorrow."

Archie grunted. "Hey," he said abruptly, jolting as though he had remembered something, "what's this gossip I hear about you getting married? And to that Smith woman! Is there any truth in it?"

"Maybe a little," Matt admitted. A precious little.

"You know she went to Noonan for her wagons?"

Matt swore. Noonan. Of all people.

"You might want to get on that," Archie advised.

"Yeah," Matt said sourly. Damn it. As if he didn't have enough to do. He didn't have time left today. He'd see Noonan tomorrow.

"I was thinking you'd snuck out the back door, honey. You took so long to come out," a voice purred as Matt stepped into the street.

He was starting to hate this town. Just when he thought things had calmed down, something crawled out from under a rock to bite him in the ass.

This time the something was Seline, who was dolled up in her Sunday best. Her gaudy, shiny, busty Sunday best. The bright pink satin caught the afternoon sunlight and clashed horribly with her hair. She'd smacked on some extra rouge too, he noticed.

"What do you want?" he sighed.

"Now, honey, that ain't no way to treat a lady." She fluttered her eyelashes at him.

Despite himself, Matt had always liked Seline. She had spirit. And there was a certain detachment in the way she approached him with her random acts of seduction that put him weirdly at ease. He'd always had the sense that she didn't give a damn about him. Any attraction was a performance. And that felt a hell of a lot safer than the temptation offered by Georgiana Bee Blunt, whose inky eyes last night had glistened with pure, instinctive, unperformed desire.

"Drop it," he told the whore. "I'm busy."

She grinned and dropped the flirtation. Immediately her body language changed, relaxed. "Me and some of the girls want to go to California," she said.

"I don't go to California."

"I know, but that stuck-up Joe Sampson won't take us." She rolled her eyes. "He said he doesn't trade in whores."

"Neither do I." Matt started walking back to the square. Seline followed along.

"There's a hell of a trade to be done on those goldfields," she said, her shiny pink skirt swinging as she skipped alongside him. "Do you have any idea how many men are out there, and how few women?"

Matt grunted. He had no intention of taking whores on his train.

"There's a fortune to be made! And I'm tired of spreading my legs for the profit of other people. I want to start my own place. For the profit of *me*. I have the girls. I have the money to set us up. Now I just need someone to take us." She gave him a look. "Someone I trust, who ain't going to abuse us."

"I don't go to California," he repeated. He stopped, frustrated. He could hardly walk into the town square trailing a whore.

"I know. But you could talk to your man Joe, surely? Have you seen the group he's got together? It's almost all men. All of them headed for the goldfields! I could make a fortune on the trail alone! Wait!" she said, sounding frustrated when he tried to walk away. "Listen! Just listen, that's all I ask. You know what a party of men is like—that many men: dozens and dozens of single men out on the trail, without the comfort of women. You know we could be doing you a great service, keeping them all placid."

Matt grunted.

"Just *talk* to him, honey," Seline pleaded. "That's all I ask."

Matt sighed. "It won't do any good, Seline. Neither of us wants whores in our party."

She scowled at that. "Don't you go getting up on your high horse, Matthew Slater. Just because you never visit a whore, don't mean you got a right to judge me and the girls. You think we *chose* this life? You think any girl in her right mind dreams of becoming a whore? But I'll be damned if I'll be looked down on. If you're going to look down on anyone, you can look down on the dirty bastards who pay us. The ones with wives." She caught herself and took a deep breath. He watched her expression become composed again. "Those men in Sampson's party are mostly single. None of them would begrudge him taking us along. We ain't likely to upset anyone's sense of common decency."

"He travels along with my party, Seline. I got families. Hell, I even got a priest."

"Well, he shouldn't be complaining. Mary Magdalene was a whore, wasn't she? And she's a goddamn saint!"

Matt sighed. "I'll ask him. But that's all I'll do. And I can pretty much guarantee that he's going to say no."

She didn't look happy about it, but she didn't look surprised either. "Just take a look at his books when you talk to him," she said quietly, "and see how many are men on their own-some, and think about what I said. You might run into trouble with that many single men, that many rough-and-ready gold diggers on the trail along with your decent folks. And your *priest*." She tossed her head and pranced off, the pink bell of her skirt swinging.

Matt did think about it. He'd had a particularly hairy trip one year when he'd made the mistake of not balancing out his party with enough families. She was right. Too many single men could make for a hard trip. But he wasn't about to talk to Joe today. He'd wait and hope Seline found another party to join first.

He headed for the square, feeling like his life had become just one damn mess after another.

GEORGIANA HADN'T MANAGED to speak to Matt since Mrs. Tilly's. It wasn't for lack of trying. But the man was slipperier than Wilby wet from the bathtub. Straight after the meeting, he'd left with Blue Bonnet, of all people. Georgiana had gone back to meet him at the hotel, just as Mr. Doyle told her to. He'd said Matt would see her later at the hotel. But he hadn't come. She'd waited all afternoon. By that point she'd been a little irritated. But even though the children begged her to go back to the cook-house for dinner, she stayed at the hotel instead, just in case. He still hadn't come. She'd stabbed at the dry mutton and lumpy gravy, blaming him for their unappetizing dinner. She certainly wouldn't be eating Mrs. Bulfinch's cooking if it weren't for him. Breakfast was bad enough, but the things that woman could do with a roast beggared belief.

By the time she hauled the children up to bed, she was in a filthy temper. She'd sat around *all day*. Well, most of the day. The afternoon and evening, anyway. Because he'd asked her to. Because of him she hadn't gone back to Mr. Noonan's to sort out her wagons; she hadn't bought a cow or a kettle or any of the other things on his wretched list; she hadn't done *anything* except sit on Mrs. Bulfinch's porch, in Mrs. Bulfinch's parlor, and in Mrs. Bulfinch's dining room. Not only was it stuffy and boring, but she'd had to deal with all the men she'd rejected. She'd started out polite and ended up quite snappish. She blamed Matt Slater for that too.

She was short with the children as she helped them wash and dress for bed. She had to count to ten at least a dozen times to stop herself from shouting at them. When Susannah burst into tears because Georgiana wouldn't sing her a lullaby, she was quite at her wit's end.

"I can't," she tried to explain to her daughter. "You know I always fall asleep when I sing to you, and I have to stay up so I can talk to Mr. Slater."

"He don't seem to want to talk to you," Phin said, his voice muffled by his pillow.

"Doesn't. He *doesn't* seem to," she corrected him, trying not to feel the bite of his words. "*Don't* is vulgar."

"People around here say *don't*," he defended himself.

"Well, we're not from here, are we? And we're certainly not staying here."

Susannah had no patience with their conversation and kept crying for a lullaby. In the end, Georgiana bribed the twins to sing to her in exchange for buying them the marbles they'd coveted at the store.

"You have to sing at least five songs, or no marbles," she warned. "And no short songs! If it's 'Twinkle, Twinkle, Little Star,' you have to sing it through at least three times."

They groaned but wanted the marbles enough to do as she asked.

Georgiana left them to it and went into her own room, which opened onto the hallway. She pulled the desk chair up to the door and opened it a crack. From where she sat, she had a clear view of Matt Slater's door. There was no way he was getting past her.

Or so she thought.

She must have dozed off sometime after the second hour. She woke suddenly to a very still house. She could hear the ticking of the grandfather clock downstairs. It must be very late. Her door was closed, she realized. Had she knocked it when she'd fallen asleep? Or had he come along and seen her and closed the door on her?

Georgiana felt even more irritable than before. She was stiff from her odd position in the chair. She got up and checked on the children. They were fast asleep. She turned down their lamp and headed crankily back to her own bed. The clock said it was after midnight. Midnight!

That wretch had told her to wait at the hotel and he'd speak to her there! And then he'd left her to sit and wait until midnight!

But he hadn't said exactly *when* he'd be at the hotel, she realized. He'd only said *later*; he might have meant tomorrow. She scowled. No. He must have known how she'd interpret it. It was just a cheap ploy to keep her out of his way. He'd been very short with her this morning, and then he'd sent Mr. Doyle over to shoo her away, instead of speaking to her himself. Was he mad at her?

Was it because of the kiss?

He had no cause to be cold with her. The whole pretend engagement thing was *his* fault in the first place. As was the kiss.

He had no right punishing her for his faults!

Georgiana cocked her head. She thought she'd heard the faint sound of male voices. Was he awake? She opened her door. Yes, there were definitely voices talking behind his closed door.

He thought he could avoid her, did he?

Well, we'd see about that.

She marched over and knocked. The murmur of voices fell silent. She knocked again.

Silence.

Now she was really irked.

She knocked louder, not caring if she woke the whole hotel. "Mr. Slater?" she called. "It's me."

She heard whispers. *Not now . . . Get rid of her . . .*

That made her mad enough to want to kick the door down.

Get rid of her? Ha. She'd like to see him try. "I know you're in there," she said, slapping the flat of her hand against the door.

She heard soft footsteps and a clicking sound, like a door closing. She slapped again. Harder.

The door opened as her hand came down a third time, and she went stumbling over the threshold. Right into a grumpy-looking man. A starkly handsome, angular, completely grumpy-looking man.

He was terrifying.

It didn't help that the lamplight was low, casting his face into shadow. He loomed over her, still as glass.

"Can I help you?" His voice was flat, with an oddly formal accent.

"I'm looking for Matt Slater," she said, breathless, stepping away from him and trying to regain her balance.

"He's not here."

That made her blood boil, and in her anger, she totally forgot that the man in front of her was terrifying. "He is! I heard him!" she insisted.

"No." The man was like a granite cliff. He had absolutely no expression.

Georgiana couldn't keep her mouth from dropping open at the sheer gall of it. Out of habit, she started to count to ten to control her temper. Then stopped herself. She had every right to be angry after waiting around all day for a man who hadn't come when he said he would, and who was now *hiding from her*. Like a coward. "I know he's here," she said darkly. "I *heard* him."

"You are mistaken."

"I'm *not*," she said through gritted teeth. She pushed past him, barely noticing that he didn't really try to stop her. "I know he's in there!" She headed straight for the door on the wall opposite. The room was a mirror image of her own, so she assumed it led to a second bedroom.

She was right.

"Aha! I *knew* you were here!" she cried when she saw Matt Slater standing by one of the twin brass beds. She threw a triumphant look over her shoulder at the man who'd lied to her.

"You didn't try very hard to get rid of her," Matt complained to his friend.

The man shrugged. "I'm not even supposed to be out of bed," he said. Now that Georgiana was on this side of the door, she could see that he wasn't too steady on his feet. He closed the door and staggered back to his bed. "Close that door if you're going to talk. And keep your voices down. It's the middle of the night." He pulled the covers up over his head.

Matt sighed. "Listen, Mrs. Smith or Mrs. Blunt or whatever your name is, my brother ain't well. Off you go."

"Oh no. No, no, no, no." Georgiana stepped into his room with him and closed the door behind her. Her temper was still up, enough that she didn't stop to think about the wisdom of being alone with him in his bedroom. Or perhaps, she thought later, she'd known deep down what would happen and had secretly *wanted* it to happen . . .

"Listen, lady, it's been a long day."

"Indeed it has. And I have spent that long day sitting downstairs, waiting for you to come, like you said you would."

He blanched. "Would you believe me if I said that something came up?"

"No," she said bluntly.

"Look. I'm sorry I kept you waiting, but this ain't right, you being in here with me like this."

"Oh no?" Georgiana could see she was making him uncomfortable. He'd backed up until he was hard against the other bed. "Even though I'm your fiancée?" She sat down on the bed closest to her.

"People will gossip," he said tightly.

She crossed her ankles, folded her hands in her lap and fixed him with a patient look. She was quite enjoying how nervous he looked and had no plans to move without getting what she came for.

He sighed. "What do you want?"

"I merely want to have the conversation we were supposed to have this afternoon." She didn't care if he hadn't specified the afternoon. She'd been *waiting*.

"We can have it first thing in the morning," he promised. "I'll have breakfast with you."

"Oh no," she said. "I want it now."

"Well, I don't." There was a flash of temper on that darkly stubbled face. Somehow, it only made him more attractive.

She brushed the thought away. She wasn't here for that non-sense. She was here to do business. "I waited in this hotel for over eleven hours," she said coldly, "and I don't plan to wait a minute longer. Now, you can stand there arguing with me and wasting more of my time and yours, or you can answer my questions and get the conversation over and done with."

Matt rubbed at his eyes. He looked very, very tired.

"Answer her damn questions!" a voice called from the other room. "Some of us want to sleep tonight!"

Matt scowled at the closed door and muttered something under his breath. "Fine," he snapped. "What do you want?"

Georgiana pulled the annotated list from her pocket. She'd made notes this afternoon, in preparation for their meeting.

Matt saw the scribbles and groaned.

She gave him a prim look. "Don't worry," she said, "we don't have to get through all of it tonight. Although," she warned, "I won't leave unless you promise to help me with the rest of it tomorrow. At breakfast."

"Lady, you're bossier than you look."

There was a pounding against the wall.

Matt scowled. "Sick, my ass," she heard him mutter. "Fine," he sighed. "I'll answer one question now, and we can do the rest over breakfast."

Georgiana knew exactly which question she wanted to ask. It was the reason she'd waited all day. "Show me the map," she said. "I want to see the California Trail." She was desperate to know every step of the trail that lay between her and her son.

THE MAP WAS so big it took up most of the single bed. Georgiana bent over it as Matt showed her the trail, starting with where it branched off from Fort Hall.

"Do they sell maps like this in town?" she asked, when he was spreading it out.

He gave her an odd look. "What do you need with a map? Joe Sampson knows the way like the back of his hand. He'll get you there right enough."

"I just want one," she said stubbornly. For insurance.

But she also wanted one just to look at when she was sleep-less in the long, anxious nights, to reassure her that the trail led inevitably to Leo. Just the idea of owning a map made her feel calmer; it was a solid connection to her son.

Matt was still giving her an odd look. "They sell them at the store. Not as detailed as this. But there's plenty of demand for them these days."

Of course there was.

"Tell me about the trail," she asked, bending low to peer at the landmarks on the map. "Just from here." She pressed the pad of her finger into the black dot of Fort Hall.

"I don't know the California Trail as well as mine," he admitted, "but I've been in some rescue parties along it."

She shivered. Rescue parties? That didn't sound good.

He leaned over the map beside her. "It's longer than the Oregon Trail. Almost three thousand miles."

"Three thousand?" Georgiana couldn't keep the shock from her voice.

She should have known that, shouldn't she? She realized how woefully ignorant and underprepared she was as Matt talked her through the trail that ran south from Fort Hall. "After we split here by the Snake River, Joe'll take you down along the Raft River here, to the City of Rocks." The names coming out of his mouth sounded mythical. It was difficult to believe she'd be walking through all of these places in a few months' time. She watched as his finger traced a network of small rivers until it reached a larger one called the Humboldt. He tapped this longer line. "You follow this through the Great Basin until it peters out." And it did peter out, she saw; a river that ended in the middle of nowhere. "This," he said seriously, when his finger ran off the end of the river, "is where it dies in the flats. And where you hit the Forty Mile Desert."

Oh, she really didn't like the sound of that. And she liked even less the look of the crinkles representing the Sierra Nevada mountain range.

"That's where the Donner party was stranded, wasn't it?" she asked anxiously.

He shot her a look. "It's a busier trail now," he said. "Since the gold rush, the trail bustles all season. It's hard to get stranded with that many people going to and fro."

"But if the weather turns, like it did for them . . ."

"They were stupid," Matt said firmly. "They went off trail, and they didn't have a proper guide. Joe's one of the best. I'd trust him with my life."

She nodded but still felt uneasy as she took in the vast distances represented by the lines and crinkles and dots. She had such a long way to go . . .

"I was at Mrs. Tilly's again late this afternoon," Matt said quietly. She was abruptly aware of how close they were standing. "She found out about us."

She looked up at him, but his gaze was firmly fixed on the map. Us. The word made her break out in goosebumps. *Us.*

He traced his finger along the area of the goldfields. "She told me why you're going to California."

Georgiana froze. "What do you mean?"

He looked up. His face was grave. "She told me about your son."

Georgiana's heart squeezed. "Oh." All Mrs. Tilly knew was that Georgiana *had* a son and that he was waiting for her, alone, in California. She didn't know anything about Wendell and Kipp and their horrid puppet master, Hec Boehm. The monster who had her son.

"It's a powerful long distance between a mother and her child." The tenderness in his voice was her undoing. The wretched tears were back, pricking at her. And here she'd almost managed a whole day without crying . . .

She kept her face averted. The map swam before her. It *was* a powerful long distance, made all the worse by not knowing how Leo was being treated. Was he locked up or free? Were they caring for him or abusing him?

He must be so scared . . .

The tears fell in earnest, splattering against the map.

"I'm sorry," she apologized, rubbing at them with her thumb. "I don't want to ruin your map." Matt caught her hand and stopped her.

"Don't worry about the damn map."

She tried to get hold of herself, but it was hard once the tears had started. It was like working a water pump: once the water was gushing, it was gushing. She used her free hand to swipe at her cheeks. She felt terribly exposed.

"How old is he?" Matt asked her. He hadn't let go of her hand. His fingers were warm where they curled around hers.

"Twelve."

"You must have had him when you were still in the schoolroom," he said, sounding shocked.

"Almost." She sniffed and tried to gain control. This man had seen her cry far too often. And she'd only met him a few times; at this rate he'd think she did nothing but cry. "I was seventeen."

"What's his name, your son?" His thumb was stroking the back of her hand. She didn't think he was aware he was doing it.

Their voices were hushed, and they were standing so close over the map that she could feel the warmth of his breath on her cheek when he spoke. The air was charged again, like last night in the laundry. Georgiana was finding it hard to breathe.

"Leo," she said, her voice unsteady.

"Mrs. Tilly said he's with your people?"

Georgiana pressed her lips together and nodded. She couldn't bring herself to say the lie aloud. They *weren't* her people. She'd never met them.

"I ain't going to lie to you, lady," he said, his voice painfully gentle. "It ain't an easy trail. But, you do as Joe and I tell you, and we'll get you there safe. You and all your little ones." He pulled a face. "I'll even get those cousins of yours there safe."

She was startled into a laugh. It must have sounded a little hysterical, because he gave her hand a squeeze to reassure her.

"Here," he said, releasing her hand and reaching for his map. He rolled it up and held it out to her. "Take it."

"I can't take your map." She brushed away the last of her tears. "You need it."

"I have another one. The one I had at Mrs. Tilly's today. I keep it there for my Thursday speeches." He pressed the map into her hand. "Take it. Really. I don't need it."

"Thank you," she said shakily, taking the map.

He really was the most bewildering man: rough and irritable one minute, gentle and kind the next. He seemed boyish again, like he had last night, his hair tumbling over his forehead as he looked up at her through those thick black eye-lashes. When she was with him, she didn't feel so scared. She felt something else, something like safety but more exciting. Her stomach was buzzing, her heart tripped over itself, and she was aware of every inch of her own skin.

In that moment, as she took the map from him, Georgiana knew precisely why she'd come to find him tonight. She knew why she'd forced herself into his room, rather than waiting to see him in the morning. It was because she'd thought of nothing but kissing him all day. She felt like a giddy girl. She wanted nothing so much as to find a quiet corner where she could hide away with him and kiss him for hours. As though she wasn't a responsible single mother of five, but a blushing young debu-tante, stealing off with a daring young man at a party.

She'd never thought of herself as brave or bold. Foolhardy, perhaps. And so it was probably foolhardiness that made her kiss him.

She stretched up on tiptoe and pressed a light-as-a-feather thank-you kiss on his lips. She felt him jump slightly.

"Thank you," she whispered again, against his lips.

She kept the kiss light, instinctively knowing anything more might scare him off. She saw his eyelashes flutter. He looked the way she felt. Mesmerized, stupid with this slowly uncoiling desire that seemed to unleash itself whenever they were together. The feeling was so much nicer than the swollen, incompetent grief she lived with; it was a beautiful, magical distraction from the horrifying facts of her life.

The shimmery, shivery feeling transformed the world; it brought it into sharp relief. In the laundry . . . outside the breakfast room . . . as she watched him give that talk at Mrs. Tilly's . . . as she'd waited for him at the hotel, pacing, anxious, wound up . . . from that very first time she saw him through the window as he hitched his animals, she'd felt *different*. The sod-den helpless sense of her life being over, of just going through the motions, was gone, and in its place, she was vibrant again. She was Georgiana again. Not Mrs. Leonard Blunt. Not Mrs. Smith. Not Mother. She was just Georgiana, and there was a world of possibility at her feet. When this feeling shimmered to life, she felt as though her life was just beginning.

This was what she'd wanted when she'd burst into his room. She wanted to come to life.

Georgiana kissed him slowly, as she'd imagined doing all day long, her mouth slanting across his as she stretched against him. Her free hand slid up his chest. She felt him tremble. His eyelids fluttered closed, and she felt an intoxicating sense of power. She'd half expected him to shove her away, especially after his appalled reaction last night. And he wasn't drunk this time.

But he didn't push her aside. He stood, silent, frozen, and let her kiss him. His lips were soft under hers, accepting her movements. There was none of the hunger of the night before. Just gentleness. Sweetness.

Her fingertips ran over his open collar, across the hot skin of his neck, lingering at the feel of his surging pulse; her touch trailed up his nape, her fingers threading through his hair, pulling him down harder against her mouth. Bolder, she touched the tip of her tongue to his lips. She felt him jerk slightly, and then his mouth opened for her. She traced his lower lip with her tongue. The feel of him trembling against her was one of the most erotic things she'd ever experienced. The sense of him being leashed, pulsing, aroused but utterly restrained.

She had a feeling that any moment the dam might break, and all that desire would come crashing down on her as he lost control.

But he didn't lose control, not yet.

Georgiana was hot, melting, as she slid her tongue into his mouth. As her tongue touched his, he took hold of her shoulders and pulled her harder against him. She felt the rolled-up map crush between their bodies. She couldn't get close enough. He was kissing her back now, his tongue entering her. He caught her lower lip between his teeth and gave it a slow suck. She could barely keep on her feet, the force of her desire was so strong.

"Goddamn it!"

She didn't know what happened. One minute she was blissfully drugged, being kissed to within an inch of her sanity, and the next she was being marched out. He had her by the arm as he dragged her out of his bedroom, through his friend's room, and all but flung her into the hallway.

"Stop that!" he ordered, jabbing his finger in her face.

Georgiana couldn't think to reply. She was still lost in the warm haze of their kiss. She wasn't quite sure how they'd gone from there, to here.

"No kissing," he growled at her. Then he slammed the door in her face.

She frowned. *I beg your pardon?*

She rapped sharply at the door. She heard his friend curse.

The door flung open again. "What?" Matt snapped at her. He looked utterly delicious, with his hair ruffled from her fingers, his face flushed, his eyes still foggy with desire.

"Are we still having breakfast?" she asked primly.

He scowled. "I said we were, didn't I?" The door slammed again.

Georgiana smiled.

She should feel insulted, but she didn't.

Because what she'd seen in his eyes wasn't disgust or dislike. It was pure, unadulterated fear. He was *scared* of her. Of their kiss. Of that throbbing energy that began to beat whenever they were alone together. That shivery, delicious feeling.

Georgiana drifted off to her bed in a haze of desire. Somehow, his fear made her feel less afraid. She didn't know why. Tonight, she didn't care why. Tonight, she was just happy to feel something other than fear and worry. She sat in bed with the map, staring at the crumpled waxy paper, but seeing only a pair of golden eyes and a swollen, well-kissed Cupid's bow mouth.

❧ 14 ❧

H E COULDN'T GET rid of her. She was stubborn as all hell. For some reason, Matt hadn't expected that. She might look like a china doll, but she was ornerier than his old donkey. No matter how many times he tried to shake her off, she just looked at him with those prairie flax eyes and kept on following along.

She'd left her children with Mrs. Tilly long before Matt emerged from his room the next morning, and she was lying in wait for him. She'd pulled her chair into the hall and was calmly sitting there outside his door, reading a book. She was in another black dress, this one shiny, with a bunch of ruffles at the hem. Her mourning dresses were fancier than any party dresses he'd ever seen. Today she had a silly little bonnet perched on the back of her head and a filmy black veil that fell all the way to the hem of her dress. She looked like she was sitting inside a cloud. Instead of muting her, all that black made her skin glow and her eyes seem even bluer.

He scowled.

"Mrs. Tilly is up baking before dawn," Georgiana told him cheerfully, "so I took the children there first thing. They love to help her bake. I thought we'd get more done without them." She snapped her book closed. It was one of those stupid dime novels, he saw. There was a black-and-white drawing of a fearsome Indian on the front.

"When I was out and about yesterday, I saw the cookhouse does breakfast, if you'd rather go there?" She kept chattering as she put the chair and the book back in her room and locked the door.

He'd rather not go anywhere with her.

He was sullen as they went downstairs, but it didn't seem

to discourage her. She chattered away, happy as a lark. He didn't know what she had to be so happy about. They were in a hell of a bind. How were they supposed to get through the next few months when they couldn't get through half an hour in each other's company without . . . *NO*. Don't think about it. He'd lost another night's sleep to sweaty, fretful dreams of touching her, kissing her, unbuttoning her, cupping her . . .

Stop.

Hell. Being with her was torture. The *smell* of her. She didn't smell like anyone he'd ever met. She had this light, zingy fragrance to her. Expensive soap, he thought sourly. Or some kind of perfume. Whatever it was, it drove him nuts. Just a waft of it made his body tingle. The smell was all tangled up in the sensation of kissing her, the feel of her tongue . . .

STOP.

He was sweating with the effort of not thinking about it. He barely heard a word she said as she sailed out into the early blush of morning. The town was just jingling to life beneath the peachy sky.

"I'll catch up to you," he said gruffly. "I have to take care of the animals first."

"Oh, I'll come with you."

He wished she wouldn't. But she followed along cheerfully enough as he skirted the hackberry bushes around the side of the hotel. Matt saw the doc's wife, Mrs. Barry, pause in the yard next door to watch them. He sighed.

"I brought the list you made us," she said, as they reached the stable. She fished in some secret pocket in all that shiny skirt and brought out his list. "What was your fee for assisting with the purchases?"

He scowled at her. He wasn't about to charge her. "How'd that look?" he said. "Charging my fiancée for helping her?"

She blinked. "No one has to know. It doesn't seem polite not to pay you. We can keep it entirely between us."

Us. He didn't like that word. It gave him queer feelings.

Dog was whining for attention. Matt let him out of the stall, and he immediately jumped up and licked at Matt's face. He was a social dog and wasn't enjoying being exiled from Deathrider.

"Oh my!" He heard a rustle of skirts as Georgiana scurried backward, away from the dog.

"He ain't dangerous," Matt said.

She looked dubious. Matt took Dog by the scruff and walked him over to Georgiana. "Here, Dog, this is our friend." He gestured for her to hold out her hand. "Let him sniff you."

Nervously, she did as he asked. Dog gave her a good sniff.

"He looks like a wolf," she said anxiously, as Dog's wet nose prodded her palm.

"Nah. He's an Indian dog. They're good working animals." He slapped Dog on the haunches. The dog shivered with delight and barked, rubbing his head against Matt's leg. "We'll bring him along with us today. It ain't right for him to be alone all the time like this."

She brightened at his words, and he flinched. Hell. He'd just said the "us" word. And said he'd be spending the day with her. What kind of idiot was he?

The thing was, he thought as he fed his animals, some idiot part of him *wanted* to spend the day with her. Was even looking forward to it.

It was the same idiot part of him that had taken care to shave this morning, rather than let his beard grow out as he'd planned. Deathrider, still pale but clearly on the mend, had no end of fun poking at Matt as he stood at the shaving mirror.

"Pass on my regards to the missus."

Matt had flicked a handful of soapy water at him, but it hadn't discouraged him. The sight of Matt prettying himself up was just too tempting a target.

Matt didn't know what was wrong with him. It was just a kiss or two.

An *unbelievable* kiss or two. And a couple of nights of the dirtiest dreams he'd ever had.

He stole a glance at Georgiana. She'd come all the way into the shadowy stable and was scratching Fernando's ears. The crotchety old donkey was all but rolling his eyes with pleasure. Matt felt a stab of envy.

"It's an enormous job, running a wagon train, isn't it?" she said. "How long have you been doing it?"

"Long enough." He felt stupidly bashful. Talking to women

wasn't his strong suit at the best of times, but right now it felt nigh on impossible. How was he supposed to think, let alone talk, when all he wanted to do was lift her off her feet and carry her up to the hayloft? He wanted to throw her in the straw and spend the morning kissing her. She got a look on her face when she was being kissed that made him wilder than a bull. Her blue eyes got all hazy and soft, and her mouth was like an overripe raspberry, all plumped up and juicy. And then there was the feel of her body against his. He imagined how it would feel, if he could lay against her up there in the hay. Last night she'd run her hand up him; today he wanted to run his hands down her.

Oh, this was going to be rough.

"I need to check my wagons," she was saying sheepishly. "After listening to you yesterday, I'm not sure they'll meet your specifications."

Wagons. Yes, think about wagons. Forget the damn hayloft.

"I heard you went to Noonan," he said, not looking at her. He finished with the animals and clicked at Dog to follow. The dog was beside himself with joy to come along and ran in wide circles as they left the yard, sniffing everything he could see.

"When I got here, I was told that wagons can take up to six weeks to build, so I thought I should order some immediately." She was a black blur at the corner of his vision. Her veil was so light it trailed behind her in the air. "His prices seemed reasonable." She shrugged. "I must say, I had no idea what I was looking for."

"Noonan ain't the most reliable of wainwrights," he told her. He relaxed slightly as they fell into talking about wagons. It was easier when he didn't look at her.

Independence was turning on a bright and crisp spring day, and the morning air was full of the smell of apple blossoms and fresh-cooked bacon and biscuits. They continued their talk of wagons over breakfast. The coffee and vittles were much better at the cookhouse than at the hotel, and he had three helpings. She lifted her veil to eat, which made him nervous again, but the busyness of the cookhouse helped. A few people came up to him to ask questions about joining his party. He was comfortable with the topic of traveling and after a while managed to banish any thoughts of kissing her.

All in all, it was a surprisingly enjoyable morning. They sorted out her wagons, went to Cavil's and started checking things off the list, and by lunchtime, they were purchasing her a milk cow and a couple of goats. Once the animals were stabled back at the hotel (for a ridiculous fee), Matt locked Dog back up with Pablo and tried to excuse himself. But wouldn't you know it, she wouldn't take no for an answer. She tagged right along with him as he headed for the town square to get on with his business. Word had spread about their engagement, and wherever they went, people stared. Many offered their congratulations. There were a lot of smirks. There were also a lot of irritated rejected suitors; a couple of them gave Matt such black looks he had half a mind to go back to the hotel for his rifle. Just in case.

Josiah Sampson was grinning like a fool when he saw them coming across the square. They were pretty hard to miss, as Georgiana's skirts were as big as a church bell. She parted the crowds like Moses parting the Red Sea. Matt braced himself for the teasing; he'd deliberately avoided introducing her to Joe yesterday. He took enough grief from Deathrider without adding more from Joe. At least Matt's brothers weren't here— Tom and Luke would be merciless; Matt hoped they'd never find out about this whole situation.

Of course, now that she was here with Matt in the square, Joe made sure to introduce himself to the future Mrs. Slater. He gave Matt a cheeky wink as he complimented him on his taste. Matt scowled and went to help Seb, who'd been working the square alone all morning. From the corner of his eye, he watched as Georgiana fell into an animated discussion with Joe about the California Trail. Matt surprised himself by feeling an unexpected stab of jealousy.

He looked at Joe with fresh eyes. He was strapping, smart, good-looking, charming, unmarried . . . and headed for California. By the way he was staring into those big blue eyes, he might not be averse to the idea of marriage either.

Matt felt like punching him.

Which was downright stupid, as he *wanted* her to find someone to marry. Someone who wasn't him. And Joe was a nice guy.

So why was he downright happy when that idiot Wendell

Todd came barging into the square, inserting himself right in the middle of Georgiana and Joe's conversation? He only got happier when the idiot pulled out a map and dragged Georgiana away from Joe Sampson and over to the low limb of the sycamore. Wendell spread the map along the limb and started talking a mile a minute, jabbing at some route on the pages before him. Matt should have felt sorry for her, should maybe even have gone over there to rescue her, but he didn't. He felt relieved. While she was tangled up talking to that goose, she wasn't bewitching Joe, and Matt was free to catch up on business.

"WHERE ARE WE going now?"

We. First it was "us" and now it was "we"!

"I don't know where *you're* going, but *I'm* going to Mrs. Tilly's for my afternoon meetings." Matt plowed on, leaving her to trot along behind, trailing her filmy black cloud.

"Oh good, we can order some sandwiches. No wonder you have such a healthy appetite, with all of this running around and not eating luncheon until three!"

Matt picked up the pace. He *didn't* usually leave eating until three. He'd just been hoping to shake her before leaving the town square; he'd expected she'd get bored standing around under the sycamore and leave. But she hadn't. She'd outwitted Wendell quicker than Matt could follow. One minute they'd been bent over the map together, and the next Wendell was gone and Georgiana was standing at Matt's elbow.

"I sent him off with the list," she explained, when she saw his quizzical expression. "He did so want to help, and there's so much we need."

"You trust him with your money?" Matt thought that was the dumbest thing he'd ever heard.

"Of course not. He said he'd run an account in his name and I could settle it later. That way I can check everything matches up and all items are accounted for."

Matt grunted. She was smart.

She was also distracting as all hell. It had been near impossible for him to concentrate as she stood next to him, listening to everything he said, watching everything he did. The smell of her drove him crazy.

"Don't you have better things to do?" he'd snapped eventually.

"Not really." She had the nerve to smile at him.

"Maybe you could find something," he said shortly. "I have business to attend to."

"I won't get in your way," she insisted, those blue eyes guileless. "I'm learning a lot listening to you."

He didn't know how. He felt like he was rambling like a witless idiot. Their easy companionship of the morning had evaporated. Probably because they weren't engaged in a task together—she was just *looking* at him.

She was still looking at him now as she trotted along behind. He could *feel* it.

"Wendell says he and Kipp will drive my wagons," she said breathlessly, as she struggled to keep up. "Will I need to hire any help apart from them?"

"Help with what?"

"Well, listening to you talking to people today, there's an awful lot: driving every day, milking the cow, digging the wagons out when they're stuck, fording rivers, fixing the wheels when they break . . . ever so much."

"You and the kids can do a lot of that." He stole a glance to see what her reaction was to that. Grim, by the look of it.

"Oh. Of course." There was a brief pause. "But I don't know how to milk a cow or fix a wheel . . ."

"You can learn." He sighed as he climbed the stairs of Mrs. Tilly's front porch. "Listen, lady, if you have money to splash around, you can hire a girl to help you with the kids and the animals and the cooking, and you can hire another man to help with the rest. Or"—he threw her a pointed look—"you can save your pennies, roll up your sleeves and work like the rest of us."

He saw her chin go up at that. There was that stubbornness again. Good. It would serve her well out there on the plains.

"Matthew!" Mrs. Tilly all but flew across the room when she caught sight of him. She was in a flap about something. Or, rather, someone.

Seline.

"Please," Mrs. Tilly said desperately, "get her out of here. She's offending my guests!"

The whore was in her Sunday best again, only this time she'd added some enormous ostrich feathers to her bonnet. They curled around her face and flapped in the air at least two feet over her head. Everyone in the tearoom was staring at her.

"Why, Matt Slater," she said sweetly, "I've been waiting for you."

Matt heard Georgiana's horrified intake of breath. Her gaze was riveted on the whore's plunging neckline. Seline heard her too, and her painted lips broke into a grin.

"Well, hello again, honey." The feathers danced as she inclined her head. "I hear congratulations are in order." Her gaze swept over Matt, lingering here and there in a way that made him mighty uncomfortable. "You sure made a fine choice."

If looks could kill, Matt thought Georgiana's stare would have been the end of Seline.

"Please get her out of here," Mrs. Tilly begged.

Seline lifted her nose in the air, as imperious as a princess. "I got legitimate business with him, missus, and this is where he keeps his office, so this is where we're doing business. My money's as good as anyone's." She gave them an insouciant wink and drawled, "Although I bet you never heard of a whore paying for it before."

The ladies gasped, and Seline gave a throaty laugh. "Don't worry, honey," she told Georgiana. "I'll just warm him up for you. I promise not to wear him out."

Georgiana had turned a fierce shade of red. Matt took pity on her.

"She just wants to join our train," he told Georgiana. "That's all. There's nothing else going on." He didn't know why he felt the need to reassure her. She wasn't his *real* fiancée. He had every right to see a whore if he wanted. Although maybe not this publicly. The room was full of people gawking, and he guessed the town would be humming with gossip in no time. *Matt Slater snagged the rich widow Smith and then rubbed her nose in his relations with a whore.* Well, damn the gossips. None of this was his fault.

"At least see her in the back room," Mrs. Tilly pleaded.

"C'mon, Seline." Matt started for the room he used for his office.

"Not without a chaperone," Mrs. Tilly squeaked.

"I'll go." Georgiana inserted herself neatly between Matt and the whore.

Matt groaned. "You can't keep following me."

"I believe, as your fiancée, it's in my best interests to do so in this instance," she said with icy formality.

"I don't mind," Seline told him.

"*I* mind."

But they didn't listen to him; both of them swept into the small back parlor, their enormous skirts just about filling the room. It was like he hadn't even spoken.

"What do you want, Seline?" he snapped when he squeezed in between their skirts.

"Aren't you going to offer me tea?" She sat down with a rustle of her bright pink skirt.

"No."

"Fine." She pursed her painted lips. "I have an offer for you."

Georgiana frowned and Seline laughed.

"Don't worry, honey, it ain't that kind of offer."

"Get to the point, Seline," Matt ordered.

"The *point*," Seline said, dropping the coyness, "is that I want to join your wagon train."

"Joe's train," Matt corrected.

"Which *you* can get me on," she countered. "And *you*, for some reason, are being contrary."

Matt wasn't about to have this conversation under Georgiana's disapproving blue gaze. "You were right," he told her abruptly. "We're long overdue for luncheon. Would you mind ordering us tea and sandwiches from Mrs. Tilly? Have her put it on my account."

She looked suspicious.

"I prefer coffee. And I take it with cream," Seline said sweetly, "if you could make sure she sends cream and not milk. Thank you very much."

That didn't help. Georgiana was looking stubborner than a bull now.

Matt managed to find what little charm he possessed. "Please," he said. "I would greatly appreciate it."

She was a smart woman. She knew she was being managed. But she also couldn't think of a reason to protest, since

the sandwiches were her idea in the first place. He saw the
black look she gave them as she left the room. He didn't imagine they had much time; she'd move as fast as she could to get
back in here before she missed anything. She didn't trust Seline one bit. And why should she?

Although why she cared was beyond Matt. They weren't
actually engaged.

"Speak quickly," Matt ordered Seline.

"My money is good." She pulled out a drawstring bag and
dumped it on the desk in front of him. It made a solid noise as
it hit. "There ought to be enough in there to get you over the
stumbling block of my profession."

Matt picked it up and untied the rawhide cord. There certainly was.

"There's more for Mr. Sampson, if you ain't of a mind to
share with him."

"I'd share," Matt said. Taking any more from her would be
highway robbery. He retied the cord and handed the bag back to
her. She pouted. "Take it," he insisted. "Let me see how it goes
with Joe. You can pay me if I succeed."

She squealed and threw herself at him. He fought her off,
keeping her firmly at arm's length. "You won't regret this," she
said.

He already did. How was he going to explain this to Joe?

"Come and see me tonight at the Bunkhouse?" Seline
asked coyly.

"So you can earn back some of that money?"

"Honey, I'm so good, I'll earn it *all* back."

Matt rolled his eyes. The woman was incorrigible.

"WHAT'S THE BUNKHOUSE?" Georgiana asked Becky, as she
watched the children clean up their latest kitchen catastrophe.

"Where did you hear about that?" Becky giggled. She was
friendly again now that she knew Georgiana was engaged to
Matt Slater and had no romantic interest whatsoever in Pierre
LeFoy.

Georgiana shrugged. "Does it matter? What is it?"

Becky lowered her voice. "It's a bordello."

Georgiana had suspected as much. "Where is it?"

"Just around the corner. It used to be an actual bunkhouse,

but when the whorehouse burned down a few years ago, the whores just moved into Ralph's Bunkhouse and turned it into a whorehouse. Ralph up and married the madam. They fight like a cat and dog; you can hear them some nights, going at it like they're going to murder each other. My money would be on her though. She's bigger than he is."

Come and see me tonight at the Bunkhouse?

She hadn't heard his response. Had he nodded? Or shaken his head in the negative? It was eating Georgiana up inside, not knowing if he was going to see the whore tonight or not.

"Mrs. Smith?" Becky had to repeat her name a few times before she managed to break into Georgiana's thoughts. The girl was looking bashful. "I was wondering if you could show me how you do your hair like that? For the dance tomorrow night . . ."

Georgiana blinked. The dance?

"I was thinking, now that I'm eighteen, I could wear my hair up . . . the way you do. Pierre said he'd dance every dance with me," she sighed.

The dance. That's right. Matt had said there was a dance every Saturday, and that their group would meet under the sycamore. Georgiana took in the girl's shining eyes and shy excitement, and felt a bittersweet envy. She wished she were still young and unbruised by love. The girl had no idea how painful a hurt heart could be.

"Of course I will," Georgiana promised. Because what else could she do? She didn't want to discourage the girl. After all, the risk also came with soaring joy. Her mind drifted to Matt's kisses. And perhaps the joy was worth the pain that came afterward.

❧ 15 ❧

OH, *NOW* HE came! Georgiana spotted Matt the minute he walked into the lantern light under the sycamore. What time did he think this was? She'd been at the wretched dance for more than two and a half hours! She'd been *waiting* for him. And now it was late and time to take the children home to bed! She'd even come out of mourning for this, she thought sourly. Well, not so much for this as for *him*.

Georgiana had been pinning up Becky's hair like she'd promised when she'd been overtaken by the urge to play fairy godmother and lend her a gown. Becky's best dress had been a sad, well-worn affair, and her forlorn attempt to brighten it up with a corsage of tissue paper roses had pinched Georgiana's heart. So she'd dug through her trunks to find an old gown she could lend the girl. Her trunks were full of gowns she couldn't wear anymore. She'd been in mourning for *years*. First for her mother and then for Leonard. She hadn't been able to bring herself to leave her gowns behind, even if she couldn't wear them; now she was glad she had brought them: someone might as well enjoy them.

Georgiana had felt such a bolt of envy when Becky was decked out in all of her borrowed finery. The girl looked lovely. While Georgiana looked like a gargoyle. Impulsively, she decided to ditch her black dress and come out of mourning. After all, she was at the gateway to the frontier—who cared if she was in black or not *here*?

Deep down she knew her decision had more than a little to do with the thought of seeing Matt Slater at the dance. What would he think when he saw her in something becoming—something that wasn't black and high necked and stuffy?

Would he get that look again? The one he got when he wanted to kiss her?

She bet he would.

She'd been soaring with hope and girlish excitement as she and Becky bustled the children along to the town square. She'd been charmed by the lanterns and the music and the rustic vision of the lively dance, craning her neck to catch sight of Matt. Would he be dressed up too? Would he be nervous? Would he ask her to dance? Her heart raced and skipped.

But the wretched man hadn't been there. She'd kept her spirits up for a good hour or more, searching for him, too distracted to keep a conversation going. But after the second hour, she realized he probably wasn't coming. And then a horrid thought weaseled in: Was he at the Bunkhouse? With that whore?

When he arrived at the dance, she was across the square, sitting at a table with Becky and a woman from New York. The woman was buying them jugs of rum punch and telling outrageous stories. She was pretty and vivacious and shockingly confident for a woman alone; she talked a mile a minute and peppered them with questions about themselves. Georgiana was really quite tipsy after all the cups of punch and had trouble following the conversation. Wilby was half asleep on her lap, his thumb in his mouth and one hand playing with the curls over Georgiana's ear.

"Well, look who's here," she said crankily when she spotted Matt.

Becky and the woman turned to look.

"Is that the man from your fortune?" The redheaded New Yorker craned her neck, trying to get a better look.

"That's her *fiancé*," Becky giggled. "But who knows if it's the same man as in the fortune."

They'd met the redhead while they were waiting in line to have their fortunes told. The redhead wasn't waiting for a fortune; she was just being friendly. She'd struck up a conversation and asked to join them. Georgiana had missed her name, and after a while it was too awkward to ask again.

"I don't know anyone else," the woman had said ruefully as she tagged along. "I only got to town yesterday."

Georgiana liked her. She was brash. And certainly a lot
more fun than Becky was. The girl had done nothing but
moon and mope over LeFoy all night. The redhead also had a
welcome talent for helping Georgiana to dodge Wendell Todd.
She'd just sent Wendell back to the hotel to fetch a blanket for
Wilby. Before that he'd been on multiple errands, for plates of
barbecue and jugs of punch, to check on the children, to request songs from the fiddle player. If it hadn't been for the redhead's ingenuity, Georgiana might have had to suffer his
attentions all night long.

"Well, let's hope this Matt Slater is the man from your fortune. After all, she did say he'd be tall, dark and handsome,
and it certainly looks like he is." The redhead was smirking as
she sized Matt up.

He certainly was. Georgiana watched as he shook hands
with people. He was the size of a *tree*. And he looked very fine
in his nice clean shirt. Very, very, *very* fine.

Although he'd look even finer without it.

Oh my. She'd had too much to drink. She pushed her glass
away. She needed to remember that she was mad at him. And
for a very good reason: because he'd rather spend the night
with a whore than be here at the dance with her.

"She said he'd take you far, didn't she?" the redhead teased.
"I suppose Oregon is far enough?"

Georgiana pulled a face. "She hardly needed to be a
fortune-teller to know that much. Everyone in town must
know about us," she said. "She knew very well who I was marrying and where we were going."

The redhead laughed. "Well, you did advertise in the paper.
That's a sure way of letting people know."

"You know about my advertisement? Even though you only
got into town yesterday?" Georgiana groaned. "I must be top
of the gossip list!"

"The very top," the redhead agreed. "The Notorious
Widow Smith and her Mail-Order Groom."

"You make me sound like I belong in one of those dime
novels!"

The redhead laughed. "Maybe you do!"

"We should go over there," Becky suggested. Her gaze was
fixed on LeFoy, who was talking to Matt. Her fortune had

promised a long journey with love as the reward. It wasn't too different from Georgiana's, only hers had her winning love at the end of her journey, rather than at the beginning.

"That means I'm going with him to California!" Becky had said excitedly as they'd left Mrs. Ware, the ersatz fortune-teller.

Georgiana hadn't had the heart to ask her how that was going to work. It wasn't like Mrs. Tilly was going to let her tag along after a strange man, all the way across the country, all on her own.

"Come on," Becky pleaded, standing up and straightening the big pink skirt with its big pink bows. "Quickly!"

"The journey begins," the redhead called after her as she started for the sycamore. Georgiana struggled to get to her feet without dropping Wilby. He hooked his arm around the back of her neck and burrowed his face into her bodice. He was getting heavy. Georgiana and the redhead skirted the dance floor, which was bouncing with people. "Do you think the fortune-teller would have seen a dark, handsome man in my future too?" the redhead asked cheerfully.

"Probably. One who'll take you on a journey," Georgiana said dryly. She was getting nervous as they approached the sycamore, aware of how disheveled she looked. They'd danced and toured all the stalls around the edge of the dusty square; she'd perspired and drunk too much punch and was looking nowhere near as fine as she had at the beginning of the night. Her beautiful dress was dusty, not to mention crushed under the weight of Wilby.

Up close, Matt was disheveled too, she saw. His hair was messy, and his shirt was damp with perspiration. He looked like he might have run all the way here.

Or been exerting himself with that whore.

The sick, jealous feeling was all too familiar to Georgiana. It was a horrid feeling. One she'd hoped never to feel again, and she hated him for making her feel it.

Georgiana stopped short of the sycamore, her nerves and jealousy getting the best of her.

She didn't have to do this. She could just gather the children and go back to the hotel. She didn't have to put herself in his orbit; she didn't have to stand near him and feel the zing of desire; she didn't have to face the horrid thoughts about where he'd been tonight and who he'd been kissing. She could just take herself away and remember the lesson Leonard had taught her.

Love was for fools.

But then Matt looked at her, and all the thoughts fled from her head. The wind ruffled his hair, and his eyes were pools of darkness in the lantern light. His gaze skimmed over her, taking in the dress, the beribboned curls, the boy in her arms.

Time grew slow and heavy. Georgiana felt like she was trapped, like an insect enveloped in a slow-moving tide of sap. He walked toward her and her heart stumbled.

"Do you need help?"

Of course she did. She was clearly losing her mind. He made her forget all her plans, all her resolutions. Because of him, she was standing here in an inappropriately fancy dress, pretending to be engaged to him instead of actually finding a husband, fantasizing about kissing him and touching him and doing all sorts of sinful things . . . while her problems sat there in the corner, gathering dust, unsolved.

"Hold on." Matt turned on his heel and left.

What was he doing?

Being wonderful, that's what he was doing. He'd crossed to one of the stalls, where he purchased a big, beautiful padded quilt. She watched in astonishment as he returned and laid it out at the base of the sycamore, forming it into a Wilby-sized cocoon. He took the sleepy boy out of her arms. Wilby struggled for a moment, but only until Matt laid him in the cushiony bed of the quilt.

Oh. Georgiana hadn't felt this before. This was an entirely new feeling: a keen tenderness that brought tears to her eyes.

It was something about the way those big hands, swollen with muscle, gently tucked the quilt around the boy's little shoulders, something about the way Wilby's heavy-lidded eyes slid closed, utterly trusting, utterly safe.

"I brought two, just in case!" Wendell's eager voice broke into her thoughts.

He was standing there, proudly, holding out two of Mrs. Bulfinch's scratchy woolen blankets. Then he saw Matt bent over Wilby and the quilt and scowled.

"Slater!" He dropped the blankets at Matt's feet. "Can I have a word with you? In private?"

"Well," the redhead murmured to Georgiana as they watched Matt sigh and follow Wendell to a more private spot. "I must say, if he is the man your fortune meant, you're one lucky woman."

"What are you doing?" Wendell gave Matt a shove the minute they were out of sight of the sycamore. "The deal is you give me a chance to win her over, not *you* go winning her over. What are you playing at?"

"I was just making the kid comfortable." Matt tried to keep his temper in check. Wendell had no idea how close he was to a thumping. Matt wasn't really in the mood to have a lovesick Wendell Todd berating him.

"You were just making the kid comfortable? And how in hell are my blankets supposed to compete with a quilt like that?"

"Listen. You wanted me to get pretend engaged, and I got pretend engaged. You're the one who has to go woo her, so stop your whining and go and woo her."

"It'd be easier if you'd back off and let me!"

"I ain't been here all night!" Matt snapped. "You've had plenty of time."

Wendell looked really black at that. "You turned up just when I had her primed, that's all!"

"Primed?"

"Just stay away from her," Wendell growled, "and let me work my magic." He stormed off.

The only magic that idiot had was the power of repulsion. Matt set after him. He wasn't about to be chased away from his own damn party.

Wendell had all the charm of an outhouse. While Matt kept his distance, trying to focus on getting to know the emigrants in his party, he couldn't help but watch Wendell in action. Men surrounded Georgiana, and Wendell had a hard job elbowing his way through to her side. It was no wonder. She didn't look like anything that belonged on earth. Is that how all women looked back east, or was she special even there? Any other woman Matt knew would have been outshone by that dress, which was fancy in the extreme. But Georgiana seemed to glow in it, her beautiful white shoulders rising from the lace, her long neck elegant, the charm of her face accentuated by the ribbons and curls of her fussy hairstyle. Rather than being swallowed by all her finery, it merely served to draw attention to her incredible loveliness.

Hell. Since when did he think about gowns and ribbons and pretty faces?

Matt resolutely turned his back on her. She had all the suitors she needed there, as well as Outhouse Wendell. She'd be able to find a husband among their number in the next few months. Meanwhile, he had a business to run.

"Ain't you going to ask your missus to dance?" Seb asked, noticing how Matt kept well away from her.

"I don't dance," Matt said shortly. It was an enormous effort not to look at her.

"I'm sure she could teach you."

"I've got better things to do." He moved on to the next cluster of people, who were gleefully gossiping about a certain goddamn Indian.

"Slater! You were there!" Joe Sampson gestured him forward. "You saw the Plague of the West get shot in Kearney, didn't you?" He beamed at the redheaded woman standing next to him, the woman who'd been with Georgiana and Becky all night. He seemed smitten, Matt noticed. Good. That might keep him away from Georgiana.

"I did," Matt agreed. "Saw him shot stone-cold dead." Matt wasn't normally one to gossip, but this was one story he'd been taking care to spread. He was more than happy to tell the tale; the more people heard it, the more people spread the news that the Plague of the West was dead and gone. By the time they rolled out of Independence in a couple of weeks, Deathrider could come along and no one would suspect who he was.

"I heard he turned into a wolf," the redhead said lightly.

Matt shrugged. He didn't know where the idea had first come from, but people sure did seem to warm to it. He didn't know how they could even consider it, it was so dumb, but they did. With relish. "Maybe he did. But if so, he turned back into a body afterward, because I buried it."

"I've read all those books," Herb Tasker said, "and I find it hard to believe that someone could shoot him that easily. I reckon you got the wrong Indian."

"I knew him a long time. It was definitely him," Matt said tightly.

"You were friends?"

He didn't like the way that redhead was looking at him. She was sharp, like a bird of prey.

"We traveled together sometimes."

"Are you an outlaw too, Mr. Slater?" she teased. Only it wasn't all teasing. There was a thread of malice in it.

"Matt's no outlaw!" Matt's defender was no other than Phineas Fairchild Bee Blunt. Or his brother. He was wearing one black boot and one brown boot, so Matt couldn't tell which one he was. "You can't go calling honest gentlemen outlaws!"

"It's defamation!" his brother agreed.

Even dusty and with their faces sticky with toffee, they were like little lords. Their clipped accents just dripped disdain. Defamation. What kind of kid even knew what defamation was, let alone bandied the word about in conversation?

"I do beg your pardon." The redhead looked like she wanted to laugh, but kept her tone courteous. "I was simply surprised that Mr. Slater would travel with the Plague of the West. After all, he's a known menace."

"Was." Matt stressed the past tense. He had a hard time not defending his friend.

"You knew the Plague of the West?" The boys were in awe at that.

"Did you see him shot?"

"I heard there was blood everywhere!"

"And brains! Were there brains?"

"I bet they were *everywhere*!"

The little lords had evaporated, replaced with bloodthirsty barbarians.

"Boys! What on earth are you talking about?" Matt hadn't heard Georgiana come up behind him.

"Matt saw his friend be shot in the head!"

"What?"

"Imagine the mess!"

"Phineas!" She was furious, he saw. "Come here. Now!"

She seized the boys and dragged them a few steps away. Even though she kept her voice low, Matt and everyone else in the group could hear from her tone that she was well and truly blistering their ears.

When she brought them back to the group, they were hanging their heads. She gave them a poke.

They looked up at Matt, miserable.

"I'm very sorry," one mumbled.

"We are sorry for your loss," the other agreed.

"I do beg your pardon," Georgiana apologized to the entire group, as well as to Matt. "You must think they were raised in the wilds." She was flushed. "That was certainly no way for them to speak about your friend's death. You have our condolences," she told Matt formally. She shot the twins an evil look. "How they could speak of it that way is beyond my comprehension."

"Don't be too hard on them," the redhead told her. "It was my fault: I brought the subject up. And Mr. Slater had just finished telling us that he and the Plague of the West weren't really friends. They just traveled together." She sounded amused at the distinction.

"The Plague of the West?" Georgiana's mouth fell open. "You were friends with the Plague of the West?" She turned horrified eyes on Matt.

"No," the redhead disagreed, still sounding amused, "they just traveled together."

"You traveled with the man who shot up the Hudson's Bay trading post by Birchville?" Georgiana sounded appalled. "The man who terrorized the Fuller party the whole way along the Oregon Trail?"

"He what?" Matt had never heard such nonsense.

"I read about it! In those books!"

"Those dime novels are garbage," he snapped. He was sick to death of hearing such nonsense spouted about his friend. "There isn't even a place called Birchville out that way. It's all made up."

"Made up?" the redhead sounded shocked. "You're really going to claim that Rides with Death never terrorized the Fuller party?"

"I doubt he even heard of them!"

The redhead gave him a scornful look. "I'll have you know, I heard it from Fordham Fuller himself!"

"I don't care if you heard it from God himself; it's a lie," Matt said stubbornly. He wasn't about to stand by and let Deathrider be . . . defamed.

"How can you defend him? He was a rapist and a murderer!"

"He ain't a rapist! And if he ever murdered anyone, they probably needed murdering." Matt could have bitten his tongue off. What was he doing? He could see the shocked looks he was getting. He took a deep breath. "I'm sorry, that was out of line. But those books are pure rubbish, and I ain't going to agree they're anything else."

"Rubbish!" The redhead was irate now. "How dare you! And when that man held Susannah Fuller captive! He raped a child of thirteen!"

"Raped!" Georgiana gasped.

Matt wasn't going to be able to keep his temper if that woman accused Deathrider of raping a child. "Excuse me," he said, struggling to keep the anger out of his voice, "but it's time we got the kids to bed. It was nice to meet you, miss."

"Miss *Archer*," she told him, her voice as sharp as a needle.

Matt felt his blood turn to ice. "Archer."

She nodded.

"A.A. Archer?"

"Ava Addison Archer." Her smile made him think of a snake.

He wasn't sorry to leave her. If he'd stayed, he might have said something he'd regret. The last thing he wanted was to end up in one of her dime novels. He had no doubt it would be as the villain.

WENDELL WAS DETERMINED to help round the kids up and get them back to the hotel. He wasn't about to let Georgiana be alone with Matt, to her immense frustration. He refused to let Matt near Wilby, scooping the sleeping boy up, quilt and all.

"Do you want me to come help put them to bed?" Becky asked. She was shooting longing looks at the courthouse steps, where LeFoy and his girls were standing next to the piano.

"I can help," Matt and Wendell said simultaneously.

"Are you sure?" Becky seemed torn.

"I'll be fine," Georgiana assured her, giving her hand a squeeze. "Enjoy the dance. You look beautiful."

Becky gave her a grateful look.

"You don't need to help," Wendell told Matt sharply. "I'm more than happy to."

"As her fiancé, I think I should," Matt said, and Georgiana thought he was needling Wendell. "Besides, my hotel room is right opposite. It ain't out of my way."

Wendell scowled.

Georgiana felt immensely grateful for the charade of their engagement. The last thing she felt like was being alone with Wendell Todd, and he could hardly protest her fiancé being with her wherever she went. It made Matt the perfect shield.

"We'll meet you back at the hotel after the LeFoys finish," Phin said casually, leaning against the tree.

Susannah wailed. "I want to see them too!"

"Nice try," Matt told the twins, "but none of you are staying to watch. It's time to go."

"But they're so good," Phin complained. And it was true. As they left the square, the LeFoy girls started singing, and they were amazing.

"They'll still be good next week," Matt told the children. They pulled faces but went along.

Georgiana held Susannah's hand tightly as they walked back to the hotel. The sweet blend of the LeFoy girls' voices singing "The Rose of Alabama" drifted through the cooling night.

"I'm exhausted by this journey already, and we haven't even left yet," she said to the two men, once they'd deposited the children in the hotel room.

"Me and Kipp are more 'n happy to help get everything organized," Wendell said. He was holding his hat in his hands and giving her a sycophantic look. She remembered all too well how he'd threatened her back in New York. She didn't trust this new Wendell one bit.

"Good night," she told him firmly. But he wasn't leaving. Not while Matt was still standing in the hallway too. Matt was staring at him, waiting for him to go.

They just stood there, staring each other down.

Georgiana rolled her eyes. Men. She didn't have the energy for them tonight. Even though she'd been longing for a moment alone with Matt, it didn't look like it would happen.

"Good night," she said regretfully. And then she closed the door on them and the whole disappointing night.

❖ 16 ❖

IT ONLY TOOK a couple of weeks for Matt's party to book out, and after that, his days were full of provisioning, hiring scouts, auctioning Luke's horses and doing everything in his power to avoid Georgiana Bee Blunt. Deathrider had come through the worst of his infection and was driving Matt crazy with his constant complaining and his refusal to stay in bed. Matt was glad they'd managed to keep him locked in the room until Ava Archer had left town, or things might have got even more interesting.

"Stop fussing about it," Deathrider snapped when Matt barred him from leaving. "I've never met her! So it's not like she'd recognize me."

"Just because you haven't met her, don't mean she hasn't *seen* you. And I didn't go through this whole circus for you to get found alive now."

He was such a pain in the ass. He was still running fevers and battling headaches, which made him ornerier than a bee-stung bear, but he refused to stay put in the room. He spent the day following Matt about, making a general nuisance of himself; he poked into Matt's business, criticized him constantly and seemed peevishly entertained by Matt's fake engagement. He was at great pains to update Matt on what his fiancée was up to at all times.

"I don't want to know," Matt snapped at least a hundred times.

"Yes, you do. You just don't want anyone else to know that you want to know."

"That's the most wrongheaded thing I ever heard."

"It is. But then, you're a wrongheaded person."

"That ain't what I meant!"

"Wendell's teaching her how to fire a rifle," the ornery Indian said one day, helping himself to Matt's coffeepot. Matt was closeted up in his office at Mrs. Tilly's, trying to make the account that had just arrived from Cavil's add up. He had a feeling he'd been overcharged on flour again.

"He what?" Matt looked up sharply.

"He's teaching her how to shoot. She's in those new travel clothes that she and Mrs. Tilly's girl sewed up. They do some wonders for her figure."

Matt glared at him.

Deathrider shrugged. "Wait till you see. It's not something a man can fail to notice."

"Did you want something? I'm trying to work."

"I'm just here to give you your daily update. Which is, she's looking fine, and she's armed and dangerous."

"I don't care." Matt still couldn't get the numbers to add up. But that might be because he kept picturing what on earth Georgiana could be wearing that would make Deathrider say such a thing. *They do some wonders for her figure.* The woman had so many fancy clothes already. What was so special about these new ones? "Why's she learning to shoot anyhow?" he asked irritably.

"Because she's going to Oregon." Deathrider gave him a sideways look.

"California," Matt snapped. And the sooner the better. He didn't think he'd had a decent night's sleep since he met her. It was all dirty dreams all night long. It wore a man out.

"These make no sense," he growled, standing abruptly. "I'm going to ask Cavil about it in person." He grabbed his hat and was out the door, the accounts under his arm. He was aware of Deathrider following him.

"They're in the paddock behind the blacksmith's," Deathrider said.

"I don't know what you mean. I'm going to Cavil's." But Matt couldn't stop himself from taking the long way, which went straight past the blacksmith's. "I need some nails," he grumbled, but he knew Deathrider didn't believe him. Especially when he went straight past the blacksmith's and round to the back paddock.

Jesus, Mary and Joseph. Matt came to a dead stop when he

saw Georgiana, out there behind the smithy, aiming at old
cans with a rifle about half the size her body. It wasn't the rifle
that gave him pause. It was her goddamn travel clothes. In
place of her usual bell of a skirt was a narrower heavy one
that drew attention to the natural line of her hips. But it wasn't
that either that had him hot under the collar. It was the leather
vest she was wearing. The thing was obscene. It was tightly
fitted and cinched in at the waist. It was similar to the one Ava
Archer wore, but on Georgiana it looked less practical and
more . . . suggestive. The leather clung lovingly to the impres-
sive swell of her breasts. Her large, firm, thrusting breasts.
The dramatic dip of her waist beneath them only made them
seem bigger. Hell. A man couldn't look away.

Wendell Todd certainly couldn't. Matt's fists clenched.
Look at the way the idiot was staring. Especially when she
hefted the weapon and threw her shoulders back.

Goddamn it, no! He wasn't doing this.

Matt left the paddock like the devil himself was after him.
He couldn't be around her, not when she was wearing a vest
like that. He was sweating with the effort of not going over
there, throwing her over his shoulder and making for the nearest hayloft.

"You forgot your nails," Deathrider called after him.

After seeing her behind the smithy, Matt was on guard
never to run into her. Occasionally, he saw her from the corner
of his eye, always wearing that damn vest. The vest he took to
dreaming about. Only in his dreams she was wearing nothing
but the vest, the full curves of her breast swelling over the
neckline and visible through the armholes when she lifted her
arms. Which she did to pull him down to kiss her.

Goddamn, it made him itchier than a jackrabbit.

That vest was so tangled up with his lustful fantasies that
he couldn't risk seeing her in person. He spoke to her through
Wendell, which made Wendell happy. The idiot ran back and
forth between them like a messenger boy, eager to do everything he could to keep them apart, and even more eager to use
any excuse that he could to spend time with her.

"How are you going to keep this up on the trail?" Deathrider asked him the week they rolled out. The two of them were
packing the chuck wagon while Seb double-checked the tents.

Matt ignored him.

"Especially considering you're supposed to be her fiancé. People have noticed, you know. It's not normal for a man to avoid his bride-to-be. Especially when the bride-to-be is as comely as Mrs. Smith."

"It's just pretend." Matt threw a bag of corn at Deathrider, harder than he needed to. It thudded into him and Deathrider laughed.

"And I've been busy," Matt said.

"Sure. But come roll out, you'll have all those long days, with nothing to do but travel. Together."

"Piloting a train is busy work," Matt grunted.

"You might wear yourself out so you can get some sleep, at least," his friend said dryly. "I'm only glad I won't have to listen to you toss and turn when we're on the trail. Those hotel bed springs squeal like an angry pig."

They squealed again that night. And all the nights until they left Independence. Despite working himself ragged all day, getting every supply wagon packed and checked and visiting with all his people to make sure they were ready to go, he couldn't sleep. The last night in town was the worst night yet. He didn't even *almost* sleep. And it was mostly due to the very last visit he'd paid.

He'd left it till last because he couldn't quite face it, but that had turned out to be an immense mistake, because it meant he'd come knocking so late. Being alone with her in the quiet of the house, by the flicker of lamplight, had been a challenge, to say the least. He'd known it was foolhardy the minute she'd opened her door. She'd been brushing her hair and still had the hairbrush in her hand. He'd never seen her with her hair down before, and the sight took his breath away. It was like getting kicked in the stomach by a mule.

Her glossy dark curls fell heavily down her back and over her shoulders. Shorter curls clung to her face and neck. He had the urge to reach out and touch them. He had to clasp his hands behind his back to stop himself from giving in to the urge. At least she wasn't wearing that leather vest. That would have been his complete undoing.

"Matt," she said softly. She was clearly surprised to see him, as they hadn't spoken directly in days, maybe weeks.

"I need to check your wagons," he said curtly.

"I beg your pardon?"

He scowled. He'd thought it would get easier being around her after not seeing her for a while. It hadn't. It was worse than ever. God, he wanted to kiss her.

"Your wagons," he managed to say. "I just need to check you're all packed properly. Go over any last-minute questions."

"Oh. Of course." She frowned. "But surely you spoke to Wendell about it?"

Wendell. She said his name like he was already her husband.

Well, that was his own fault. He was the one shoving them together.

Like he was supposed to. That was the deal. Damn it.

"I did. But they're your wagons, and I think you should know what's happening with them. I'd hate for you to get out on the trail and for something to be missing."

"Oh." She glanced over her shoulder. "It's very late . . . "

"I had a lot of people to get through." He was brusque.

"Of course. Just hold on a moment while I get my wrap."

It was easier in the street than in the hall, as people were out and about, packing and repacking. At least he wasn't alone with her now.

"These are your two?" he asked as he approached the two biggest wagons on the street. He knew perfectly well that they were her wagons.

"Is Wendell asleep?" Georgiana asked Kipp, who was guarding them. "Matt wants to just check over our wagons."

"He's taking the next shift." The boy eyed Matt. "Why's he need to be poking through our stuff?"

"*Her* stuff," Matt corrected. "It's a service I offer. Don't worry, there's no extra charge." He hauled himself up onto the seat of the front wagon. He'd done the final check on it with Wendell before he let her pay Noonan for it. As usual, Noonan had done a slapdash job and had needed to make adjustments before Matt was happy.

Georgiana's lead wagon was a massive hickory-framed prairie schooner, filled to the brim with supplies and trunks. He checked everything was strapped down and made sure the waterproofing was tight.

"Where's your tools?" he asked.

"Other wagon," Kipp said sulkily.

"No. You need some in each. Just in case. What if something happens to the other wagon?"

"Like what?" Kipp sneered.

"Like it gets smashed to bits in a river crossing."

"Oh my." Georgiana shivered and pulled her wrap tighter. "Would that really happen?"

"Or you might get separated. It's best to be prepared. You got the food divided between the wagons, like I told you?"

"Yes," Georgiana said before Kipp could answer. "The children and I helped with that this afternoon. That was on your list of instructions."

"Good. Let's go through your tools and see what we'll put in this wagon."

Georgiana followed him to the second wagon.

"These all your tents?" he asked.

Georgiana bit her lip. "I suppose we should move half of those to the first wagon too?"

He nodded. "And half the bedding. You don't want to be caught out." He saw the quilt he'd bought Wilby at the dance, neatly folded.

Together they readjusted the loads, moving things back and forth between the wagons to cover all of the "just in case" eventualities he could think of.

"I must say, Mr. Slater, you are very prepared," she said when they'd finished the night's work.

"Have to be," he told her as he tied the canvas cover down tighter. "It can be deadly out there. I don't like to take chances."

The moon had risen over the rooftops, silvering the street. He watched as people scurried about, packing. The night before a roll out always had a strange cast to it. The streets were busy late into the night, and there were the sounds of hushed voices, hammers fixing the last bits and pieces, horses whickering uneasily, oxen lowing. Expectation walked the streets, and no one slept well.

"Thank you for looking after us," Georgiana said. "You're so thorough. It puts me at ease." She didn't look at ease.

"It's my job." He was being ungracious, but he couldn't

seem to help himself. "Your wagons look good now," he said gruffly. "You need anything?" he asked Kipp.

"Only some sleep," the boy sneered.

"I'll send some coffee out for you. Mrs. Bulfinch keeps a maid on all night the night before a roll out. It's a busy night. At least you're not like poor Trent there." Matt gestured to a man halfway down the street who had his belongings strewn everywhere, while his wagon gaped like an empty mouth. "He's had to repack his whole wagon."

"Why?" Georgiana asked.

"Packed the food right in the middle, where he couldn't get to it. He seemed to think he'd have time to unpack and repack every night. Doesn't seem to realize unpacking is the last thing you feel like doing after a long day traveling."

Kipp didn't show any sign of sympathy.

"Roll out is just after dawn," Matt told them. "I'll be here after four to help you with your animals."

"Four," Georgiana said numbly as she followed him back into the hotel.

"That's right, missus. And you'd best get used to those hours as we'll be rolling out every morning around dawn. We need to use every ounce of daylight we can if we want to make Oregon before the leaves fall."

"California," she corrected softly.

Goddamn. Why did he feel it like an elbow in the ribs every time he thought of her in California?

It didn't matter. He didn't care, he told himself fiercely. He didn't care one bit.

He bid her farewell at their shared landing, aware of the way her gaze followed him longingly.

He closed the door between them and went to bed. Deathrider was awake but was wise enough not to comment.

❧ 17 ❧

HE WAS BRINGING his whore with him! Georgiana couldn't believe the nerve of him.

She hadn't slept more than a couple of hours, and it had been an exhausting morning. She felt like she'd done an entire day's work before the sun was even up. For once, the twins had actually been helpful. Excited about the adventure ahead, they'd even slept in their clothes, so they could bound straight out of bed and head down to the wagons. It proved much harder to get Susannah and Wilby out of bed. In the end, Georgiana left them sleeping while she finished all her other chores. Nearly everything was packed already, so clearing out the hotel rooms didn't take long. She'd dressed in her new clothes, which were far easier to don without a maid than her old gowns, most of which buttoned up the back and took forever to wrestle with. She'd made the traveling outfits herself, with Becky's help, and she was pretty proud of them. She'd done quite a lot of needlework in the past but only frivolous things; this had been far more rewarding. She'd also done as Matt's list instructed and bought new boots for herself and the children, and invested in shoe repair materials. Apparently, they'd be doing so much walking over the summer that their shoes would need constant maintenance. His attention to detail was incredible, she thought as she checked over the list before she left the hotel room. She dreaded to think of the disasters he must have endured to warrant some of the things on that list.

By the time she got downstairs, it was quarter to four and the hotel was bustling. Even the people not heading out were up, having a look-see at what a roll out looked like. It looked busy, that was for sure. Matt's group was one of the first to leave for the season, so Georgiana didn't know if theirs was normal or not. She'd only seen one other roll out, and that one had been enormous. The dust had hung over the streets all day in their wake.

Mrs. Bulfinch had a full breakfast on, which she charged double prices for, as she had to be up half the night making it, she grumbled. Georgiana was too nervous to stomach breakfast, and she saw the twins clearly felt the same. They were out on the street running around with the LeFoy girls, their excited voices carrying in the clear night air. The spectators stood by the dining room window and on the porch, yawning and drinking coffee. Coffee. That was what she needed. Despite being keyed up, her body felt slow and tired. Georgiana fetched a pot of coffee and some tin mugs from Mrs. Bulfinch. She'd settled the account the night before, so Mrs. Bulfinch demanded she pay on the spot for the coffee. Georgiana wouldn't be sorry to see the back of the tightfisted hotelier. Although she was sure she'd miss the brass bed upstairs pretty quickly after a night or two of sleeping on the hard ground.

Matt Slater was up already of course. His animals were lined up at the hitching rail directly in front of the hotel. His strange brother was up too, still looking thin and surly from his recent illness. Matt was arguing with him, and their wolf-like dog was circling them nervously, looking back and forth between them. Tom Slater looked as immovable as a rock. It just made Matt frown more and gesture harder, but whatever was happening, Tom didn't seem to be budging. Eventually, Matt seemed to have enough and stomped off.

"He's used to getting his way," his brother told Georgiana as she descended the porch steps and passed in front of him. "Youngest child."

She smiled politely. Tom Slater made her anxious. There was something in his stillness that was utterly unnerving, and his eerie pale eyes followed you a little too closely. He put Georgiana in mind of a snake: coiled, ready to strike.

"Would you like a coffee?" she offered.

"You're very thoughtful," he said, after he'd accepted her offer. "My brother is a lucky man."

Georgiana was startled. Surely, he knew the engagement

was a sham? Matt must have told his own brother. It was hard to tell if he was being serious or facetious; he was near impossible to read. She was glad to get away from him. She busied herself pouring coffee for Wendell and Kipp, and then rounded up the boys and had them help fetching the last of the belongings from upstairs.

"I don't see why Sooky gets to sleep in," Philip complained.

"You don't mind if we wake her, do you, Ma?"

"It's Mother, not Ma. And leave your sister be. You focus on your own jobs and leave your sister to me."

"Yes, Ma."

She rolled her eyes. They were the most contrary creatures. Still, she mustn't complain—at least they were eager to help this morning. Although she was sure she'd hear Susannah screaming bloody murder any minute now as the twins dragged her out of bed.

"Animals," Matt said curtly, as he rounded her up. "We need to get your animals harnessed. I've got to sort three other parties after you and get to the town square before five."

"Wendell and Kipp are looking after—"

"They're your animals." He cut her off and swept her along to the pens at the end of the street, behind the hostler's. "You need to know what you're doing."

"Just in case?" she said wryly.

"Just in case." He was clearly tense this morning.

Georgiana eyed her oxen with distaste. They were huge, slobbery, misshapen animals, nothing like the cows back home. Their new milk cow, Bella, was narrow and sweet looking in comparison. She and Sissy, the goat, were waiting patiently in the next pen. Matt had not looked impressed when she and the children had named them.

"They ain't pets," he'd said.

"They're sort of pets," Georgiana had countered. "And if they're going to be giving us milk, I think we should treat them with at least a little respect."

"I had a house cat when I was a girl," Georgiana said mildly now, as he held open the gate to the pens for her. "And of course a horse . . . " She cleared her throat. "But I must say, I have no experience with working animals like these."

"It's not that much different to a cat." He closed the gate behind her.

So he had a sense of humor after all. It had been hard to tell these last few weeks.

He had Wendell and Kipp harness up the second team, and made her harness the animals for the lead wagon. He refused to listen when she suggested she could watch him do it. So she could learn.

"You'll learn quicker if you do it yourself," was all he said.

It was even harder than she'd thought it would be, but he was a patient teacher. She dropped the harnesses and shied away from the bulk of the oxen when they moved. They were enormous. The front two had giant curling horns that looked like they could impale her if the oxen so much as shook their heads.

She protested when he told her to lead them back to her wagon, but he ignored her and went to check on Wendell.

She twisted the lead around her fist and gave the yoke a pull. The two animals in front rolled their eyes at her. She pulled again. One opened its mouth in a slobbery great yawn.

"Come," she ordered, pulling again.

"You have to be tougher than that. They ain't bright," Matt called.

She flushed. He'd been watching her.

"Move!" She used the scary voice she usually saved for the twins and pulled on the lead with all her weight. This time they moved forward a step before stopping.

Matt took pity on her and gave the lead animal closest to him a slap, yelling, "Ha!"

Georgiana flinched, expecting the team to stampede. But they were ponderous animals and merely lurched forward, plodding toward the gate.

"Unwrap that thing from your hand!" Matt called. "Or if they run, you'll be dragged to your death!"

She seriously doubted these beasts were capable of running, but she did as she was told. Luckily, it was a straight line from the pen to the wagon, because she didn't think she would be able to steer them. It was also lucky that they were so slow, as Matt was able to catch up and help her before she had to get them to stop. He then taught her how to harness them to the wagon. It wasn't hard, just awkward. And it meant Georgiana had to get right up close to the ugly beasts.

"You'll get used to it," he told her.

She sincerely hoped not. She hoped Wendell and Kipp would be doing most of the harnessing. In return, she would cook for them. Once she'd learned to cook.

It couldn't be too hard. People did it all the time. And Mrs. Tilly had written out a bunch of easy recipes for her.

"I'll meet you at the town square," Matt called over his shoulder as he moved along to his next job. "Don't forget: you're to go to the front of the courthouse steps, on the right by the horse trough."

Georgiana felt disgruntled as she watched him go. She didn't like the curtness of their interactions these days. Although they were safer than those breathless encounters in the lamplight, which only ended in kisses. This was better, she reassured herself. Especially after that horrid night at the dance when she'd made a fool of herself dressing up for him, while he was off with his whore.

"You ready?" Wendell interrupted her thoughts, appearing at her side.

Oh my. It was time to go.

"Boys!" She called the twins down from the lead wagon, where they were stashing the bags they'd brought down from upstairs. "Go to the outhouse, please! I don't imagine we'll be stopping for a while."

"We'll be stopping in the town square."

"You saw that group that headed out last week." Phin's voice dripped disdain. "They were hours in the square before they left."

"Listen to your mother," Wendell cautioned them.

They ignored him.

"Just do it, please," she sighed. "Or I'll make you ride with your sister all day."

That worked. They were off the wagon and tearing round the side of the hotel to the outhouse. She left them to it and ran upstairs to rouse Susannah and Wilby. She managed to get Susannah up and dressed without too much trouble, but Wilby was still dead to the world. She did her best to dress his sleepy, floppy body and then carried him downstairs. Susannah followed along behind, dragging their bag.

"I'm hungry, Mama."

"I know, petal. We'll get something to eat in a moment."

Wendell helped her make a nest out of the quilt just behind the buckboard. They'd kept a tiny space free, specifically for this purpose, as they'd assumed Wilby and Susannah wouldn't be walking as much as Georgiana and the twins.

Once Wilby was tucked in, Georgiana escorted Susannah to the outhouse, and then they washed their faces and hands in the laundry and bought some biscuits from Mrs. Bulfinch. The old woman even charged them for the napkin she wrapped the biscuits in.

"Best eat it all," Georgiana warned her daughter. "Each crumb you drop is worth a small fortune."

Her heart was pounding as she handed Susannah up and checked on the twins, who were sitting on the bench of the second wagon with Kipp.

"Well, here we go," she said, handing them each a couple of biscuits. Grudgingly, she gave one to Kipp too.

"You didn't get jam or butter?" Phin complained.

"I couldn't afford it," she said dryly.

"Can we carry the rifle?" he asked.

"No." She felt anxious as she made to leave them. "Are you sure you don't want to ride up front with me?"

Kipp looked hopeful they'd agree, but they didn't. She fretted over leaving them. It was hitting her now, what they were about to do. It was insane, wasn't it? Dragging four young children along such a hard road. But what choice did she have?

Her chest felt tight. Today they were finally leaving to go and get Leo. It was easier to think about him, now that she was on her way. Moving felt better than sitting still.

"Be good," she warned the twins. "And you remember what Mr. Slater said: children die all the time from falling off wagons and going under the wheels." She stole a glance at the giant ironclad wheels and shuddered. "You be extra careful. I don't want to lose you as well."

"What do you mean 'as well'? You haven't lost anyone."

Leo.

"She means our father, you idiot," Philip told him.

"Just be careful," she repeated. Would they be safe with Kipp? Maybe they should come with her?

She heard a "Ha!" and the Barrys' wagon rolled out. Tom Slater rode with them. His horse was tethered behind, with the Barrys' other animals, and he didn't look happy about it, but the doc wouldn't let him ride yet.

A cheer went up from the spectators on the porch of the hotel as the first wagon rolled.

"You ready?" Wendell called.

"You'll see us at the square, Ma," Philip said patiently. "It's only a couple of blocks away."

"Mother, not Ma." She patted his knee and left for her own wagon.

Susannah was sitting stiffly next to Wendell, shivering in the cool night air. It was still black as pitch. Wendell had a lantern hung on the wagon frame by his head. It cast a pool of golden light around them. He didn't help her into the wagon; it didn't even seem to occur to him to do so. She used the wheel hub to climb up and settled on the bench, pulling Susannah close. She checked on Wilby, who was still asleep in his quilt nest.

Oh my. This was really happening.

Another cheer went up from the hotel as they rolled forward. People held their coffee cups aloft in salute.

"Happy trails!" someone called.

Forget happy. Just let them be *safe* trails. Georgiana took a deep breath and straightened her spine as they rolled on through the dark streets. People stood at windows and clustered on porches, waving as they passed.

The wagon shuddered and creaked. It wasn't going to be a comfortable ride, Georgiana realized. She understood now why Matt had told them they'd be walking the whole way. She felt like her teeth might well rattle right out of her head. The shuddering woke Wilby, who began to whine. Georgiana leaned over and stroked his head. He stuck his lower lip out and looked like he might cry. But she managed to soothe him, and soon he pulled himself up to look over the tray and out at the big, old, ugly behinds of the oxen.

"Horse!" he said, pointing.

"Ox," she corrected. "Remember our oxen? The big cows?" Her voice was all shaky from the movement of the horrid wagon.

Oh my. As they rolled into the square, Georgiana began to get an idea of the scale of the enterprise. Matt and Josiah Sampson were on the courthouse steps, directing traffic. Their scouts did the legwork, talking to the drivers as they rolled into the square, directing them where to park their wagons. There were more wagons than could possibly ever fit into the square. As the first pale green wash began to spread on the eastern horizon, the wagons built up, snaking back through the streets in all directions. The scouts ran along the rows, giving orders.

Georgiana's wagons were right at the front, close to the courthouse steps, near Matt's chuck wagon, which Sebastian Doyle was driving.

"We're going to be here awhile, I reckon," Wendell observed, standing on the seat and peering over the sea of white canvas hoops, which glowed in the predawn light.

The square looked like nothing so much as a busy harbor, seething with yachts at full sail. Clumsy, bulky yachts.

People were climbing down from their wagons and stretching their legs. The twins wasted no time in joining them and belting past Georgiana, up the courthouse steps, to look at the view. She climbed down too but asked Susannah and Wilby to stay where they were. She didn't want to lose them in the crowds. There were hundreds and hundreds of people.

"It always seemed like chaos watching a roll out," Mrs. Barry, the doctor's wife, said, joining Georgiana, "but I must say, it seems even worse being *in* it!"

Georgiana had met the woman a couple of times before at the Saturday night dances. She was a calm, practical woman, with a round face and a gentle manner.

"It looks like we'll be traveling together," Mrs. Barry said with a smile. "It's kind of Matt to put us up the front of the line. I imagine the dust is horrendous farther back."

"I imagine so." Georgiana pulled a face and looked up at the clouds of dust hanging in the air above them. She supposed it *was* kind of him to let them ride up front. Although, it would also be expected, since she was supposed to be his fiancée.

"I don't envy him," Doctor Barry said, as the three of them watched Matt organizing things from the courthouse steps.

"Maybe not. But don't pity him either," Tom Slater drawled. He was slouched back on the seat of the Barrys' wagon. "He thrives on it. If you're going to pity anyone, it should be me."

"You stay right where you are," Mrs. Barry scolded, "or your brother will have my hide."

"Did I hear he was bitten by a snake?" Georgiana whispered, when Tom Slater had turned his attention back to the courthouse steps. "I do worry about the children," she admitted. "Do you have any advice about snakes, Doctor?"

"Don't go near them?" Doctor Barry suggested. "In fact, stay away from all the wildlife. Including him." The doctor nodded his head at Tom Slater. "He's an ill-tempered critter."

Tom heard them and, surprisingly, smiled. He looked different when he smiled. Less terrifying. But he didn't look like Matt in the slightest.

"Would anyone like some coffee?" Mrs. Barry asked. "I brought the pot and a jug of cream. We'd best use the cream, as it won't last."

They clustered together, drinking Mrs. Barry's coffee and watching the chaos around them. Slowly, they saw order form in the chaos and found themselves clumped with a bunch of other wagons. By the time Matt came to talk to them, the green wash on the horizon was turning rosy orange. The twins followed him and even climbed up on the chuck wagon beside him when he leapt up to address the wagons nearby. All around the square, Georgiana could see his scouts doing the same thing, swinging up onto the backs of wagons to address smaller groups within the whole. Like a round, she heard voice after voice call:

"Listen up, the following parties!"

And that was when Georgiana saw the whore. She was standing on the seat of a wagon, right near the edge of the square, on the fringe of wagons over near the sycamore tree. Her unmistakable bright red hair blazed in the lamplight from the lantern she was holding, and her bonnet streamed garish purple ribbons. Her dress was completely inappropriate to the occasion, with ribbons galore. She was smiling like a contented cat.

He'd brought his *whore*!

Georgiana felt like someone had poured ice water down her back. How *dare* he. Pain and rage competed. *Why* would he? How *could* he?

"Listen up, the following parties!" Matt called. "Smith, Barry, Ahlström, Blomgren, Nilsson, Klein, Berger, Turner, Colicut, Hill!"

The crowd around Georgiana grew hushed, but she couldn't look away from the whore. Seline turned and whispered something to someone next to her, and that's when Georgiana realized it wasn't just *one* whore, but a whole wagon full of them. They were like a bunch of parrots, in their too-bright dresses and feathers and ribbons. It was scandalous. She turned to glare at Matt, revising her opinion of him. What kind of party *was* this?

"You're with the lead group," Matt continued, oblivious to Georgiana's ire. "Seb here is your man." Matt pointed at Doyle, who gave them a wave. "He's driving the chuck wagon, and you're to fall in behind. You can ride two to three wagons across when there's room permitting, more when we're on the plains, but sometimes it will have to be single file, particularly when we're crossing rivers." Matt's voice carried easily. "The Barrys will go first, followed by the Smiths, then the rest of you can sort yourselves out." As he spoke, the first spear of sunshine broke between the buildings.

"I suggest staying in your wagons until we're free of the town. After that, you may prefer to walk or ride. Seb will lead out in just a moment, so get yourselves ready. I'll be sending two scouts on ahead while I wait here until the train is out. After our party is out, Joe Sampson's will be rolling, so please keep moving. Do not stop. We need to keep going until both parties are well clear of the town; I'll catch up with you by the time we stop for the noon meal. Have a good morning."

There were cheers and a smattering of applause as he jumped down from the chuck wagon. The tension in the square was palpable.

Mrs. Barry gathered up her cups, and Georgiana shooed the twins back to their wagon, reiterating all her warnings about being careful and not falling under the wheels. Wilby had climbed over the tray and onto the bench next to Susannah. Georgiana made sure to issue the same warnings and to keep them tightly sandwiched between herself and Wendell.

Matt ran up the courthouse steps and conferred briefly with Josiah Sampson. The square was full of the jingle of bridles and the creak of wagons and the low chatter of voices. Georgiana felt a moment of panic. Once they rolled out, they couldn't turn back . . .

The sound of a gunshot made her jump.

It was Matt, standing on the steps, firing into the air. At the sound of the shot, a bugle sounded. It was a sound they'd be familiar with before long. The bugle called the morning roll out, and the stops along the way. Seb yelled "Ha!" and the chuck wagon lurched forward. The Barrys' wagon followed, and then Wendell was whipping the oxen, and Georgiana held on tight to Wilby as they jolted into motion. The wagon shuddered and rattled, and a great cheer rose from the square.

"We're off!" someone yelled.

"See you in Oregon!"

"California!"

"Oregon!"

The cheer swelled. It was joined by excited gunfire.

"What are those fools doing?" Wendell grumped. "Someone'll be shot in the head with all those bullets raining down."

Georgiana looked anxiously skyward, but they seemed to be out of danger.

As they left the square, people lined the roads, waving the party off. They leaned out of windows in their nightclothes or stood in the doorways with their morning coffee while their children and dogs chased alongside the wagons.

"Say good-bye to civilization," Wendell said cheerfully. "You won't see anything like it for a good long while."

"There aren't *any* towns?" Susannah asked.

"Nope." Wendell slouched back in the seat, settling in for a long drive. "Only a trading post or two and the odd fort. No towns like this. Not till we get to California."

Georgiana and Susannah took in their last look of civilization, both of them subdued. No more stores and tearooms, no more hotels and dances, no more cookhouses and no more beds with feather mattresses. No more baths, no more decent food, no more quiet days. There was just the shudder of the wagon and the unknown of sleeping in a tent on the hard ground . . .

By the time the spectacular golden sunrise had faded into a fresh blue day, and the town had given way to the scrubby Missouri wilderness, Wilby and Susannah were bored and squirming. Eventually, Georgiana grew tired of fretting about them falling off the wagon and deposited them both in the tray behind the bench.

"It's hot back here," Susannah complained.

"I'm bored!" Wilby joined in.

"Listen," Georgiana pleaded, "this is the first morning of a very long journey. I'm sure you'll get used to it eventually. Watch the scenery. Maybe you can walk after lunch. Susannah, isn't your slate and chalk back there? Why don't you draw things for your brother?"

They did as she asked, but without enthusiasm. As she listened to the squeal of the chalk, Georgiana felt it was going to be a long trip.

❧ 18 ❧

"OF COURSE YOU put us at the *back*," Seline complained, when Matt rode past her wagon.

"Just be grateful you get to come along," Matt told her. "Joe ain't happy about it."

"Tell Joe we'll give him a freebie to make up for it," one of the other whores giggled.

"You tell him. You're in his party. I'm off now." He turned Pablo and circled back, fixing Seline with a serious look. "I've gone out on a limb for you on this one," he told her. "Joe is a good guy. Don't be making trouble for him, you hear?"

"Honey, we'll *save* him trouble," Seline scoffed. "We'll keep all these 'uns peaceful." She gestured to the groups of men milling about. Nearly all of Joe's party was made up of men, some single and others who'd left their families home while they went to make their fortune. The ones nearest to the whores were giving them a close inspection.

"See that you do," Matt warned, "and do as you're told."

Seline nodded and gave him an angelic smile. "You might not be as cuddly as your brother, Slater, but you're a damn fine man. I appreciate all you've done. Even if we do have to ride right at the back in all this dust."

"Good luck," he said, and kicked Pablo into a gallop. He waved at Joe as he rode by the courthouse steps. The last of his wagons were just trundling out of the square. Joe would give them ten or fifteen minutes, and then send his chuck wagon and first group after them.

Matt kicked Pablo hard in the ribs to speed him along. He was glad to finally be rolling out, even though he didn't feel nearly rested enough for the long trip ahead. Rest wasn't in the cards this year. Nothing much he could do about that. He was glad to leave this mad town behind, even if he had to take some of the mad people with him. He could rest up when he got back home. He was thinking that after this last nightmarish year he might take a season or two off and stay put at home in Utopia for a while. Get away from the gunslingers and emigrants. Have some peace and quiet.

He felt the tension in his shoulders loosening as he left the town behind. Deathrider was almost well again, Georgiana Bee Blunt was on her way to being out of his life: things were looking up. He stopped alongside each wagon as he rode, having a brief chat with the folks inside. He seemed to have chosen nice folks this year. They were all settlers, not like the rougher sorts back in the square, who were aiming for California gold country. These folks were mostly families looking for a better life.

A wagon train was a funny thing. It was almost a living creature. You started it rolling and it just kept rolling along, as though it had a mind of its own. The chuck wagon was the thinking head of it, and when the chuck wagon stopped, gradually the rest of the body caught up and the halt rippled on down the line. Matt still wasn't anywhere near the front when he heard the distant call of the bugle, and there was a slow ripple as the wagons rolled to a stop for the noon meal. He'd been too busy chatting. There were close on 200 wagons in his train this year, and he wanted to take time to get to know the people in them.

"You're a long way from your chuck wagon," Henrick Shott told Matt as they ground to a halt. "How about you stop and take the meal with us?"

"That sounds like a pleasure," Matt agreed. This was how it usually went, and he'd been expecting to lunch with someone mid-train. But he couldn't help feeling a pang, thinking about Wendell Todd lunching with Georgiana up there at the front. Stupid. But he couldn't shake the petty little envy. The feeling was so persistent and so distracting that he barely heard a word anyone said as he ate.

"YOU DON'T THINK he's lost?"

Seb Doyle laughed at her. "Matt? Lost?" He just about split his sides. "Lady, you got no idea who you're marrying if you can ask a question like that! Matt don't get lost. Not ever. You could blindfold him and drop him in the middle of the Lava Lands and he'd find his way out." He shook his head. "Lost!"

"I just thought he should be back by now," she said lamely.

She was stretching the kinks out of her legs while Seb built a cook fire for them. All along the line behind them, she could see similar fires being built. A huge billow of reddish gold dust rose into the blue sky above them; it hung, unmoving, in the still air. Soon, pale curls of woodsmoke mingled in with the dust.

"Best get your vittles ready. I'll have the fire up by the time you're back from your wagon," Seb advised. "We don't stop long, so you don't want to be wasting time."

Georgiana pulled a face. She supposed it was time to test her nonexistent cooking skills. She sighed and made for the back of the second wagon. She'd stashed the hard-backed ledger Mrs. Tilly had given her for a recipe book in the burlap bag with the cook pot. She lowered the back gate of the wagon and reached for the bag. As she did, she heard a sneeze.

"Boys! I told you not to climb around in there!" she snapped. Honestly. They never listened.

But then she heard their voices drifting over from the Colicuts' wagon behind her. She turned. There they were, making friends with the three Colicut boys.

"Susannah?" she turned back to the wagon. It wasn't like her daughter to go climbing around. She was usually so prissy and well-behaved.

There was silence in the wagon. Georgiana tilted her head. "Kipp?"

Nothing. Maybe she'd imagined it. She pulled the cooking utensils free of the wagon. They clanked as they fell to the ground. She fussed inside until she found the recipe book. She had no idea which ingredients to get until she worked out what to cook. Mrs. Tilly had filled the first few pages with some simple recipes for her.

"You can get more recipes from some of the other women as you journey," Mrs. Tilly had said cheerfully. "By the time you get to Oregon, I'm sure you'll have filled every page. And it will be a nice way to get to know people, won't it?"

Georgiana didn't know about that. Truth be told, she found

the idea of cooking quite daunting. Especially as her failures would be public.

She flipped through the book, trying to find something quick. None of the biscuits or breads or stews could be done in the brief time she had to make lunch. Lovely Mrs. Tilly had written some handy hints on the inside cover, she saw, including one Georgiana filed away for later tonight: *Make double serving of evening meal, so you can reheat leftovers for lunch the next day.* Yes, she'd do that. Reheating sounded far easier than actual cooking. But it didn't help her now, as she had nothing made that she could reheat.

Here was a possibility though. Fried tomatoes and bacon. How hard could that be? And she'd bought some loaves of bread from Mrs. Tilly to see them through the first few days of traveling. Tomatoes, bacon and bread. That was a meal. And frying didn't seem too daunting. You just threw it all in the pan. She dug out the pan.

Finding the bacon proved harder. It was packed in there somewhere, but she hadn't packed this wagon herself, so she wasn't sure where. She had to haul herself up to try and find it. She was glad no one was with her to witness her clumsy climb in.

It was as she rummaged about that she heard the next sneeze. It was definitely a sneeze, and it was definitely right here in the wagon with her.

"Susannah!" It had to be her daughter. It was definitely female. Although, what on earth Susannah would be doing in here was beyond her.

"Susannah, you get out here right this minute!"

Silence.

"I really don't have the patience for this." Georgiana began yanking things about, trying to find her. As she hefted a sack of coffee beans, she was astonished to uncover the corner of a patchwork quilt. The tents and bedding were stashed right by the end of the wagon, near the back. What was a quilt doing here? What was her daughter up to?

The sneeze sounded again, and the quilt jumped. Georgiana pulled it, and it came away, revealing a stowaway.

"Becky!"

The girl looked utterly horrified to be discovered. "You

weren't supposed to see me until tonight!" she wailed. "Please don't send me back!"

"How did you fit in here?" Georgiana was astonished as she peered into the crack between the barrels. The girl was crammed into a nook that could barely have accommodated Wilby.

"It hasn't been comfortable," Becky admitted.

"Come out of there." Georgiana wriggled out of the wagon, making way for Becky to follow. Only, the girl's legs had gone to sleep under her, and when she tried to move, she was seized with agonizing pins and needles. She sprawled on top of the baggage, whimpering.

"Mrs. Tilly will be beside herself with worry," Georgiana scolded, as she watched the girl trying to massage the feeling back into her legs.

"I left her a note," Becky protested. "She'll understand. She always knew I wouldn't stay forever."

Georgiana shook her head. "Are you chasing after LeFoy?" she asked, already knowing the answer. "You do know he's not even in this group?"

Becky looked sheepish. "But he *is* traveling close by."

"You can't go running off with a strange man like this!" Georgiana conveniently ignored the fact that she had been trying to do much the same thing by placing her advertisement.

"I'm not," Becky insisted, finally wriggling out of the wagon after Georgiana. "I'm running off with *you*." She gave Georgiana a hopeful look. "I can help you with the children." Her gaze dropped to the recipe book Georgiana was still holding. "And I can cook!"

Georgiana shook her head. She heard Matt's voice in her head: *Roll up your sleeves and work like the rest of us.* He was right. Mrs. Barry didn't have a girl helping her, and neither did Mrs. Colicut or Mrs. Klein or Mrs. Blomgren. "I'm going to learn," she said firmly. "And I'm perfectly capable of looking after my children myself. You have to go back. Poor Mrs. Tilly."

"I can *teach* you to cook, then," Becky begged. "And of course you're perfectly capable, but everyone needs help sometimes. And those twins . . . " Becky trailed off significantly. "Besides, I'm not asking to stay with you all the way to Oregon. I'm planning to be married by then."

"Married!"

"Yes." Becky lifted her chin stubbornly. "I have all summer to get him to fall in love with me. And even if he hasn't quite yet by then, he has children too. I bet he needs a wife."

Georgiana sighed. Becky was so young.

"Please, Mrs. Smith. I'm ever so useful!" Becky's eyes were pleading. "And I love him!" she said. "I really do. And I'll earn my keep."

"Mrs. Tilly . . ."

"Isn't my family," Becky finished, cutting her off. "She was so good to me, taking me in when my family passed away, but we were heading west, and she always knew I'd finish the journey one day."

"How are you doing, missus?" Seb hollered from the cook fire. "You're running out of time!"

Georgiana sighed. She hadn't provisioned for Becky . . . But then, she'd bought more than the list had specified, because she'd had Matt's voice in her head: *Just in case.*

"Fine," she said, thrusting the frying pan at Becky, "but only if you make lunch."

"WHERE THE HELL did she come from?" Matt asked, when he finally reached the head of the train, sometime just before sunset.

Becky was walking along next to Georgiana, off to the side of the wagons, away from the dust. The twins had long tired of walking with them and were sitting up next to Wendell. Susannah and Wilby were asleep in their nook in the tray.

"She's a stowaway," Georgiana said calmly. She was long since used to Becky's presence. Today seemed like it had lasted for more than a week. She barely even remembered discovering the girl in the wagon; it felt like Becky had been with them all along.

Matt grunted. "She didn't pay to come."

"I'll pay for her," Georgiana told him. Becky had already proved her usefulness, feeding them all and helping with the children. The children had already been a bigger challenge on the journey than Georgiana had anticipated. It was only the first day, and the younger ones were bored and uncomfortable, and the twins were in constant danger of serious injury or of getting lost. Becky was a godsend, distracting the two little ones and helping to keep track of the boys. She was also company on the walk. She was so thrilled that Georgiana hadn't sent her back to Independence that she chattered away merrily. It was a welcome distraction from the pain in Georgiana's feet.

Mrs. Barry had joined them walking very briefly, but she still preferred the wagon at this stage. And the Scandinavian women didn't speak enough English yet to be good traveling companions. Mrs. Colicut, the southern woman with all the children, was too busy with her brood to be able to talk much either.

By sunset, when Matt rode up, Becky and Georgiana weren't talking much themselves. They plodded along, watching the way the dust clouds turned golden as the late sunlight fell through them in thick wedges. Matt, on the other hand, was easy in the saddle, dusty and sweaty and looking far too energetic for this end of a long day.

"I can pay you when we stop tonight," Georgiana promised.

"Looks like you got yourself some hired help after all," he said, and then he rode off to join the chuck wagon.

Georgiana winced. He thought she was a spoiled little rich girl.

Well, she *was*. Or rather she used to be. And if she could afford it now, she most certainly would have brought a team of nannies and cooks and helpers with her, she thought longingly.

"He's a mighty handsome man, isn't he?" Becky said. "I would never have known it when he was under all that beard."

"You think he's handsome?" Georgiana feigned indifference, even though she couldn't tear her gaze from his broad back.

"Not as handsome as Pierre," Becky said loyally, "but very close."

It took all Georgiana's willpower not to laugh. Pierre Le-Foy wasn't anywhere near Matt Slater when it came to looks. They were almost different species!

Speaking of Matt Slater, where was he going *now*? There had to be less than an hour of daylight left, yet he was cantering off toward the horizon. For the love of God, weren't they ever going to stop?

They did eventually, but not until Georgiana had just about walked herself to the edge of death. Her legs were trembling from all the exertion.

Matt cantered back into sight after fifteen minutes or so, and then he led them to a river; they followed along beside it for quite a long while before he called a halt. The cool air rising from the waters was bliss; Georgiana could feel it slipping against her skin. She would have collapsed right beside it, if Matt, that horrible man, hadn't ridden past, snapping at them to circle the wagons and corral the animals in the center. There were too many of them to make one large circle, so instead they formed a few smaller ones; Georgiana's lead group of ten wagons joined up with the second and third groups. The circle they made was big enough to form a substantial paddock for the animals.

She was quite happy to let Wendell and Kipp see to the livestock and the tents while she and Becky prepared the evening meal. At least she was until the men had finished and were sprawled by the fire. At that point she realized that the women's work would last far into the night: once they'd fed everyone and done the dishes, she'd still have to put the children to bed. Bed. Oh my, how she was longing to just crawl under a quilt and sleep.

She eyed her children, who were snuggled up under blankets and quilts around the fire. All four of them were heavy eyed with exhaustion.

"You know," Tom Slater drawled, as he watched Georgiana struggle with the cook pot, "it makes no sense you cooking for your lot and Seb cooking for me and Matt. Not when you're marrying Matt. That just doesn't seem natural."

Georgiana shot him a dirty look. She didn't fancy having to cook for *more* people than she already had to. Look at him sitting there, shelling peanuts, his legs stretched out before him, while she had to go haul water and slave over the cook fire.

"It seems to me that we should pool our resources," Tom said, flicking a peanut shell into the fire.

"Be quiet," Matt warned his brother.

Georgiana jumped. She hadn't realized he was there. He was just outside the circle of firelight, his eyes fixed on her. How long had he been there?

"You shouldn't talk to your lady that way," Tom scolded.

"I was talking to *you*."

"What do you think, Seb?" Tom continued, as though Matt hadn't spoken. "We can cook half the time and she can cook half the time?"

"Sounds good to me," Seb said as he dropped the burlap sack he was carrying. It thudded to the ground, and a potato rolled out. "I wouldn't mind a night off here and there."

Georgiana looked at Tom in shock. Was he actually being *nice* to her? She hadn't been expecting that from him. Was he really suggesting she wouldn't have to cook every night? Because that was music to her ears.

"I'm happy to do a night a week," Tom said, stretching out, "and Matt's a decent cook."

Of course he was. Georgiana stole a look at him. Was there anything he couldn't do?

"So with me, Seb, Matt, Mrs. Smith and Becky here, that's five of us."

"I can cook," Wendell interrupted belligerently.

"Not well," Kipp said.

Wendell looked furious at the slur. "I bet I'm as good as Slater."

"There you go," Tom said. "With Wendy here, we're six. That just leaves the Sabbath, and maybe we can have leftovers on Sundays."

"It's Wendell," Wendell growled, "not Wendy."

"I'd be happy to join in with you," Mrs. Barry said from where she stood at the cook fire. "That is, if you don't mind?"

"There you go," Tom told Matt smugly. "It looks like I'm almost as good at organizing things as you are. Mrs. Barry makes seven. This way none of us needs to cook more than one night a week. And," he added, with relish, "we can all eat together. Like one big, happy family." His gaze drifted back and forth between Matt and Georgiana.

Matt scowled at him.

Oh, she could have kissed Tom Slater, even if he was a scary man. She wouldn't have to cook every night! The thought of slumping down by the fire and resting her feet at the end of the day sounded like heaven.

As did the thought of eating with Matt Slater every night. It was a thought that sent a delicious thrill through her. It was a thrill that was completely oblivious to her better sense. It didn't

care that he had avoided her like the plague these last weeks, or
that he preferred the company of whores. Some stubborn part
of her was desperate to be in his company. And, after the exhaustion and monotony of the day, she was glad to give in to it.

"Who cooks tonight, then?" Matt growled. He didn't look
at all happy about this arrangement.

"Let's do it together," Tom said cheerfully, "in honor of our
first night. Why don't you help your lovely fiancée fill that
cook pot with water from the stream, little brother? It's just
about bigger than she is."

Georgiana heard him muttering under his breath, but he
came along. Her heart pounded as he snatched the cook pot
off her and led her to the stream.

"You don't need to come," he snapped. "I'll bring it to you
when it's full."

"I don't mind." In truth, she couldn't have stopped herself
from following him. Her heart was racing and her hands were
sweating and she wanted nothing more than to be alone with
him at the stream. *Stupid, stupid, stupid. Don't* do *this to
yourself. Oh, shut up. Shut up and allow me this* one *moment
of happiness today.* Because it *was* happiness to be near him.
Even when he didn't seem happy to be near her.

"Did it go well today?" she asked nervously as they stepped
beyond the firelight and into the blue evening. The sound of
flowing water ran like music through the night.

"As well as it could," he said shortly. He filled the cook pot,
bending down on one knee over the stream. He wasn't wearing
his hat, and his dark hair was curling against his neck.

"My feet have never hurt so much in my whole life," she
admitted. She was nervous and rambling, and she kept rambling, about her sore legs and how many miles lay ahead of
them, but she couldn't stop herself. She was too tired to be
composed.

He stood and looked at her.

"Oh, that must be heavy," she said, looking at the cook pot
brimful of water.

He didn't say anything.

"I could never have carried it," she babbled. "I would have
had to make several trips with a pitcher." She pressed her lips

together. "I'm sorry, I'm blathering on. It's just," she blurted, "you make me nervous."

His eyebrows shot up. She'd shocked him.

She'd shocked herself. She certainly hadn't expected to tell him the truth. She was just so tired. And she had a deep-body memory of the comfort of his arms. She wanted comfort tonight.

She'd regret this tomorrow. Tomorrow, after she'd slept, she'd care again about the whore and about the fact that she shouldn't get attached because she'd have to say good-bye to him at Fort Hall. But now wasn't tomorrow.

Georgiana took a deep breath and simply told the truth. "I missed you these last few weeks."

Now he looked worse than shocked. She plowed on.

"I'm sorry, I know this is awkward. I know we had . . . a couple of . . . *moments* . . . that complicated things." She cleared her throat. "And I know that you don't want to be around me anymore. I mean, you've made that perfectly clear."

He wasn't saying anything. He wasn't so much as moving. Georgiana shriveled with embarrassment but couldn't stop herself from talking.

"But it's a long journey, Mr. Slater, and we're traveling practically in each other's pockets. Pretending to be engaged, of all things." She laughed nervously. Oh God. He was like a statue. This was so humiliating. "I just thought perhaps we could find a way forward, so things aren't so awkward? We could treat it more like a business arrangement? Act like we're associates? Or friends?"

And that way she could see him again. They could talk. And maybe, in an unguarded moment, she might feel his arms around her again, his lips on hers . . .

She was mad. Truly, deeply mad.

She swallowed and waited for his reply.

"This is heavy," he said gruffly. And then he pushed past her and walked back to the cook fire, and she just about died of shame.

❧ 19 ❧

E VEN THOUGH SHE'D never slept in a tent in her life, even though the ground was hard and there were strange noises in the night beyond the canvas, even though the children snored and Wilby flailed about, Georgiana had the best night's sleep she'd had for weeks. Mostly because of the brief conversation she'd had before going to bed.

She'd been heading into the tent when he'd stopped her. The children were long asleep, and the campfire had been damped down for the night. Tom Slater had fallen asleep wrapped in an Indian blanket by the fire, and everyone else was retiring, except for those on the first shift of guard duty. The only sounds were the stream and the soft voices drifting from other fires farther off.

"Georgiana." It was the first time Matt had said her name. The sound of it from his lips had made her quiver.

She'd pasted a polite smile on her lips, still not recovered from the humiliation by the stream. "Yes?"

He approached, radiating discomfort. He was a long, bulky shadow in the darkness. "I've been thinking about what you said before," he said huskily. He sounded apprehensive.

Georgiana felt ill. Could this situation get more embarrassing? "Please," she begged, "forget I said anything. I was over-tired from the day."

"Of course." He cleared his throat. "But . . . you meant it?"

Oh God. Of course she did. Otherwise, she wouldn't be standing here *dying* of embarrassment, would she? At least it was too dark for him to see her expression.

She heard him breathing in the darkness. She couldn't make out his expression either.

"Yes," he said abruptly.

"Yes?"

"Yes. Yes, I think we can be associates." He paused. "Friends."

She hadn't been expecting that.

"If the offer still stands," he said lamely.

"Of course." Oh, the relief.

"You were right. We have had a few . . . *moments.* And we both know they can't happen again. And I think it's unlikely they *will* happen again, considering our lack of privacy here."

What was the madman talking about? Look at them right this minute, alone in the darkness! It didn't get much more private than this. Admittedly, there were people only a few feet away, but it was pitch-black out here. He could kiss her and no one would ever know . . .

And yet, Georgiana knew that if he kissed her now, any chance of their being friends would evaporate. For whatever reason, he was spooked by his attraction to her. And she didn't want to scare him away. These last weeks had been torture, with him just across the hall but totally out of reach.

Like Leo. Beyond her grasp.

No. Don't think of Leo. She could barely move for fear when she thought of Leo. It was easier to push it away. But the pain of being cut off from Leo certainly seemed to heighten whatever this mixed-up feeling of longing-loss was from being cut off from Matt.

"So, yes," he continued, more talkative under this cover of darkness than usual, "I think we can negotiate a new relationship. One without . . . *moments.*"

"Yes," she said, able to keep the regret from her voice, even though it was the moments she liked. The moments she longed for. But of course, the moments weren't good for their situation. And they both knew it.

"I'll see you in the morning," he said.

"Yes."

The air between them thrummed with that tension they had, that charge, that silent anticipation. Wasn't this almost a moment?

If it was, it was the kind they could pretend hadn't happened.

"Good night, Georgiana."

She shivered at the sound of her name.

"Good night, Matt."

Did he shiver too? She hoped so. Just as she hoped that as he walked away he felt the same keen disappointment she felt, but also that strange feeling of elation that floated just above it. Because when they stepped out of their tents tomorrow, they would be starting again. As friends.

IT WAS A little awkward at first. But only for a few days. The fact that they only saw each other in groups helped, as there was always plenty of distraction. They lapsed into a distant but friendly relationship, not dissimilar to the one he had with Mrs. Barry. He wasn't around much for there to be any risk of intimacy. He was off, up and down the line, out in front, scouting, helping with broken wagons and lame animals, fetching the doctor for people who had blisters. Which included Georgiana after a couple of days of walking.

He'd happened to be near when she'd eased her boots off after washing the evening dishes. She'd gone down to the river to wash up and had taken the opportunity to soak her battered feet. She'd thought she was alone; she eased her boots off to slip her poor feet in the cool water and had heard him curse. He was behind her, an empty pitcher dangling from his hand.

"What in hell is that?" he demanded, looking at her mangled feet, with their suppurating blisters.

"Nothing." She hurriedly plunged her feet into the stream, out of his sight. She didn't want him to see how weak she was. She already knew what he thought of her—that she was a pampered little miss—and she didn't particularly want to confirm his opinion of her.

"You wait there," he snapped.

"Why?" But he was already gone. When he came back, he was dragging Doctor Barry with him.

"Look at her feet," he ordered.

Georgiana flushed. He sounded disgusted.

"Well, you certainly have done some damage, haven't you?" the doctor said mildly, when she'd lifted them from the water. "It's good you've cleaned them, but it would actually be best not to get them wet for a while. We want those sores to dry out." He looked up at her. "That means no shoes for a while either."

"No shoes!" But how was she going to walk? She groaned. As bad as walking was, riding in the shuddery wagon was infinitely worse.

"Jesus, woman," Matt snapped.

She squealed as he bent down and hauled her from the ground. He carried her back to the camp, ignoring her protests.

"The pots and dishes are back there!"

"I'll go back and get them later," he growled. "What in hell were you thinking? Were you trying to make yourself lame?"

"It must have been the new boots," Georgiana mumbled.

"Didn't you wear them in?" He seemed furious at her stupidity.

Georgiana flushed.

"And I bet you ain't walked like this in your entire life before," he railed. "A smart woman would build up to a full day's walking, not plow along on tender feet."

"You're right." Georgiana's eyes filled with tears. She *wasn't* smart. And her feet *were* tender. In fact, they hurt beyond belief.

"Don't cry," he said, appalled. "Why do you always cry?"

"I *don't*," she said, feeling a spurt of anger.

"You cry a lot."

"I cry when it's appropriate! I've had a lot to cry about lately."

"Boys," he called to the twins when he stepped back into the light of the campfire, "bring me that big quilt you're using. Your ma needs it." They came running, and he put them to work spreading it out for her and fetching cushions from their tent. Then he set her down, gently, as though she might break.

"You're not to move," he snapped at her. "When it's time to go to bed, you call me and I'll carry you."

Georgiana could see Tom Slater watching them from across the fire. He looked amused.

"I can walk," she protested.

"No, you damn well can't. And you're not to walk anywhere for the next few days, you hear me? Not anywhere.

You're to let these two look after you." He jabbed a finger at the twins. "Which you're to do," he told the boys. "You fetch her food, and you make sure she stays put in that wagon."

"I hate the wagon!" Georgiana complained.

"Bad luck. You'll hate being lame worse if you don't keep off those feet."

"I really think you're taking this a bit too far," Georgiana said. "Surely, I can still walk a little bit?" she asked the doctor.

Doctor Barry held his hands up and shook his head. "Far be it from me to get between a man and his wife-to-be."

"It ain't going to be easy keeping her in the wagon," Phin said thoughtfully, adopting the western drawl he put on when he was trying to sound like Matt. "Perhaps we should have the rifle?"

Matt choked. "Why? You planning to shoot her if she don't stay put?"

"No rifle!" Georgiana snapped. "I don't know how many times I have to tell you: you're not to go anywhere near it!"

"Maybe we could tie her down?" Philip suggested.

"You hear that?" Matt told her. "If you don't stay put in that wagon, they'll tie you down. Or shoot you."

She glared at him as he left.

"Get your ma a cup of tea," he ordered the boys over his shoulder as he left. They jumped to it.

They never seemed to listen to *her* that way. Georgiana sighed in disgust and flopped back against the cushions. She hated to admit it, but it was lovely to be looked after for a while. And her feet really did hurt. Maybe she could take a nap. The fire was so warm, and the quilt was so comfortable, and she was very, very tired.

Maybe it wouldn't be so bad traveling in the wagon for a little while.

IT WAS WORSE than bad. It was unbearable.

She hated that wagon. The bench was hard, the road was rough, and she was rattled from her eyeballs to the balls of her feet. Her jaw ached from clenching her teeth so they wouldn't clack together. It was the most god-awful way to travel. Her feet were propped up on the buckboard in front of her, and, wouldn't you know it, they got sunburned the first day, adding to her pain. After that, she kept a blanket over them. But that was hot and miserable too.

"She's making everyone's life a misery," Phin told Matt cheerfully as they helped him cook. Matt had them rubbing coffee grounds into a haunch of salted beefsteak.

They hadn't helped *her* cook, Georgiana thought grumpily, and if she'd asked them to, they would have run off. And who put *coffee* in food?

Although, it tasted wonderful, she had to admit. She didn't like the fact that he could cook so well. It didn't seem fair that he was so capable at *everything*, especially when she was sitting here like a fool, with her burned and blistered feet. And his steaks made her rock-hard corn fritters look very poor in comparison.

"How long do we have to ride up here with her?" Philip moaned when Matt pulled up alongside the wagon the next morning. The twins were struggling with Wilby, who was no longer content to sit still in his nest, but clambered around, trying to entertain himself. Georgiana was in constant terror he would fall and go under the wheels, and Philip, who was Wilby's favorite, was the one who bore the brunt of the toddler's boredom. The worst bits were the river crossings. Even though they were just small waterways at this point, they were torturous for Georgiana, especially as Matt wouldn't let her do anything. Sitting on the bench, helpless, made the entire procedure nerve-racking in the extreme. Wilby and Susannah couldn't swim, so she kept close hold of them, the backs of their clothes bunched in her fists. Wilby had struggled the entire way across the Blue, the Wakarusa, the Kansas and the Vermillion, and had almost thrown himself into the Little Blue, thrashing about and indulging in an earsplitting tantrum when his mother wouldn't let go of him.

"Wilby needs a cage," Phin suggested now as Matt's horse fell into a trot beside the wagon.

"No!" Wilby shouted.

"Can we put Ma in one too?" Philip asked. "She's almost as bad."

"Mother," Georgiana corrected sharply. She hated being

called Ma. Although, to be honest, today she hated everything. The wagon made her that grumpy.

"Bored!" Wilby complained for the six hundredth time that day.

"We're all bored," Georgiana snapped.

Matt sighed. "We ain't even two weeks out," he said. "You cain't be bored already."

"Bored!" Wilby yelled.

"I'm bored of you yelling 'bored,'" Phin countered.

"You lot will have murdered one another before we even reach the Platte."

"If we're lucky," Wendell said under his breath.

They glared at him.

After a few days of riding with them, Wendell had learned to mostly keep his mouth shut. Becky had decamped to the other wagon; riding with Kipp was preferable to riding with the warring Smiths. Even Wendell was suffering. He'd originally tried to use the time to cozy up to Georgiana, but her temper was filthy ever since she'd hurt her feet, and she didn't do anything but give surly one-word answers to his questions. So he'd stopped talking and had fallen into the trance of driving for hour after mind-numbing hour.

Matt sized them all up, looking vaguely amused. "Wendell, after the noon break, you and I are going to swap."

"Huh?" Wendell squinted at him. "Whaddya mean?"

"I mean, you can ride your horse this afternoon. I'm sure the Kleins would appreciate some help herding their livestock, and I bet you could do with a change of scene."

Wendell visibly brightened at the idea.

Georgiana scowled. She wished she could ride too. But no, she was stuck here in this horrid wagon. Why hadn't she thought to buy a horse back in Independence?

Because they were expensive and she'd never dreamed the wagon would be *this* uncomfortable.

"And *you*," Matt said, fixing Georgiana with an impatient look, "are going to learn to drive this vehicle."

"I beg your pardon?"

"It will give you something to do. You and Wendell can take turns driving, and that way you'll have something to occupy yourself with and he can get out on his horse for half the day. He'd be useful with the loose animals during the river crossings."

"Goddamn it! We should have bought horses, Ma!" Phin kicked the boards at his feet. "We *told* you we should have bought horses."

"Phineas! Watch your language!"

"If we had horses, *we* could herd the stock too," Philip complained. "Without them, all we can do all day is ride on this thing . . . "

"Or *walk*," Phin said the word like it was a personal debasement. "It's goddamn stupid."

"Hey!" Matt growled. "You don't talk to your ma that way. *Ever*. I won't have anyone in my party speaking to *any* woman in that manner. Is that clear? And don't blaspheme."

Phin flushed.

"Is that clear?" Matt asked sternly.

"Yes, sir," Phin mumbled.

"Apologize to you mother."

"I'm sorry." Phin was turning redder by the minute. He gave Georgiana a shamefaced look. "I won't do it again."

"I should hope not," Georgiana said, "but thank you for apologizing." She sighed. "I don't agree with the manner in which you said it, but I agree: I wish I'd bought a horse or two as well. They're just so expensive . . ."

"You can all ride?" Matt asked, eyeing the boys.

"Of course we can ride." Phin's chin went up, and he gave Matt an imperious look. "We're superior horsemen."

"They can all ride, except Wilby," Georgiana agreed. They'd had a fine stable of horses once. Before they'd had to be sold off to pay Leonard's debts.

"Wilby wants to ride!" Wilby held his arms out to Matt. Philip held on tight to his squirming body, and Georgiana grabbed a handful of his shirt. He looked about ready to launch himself at Matt.

"If you don't sit still, we're going to get that cage!" Phin threatened his brother.

Wilby let out an enraged scream.

"Stop!" Georgiana warned him. "Stop, or you can go straight back to your quilt."

He screamed louder.

"Enough!" Matt bellowed. Wilby shut up immediately, his eyes wide. "That's enough. Wilby, you make that noise again, you'll be in the back of that wagon for the rest of the trip."

Wilby tilted his head, as though he was weighing up the choice.

"But if you promise to be good and quiet, and to listen to your mother, I'll take you for a ride."

"What! How come *he* gets to ride!" Phin was incensed.

"He's too little to walk," Matt said curtly. "You two, on the other hand, are going to get down from there and walk off some of your energy and attitude."

The twins scowled.

"The exercise will be good for you. And it will give your mother a break. Get down. Now."

Georgiana watched, astonished, as the boys did as they were told and jumped from the slow-trundling wagon. She added child-wrangling to Matt's skills.

Tom Slater's dog saw the twins and came bounding over to play with them. That cheered the boys up, and they went out hunting for sticks to throw.

"Ride!" Wilby yelled, holding his arms out to Matt.

"Only if you promise not to yell anymore and to be nice to your ma."

"Yes!"

"That's still yelling."

Georgiana swore she could see the ghost of a smile on Matt's lips.

"Yes," Wilby whispered in a mousy little voice.

"All right, then." Matt leaned over and plucked Wilby away from Georgiana. The boy went rigid with delight as Matt sat him on the saddle. Wilby grabbed the pommel with both pudgy hands and beamed.

Georgiana felt a pang of envy. So did Susannah, judging by her expression. Poor Susannah. She was so quiet and so well-behaved that she was often totally forgotten. Georgiana stroked her cheek, and the girl tried to smile. But her gaze never left the horse.

"He's good with children, ain't he?" Wendell said glumly as Matt rode off with Wilby.

Yes. He was. Look at how firmly he held Wilby in the saddle, and look at the way Wilby laughed with joy, for the first time all day. Look at how the twins jogged along, throwing a stick for the dog to fetch, talking happily with the Colicut boys. He'd seen their disgruntlement and he'd dealt with it.

And after lunch, he dealt with hers. Not in the way she would have wished, but it was still an improvement on the rest of her day. And she got to sit next to Matt for an hour or so, alone. Or as close to alone as it was possible to get, considering the circumstances.

Matt had sent Wendell off on his horse. The man had lit out like his tail was on fire, he was so glad to get away from the bickering Blunts. Wilby had been worn out by his ride and was asleep in the back, while Susannah was contentedly feeding bits of apple to Matt's horse, which was tethered to the wagon hoop beside her. She was talking to the animal like it was a pet as it trotted along. The twins were off with the Colicut boys and the dog again, rejuvenated after lunch.

Matt, meanwhile, was teaching Georgiana how to drive. He handed her the rod, which she looked at distastefully. She didn't like the idea of whipping animals.

"It's not to whip them," he said, exasperated, when she said so. "It's to goad them along."

"I think that's just splitting hairs," she said stubbornly. "I *have* been sitting here, watching Wendell. I think I know what whipping is."

"It's your rod. Use it as you see fit," he replied, shaking his head at her crankiness. "Maybe Wendell uses a heavy hand, but that doesn't mean you have to. But you'll at least have to tap them, so they know to listen to you."

The rod was light and supple in her hand. She did a practice swipe or two.

"You know the commands?" Matt asked.

Oh. She should have paid more attention. "Giddyup?" she said tentatively.

He nodded. "That's right."

"And . . . whoa?" She hoped that was a command and wasn't just something Wendell shouted.

He nodded again. "And the others?"

She assumed *Get on, you cross-patched ballbags* wasn't an official command, and neither was *What in Sam Hill are you doing, you useless grunters?*

He took pity on her. "Get or giddyup is for go; whoa is for stop; back means back up; gee means turn right; and haw means turn left. Got it?"

She nodded. She'd keep Wendell's "cross-patched ball-bags" up her sleeve, should these not work.

"What are you smiling at?"

"Nothing." She pressed her lips together. She had an urge to yell, *Giddyup, you useless grunters!* just to see the look on Matt's face. But of course she didn't. Ladies didn't do such things.

"Off you go, then," he said, as the bugle sounded and the chuck wagon rolled out. The scouts galloped off in advance.

Georgiana tapped the rod on the oxen's backs. "Get!" she called.

"Lady, you have to be louder than that or they won't hear you over the sound of the flies."

Georgiana wasn't about to be embarrassed by a bunch of useless grunters. She flicked the rod and yelled, "Get!"

Susannah jumped a mile.

The oxen didn't even move.

"Hit them harder," Matt suggested. "They cain't feel a little flick like that. Don't worry, it won't hurt them." He held her wrist and flicked it for her. Just a little bit sharper. She saw the ox hide twitch under it.

"Get!" she called, flicking with the same strength he'd used. This time they moved. Georgiana had driven a phaeton before, and this wasn't too different; it was just clumsier and slower, and the animals weren't terribly responsive. She didn't need to do much except hold the reins while they plodded along.

"Nice work, old hoss." Matt sprawled back in the seat and stretched his legs out as far as he could. Georgiana had never seen him quite as relaxed as this before. The farther they traveled from Independence, the calmer he seemed. He was less terse and more playful. Lighter of spirit.

Sitting in the warm afternoon sun, with him half dozing beside her, the children busy or sleepy and the reins supple in her hands, the afternoon was almost peaceful. Georgiana was surprised to find she was enjoying herself.

Susannah foss rummaged around in back, looking for more treats for the horse.

"You'll make him fat," Matt teased the little girl.

"Don't waste all our apples," Georgiana warned.

"They're only old ones." Susannah held up the wizened last season's fruit.

"We only have old ones," Georgiana complained. "It's that time of year."

"Just one more?"

"Pablo will love you," Matt said, as the horse devoured the apple with one whiskery nibble against Susannah's open palm.

"He's lovely," Susannah said, rubbing his nose as he plodded alongside the wagon.

"He ain't too pretty and he ain't too bright, but he's a hard worker."

"That's what Mother said she wanted in a husband," Susannah said with a giggle.

Georgiana blushed and gave her daughter a warning look.

"I thought the advertisement said frontiersman," Matt said.

"Well, she could hardly say she didn't want a handsome man in an advert, could she?" Susannah told him primly.

"No," Georgiana said through gritted teeth, "some things are private." Children. How did they manage to find the worst possible times to say the most embarrassing things?

"What else did your mother want in a husband?" Matt asked curiously. He sounded amused.

"I really don't see that this is an appropriate conversation," Georgiana said tightly.

"Don't listen to her," Matt told Susannah, leaning around Georgiana to get a better look at the girl's face. "I am marrying her, after all. It would be helpful to know what she expects from me."

Susannah nodded as though that made perfect sense. And Georgiana could hardly protest that he *wasn't* going to marry her, could she? How would she explain *that* to an eight-year-old?

She contented herself with scooting forward on the seat, to block his view of her daughter. He just leaned the other way and looked behind her back.

"We helped write the advertisement too," Susannah said proudly.

"Oh? What did you *and* your mother want?"

"Well," Susannah said thoughtfully, "the boys thought being able to wrestle a bear would be helpful. And owning a gun, of course. Do you have a gun?"

Georgiana would have protested, but the oxen chose that moment to veer off course, and she had to practice yelling "Haw!" and flicking the rod. The stubborn animals didn't listen, and before long, the flicking had become a bit of whipping. Just lightly. But still. She didn't feel good about it.

"I have two guns, since you ask," Matt said, leaning back on his elbows and watching Georgiana struggle to control the team. He didn't lift a finger to help. "A hunting rifle and a pistol." He paused. "I cain't say I've ever wrestled a bear though. Although I have seen lots of them."

"You have? Were they friendly bears? Is that why you didn't wrestle them?"

Georgiana eavesdropped madly, even as she struggled with the team.

"I just didn't see much point in wrestling them, I guess," he said with a shrug. "They were just going on about their business."

"What business?"

"Well, the last one I saw was a mama bear with two cubs, and she was teaching them to fish."

Susannah was captivated as he described the scene. So was Georgiana.

"And the first rule of wrestling bears," he said in mock seriousness, "is never mess with a mama bear. Ain't no one getting between a mama bear and her cubs."

Susannah nodded as though this was sage advice. Which Georgiana supposed it was. Not that she'd be going near any bear, ever, mama bear or not.

"Watch where you're going," he warned, reaching out to tug on Georgiana's hand. His skin was warm on hers. "Or you'll hit the brush there."

"What else did she want in a husband?" Matt asked, letting go of her hand as the oxen fell back into line. "A not-too-pretty, not-too-bright, hardworking gun owner who wrestles bears . . . and what else?"

"Are we still doing this?" Georgiana exclaimed. "I mean, really!"

"Really, what? I think this is important."

Was he teasing? She darted a look at him. He was! He was making fun of her!

"Don't you think it's important, Susannah?" He winked at the girl. "A man ought to be able to please his bride."

His bride. Georgiana shivered at that. Like a fool. As though he *meant* it. Which, of course, he didn't; he was just entertaining himself at her expense.

"She doesn't want a charming man," Susannah confided.

"Susannah!"

"Hush and drive," Matt scolded. "Or you'll run us into a tree."

"There aren't any trees out here."

"I'm sure you'll find one, the way you're driving."

"I'm doing *well*, thank you very much!"

"You'd do better if you'd stop talking and concentrate." He waved her quiet and gave Susannah his full attention. "Why no charming men? I thought ladies liked charm."

"Apparently, my father was charming."

"Apparently? You don't know? Or you didn't find him charming?"

"I don't really remember him," Susannah said wistfully. "I only saw him twice, and the last time I was only five."

Georgiana kept her eyes fixed on the oxen's behinds. She swallowed hard, well aware she was turning as red as a tomato. She felt terribly exposed.

"But everyone said he was charming," Susannah continued. "My grandmother used to say he could charm the birds from the trees. And then make a pie of them."

"Oh." Matt didn't seem to know what to do with that. "Charm isn't always bad," he said quietly. "My brother is charming, and he's a decent man. Don't tell him I ever said that, mind. He has a big enough head as it is, and we've got no call making it any bigger."

"My father was decent," Susannah said stubbornly.

"Of course. I didn't mean to imply otherwise." Matt cleared his throat. "I was just saying my brother could charm the birds from the trees too. Only he don't bake 'em into pies."

"Is Tom an older brother or a younger brother?" Susannah asked.

Georgiana held her breath. She was dying of curiosity about Matt. All she knew about him was that he was from Oregon, ran wagon trains, had a scary-looking brother and magic eyes, and kissed like an angel . . . or a devil . . .

"Both my brothers are older." He paused. "But I'm talking about Luke, my oldest brother. Tom is . . . something else again."

"Older brothers are *hard*," Susannah commiserated.

"Yes, they are." They exchanged sympathetic looks. "So, no charm? What else do I need to know? What does your mother's husband need to be?"

"He needs to be tough. So he can help us get Leo."

"Enough!" Georgiana couldn't let this go any further. She had no desire for Matt Slater to know all her secret business, and there was no telling what Susannah would say. "This has gone far enough," she said firmly. "If you want to know what I want in a husband, you can ask me. In private."

He was watching her closely. "Fair enough."

"Don't worry, Mr. Slater," Susannah confided, leaning over Georgiana to speak to him, "I think you're going to make a perfect husband. We all like you very much."

Now the shoe was on the other foot and *he* flushed. Good. She felt no pity for him at all after that performance.

"Your ma seems to have got the hang of driving a team," Matt said, trying to break the embarrassed silence. "You like to ride, Susannah?"

"What?" Georgiana's head snapped around. "What are you talking about?"

"Watch where you're going," he said patiently. "I thought Susannah might like to come for a ride, like Wilby did this morning?"

"Oh yes!" Susannah cried.

"But what about me?" Georgiana felt panicked at the thought of being left alone in the wagon. What if something happened? What if she couldn't control the oxen? Wilby was in the back! He might get hurt.

"Oh." Susannah completely misunderstood her. "I'm sure Mr. Slater can take you for a ride as well?" she suggested innocently. "When Wendell comes back?"

"No," Georgiana blurted. "I can't do this without help!"

"Of course you can," Matt said blithely. "If all those people can do it, you can do it." He waved a hand at the snaking line of wagons behind them.

She didn't know how to argue with that.

"We won't go far," Matt promised. And then he jumped off the wagon, mounted Pablo and took her daughter, leaving her all alone on the high seat of the wagon, reins and rod in hand.

All sense of peace and contentment fled now that everyone was out riding except for her. Well, her and Wilby. But he was happily cocooned in his quilt, and she was out here on this spine-jarring seat, sweating in the sun, her skin prickling in fear that she would lose control of the situation.

Although, she thought helplessly, as she watched Matt and Susannah galloping off into the dust cloud, it was possible that she'd already lost control of the situation.

❧ 20 ❧

"WHAT IS *THAT*?" Georgiana could barely speak for the shock. She hadn't slept well. Again. She'd wriggled out of the tent before dawn, planning to wash her face in the river and have a quiet moment or two alone before the children exploded out of the tent for the day. She'd been expecting to find the camp still sleeping. She hadn't been expecting *this*.

Standing in front of her tent was Matt Slater. And he wasn't alone.

"What are those?" Georgiana sputtered.

"Horses."

"I can see that."

Standing behind him was a veritable herd of paint horses. Their speckled white hides glowed in the wash of predawn light. One of them nudged Matt's arm impatiently.

She'd spent a sleepless night stewing over where he was. With his whore, she suspected, way down the back of the line. He'd disappeared yesterday and not come back for supper. Her mood had blackened by the minute, as she pictured him dining with Seline, and then following her into her tent. Georgiana had been prepared to freeze him with icy disdain when he returned.

But now here he was with a pack of horses.

"Why are they outside my tent?" Georgiana pushed her hair out of her face and pulled her shawl tighter. It was hard to maintain an icy disdain when she was a disheveled mess. But she tried.

He flushed. He looked both embarrassed and mighty pleased with himself. "They're for you." He held out the reins. "They were supposed to be a surprise."

The combination of lack of sleep, lack of coffee and shock made it hard to understand what was happening.

Horses.

"You bought me horses?" she said dumbly.

He nodded, still looking immensely pleased with himself. Behind him, the Indian ponies shifted restlessly. They were fine paints, speckled brown and white, with bright, curious eyes.

"You can't buy me horses!" Georgiana protested.

"Well, I did. I rode to Fort Leavenworth yesterday and got these. They ain't the fanciest, but they'll do. I picked up some tack as well. Just old stuff, but it'll do."

"I can't afford horses," Georgiana protested.

He frowned, confused. "They're already bought."

"I can't accept horses as a *gift*!"

"Why in hell not?" Now he was frowning in earnest. It clearly wasn't the reaction he'd been expecting.

"What will people think?" Georgiana said, turning red. She tried to calculate what the animals must have cost.

"They'll think you were my fiancée and I bought you horses."

"You don't understand," she said, trying to breathe calmly. "It just isn't done to give a lady such an expensive gift. It puts me in your debt."

"You're already in my debt. You got me to pretend to be engaged to you, remember?"

She blinked. She didn't really have a response to that one.

"You wanted to ride," he reminded her, thrusting the reins into her hands. He had a sulky face on now, like a chastened child.

"Wait!" she called, dashing after him as he left; he was clearly upset at her lack of pleasure. The ponies came along with her. "I'm sorry! I didn't mean to offend you. I was just . . . surprised." This meant he hadn't been with his whore, she realized suddenly. In fact . . . quite the opposite . . . this meant he'd been thinking about *Georgiana* the entire time he'd been gone . . . . "Please stop!"

He stopped. He could barely meet her eye.

She bit her lip. He looked very vulnerable, standing there

in the predawn light. Oh my. He must have ridden all night to surprise her, and she'd been such a churl.

"You got me horses," she said numbly, not knowing what else to say.

He shrugged, still not meeting her eye. "You wanted to ride. And I thought the children would be happier riding too. You don't have to keep them." He scratched at his stubbled jaw. "I ain't had much to do with ladies. I didn't mean nothing improper by it."

"No, of course not," she said quickly.

"If it makes things less awkward, you can just have a loan of them. You don't have to keep them. That way you won't be . . . what was it? In my debt?"

"As you said, I'm already in your debt," Georgiana said, "but yes, borrowing them might be better. It would be a terribly generous gift."

One of the horses whickered, as if in agreement.

Georgiana sighed. "We're always at such cross-purposes, aren't we, you and I? All I want is for us to be friends."

"We are," Matt said, giving her an exasperated look. "I just rode for miles to get you horses. I don't do that for people I don't call friends."

"You gave me *horses*!" It was just sinking in, what he'd done for her. "You went to Fort Leavenworth to get us *horses*." Her eyes filled with tears.

"Don't do that!" He looked horrified. "It was supposed to make you *happy*."

"It does!" It was the most thoughtful thing anyone had ever done for her. How she'd envied the children their rides with him . . . How she'd longed to be free of the wagon . . . How she'd looked at the wide-open spaces and the broad sky and imagined tearing along on a horse of her own. And he'd *known*.

Not only had he known, but he'd ridden miles out of his way to buy her a horse of her own.

"I went to get you one, but when I was there, I suddenly thought the children might be upset if you got to ride and they didn't . . ." he admitted. "And that little girl of yours has the making of a real horsewoman."

"She really does," Georgiana agreed, still trying to control her tears. "She loved riding, before we had to sell her pony."

"So I got you one each." He paused. "Except Wilby." He was looking guilty again. He cleared his throat. "And then I got worried that Wilby would get upset . . ."

"He probably will." Georgiana pulled a face. "But he gets upset about everything. He's just at that age."

"Well . . ." He was looking painfully guilty again.

"Well?"

"I might have got him something else. I just thought I'd best ask you about it before I gave it to him. Horses is one thing, but . . ."

"But what?"

"Wait here."

What on earth had he brought for Wilby? Georgiana watched as he jogged back to the chuck wagon, where his own horse was tethered. It was still too dark and the breaking light too watery for Georgiana to make out what he was doing.

When he came back, he had something cradled in his arms.

"You got him a puppy!"

It was a brindle and black ball of fuzz, with ears that flopped close to its head and markings above its eyes that made it look like it was frowning fiercely. Despite its adorable frown, it was shivering with delight as Georgiana petted it. It licked her hand enthusiastically, its fuzzy tail thumping against Matt's body.

"You don't mind?" Matt seemed concerned. "I thought it could keep him company in the wagon."

"I don't mind." She couldn't suppress the tears this time, and they rolled happily. "It's the sweetest thing anyone could ever do."

"It ain't pedigree, mind," he warned. "It's just a mutt."

"It's perfect! *You're* perfect!"

He seemed even more appalled by the praise than by her tears. He didn't know what to do with her thanks and suffered it with a disgruntled expression.

If he found her gratitude hard to take, he was positively bowled over by the children, who were beside themselves at the gifts. They could barely eat breakfast, they were so excited. They kept their animals close and helped Matt feed and water them and get them saddled up, chattering the whole time. The puppy's body was as long as Wilby's as he carried it about with him, its pink tongue lolling out of its mouth with joy.

"I'm calling my horse Hercules!" Philip announced.

"Mine's going to be Princess," Susannah said.

"That's the dumbest name ever. Besides, I think your horse is a boy." Phin was disgusted.

"Then he can be a boy Princess."

"That's a prince, stupid."

"Leave her alone," Georgiana ordered, "or I won't let you ride the horses today."

"I'm calling mine Eagle." Phin took no notice of her.

"And you thought Princess was dumb," Susannah said under her breath. Georgiana heard Matt stifle a laugh.

"And what are you calling your puppy, honey?" Georgiana asked Wilby.

"Woof!"

"That's right, puppies go 'woof.'"

"No! Woof!" He pointed at the puppy, which was crouched in front of him, barking excitedly.

"I think Wilby wins the dumbest name competition," Philip said.

"Your mother hasn't named hers yet," Matt protested. "How do you know hers won't be dumber?"

Georgiana pursed her lips. "Well, I like that."

"What *are* you calling your horse?"

"Wishes," Georgiana said quickly, before the boys could make any suggestions.

"If wishes were horses?" Matt laughed. His awkwardness had slowly given way to relief and then pleasure. He seemed to genuinely enjoy their happiness.

"She was. And she is," Georgiana replied gleefully. "My wish was a horse and here she is." Although, she thought ruefully, she might have wished for a sidesaddle too. She'd have to sew a pair of riding pants. Until then, she wasn't about to be bound to the wagon simply because she didn't own a pair. Instead, she begged to borrow a pair of Doc Barry's trousers off Mrs. Barry, with the promise she'd return them as soon as possible.

"Oh, don't rush," Mrs. Barry laughed. "This old pair barely buttons up anymore. I'm sure they'll fit again in another couple of weeks, after all this exertion, but for now he can't wear them."

Georgiana put them on under her skirts, and the moment the wagons were packed and Becky had charge of Wilby and Woof, she swung into the saddle. She didn't know who was giddier, herself or the children, as they rode out at the sound of the bugle.

"You all want to come and scout with me?" Matt asked them when they drew up alongside the chuck wagon. "You have to obey me, mind. No running off ahead."

"Ma, we should bring the rifle," Phin called. He was trying to kick Hercules into a gallop, but the paint was refusing to cooperate, staying close to its herd.

"I got docile animals," Matt confided to Georgiana as they drew ahead of the wagon train. "Yours is the only one with any real spirit. I thought that was safer."

It certainly was, considering the nature of her sons. They would have had their horses jumping canyons if it was up to them. As it was, they wouldn't stop hounding her for the rifle, so they could shoot at muskrats.

Georgiana ignored them, and after a while they hushed up and instead rode alongside the river, looking for beaver dams.

Susannah stayed with Matt and Georgiana as they forged ahead.

"What are we looking for?" Georgiana asked. My, but it felt good to move. The plains stretched before them, shining in the morning sun, without the patina of dust she was used to. The dust was behind them, with the train.

"We're going to find a place to cross the Big Blue," Matt told her. He was easy in the saddle and loose with his smiles. And, oh, that man could smile.

Georgiana kicked Wishes into a trot as she and the children followed Matt along the tributary of the Kansas River, looking for a place to cross.

THE HORSES MADE a world of difference. There was nothing in the world as good for the soul as riding free on the plains. The enormous arc of sky above them shone gold and blue during the morning, was streaked with pink and orange at dusk, and was stacked with billowing clouds when the rains blew

across the far horizon. It was the most gorgeous sight. The air
away from the train was fresh and clear, and spring warmed
around them into a glorious early summer. Georgiana and the
children blossomed as May passed into June and the train
passed deep into the plains. They worked harder than they'd
worked in their lives: herding animals, scouting trails, crossing rivers, pitching tents, gathering firewood, hunting, cooking, driving. Even Becky and the children learned to drive the
wagons, and soon they were all sharing the work. Only Wilby
escaped lightly, but even he was put to work shelling peas and
nuts and doing other menial work in the back of the wagon.
After an initial kickup, he seemed happy enough to stay occupied, especially when Woof was curled up beside him.

    There were places along the trail that were too beautiful to
be believed. There was Alcove Springs with its verdant growth
and rushing waterfall, where they spent a night and the children bathed under the silvery cold splashing of the falls. And
then after a month on the trail they reached the vast stretch of
land around the fork of the Platte, where grassland spread as
far as the eye could see. It brought to mind the encyclopedia
Georgiana's father had shown her when she was a child, with
its pictures of the wild plains of Africa. She half expected to
see a giraffe or an elephant lumber by. These plains were similarly wild and sunstruck, only in place of the giraffes and ele-
phants there were antelope and prairie dogs, coyotes, cougars,
buffalo and bears. Eagles soared overhead, and otters gamboled
in the streams and rivers. It was like nowhere Georgiana had
seen before. It was magnificent.

    The Platte itself was a silty expanse of muddy-looking wa-
ter, befouled in places by the buffalo.

    "Might as well take advantage," Matt said one afternoon,
when they saw a herd off on the horizon.

    The train paused for a day, and Matt had his entire group
form a giant circle with their wagons. The men went out hunting, and the women built large cook fires in an adjacent field
of grass. Phin and Flip (as Wilby now had everyone calling
Philip) yelled bloody murder when Matt and Georgiana
wouldn't let them go hunting with the men. They collected
buffalo chips for the fire with ill grace and grumbled the entire
day, as the women washed clothes in the river and prepared for

the night's feast. It was only when Matt let them help him with the butchery in the afternoon that they cheered up, and they returned with the buffalo steaks for their mother, covered in blood and feeling like men.

Georgiana tried not to laugh as they swaggered about the fire. Matt winked at her when he returned to find them lording it over their siblings. Susannah was utterly unimpressed. She'd spent the afternoon peeling potatoes and felt that she'd worked at least as hard as they had.

And that night, one month out of Independence, they feasted on roast buffalo and mixed with people from farther down the train. Jugs of whiskey and kegs of beer were rolled out, and people pulled out accordions and fiddles and guitars. The purple June night was luscious with the smell of grass and flowing water and roast meat, and a full golden moon hung heavy in the sky. It was a fine night to be alive, and their spirits were high.

After people had eaten their fill of the buffalo, there were puddings and cookies and pies. And the LeFoy girls sang while people danced. Georgiana danced with every man she knew, and many she didn't. She danced with Wendell Todd several times, even though he trod on her toes. She danced with gold miners and scouts, a reverend and an ex-army captain. But not Matt Slater, who didn't seem to care for dancing. He drifted around talking to people, but Georgiana didn't see him dance with a single person.

She was slightly tipsy from Mrs. Barry's rather intoxicating apple cider and found herself looking for him in the crowd. All of these other men were fine to dance with, but the only man she really wanted was Matt.

"He's over there," Della Barry said, winking at her. "Here"—she held out another nip of cider—"for courage." It hadn't escaped anyone's notice that Matt was friendly but not *too* friendly with his wife-to-be. "Good luck!" she called after Georgiana as she gathered her skirts and trotted off in Matt's direction.

"You haven't danced with me," Georgiana announced, barreling into him as he left one group and headed for another.

"I don't reckon you need me," he said dryly. "You seem to have plenty of men willing to dance with you."

"But I want to dance with *you*." Oh, her tongue was loose tonight.

"I don't dance," he said.

"Of course you do. Everybody dances."

"Not this body."

Georgiana frowned. "Don't they dance in Oregon?"

He was startled into a laugh. "Of course they do. I just never learned, that's all."

"What's to learn?" Georgiana pointed at the chaos. "This isn't like proper dancing. It's not like they're doing reels. Come on." She grabbed his hand and dragged him into the crowd. "Besides, no one's looking!"

But they were. A cheer went up as Matt and Georgiana entered the fray.

"Thought you'd never dance with her, Slater!"

Matt looked ready to bolt, but Georgiana kept a tight grip on him.

"Here." She put one of his hands on her waist and clasped the other one. "Now just move your feet." She gave him an encouraging smile. "See! You're doing it!"

Only, he wasn't really. He was really just standing still while she jerked him around. But then the song ended and a slower one started.

"This will be easier," she said, inching closer and tilting her head up to look at him. Oh my, he was a beautiful man. The moonlight cast the planes of his face into sharp relief, and his eyes were endless dark pools in the silvery night.

"This don't feel easier," he said huskily.

"Not even if I do this?" She stepped even closer. "Now you barely even need to move."

She could feel the heat radiating off his body. He smelled of soap and beer and apples. His hand was rough and warm and trembling in hers. His shirt was unbuttoned at the neck, and she could see swirls of dark hair. She remembered the sight of him standing in the bath at Mrs. Bulfinch's hotel, the way that hair trailed over a hard-packed stomach, down to . . .

"I'm scairt I'll tread on your toes," he said. His voice was tight. With nerves? With desire? Or both?

She herself was liquid with desire, but oddly, she didn't feel nervous in the least. In fact, the closer she got to him, the less nervous she felt. "Don't worry, my feet are so numb from Wendell stepping all over them that I doubt I'd even feel it."

His expression clouded at that. "You're getting along with him better now?"

"Better than expected. Thank you for that."

He looked startled. "Why thank me?"

"Because you obviously spoke to him. He's been nice as pie since you did."

Matt didn't respond to that, and they continued their awkward shuffling dance in silence. Georgiana noticed he didn't pull away when the music ended and another slow song started, so she took full advantage and crept all the way up to him, laying her head on his chest. He froze. Again. Just as he had back at the hotel that first night in the laundry. Georgiana could hear his heart thundering against her ear, but he didn't move away. In fact, he didn't move at all. So Georgiana stayed there and swayed to the music until she clumsily joined her. She could feel his hand pressing into her back and his legs bumping against hers. She closed her eyes and concentrated on the feel of him and the smell of him. While they danced, time fell away. There was no California and no Oregon, no Leonard and no children, nothing but her and Matt and this warm, heavenly feeling. Of being safe. Held. Treasured.

She wished the song would never end.

⋆ 21 ⋆

MATT DIDN'T KNOW what in hell was happening to him. It didn't matter where he went or what he was doing, all he could think about was Georgiana Bee Blunt. Or "Mrs. Smith," as everyone still called her, even though she wasn't hiding from Wendell and Kipp anymore. He was like a drunk, spending all day thinking about the next drink. He found himself seeking her out, even when he had better things to do. She made him act like he was someone else. Someone who lathered up and shaved every night. Someone who looked forward to riding with a pack of children. Someone who *danced*.

He must have danced with her a dozen times at the buffalo roast, and he didn't even dance.

He tried to keep well away from her the next day, but he didn't last even half an hour. He was supposed to be checking that everyone was getting ready for the river crossing, and technically, he was. It was just that he made the mistake of stopping by her wagon first . . . and he didn't manage to tear himself away until they'd removed all of the wheels and attached the buffalo hides for extra waterproofing; he found a way to hold her hands as she pulled the hides, catching her incredible blue eyes, seeing her smile. By then, he was running behind schedule.

The Platte wasn't a forgiving river at this time of year, and he couldn't afford to be distracted. But distracted he was. She and the children gave him multiple heart attacks as they navigated the rushing river. Georgiana was in her lead wagon with Wendell, Wilby and Susannah, while the twins were back with Becky and Kipp. This was the first crossing where he'd instructed people to remove their wagon wheels and to use their wagons as makeshift rafts, and he was tense as he watched their ox teams drag them across. Of course they got across safely, but not without him suffering a bad case of cold sweats and weak knees. What was *wrong* with him?

Deathrider had an opinion on that.

"You should marry her for real," the Indian said. He was finally well enough to ride for short periods and was out scouting the tablelands of the North Fork with Matt. He'd lost a lot of weight but was finally back to his cool, terrifyingly collected self.

"What are you talking about?"

Deathrider gave him a sideways look. "Your pretend fiancée. You should marry her for real."

"Have you been at Seb's moonshine?"

"It makes sense to marry her. She likes you, you like her; she's looking for a husband, you don't have a wife."

"That ain't something I mind."

"Maybe not. But you probably wouldn't mind having one either."

"You *have* been at his moonshine." Matt galloped ahead to get away from his talk of wives. Matt didn't want a wife. A wife wouldn't fit. He spent his life traveling, wandering across the country, captaining trains like this one.

But only because he had nothing better to do. Matt's grip tightened on the reins. It was true. He was only here because he had nowhere else to be, only traveling because he had nowhere to stop. Oh, he was welcome in his brother's home, but it was his *brother's* home, not his.

Why not build his own?

It had never really struck him as a possibility before.

Ah hell, it *wasn't* a possibility. He couldn't be taking on a woman and her pack of kids. He didn't know anything about children!

Except that they were strange and loud and often very funny.

And having them follow him around gave him an oddly pleasant feeling. A feeling of being needed.

"Parikitaru village ahead," Deathrider called, interrupting his thoughts.

Matt shook his head to clear it. They were ridiculous thoughts. They were also impossible to shake off. As he and Deathrider entered the Pawnee camp, Matt found his gaze drawn to the children, who stood watching the strangers with large eyes. He saw the earth dwellings, with their signs of comfortable daily family life. Stray images wandered into his mind of what daily life with Georgiana might look like. Perhaps they could build a house like his brother's in the wooded foothills close by Luke's property; the children could visit with Luke and Alex's girls; they could drive to church together; they could . . .

Hell. What was wrong with him?

Family life wasn't for him.

He wrenched his mind back to the moment and tried to focus while Deathrider greeted Red Eagle. The village chief was flanked by warriors, all bearing the mohawk that marked the tribe. Matt nodded to the men he knew and kept respectfully behind Deathrider, letting him speak for Matt's train.

"They're happy to do some trade," Deathrider told Matt as they left the village. Their next task was to find a place for the train to camp for the night. "But he worries our train is too large and that we'll cause trouble. I said we'd lead the wagons away from the village."

"Of course. We'll stay clear until we're farther upriver." Matt didn't blame them. The monster trains coming across the plains these last two seasons were full of rowdy gold-seeking men. They didn't behave the same way the settlers did. Not that the settlers always behaved well either.

"I said I would arrange a meeting place, so none of our people come to their village. I gave him our word." Deathrider fixed Matt with a cool stare.

"Your word is my word," Matt agreed. He'd have his scouts go down the line tonight and tell everyone firmly not to violate the agreement. He had no intention of antagonizing the Pawnee. He'd seen them in battle before, from a distance, against the Sioux and the Cheyenne, and he had no desire to see it up close.

He wondered if Georgiana would be interested in trading with them . . .

Ah hell, he was doing it again. He scowled and turned his mind to getting his job done for the day. And then he rewarded himself for not thinking about her for a few hours by taking her and the children to trade.

"These will be so warm to sleep in," Georgiana said with great satisfaction, as they rode back to camp with a great pile of soft buffalo robes. Matt had images of her naked body wrapped in the robe. He imagined sliding a hand through the opening of the robe and down her smooth, warm body.

"Just marry her," Deathrider sighed, when he found Matt riding hard in front of the train the next morning, galloping as though pursued by the devil himself.

"I can't."

"Of course you can."

"I can't. There's Wendell," Matt growled by way of explanation.

"You mean Wendy's threats back in Independence?" Deathrider shrugged. "So what if he knows who I am? Who's he going to tell out here? I'm well enough to look after myself again, and we're well clear of Independence. I'll be gone anyway once we hit Arapaho country. It's been too long since I've seen Two Bears." His gaze drifted to the horizon. Two Bears was his adopted father.

"You have a serious death wish," Matt snapped. "You realize if word gets out that you're still alive, you'll go right back to being a hunting trophy? Do you want all those gunslingers after you again? It's better if you stay dead." He had vivid memories of their nightmarish winter. "The last thing we want is Wendell spreading the word that you're alive."

Deathrider shrugged again. "They might not believe him, especially now all these people have accepted me as your brother. For all intents and purposes, I'm Tom Slater now. Besides, I hear that Archer woman is writing a book about the bloody slaughter of the Plague of the West. A book like that should spread word of my death quick enough." His expression turned grim. "And people do seem to accept those books as gospel truth."

"How do you know she's writing any such thing?" Sometimes Matt could throttle him. Why didn't he ever take the easy path? "For all you know, she'll write that you turned into a wolf and are roaming the plains, terrorizing emigrants with your supernatural powers."

That brought the ghost of a smile. "I heard it from Seline," Deathrider said. "The Archer woman was digging for stories."

Matt sighed. He could only imagine what that conversation had been like.

"Seline was nice enough to give her the blood and gore version of my death. Blood and gore sells, you know."

Matt rolled his eyes. Seline was causing him no end of trouble back there at the end of the train. Joe was about ready to cut the wagons of whores loose, and it took all Matt's diplomacy to keep him from doing it.

"I gave Seline a few dollars to keep spreading the word," Deathrider said, "and I promise to stay looking this white and go by another name, if you're worried about me. So don't be using me as an excuse not to marry the woman."

Marry the woman! Goddamn it. He wasn't the marrying type!

She wasn't even the type of woman he'd marry, he thought grumpily as they traveled on over the tablelands. If he got married, he'd marry a practical woman, not a china doll. He'd marry someone capable, honest, hardworking . . .

Only, as they traveled, she seemed less and less like a china doll. Her skin grew freckled from the sun, and her hands roughened up from work. She grew leaner from all the riding and walking, and she was always one of the first up in the morning and one of the last to sit down in the evening. When they had to lower the wagons down into Ash Hollow by rope, so they didn't careen down the steep hill, she was right there with the others, working the ropes. When they reached Courthouse Rock and Jail Rock, she climbed them with the children, looking off into the distance at the snow-topped Laramie Mountains with a proud grin on her face. She made friends with the other women and swapped recipes and chattered with them as they laundered clothes in the river. And she rode like a demon. He'd never seen a woman so capable in the saddle, nor one who loved it so much. She seemed a different person to the woman he'd met back in Independence. A much happier person.

"Just marry her, you idiot," Deathrider said one last time when he bid Matt farewell at Scotts Bluff. He was leaving them before they reached Fort Laramie. The army had taken over the fort in June to protect the swelling tide of emigrants from the Sioux, and Deathrider had no desire to mingle with army types. Matt had known he'd be off eventually but was surprised to receive a proper good-bye. It wasn't Deathrider's way to say farewells. Usually, he just slunk off in the night. Farther west, they called him the Ghost of the Trails, and he was a restless ghost, one who appeared and disappeared at will. But he and Matt had been through hell together, and a farewell seemed fitting. Also, he wanted to press his point one more time.

"You've no reason to torture yourself," Deathrider said. They were sitting at the base of the bluff, looking down at the campsite below. The cook fires sent threads of smoke into the indigo sky. "She's a good woman. And more beautiful than most. Some might see the children as a problem, but the way I see it, they show her to be fertile. And a decent mother." Deathrider regarded him curiously. "I don't understand what's holding you back. With your brother, I understood—he was too stupid to see what was in front of his eyes—but with you . . ."

Matt frowned. Below, he could see her tent glowing and shadows moving against the canvas.

"You haven't slept properly since you met her," Deathrider said. "You're about out of your mind with lust. But it's not just lust. Lust is an easy itch to scratch. You've got something worse than lust."

"It ain't your business," Matt warned him.

"No. Only you saved my life, Slater, and that makes us brothers. I want my brother to be happy." He rested a hand on Matt's shoulder as he stood. "The next stop is Fort Laramie. It would be a decent place to have a wedding." He began descending the slope toward his waiting animals. "I'll see you," he said. And then he melted away, as he had so many times before, and Matt was on his own for the first time in more than a year.

He'd grown used to the Indian being there. It was familiar. It reminded him of his childhood; like Deathrider, his brothers were quiet but constant presences, and, for all their difficulties, they had his back. Even when he was alone, he always knew he wasn't really alone. If he was in trouble, all he had to do was send for one of his brothers.

Not like her. He watched the shadows dance in Georgiana's

tent. She was genuinely alone, with no one to call on for help. And she handled it with nerve, he thought admiringly. She'd come out on this journey, knowing nothing about the trail, completely unprepared for the hardship, but she hadn't buckled. She'd risen to the challenge, and every day she got stronger and . . . happier. More resilient.

Which was saying something, as by this point, one-third of the way into the journey, most people on the train were exhausted. The animals were tired, and the people were looking grim. He let them stop at monuments like Scotts Bluff along the way to give them a chance to rest their sore feet and recharge their spirits, but it had been a long couple of months, and their spirits weren't looking much higher tonight. Georgiana's experience seemed the opposite, Matt thought. At the beginning of the trail, she'd started out exhausted, as her new daily workload had hit her like a ton of bricks. She'd half crippled herself walking, and she was cranky and out of sorts. And then she'd settled into it. She'd stretched. She'd grown.

Not only did she accept her new roles, she seemed to thrive. To come to life.

So perhaps she wasn't the china doll he'd thought she was.

But that didn't mean that he *knew* her. There were things about her that bothered him. Secrets. Things the children almost said; things Georgiana stopped them from saying.

Marry her . . .

It was a mad thought. And yet . . .

There was no doubt that Matt wanted to bed her. He'd wanted her from the moment he saw her. But *marry* her. That was a big step, and he wasn't a man to make hasty decisions. Laramie was too soon to be making a decision that big.

And what was the rush? It wasn't like she was going anywhere. For all of Wendell's clumsy attempts at courtship, Georgiana was in no danger of being wooed on that front. Matt had a good long while to get to know her and the children better before he made up his mind.

Hell. Look at him. He was seriously considering it. *Him.* Matt Slater! The most unmarrying man he knew.

He grunted and got to his feet. Well, considering wasn't doing.

What he'd *do* was have a look at this idea from every angle.

What did marriage have to offer him? And why marry this one and not another?

And if he *did* marry her, what kind of secrets were hidden in her past? Was there anything that would come back to haunt him?

He knew how he was going to start finding out about that one, at least.

❧ 22 ❧

"LEO'S MY BROTHER," Susannah said as she helped him give the horses a scrub down when they arrived in Laramie.

They'd set up camp in the shadow of the adobe fort. The grounds around the river were lousy with emigrants and covered wagons. The last time Matt had been through, the army hadn't taken control yet and it had been a run-down trading camp. There had been tepees on the far bank, occupied last year by the Arapaho, but sometimes the Cheyenne passed through, as did the Sioux. There were no tepees to be seen this year though, and the place had a different feel. More regimented.

Matt's party had cheered at the sight of it. It was the closest thing they'd seen to civilization in six weeks or more. The trading post was still working, and the emigrants streamed in, looking especially for treats: tobacco and whiskey, rock candy and scented soap. There were even tin tubs to rent, which were busy at all hours.

"Is Leo your older brother?" Matt prodded. He kept his head down and his voice casual. Susannah had proven to be a fountain of information, as had her brothers.

"He's the eldest," Susannah said. "We don't talk about him much anymore. It upsets Mother too much."

Matt had gathered that much already. He remembered Georgiana crying over the map back in Independence. "I bet you miss him." He passed her a currying brush. She liked to make her horse pretty. While she fussed over Princess (who really should have been called Prince, but who was he to judge), Matt sorted the boys' horses for them. Even the hardy Indian ponies were thinner and tired looking. Pablo and Fernando looked weary too. He gave Fernando an ear scratch on the way past, and the donkey *hawed*.

"Rest up," he told Pablo. "We'll be here awhile." Like him, his animals had barely rested in the last year and were looking a little worse for wear. Luckily, they'd have a few days to rest.

There was work to be done here in Laramie: they needed to refit the iron tires to the wagon wheels, which had shrunken until the tires clattered off; they had to reshoe the oxen, whose hooves had split; and they needed to wash clothes and bedding, and to restock and prepare for the next part of the journey, which would include the blistering heat of July, the storms of the High Plains, and the desolation of the Lava Lands. While they worked, the horses and draught animals could gather their strength and enjoy the pastures.

"Leo was nicer than the twins," Susannah confided as she brushed Princess. "He was more like a grown up."

"And your father took him to California?"

"Yes, the last time he was back. That was more than two years ago."

Matt did the math. "Before Wilby was born." After a couple of days of talking to the children, he was forming a pretty clear picture of their father. Leonard Blunt was a phantom presence in their lives, a visitor who appeared seemingly at random, who didn't remember their birthdays, but who descended with gifts and tales of adventure in far-flung lands. The twins resented it bitterly that he had taken Leo with him and not them, while Susannah longed for the father she barely knew. A man who, apparently, got her name wrong in his letters.

"He wrote them in a rush," Susannah said, turning her back so Matt couldn't see her expression, but he could hear the hurt in her voice.

"I imagine so," Matt agreed. "It's the only way anyone could misspell such a pretty name. And the frontier is a mighty busy place."

She gave him a shy smile. He didn't want to hurt her further, so he dropped the topic and talked about horses instead, describing his brother's horse farm back home. He had a feeling Susannah would love Luke's horses.

After they'd finished with the animals, he left Susannah

crooning to her horse and hunted the twins down. He took them out with their new slingshots, which the Colicut boys had helped them make. They were hoping to shoot down a prairie dog or two, but Matt didn't fancy their chances. They were terrible shots.

After a while, he'd managed to turn the conversation to their father. "Why did he take Leo and not the rest of you?"

"Pffft." Phin made a disgusted noise. "He should have taken *us*. Leo didn't even want to go. We did."

"I can't work out why he took only one of you," Matt said, watching as they hunted for projectiles. "Why not take everyone?"

The twins exchanged a cagey look.

"She doesn't think we know," Phin admitted, "but we read all the letters."

"And we heard them arguing," Flip added.

"She doesn't think you know what?"

Flip loaded a stone into his slingshot. He sized Matt up, squinting at him. "The thing you need to know about our father," he said slowly, "is that he's not a very nice man."

Matt tried to keep his expression even. He'd gathered that much on his own, but it was a shock to hear Flip say it so baldly.

"Let's be frank," Phin said, firing at a boulder. "He's a bit of an ass." The stone fell well short of the boulder.

Trust the twins to be blunt. They were clearly as hurt as Susannah, but rather than welling with tears, they smoldered with rage. Unlike their sister, they were in no mind to protect themselves or Matt from the hard truth.

"Mother cut him off," Phin told Matt, snapping off another rock. This one flew wide, sending up a puff of dust as it hit the ground.

"Cut him off?" Matt gathered rocks and tossed them into a small pile between the twins.

"All our money was Mother's," Flip explained. He was more patient than his brother. He'd discarded his first missile and was crouched down, sifting through the rocks until he found one he liked. Matt's bet was that he'd hit the target first.

"That's why he married her," Phin said. His next rock went sailing past the boulder he was aiming at. "Just like all those men back in Independence were trying to marry her for her gold." He looked disgusted.

"She told me there wasn't any gold."

"There isn't." Phin snatched up another rock.

"Well, there is," Flip said calmly, putting his chosen projectile in the hammock of the sling. "But we have to give it away to get Leo back."

Matt's fingers clenched around the rock he'd just picked up. "What?"

Flip stood up and sighed. "It's a long story." He tossed his head to get his hair out of his eyes and met Matt's gaze. "She really hasn't told you any of this? I mean, you're marrying her."

"We're still getting to know each other," Matt said carefully.

Phin made another disgusted noise. "The whole point of getting you was so you could help us get Leo back."

Flip rolled his eyes. "Not exactly. Mother wanted someone to protect us while *she* went to get Leo."

"I *told* her she should have advertised for a bounty hunter instead of a husband." The ground around the boulder was exploding in puffs of dust as Phin hammered away at it. Not a single shot hit the boulder itself. Matt felt a pang of sympathy. The kid was racked with anger. Hurt. Fear. "At the very least," Phin continued, "she should have kept that line I wanted: *skills with firearms a must.*"

"Matt's good with guns," Flip said. "I've seen him bring down a deer from the back of a moving horse." He was as unruffled as his brother was ruffled, but Matt bet that beneath that smooth exterior were all the same feelings Phin had. There was something about the slightly bitter edge to his voice that gave it away.

"We got lucky," Phin said stubbornly. "It certainly didn't say anything about shooting in the ad."

"Good thing too." Matt tossed him a stone. "Or you would have had a hotel full of gunslingers looking to take your ma's gold. She might have ended up murdered." He watched as the kid shot wild again. He'd let him get the rage out of his system for a bit, and then he'd show him how to shoot the thing properly.

Flip, meanwhile, was lining up to take his first shot. He adjusted his stance and tested the slingshot, pulling it back a few times until it brushed his cheek. When he fired, the shot missed, but not by as much as his brother's did.

"You were asking why Father took Leo," he said calmly as he reached for another stone. "It was because Mother cut him off. We kept getting creditors coming to the door and bills in the post, and she was worried, so when he came back last time, she said she wouldn't be allowing him access to her bank account anymore, not unless he stayed in New York or took us with him."

Her bank account. Matt thoughtfully tossed a stone. "You Leavington Fairchild Bees are worth some money, huh?"

"*Were* worth some money," Phin said, grabbing the biggest stone he could find. "Before Leonard spent it all."

"You call him Leonard?"

"Phin does." Flip rolled his eyes again. "Ever since he left without us."

"He promised he'd take us!" Phin snapped.

"Since when did he ever keep his promises?"

When his next shot missed, Phin looked about ready to throw his entire slingshot at the boulder. Matt figured it was about time to step in.

"Here," he said, reaching over and plucking the slingshot from the boy's hand. "Try it this way." He encouraged Flip to keep talking as he showed them how to maintain the same position for each shot, so they could gauge the temperament of their weapons and adjust for their slingshot's idiosyncrasies.

"They had a huge fight last time he was back. It must have lasted four or five days. He called her every name under the sun, really filthy ones, but she wasn't going to budge."

Matt winced. He couldn't believe anyone could yell at Georgiana, and in front of her children. How had she not dissolved in tears? She must have been pretty angry.

"When that didn't work, he tried to charm her," Phin sneered. "He brought her flowers and acted like a total fool."

Which might explain Wilby's conception, Matt thought dryly. He felt a stab in his gut at the thought.

"She didn't give in though," Flip said. "She said it would take more than a bunch of flowers to mend a broken bridge."

Good for her. But he imagined finding herself pregnant with Wilby had built a bridge pretty quick.

"And when the flowers didn't work, that's when he said he'd take us all west with him," Phin growled.

Matt helped him adjust his aim. The boy fired and the shot grazed the edge of the boulder.

"Nice work!" Matt grinned at him. The kid looked brighter and grabbed another rock. "But why didn't he take you all with him?"

"He said it was too dangerous." That bitterness was back in Flip's voice. "He said he'd just need an advance and that he'd go ahead to buy us some land. That he'd be back for us in a couple of years, once he'd set us up in California."

"And your ma didn't like that, I bet."

Flip had been watching Matt help Phin, and he copied the instructions. His next shot grazed the boulder too. "No, she most certainly didn't."

"But he talked her around? And he and Leo went to get you all set up?"

"Not exactly."

The twins exchanged another cagey look. Matt's instincts told him there was something they were trying to hold back. He would have to approach this carefully.

"Listen," he said, putting a hand on each of their shoulders, "we're all men here."

They liked that. He could see them straightening up.

"It's important for men to talk straight amongst themselves," he said, as he met their gazes in turn. "Whatever you tell me stays between us. Shake on it?" He took his hand off Phin's shoulder and spat in his palm for good measure before offering it to the boys.

They liked that even more. Both hurriedly spat in their palms and shook his hand.

"I won't tell your ma. I won't tell anyone," Matt promised, "but you've just committed to always talking straight to me. You tell me the truth, and I'll be straight with you in return."

They exchanged another look and then took a deep breath.

"The thing is," Flip confessed, "it's our fault."

"What's your fault?"

"We gave him the key to the safe." They hung their heads.

"Go on."

They looked up. They'd clearly been expecting Matt to tear a strip off them, but he did no such thing. "Go on," he urged.

"He said he'd take us with him," Flip said glumly, "but that we couldn't go without money."

"He said we'd come back in two years to get Ma and the others, and we'd be heroes."

"We were going to help him build her a big white house in California."

"And give her a gold nugget the size of her head to repay the money we borrowed."

Matt nodded thoughtfully, careful to keep his expression neutral. "So you helped him get the money?"

They nodded, looking miserable.

"Not just the money," Flip admitted. "He took most of her jewels too. They were the thing she cried about the most."

"Especially the things Grandma Bee had left her." Phin's voice was tight. He looked on the verge of tears. "She cried a lot about those."

"Especially the diamond bee pin."

"And Leo helped you?"

They gave him a disdainful look. "Of course not. Leo's too much of a goody-goody. He would have told on us in a heart-beat if he knew what we were up to."

So Leo was more like his sister than like the twins. That was good to know. He didn't know that he could handle more boys like the twins. They were a good handful or two on their own, and Wilby looked set to follow in their footsteps; three wild boys was enough for a man to take on. Especially when he had no previous experience with little 'uns.

"Leo was no part of it," Phin said angrily. "He had no right to take our place like he did."

"I don't think he had a choice in it," Flip disagreed. "I can't imagine he would have left Mother willingly. They were close," he told Matt.

"He was a total mommy's boy," Phin said, rolling his eyes at Matt.

Judging from what he'd heard about Leo from Susannah, Matt didn't imagine Leo was a mommy's boy so much as a boy who was trying to look out for his mother; Leo seemed to have spent his life trying to fill the role of man of the family, even though he was only a child.

Just like Matt's brother Luke.

Luke had assumed care of Tom and Matt when their father died on the trail up to Oregon, even though at the time Luke could barely grow the faintest wisp of a mustache. It must have been hard, Matt realized, as he looked down at the two dark-haired devils in front of him. Funny, he'd never given it much thought before. Luke had always been a bossy, domineering, disapproving presence in Matt's life, so much so that Matt had never stopped to consider what it must have been like for him.

Hell. Imagine being saddled with two young boys when you were still a boy yourself. Imagine having to haul them along the trail, grieving for two parents lost within as many years; imagine having to find land and build a home. He remembered the three of them struggling to build that first leaky, smoky hut, not having the slightest clue what they were doing. He remembered giving Luke hell as they worked. He'd been a wildcat when he was a kid. Not unlike these two here.

It was only now that he was dealing with children on a day-to-day basis that he truly understood what his brother had done for him. How he'd sacrificed. And also cared.

Goddamn it. What was *wrong* with him? Now he was getting all sappy, and about Luke of all people!

"Father told us to pack our bags and that he'd come get us in the morning and we'd sneak out before the rest of them got up," Flip was saying.

"But when we got up, they were *gone*."

"And he'd left her a note, saying that if she cut him off, she'd be cutting Leo off too."

Hell and damnation. What a piece of work. He'd kidnapped his own *son*.

"She cried about that more than she cried about the bee pin," Flip said despondently.

Matt rested his hands on their shoulders again. "Thank you for telling me the truth."

"There's more."

Matt almost groaned. More? That poor woman.

"We got letters, telling us about the big white house and the gold claim . . ."

"And they all included notes."

"Notes?" Matt asked.

"Promissory notes. They all said, 'Pay to the order of,' and gave her instructions who to pay."

"And then we ran out of money and had to start selling the furniture to pay them."

"And when the furniture was gone, we had to sell the house," Flip said in a small voice. "It was the house Mother grew up in."

"She didn't cry that time," Phin said grimly. "She went all white and silent and didn't talk again for a couple of weeks."

"How did your father die?" Matt was almost afraid to ask. He had a feeling the selfish dog had met a bad end, borrowing from someone he shouldn't have.

"Fever."

"We found out when the debt collectors came. Someone brought a newspaper clipping with the obituary."

The rest of the story wasn't too much of a surprise. What else was going to happen when a twelve-year-old boy was left alone on a big gold claim? He fell prey to men like Wendell and Kipp, and whoever it was they were working with. The twins were more than happy to tell him all they knew.

"Apparently, the claim is in Mother's name now," Flip told Matt, "otherwise they'd just take it."

Indeed. And they probably would have killed Leo to get it.

If they needed to get the land signed over by some soft eastern widow, what better bargaining chip than her firstborn son? She was an easy target.

But now Wendell had it in his head to marry her . . . Was he trying to swipe the claim out from under the others? Because that would be a nice, tight, legal way to do it . . . Was he offering Kipp a half claim for going along with it?

Oh, who even cared? Wendell was never going to marry her, and that was the end of it.

But what would he do if *Matt* married her?

Matt had no interest in a gold claim. Money had never meant jack to him, and he couldn't see the appeal of living in one of those hellholes, sifting in streams or sinking a shaft down into the dark. He was plenty happy back in Oregon.

According to the twins, Georgiana had every intention of

signing the claim over without protest and taking her children off to live a quiet life. Although the madwoman seemed to think she could stay in the same town. She had some idea about keeping the plot of land her useless husband had bought on the main street of Mokelumne Hill and building a mercantile business. Matt didn't think she had any idea what those mining towns were like, or the kind of men she was dealing with. Or how damn pretty she was.

Not that it mattered, because if he married her, she'd be coming back to Oregon with him. Maybe he could convince Wendell that they didn't care about the gold claim and would just quietly take the boy and go? Maybe Wendell would escort them to his cronies and they could do the deal and leave?

But that wouldn't work if Wendell wanted the claim for himself. Or if he had feelings for Georgiana. He might just get shooting mad if Matt married her out from under him. Matt remembered the pistol pressed into his belly back at Mrs. Bulfinch's.

Why did everything always have to be complicated? Why couldn't he just meet a nice girl, fall in love and get married? Like his brother.

Well, maybe not like his brother. That had been plenty complicated.

Matt sighed. Ah well, it was what it was. Besides, he hadn't decided yet whether he was marrying her or not.

"**N**o!" OF COURSE she wouldn't marry him! What was the man thinking! Georgiana kept right on walking, aware that he was following her.

"I'll just keep asking till you say yes."

"You'll die asking, then," she said, exasperated.

Alistair Dugard had taken her by complete surprise. She wasn't aware he'd joined Joe Sampson's party. Apparently, he'd missed the roll out back in Independence—Georgiana didn't bother to ask why—and he'd only caught up with them again in Laramie.

"I've been working my way up the line, looking for you," he'd said when he found her. He seemed to expect her to be charmed by his attentions. She wasn't.

"I'm engaged," she told him shortly.

"Engagements can be broken."

She rolled her eyes. He was relentless. He was also pristine, his shirt as white as snow and his hair as shiny as oil. She had no idea how he looked so neat. She was spattered with mud and smelled like a cook fire; her hair was such a deplorable tangle that she'd taken to just bundling it up in a corkscrew ball and hoping for the best.

He followed along, trying his very best to win her attention, but she was too busy hunting for the twins. They'd taken to scavenging back along the trail for discarded belongings. Since they'd left Laramie, people were lightening their loads; the animals were tired, and the wagons kept getting bogged in when it rained; the heavier the wagons were, the deeper they sank, and the harder they were to dig out. And it rained a lot. Great storms swept through, complete with sky-splitting bolts of lightning and rolling claps of thunder. Curtains of rain shaded the horizon, and they watched sheets of it marching toward them over the grasslands. The wind blew unhampered by trees or shrubs, a vicious whipping force that hit them head-on and slowed their already slow progress. This leg of the journey, the weary middle third, was the hardest on their bodies and their spirits. Tired, the emigrants threw out anything they didn't absolutely need; in their wake, the trail out from Laramie was littered with trunks and tools, oak furniture and iron stoves, pots and pans. The twins had a great time scavenging, returning with "treasures" Georgiana didn't want or need.

She'd been out looking for them when she'd stumbled straight into Dugard, who now wouldn't leave her alone. He stayed with her as she rounded the twins up. They were trying to convince her to help them carry a heavy iron stove. The whole time she was arguing with the boys, Dugard acted like they were at a garden party. As she struggled back to their camp through the sloppy mud, with the twins in tow but not the stove, Dugard peppered her with small talk. She felt like lobbing a ball of mud at him.

"Would you like to take a walk along the stream?" he asked once she'd deposited the twins back at the camp. "It looks to be a lovely evening."

Georgiana stared at him incredulously. Who had time for a walk? She still had to set up the tent and start soaking the beans for tomorrow night's dinner. Not to mention that she needed to pack the buffalo jerky away properly. "I have work to do," she said tersely.

He still didn't leave. In fact, he moved right into camp and made himself such an imposition that Mrs. Barry was forced to invite him to dinner. It was too rude not to, as he was clearly in no mind to leave. He sat himself down next to Georgiana, not seeming to notice that she didn't want him to. Wendell was scowling at them from across the fire. Georgiana wished Matt was around to discourage Dugard, but he and Doc Barry were at another campsite, dealing with an outbreak of illness caused by bad drinking water. Without Matt around, Dugard made himself quite at home, staying until Georgiana could bear it no longer and retired to her tent.

The next day brought no relief. He was back bright and early, edging his wagon up alongside hers.

"What do you think you're doing?" Matt growled, riding up. Georgiana had never been so happy to see him. No, that was a lie. She was always happy to see him. "You ain't in my party," he told Dugard.

"We're all one party till Fort Hall," Dugard said heartily.

"No, we ain't." Matt clicked his fingers and pointed at the rear of the train. "Off you go, back to Joe. We cain't have you all mixing around or people'll get lost."

Dugard tried to argue, but he was no match for Matt. Georgiana relaxed as Dugard was bludgeoned into turning aside while Matt's party rolled out. But she was wrong if she thought Dugard would be that easily discouraged. He came ambling into the light of their cook fire that night and the next night and many nights afterward. He didn't seem to care in the least that Matt was there. The worst thing about him was that he got Wendell all worked up again. Just when she thought Wendell might have gone off the idea of marrying her, Dugard came along and got Wendell competitive. If Dugard sat next to her, Wendell sat on the other side; if Dugard helped her haul water, Wendell got a bucket and hauled water right alongside him; if Dugard offered her a mug of coffee, Wendell got her a bigger one.

What was *wrong* with these men? She was engaged!

Or at least she was as far as they knew.

It got so ridiculous, people started making jokes about it. Doc Barry and Seb took to calling Dugard and Wendell "Right" and "Left."

"Where's Mrs. Smith's Right-Hand Man today?"

"Chasing off after Left."

The twins exploited the situation mercilessly, slowly out-sourcing their chores to their mother's aggressive suitors. They also convinced the two men to take them hunting. Georgiana overheard them when she was up in the wagon trying to get the flour out.

"Mother wants some meat for the stew," Phin was ordering them, sounding officious. Well, that was a bald-faced lie, she thought sourly. "She wants you to take us out to see what we can shoot for the pot."

Oh good Lord! They'd do anything to get at the guns.

"No guns!" she shouted, sticking her head out the back of the wagon.

The twins glowered. They hadn't realized she was up there.

"I'll shoot you something," Wendell said eagerly.

"Good idea," Dugard agreed. "You take the boys, and I'll stay here and help Mrs. Smith."

Oh no, no, no. Georgiana had endured quite enough of Mr. Dugard. "You should both take them," she said quickly, "but no guns! They can use their slingshots."

The twins looked marginally happier about that. She felt immeasurable relief as she watched them set out on foot. That was Right and Left out of her way for a while. The grasses were several feet high, and they disappeared into them, only the top of Dugard's hat visible as they went looking for small game.

They wouldn't be gone long, Georgiana imagined. Thunderheads were massing on the horizon, giant purple monoliths that flickered with lightning. She shivered. She didn't much care for the storms out here. They were loud and violent, and she didn't feel the slightest bit safe in the tents. Distant thunder rumbled. She'd best be quick making these biscuits for the morning or she'd be making them in the rain.

"You need help with that?"

Matt took her by surprise. He'd kept his distance since Dugard had appeared, although she often caught him watching her. She hadn't realized he was back from his rounds.

"Thank you." This was one man she *was* happy to get help from. She handed over the flour and her cooking utensils. Then, to her surprise, he put them down and reached up to swing her down from the wagon. He *never* touched her. Not that she was complaining. The feel of his hands on her waist made her weak all over.

He walked her back to the fire. She expected him to leave, as he was usually busy beyond belief in the evenings, but he didn't. Instead, he helped her make the biscuits.

"You seem to have a third hand," Della Barry teased when Matt went to fetch water for her. They'd made camp a fair distance from the river today, and it was a bit of a hike.

"Matt might count as two hands," Sarah Colicut giggled.

Georgiana blushed.

"Take advantage of it," Della laughed. "I wish I had more hands!"

While Matt was gone, Georgiana quickly pinned up her stray curls. She didn't know why she bothered, as she must look a complete fright, hair mussed or not.

"I reckon we're in for a big one tonight," Matt said when he returned with the water. He poured it into a pitcher for her, so she could make her dough.

See? What was the point in fixing her hair? He hadn't so much as looked at her since he got back. He rolled up his sleeves and went to work on the dough for her, his big hands making shorter work of it than hers ever did.

"The storm, you mean?" Della asked, squinting at the horizon, where the thunderheads had gone from purple to a horrifying black. They'd assumed a surreal shape Georgiana had never seen before, stacked on top of one another in cylinders, each one wider than the last. The thunder was still a long way off, but even so, the ground rumbled. The air was perfectly still, without a breath of wind. The animals shifted skittishly in their makeshift paddock in the middle of the circled wagons. Georgiana and Della exchanged nervous looks. They felt very exposed out here on the plains.

Matt finished kneading the dough and scraped the last scraps of it off his hands. "We might empty the wagons out now. We can put the barrels and other bits and pieces in the tents and sleep in the wagons tonight. Might be best to be up off the ground."

Georgiana glanced nervously back at the approaching storm and then checked to see that Wilby and Susannah were safe. They were. Susannah was sitting reading a book, and Wilby was playing with Woof. "The boys are off hunting."

"I'll get them back," Matt said. "We still have plenty of time. That's a slow-moving storm right there. Slow but serious. I've got Seb and the scouts spreading the news and helping people make sure their goods are covered and their tents firmly pegged. You finish the biscuits, and maybe if you could all plan for dinner to be eaten in the wagons? Pack yourselves a picnic."

The women nodded anxiously.

"Put your empty containers and buckets on your wagon seats, to catch the rain. We might as well have fresh drinking water." He winked at them.

They laughed nervously. The water from the Platte was so foul with alkali dust that they had to stir in cornstarch to purify it, so they'd taken to leaving buckets out overnight, in case it rained. It certainly looked like it was about to rain now.

"Are we in for a tornado?" Sarah asked shakily.

A tornado! Georgiana looked at the towering odd-shaped clouds with new eyes. Her guidebook had said there might be tornadoes on the plains in summer, but she'd treated it as a pretty big "might." Until now.

"Cain't tell yet," Matt said. "Let's hope it passes and makes landfall somewhere else." He was so calm. As he reeled off instructions, a group gathered to listen. The light had a sickly glow to it now. Georgiana's heart was thundering in her ears. How could a scrap of canvas and wood protect them from a tornado?

"I'll get the boys, and we'll start moving things into your tent," he said, taking Georgiana by the arm when he was finished with the group. They'd scattered to start preparing for the storm. "Do you know where Becky and Kipp are?"

"I think Becky might have gone to find LeFoy again." Georgiana bit her lip. "I don't know about Kipp."

"I might have some idea where he is," Matt sighed. "I'll hunt them down after we get things in order here."

"I don't know how we're all going to fit in the wagons," Georgiana fretted as she and Della hurried about their tasks.

"We can take someone in our wagon," Della offered. "Becky maybe? I'm sure the children will want to be with you, and then the men can have your second wagon."

Georgiana accepted her offer gratefully and rushed to pack food they could eat in the wagon. She rolled up her sleeves and, with Susannah's help, managed to empty their lead wagon of the smaller barrels and tools. By the time Wendell and Dugard and the boys trailed back, she was tackling the second wagon.

"You and Kipp will need to manage the big barrels," she told Wendell, "but leave the sacks and anything that isn't waterproofed. We'll have to sleep around them."

"I'll help you," Dugard said.

"Oh no, you won't." Matt had Dugard's horse ready and waiting for him. "You'll get back to your wagon and worry about your own business." He didn't wait for Dugard to protest but tossed him the reins. "Come on, I'll escort you."

"Kipp . . ." Wendell said.

"I'll get him."

"He—"

"I know where he is." Matt cut him off. "He's where he is most nights, at the back of the train with the rest of the troublemakers."

Georgiana frowned. Where? And then she realized what was at the back of the train. The whores. She blanched.

Wait a minute. How did Matt know Kipp was there most nights? She watched Matt escort Dugard down the line, feeling sick and angry. She was such a fool. She'd actually thought he'd stopped going to see the whore.

"Hey, Ma, catch this!"

She jumped back as Phin and Flip rolled a barrel out the back of the wagon. It crashed to the ground.

"Watch your feet," Flip said belatedly.

"If you've broken that, you'll be up for a whipping!" Wendell snapped at them.

"I beg your pardon?" Georgiana stepped in front of him as he made for the twins.

"Those two need some serious discipline," Wendell warned her, "especially after the stunt they pulled out there!"

"What stunt?" Georgiana turned narrowed eyes on her twins.

They ducked back into the wagon. "Storm's coming!" they yelled. "We can talk about this later."

"What did they do?" Georgiana asked grimly, suspecting she already had an idea.

"They took Dugard's pistol right out of his holster," Wendell snapped, "and damn near shot Matt's head off when he came riding up."

"We were shooting at a pheasant!" came a disgruntled voice from behind the canvas of the wagon. "We didn't know Matt was there."

"There ain't no damn pheasants out here!"

Georgiana just about had to hold Wendell back. He looked about to launch himself into the wagon after the twins. "The storm's coming," she said tightly. As if to punctuate her words, a stiff wind skittered through the camp. It carried the sharp smell of rain and something else . . . the smell of lightning. "This can wait until we've got everything secured."

With great effort, Wendell restrained himself and gave a jerky nod. "Those two need a man's hand," he growled as he left to empty the lead wagon.

"Who does he think he is?" Phin complained, emerging from the wagon and dropping to the ground. "He's not our father."

"Even if he wants to be." Flip dropped down after him and poked at the barrel. "It ain't even broken."

"Isn't," Georgiana corrected. "It *isn't* even broken." She put her hands on her hips. "You roll that over to the tent and store it. I'll be talking to you about the gun later."

They didn't look too concerned. Georgiana would have to see about remedying that. She'd tackle them tonight, when they were trapped in the wagon with her.

"Mother, what about Princess? She doesn't fit in the wagon!" Susannah was beside herself with fear for her horse as the winds picked up. The tall grasses were rippling like a choppy sea, and they could hear the nervous whinnying of horses and the lowing of the cattle.

"Princess will be fine, darling. Horses belong in the wild."

"No!" Wilby was outraged and wrapped his arms around Woof, who was barking at the stiffening winds.

"Woof's not a horse, Wilby," Georgiana sighed. "He can hop into the wagon with us. Now, both of you keep out of the way while the big people get organized."

She and Wendell worked quickly and had most of the barrels stored by the time Kipp rode up.

"Where's Matt?" She couldn't quite keep the sharpness out of her voice. Was he still back there with the whore?

Kipp shrugged. He didn't care.

"Can you organize the animals?" she asked him.

"Don't tie them up," Seb called as he hurried by. "Leave 'em loose so they can run if they need to."

Susannah moaned. "What does that mean?"

Georgiana gave her a hug but couldn't reassure her more than that. Who knew what would happen to the horses tonight?

By the time they were organized, the thunderheads were
rolling overhead in towering spongy masses, and the wind
carried the first sprinkle of rain. The light was eerie, the colors
of a yellowing bruise, and lightning stabbed in the hearts of
the clouds above. The thunder was still distant, cracking and
rolling but making the earth shudder beneath their feet, even
from afar.

Georgiana piled their bedding into the back of the wagon,
using the buffalo hides as mattresses. Even with the trunks and
barrels cleared away, it was cramped, as the dry goods were
still in there, the sacks lining the edges of the wagon like bal-
last. Georgiana left the children to go and fetch the kettle and
to help damp the fire down, and when she returned, the twins
had built a wall down the middle of the wagon with the sacks
of sugar and flour. They'd set themselves up on the other side
of it, and Wilby was throwing himself at it and wailing.

"Let him in," Georgiana ordered.

"He can build his own room if he wants one."

Georgiana bent over the wall into their "room" and glared
at them. "I really don't think you want to be lippy with me after your behavior with the gun earlier."

"Flip!" Wilby railed, hitting his chubby fist against the
wall. She lifted him over and deposited him on their quilts
with them. She could see the canvas hadn't been drawn tight
over the front entrance. The wind was hitting the side of the
wagon at the moment, causing the canvas to push hard against
the hickory ribs of the frame, but if it swung around, the wind
would gust through the open front of the wagon like a demon.
The boys would get soaked in no time. She sighed and prepared to go out again and fix it.

"Woof!" Wilby wailed.

The puppy was sitting curled up in Susannah's lap. She
pouted as Georgiana moved to take the dog.

"Susannah's coming with Woof," Georgiana called, gesturing to her daughter. She deposited girl and dog into the
cramped space on the other side of the sacks. "Give me a minute to fix the canvas, and then I'll come back and feed you."

She could hear them all bickering as she climbed down
from the back of the wagon. The first heavy drops were falling
from the bruised sky.

"You sure you don't want me to stay in there with you?" Wendell called from the second wagon. He had one foot on the back tray and was poised to come help her.

"No," Georgiana yelled back, "we're fine!" The last thing she wanted was to spend the night with Wendell Todd. She waved him off, and he waved back, climbing up and disappearing into the wagon. The oxen were huddled together in great clumps, and the horses had gravitated to the edge of the wagon circle where they were most sheltered from the wind. A murky darkness had fallen, and lamps glowed here and there around the perimeter of the circle. The Colicuts and the Barrys, who flanked Georgiana's wagons, had already laced themselves in tight for the night.

She fought the stiff wind and climbed onto the front of the wagon, which faced into the circle and the paddock of animals. The canvas was snapping in the wind.

"Ma!" Wilby squealed with delight when he saw her appear in the opening of the hoop.

"Hello, darling." Georgiana smiled at him. The wind blew her bonnet off and it caught around her neck on its ribbons. Her hair whipped at her face. She struggled to pull the canvas tight around the hoop.

"Bye, Ma!" Wilby waved at her as she closed it. She fought to knot the cords and get the whole arrangement secure. The wind was so stiff now it was practically pushing her off the seat. She tied off the knot. The empty buckets had blown over. They weren't going to be any good for catching rain like that, and might even be dangerous projectiles, so she gathered them up to bring inside. The tents were snapping in the wind too, bent almost double, but they were as secure as they were ever going to be. There wasn't much she could do about them, except pray they lasted the night and her goods survived.

"You all right, missus?" Seb shouted, trying to be heard over the wind. He was crossing the paddock back to the chuck wagon.

She waved and nodded.

"You get in now!" Seb shooed her.

"Becky!" she shouted. "Becky hasn't come back!"

"Matt said she's staying with the LeFoys! LeFoy needs some help with the girls!"

Georgiana doubted it. It was more likely Becky was using the girls as an excuse to spend time with their father.

"And where's Matt?" She had to yell herself hoarse to be heard over the wind, which was really screeching now.

"Don't you worry about him. He'll have found shelter somewhere! Get inside!"

As if a wagon counted as "inside." And she could guess where Matt had found "shelter." Right at the back of the train with his whore. Georgiana threw the buckets into the back of the wagon and hauled herself up. The canvas was snapping hard now. What better way for a virile man like Matt to pass a stormy night than with a wagon full of whores. Even if it *was* thoroughly irresponsible of him when he was supposed to be up here protecting them. The whores weren't even in *his* party. Georgiana scowled out at the stormy plains. From the back of the wagon she had a clear view of the havoc the wind was playing in the grasslands. The seed heads tossed and flicked, the stalks bending en masse. Nets of purple lightning flickered on the horizon.

The wind made the wagon shudder and shake.

"Mama?" Susannah was terrified, peeking over the wall of sacks the twins had built. It was dark in the wagon, but Georgiana could make out enough to see her fear. The boys popped up beside her, and they looked just as scared.

"It's all right, darlings," Georgiana said with pure bravado. "We'll be nice and cozy in just a minute. Let me just light a lamp and close the back up."

Her hand was trembling as she lit the oil lamp. Maybe she should have accepted Wendell's offer. She suddenly felt very alone. And, to be honest, she was as scared as the children were. She hung the lantern from the hook above and turned to the task of lacing them in.

"Do you have to close it all the way?" Phin said quickly. She was surprised to hear his voice break. She had somehow expected the twins to be less scared than the little ones. But they were only small boys, for all their spirit.

"I suppose we could leave a small opening, just for a little while." Georgiana didn't really want to close it all the way either. It felt a bit like lacing oneself into a tomb. She cleared her throat. "We'll close it up when the storm gets worse. *If* it gets worse," she corrected. "Matt said maybe it will pass us by."

As she spoke, there was an earsplitting crack of thunder and they all cried out. Heavy drops of rain spattered on the canvas hoop.

"Or maybe not," she said shakily.

The children scrambled over their wall and piled around her. She stroked their curly dark heads. Woof whined, trapped behind the wall. The twins lifted him over, and he joined in the huddle, wriggling right into the middle, onto Georgiana's lap. His sturdy little body was quivering.

"Let's eat," she said, striving for calm. "Pass the basket, Flip."

They ate ham sandwiches and listened to the rain and wind pelting the canvas. Through the opening, they watched the spikes of lightning intensify until they were a constant net of violent light, shivering in the murky night. The oil lamp swung on its hook, sending jagged shadows leaping. After a while, Georgiana took it down, as it jangled her nerves. She put it in the cook pot, paranoid it would fall and break and start a fire. The light grew even more muted once it was in the pot, but at least the shadows weren't so bad.

Soon there was no more thunder overhead. It marched onward away from them, a constant rumble and crack, but not as scary now that it wasn't right above them. The wind was far worse. It bent the canvas in between the hoops and squalled at the openings, rocking the wagon bed on its wheels. The rain had eased to a sporadic patter of heavy drops. But the air still had that charge. It fairly pulsed with threat. Georgiana resigned herself to a restless night.

"Let's put you to bed," she suggested. "The night will pass quicker if you sleep."

Susannah shook her head vigorously. "What if we blow away while we're asleep?"

"I'll stay up and keep watch," Georgiana promised. She crawled over to the wall and arranged the bedding in the makeshift room Phin and Flip had built.

"I want to stay with you," Susannah whined.

"It's safer back here, darling," Georgiana told her, hoping

she was right. The wall of sacks should be safe enough, as it was only a single sack high; there was nothing to fall over, and the boys had done such a good job of wedging the sacks together that nothing looked likely to move. "I'll be right here."

"Can you sing to us?"

"You know she always falls asleep when she sings," Flip protested, "and we need her to keep watch."

"I don't think I'll fall asleep tonight," Georgiana said dryly, "even if I sing." She tucked them in. They huddled together, the puppy curled up amongst them. Woof was anxious and kept licking their faces and wriggling about. But he seemed to comfort them, and all four of them reached out to rest a hand on him.

"Do you think Princess is all right?" Susannah asked in a small voice.

"Princess is an Indian horse. He's used to this weather," a voice said from the back opening.

They all screamed.

"Oh my Lord, you scared me to death," Georgiana said, pressing a hand to her heart.

It was Matt, peering in at them from the windy darkness. He was drenched, his hat limp, his face shining wet in the low lamplight.

He wasn't with the whore. Georgiana went slack with relief. She'd been fighting images of him cozied up in a wagon just like this, but with a bunch of women.

"Just checking you're all right."

She wasn't all right at all. She was terrified . . . but having to pretend otherwise for the sake of the children. She wanted to throw herself into his arms and bury her face against his neck.

He could tell. She saw it in his eyes, which went all soft the way they did when he was about to be kind to her.

The night around him glared white with lightning. A clear fork spat from the sky, seeming to hit the ground right behind him. She and the children screamed. "Get in here!" she squeaked. "Quick! Before you're killed."

There was another one of those gut-churningly loud cracks of thunder, and the rain started again.

"Get in!" Georgiana grabbed his sleeve and yanked.

"You need to untie the canvas," he said mildly. "I'm a little too big to get through such a bitty hole."

The night burst white again, and the wagon shook with the force of the accompanying thunder. Her fingers fumbled with the cords as she struggled to get the opening wider for him. He pulled himself through, flopping like a beached fish, spraying mud and water. His saddlebags were swollen and heavy, thudding to the boards as they fell from his shoulder.

"Sorry 'bout that," he apologized.

The thunder sounded like it had split the earth beneath them.

"Close the back!" the children pleaded.

"No cause to worry," Matt soothed them, calmly pulling the back tight and knotting it. The rain had intensified until it sounded like they were sitting right under a waterfall. Then it got even more violent.

"I reckon that might be hail," he said mildly. "Thanks for inviting me in or I might have had my skull split open."

"How can it be hail?" Georgiana asked. "It's so hot!" Worse than hot, it was steamy in the wagon.

Matt shrugged. "I don't know, but it is. It's not uncommon out here in summer."

"But the hail will kill Princess," Susannah said, panicked.

Matt fixed her with a disappointed look. "Now, really, didn't you listen when I told you Princess was an Indian pony? He's lived his whole life on these plains. He knows what to do when it hails."

"What does he do?" Susannah asked, her eyes huge.

He was so good with the children. Georgiana didn't know how he did it, but when he was around, they were calmer, more settled. She watched them relax as they listened to him spin a story about how Indian ponies dug holes to hide in when it stormed.

"They do not!" Phin scoffed.

"You're soaked through," Georgiana interrupted. "You should get out of those clothes or you'll catch your death."

He shot her a look and she blushed.

"We'll turn our backs and you can wrap yourself in a quilt," she said primly.

"I should be going. There's room in the chuck wagon for me."

"But it's hailing!"

"It'll stop."

"We don't mind having you here," she said, a little desperately. She really didn't want to be alone again. Especially now the thunder was once more overhead and the canvas lit up with flashes of lightning. The wind sounded like a banshee. The thought of sitting here in the dark while it wailed in the depths of the night made her break out in a cold sweat. He saw her desperation and gave a little nod.

She gave him a rather shaky smile and held out a quilt for him to use. "Thank you," she said.

"How do the horses dig holes?" Susannah pestered him, as they turned their backs to give him some privacy.

Georgiana could hear the slop of his wet clothes as he peeled them off.

"I don't know, to be honest. I've never seen them do it. But I've seen the holes."

"No, you haven't!" Flip rolled his eyes.

"Sure, I have, and you have too."

She heard the suck of his wet boots as he pulled them free and the sound of water running from his body as he wiped himself down with something. His shirt perhaps. It took all of Georgiana's willpower not to steal a glance.

"I haven't seen a horse hole," Susannah said earnestly.

"Sure you have. Those big bowl-shaped holes in the mud, close by the river. We've been seeing them for months."

"Those are buffalo wallows." Phin was scornful.

"Well, sure."

Georgiana heard the rustle of the quilt as he wrapped it around himself.

"The buffalo use the holes to wallow in when they find them." He cleared his throat. "You can turn around now."

Oh my. He was about the sexiest thing Georgiana had ever seen. His wet dark hair was pushed back from his face, and his eyelashes were spiky and damp. The opening of the quilt at his throat showed gleaming brown skin and the wet dark curls of his chest hair. His bare feet poked out from under the blanket.

He had hairy toes. She had such an urge to reach over and stroke them.

But of course she didn't. Instead, she kept her eyes averted, so he wouldn't see her desire, and offered him a coffee. The kettle was cool now, but cold coffee was better than nothing. Then she busied herself draping his wet clothes over the sacks. There was no underwear, she noticed. Was he still wearing it? Or did he not wear underwear . . .

Best not follow that line of thought. She glanced at him, wrapped in the quilt, sitting on the buffalo skin she'd spread on the floor of the wagon. Oh my.

Now that he was here it didn't seem so terrifying to feel the rattle and shake of the wagon, to hear the screech of the wind and the pounding of the rain and hail. It felt cozy inside their canvas shell as the thunder cracked and the lightning forked. If he had left, she would have been dying of terror. But now that he was here, the trembling in her limbs was caused by something other than fear.

She made him a sandwich and listened as he told the children tall tales about the magical properties of Indian ponies. She felt a shiver as she realized they were getting sleepy, and when they fell asleep behind their wall, she would be as good as alone with Matt Slater. Who was crammed into a very small space with her. Naked.

✦ 24 ✦

"YOU KNOW WHAT we need?" Matt said huskily, when the last child had fallen asleep. The rain had let up, becoming a steady whisper, and the thunder rolled away again, although the lightning was still flashing behind the canvas hoop.

"What?" Georgiana had felt their familiar tension return the minute Wilby started snoring. The charge made her blood sing. She was aware of every inch of her body. Her skin prickled. It felt harder to breathe.

Matt smiled and reached for his saddlebags. As he moved his arm, the quilt fell away, revealing his chest. Whorls of dark hair circled his nipples, which were small and dusky and puckered. Her own nipples tightened in response, and she blushed. But who could blame her? She hadn't been bedded for three years.

And she wasn't about to be bedded now, she reminded herself sternly.

Shame. Look at how his muscles rippled as he moved. His arms were enormous. And the quilt was in serious danger of falling open as he rummaged around in his saddlebags. She could see his stomach flex. Oh my, it was hot in here.

"This," he said triumphantly.

She'd forgotten what they were talking about and stared, confused, at the bottle he'd pulled out.

He took their coffee mugs and poured them each a splash. It was whiskey. She could smell it.

"I don't know about you," he said, handing her a mug and pulling the quilt back up high around him until all that lovely skin disappeared from view, "but I quite like storms."

She was having trouble concentrating on what he was saying. They were in such close proximity that she could smell him. He smelled like rainwater and sweat and whiskey and coffee. She took a shaky sip of the whiskey. It burned all the way down.

"Here," he said, passing her his mug to hold. He wriggled toward the back of the wagon and opened the canvas a few inches so they could see out. "It's a shame not to get a look at the glory." He patted the wagon floor next to him. "Come and take a look."

She felt like pinching herself. Was this really happening? He'd spent most of the trip keeping out of arm's reach, and now here he was, all but naked in her wagon, coaxing her to come closer. She wriggled closer before he could change his mind.

He took his mug back. They sat in silence, watching the vast nets of lightning splitting the sky. The darkness glared purple and white, and the warm, wet winds chased over the grassland and danced through the opening of the wagon. Now that Matt was beside her and she wasn't so scared, she could see the elemental beauty of the storm. The air itself seemed to glow with trapped light, and the clouds rolled and churned above, in shades from the palest gray-violet to darkest charcoal black. The seed heads on the grasses flashed and bobbed, and threads of grass chased by on the wind.

"I ain't never seen storms like the ones that happen out here," he said softly, wrapping himself tighter and sipping at his whiskey. He had one arm out of the quilt, and Georgiana had a hard time not staring at it. His bicep was swollen with muscle. It flexed when he lifted the mug to his mouth.

"They don't have storms like this in Oregon?" She tried to gather her thoughts enough to carry on a conversation.

"We have snowstorms," he said, reaching into the cook pot and turning the lantern all the way down.

Oh my. "What are you doing?" Her voice trembled. What *was* he doing? It was pitch-dark in here now.

"It makes it easier to see the storm."

Was it her imagination or did he inch a bit closer to her in the darkness?

There was a titanic crack overhead, and she jumped.

"That was close," he said mildly.

It was more than close. It was right on top of them. The reverberations had barely diminished before it cracked again. It sounded like the world was splitting in two. The wind gusted, and it started raining again. She shivered.

"Is this how a tornado starts?" The thunder rumbled and echoed over the vast plains.

"Now, don't go worrying about that," he said, tossing back the rest of his whiskey. "There ain't nothing we can do about it. But, no, this ain't a tornado. Trust me, you'll know if one hits."

"You've been in one?"

"Close enough. This ain't anything like it," he reassured her. "If a tornado were heading for us, the wind would be so loud you couldn't talk over it. As long as you can hear me, we're all right."

"Keep talking, then," she said, laughing nervously.

He topped off their whiskey.

"Tell me about Oregon, the place where they don't have tornadoes." Georgiana tucked her legs up under her and watched the clouds flash with light. "You said you have snowstorms?"

"We have as much snow as you could want." He wasn't usually much of a talker, but just as he'd soothed the children with talk of magical digging ponies, now he soothed her with talk of Oregon. He painted a picture of his home in the foothills of the Cascades, of green summers spent fishing and trapping, of old forests and autumn leaves so bright you'd swear the trees were on fire. He told her about his brother Luke's house, the one he'd built for a woman who refused to marry him, and lived in now with a woman who'd once dressed as a man. He described the long winters and great drifts of snow, the avalanches and the Christmas dance in the Utopia town hall, which had just been finished a year or two ago. He painted a picture so vivid she almost forgot where she was.

Or she would have, if he hadn't been sitting beside her, smelling so good and radiating such warmth. The whiskey flowed through her, loosening her limbs, relaxing her guard. Oh, but she wanted to kiss him. She'd ceased watching the storm and watched him instead. Her eyes had grown used to the darkness, and she was close enough to see his face. His eyelashes were incredibly long, and they brushed his cheeks when he looked down. The groove in his cheek was so inviting she wanted to trace it with her fingertip.

"Why aren't you married?" Oh my. Where had that come from? The whiskey had loosened her tongue as much as it had loosened the rest of her.

He glanced over at her. And, oh, if he had looked sexy before, he looked even more so with that bashful look on his face. He sucked on his lower lip and she almost groaned. Did he have any idea what he did to her?

"I don't know why I never married," he said shyly, shrugging. "I never met a girl I liked, I guess."

"I suppose there aren't many women out there in the wilderness." She tried to tear her gaze away from his mouth.

"Truth be told, I ain't too good with women."

He was selling himself short there. He was plenty good, Georgiana thought, taking in his glistening golden-brown eyes and the sleek muscles of his arm. And it wasn't even his looks. It was the way he took care of everybody. He didn't even seem to know that he was doing it, but it was his natural instinct to step in when problems arose. Georgiana hadn't missed how the women of the camp followed him with their eyes, how they smiled when he was near. Even the married ones.

They fell into silence again, listening to the beat of the wind on the canvas. After a minute, she heard him clear his throat. She shifted. The tension was unbearable.

"If you want to sleep, you can rest your head against my shoulder," he said gruffly.

She didn't want to sleep at all. She'd never felt less like sleep in her entire life. But she wanted to touch him, so she crept closer.

"Hold up a minute." He adjusted his position until he had his back against the bag of coffee. She could hear the crunch of the beans under his weight. He stretched his legs out in front of him and they brushed against her. "That's better. You can come sit here. It'll be more comfortable."

Her heart pounded as she scooted over beside him. She rested her back against the sack beside him and pulled her legs up to her chest. Then, gingerly, as though he might protest, she lay her head against his shoulder. Her new position gave her a magnificent view. Not just of the night outside, but of the length of his body he exposed whenever he took a sip of whiskey. The long muscles running down the length of him, the hardness of his stomach, the line of dark hair that ran right down his belly, circling the dent of his navel, and then disappearing beneath the quilt, made her shiver. She itched to run her fingertips over that wiry, silky hair, over the velvet warmth of his skin.

Oh God. This was going to be the longest night of her life.

He hadn't even touched her and she was wet. She ached. She was more aroused than Leonard had ever managed to make her, and they were barely even touching.

"Georgiana?"

She broke out in gooseflesh when he sighed her name. "Yes?" she squeaked. She'd say nothing but "yes," no matter what he said. Her whole being was shouting *yes, yes, yes*. Just ask me: *yes*. Just touch me: *yes*.

"I think I made a mistake."

He had? How? By wasting all these weeks *not* kissing her? Yes!

"I need to get my other arm out. If you go to sleep, it'll go numb."

What? Oh. She was lying on his arm. Her cheeks were burning as she sat up so he could free himself.

"Hold on." She heard rustling. He was folding the quilt down. She could have pouted as he covered up that delicious dark line of hair and the lovely skin of his stomach. He freed both of his arms and tucked the quilt around his chest. "Do you need a blanket?" he asked.

No. No, she didn't need a blanket. What she needed was *him*.

It was like running a high fever. She felt restless and irritable and . . . hungry. She *was* hungry. For *him*. Nothing but him. It was impossible to even *think* when he was close like this.

But she didn't say any of that. She didn't want him to go bolting from the wagon, the way he'd bolted every time they'd kissed. Oh God, *look at him*. His shoulders were completely exposed now that the quilt was tucked around his chest. His collarbones were hard lines, and there was a hollow at the base of his throat. One dark curl licked up toward it.

Now when she lay against his shoulder her cheek met bare

skin. She felt him shiver. His skin was so warm. Soft. The planes of his upper chest filled her vision.

What was happening here? She shouldn't look a gift horse in the mouth . . . but how did he go from keeping her at arm's length to having her rest her cheek against his naked chest? This was an invitation, wasn't it? What else could it be?

She could see his pulse leaping in the hollow of his throat and hear the way his breath had grown jagged. Georgiana wanted to rest her hand on his chest, spreading her fingers over the tufts of hair. She wanted to stroke him, slowly, lightly, but she didn't. She lay as rigid as a pole, struggling to breathe normally, feeling him tremble beneath her cheek.

"Georgiana?" his voice was thick.

"Yes?" She titled her head back and looked up at him. His eyes were liquid with lust. It sent something uncurling low in her belly. "Yes?" she said again, her voice throaty.

His lips parted, but he couldn't seem to bring himself to speak.

The silence drew out, interminable, throbbing with their desire.

"Would you just kiss her and get it over with?" Phin's voice was like a splash of icy water. They leapt apart and turned to see the twins and Susannah watching them, their chins propped on the sacks.

"Oh, you ruined it," Susannah said, disappointed.

"They didn't need *me* to ruin it," Phin scoffed. "They can't seem to court themselves out of a paper bag."

Georgiana flushed. "How dare you spy on us! Don't you know what privacy is?"

"Privacy isn't in here with us," Flip told her, exasperated. "If you want to be kissing all over the place, you could at least do it where we don't have to watch."

There was so much wrong with that statement that Georgiana didn't even know where to start.

"We weren't kissing," Matt said gruffly. He'd wrapped himself up tight again and looked embarrassed enough to sink right through the floor.

"Only because you took so long," Phin complained. "Jeez. When I'm grown up, you won't see me hemming and hawing that way. If I like a girl, I'm just going to kiss her."

"You'll get slapped a lot, then," Susannah observed. "Girls like a little courting before you go kissing them all over the place."

Phin snorted.

"Would you all go back to bed," Georgiana said sharply. "We'll talk about your manners in the morning!"

They rolled their eyes and disappeared behind the sacks.

"Just take my advice," Phin called over the sack wall as he settled back in for the night, "and don't wait to kiss her."

"I guess at least they ain't scared of the storm anymore." Matt cleared his throat.

"I guess not." Georgiana pulled a face. It didn't look like she was getting kissed anytime soon. Matt had gone all distant again and was pulling his clothes off the sacks. "Are you going?" she asked, disappointed.

"I'd best, while there's a lull."

Damn the storm. *Now* it chose to die down on her. It wasn't even raining anymore.

"You mind turning your back?" he asked, holding up his wet pants.

She did mind, but she turned. Behind the wall she could see the three children looking up at her. Susannah gave her an apologetic look.

Wilby was definitely her favorite child, she thought crankily. He was still curled up, fast asleep with Woof. He wasn't ruining anything for her.

She heard the wet sound of Matt trying to pull his trousers back on. She doubted they were comfortable.

"Sorry I got your quilt wet."

When she turned back, he was dressed. She felt a crushing disappointment as she watched him swing over the back of the wagon.

"Hey," he said, pausing and looking through the opening at her. Lightning flashed behind him, awarding him a halo. "When this storm ends, before we ride out again . . ." he trailed off.

"Yes?" she prodded.

"You fancy packing a picnic and coming with me to scout for Willow Springs? It's not far and it might be nice to lead the train there for some fresh water." He bit his lip. "That sounds pretty silly after the amount of fresh water we got tonight." He looked up at the sky.

"No," she protested, before he could withdraw his invitation. "I'd love to go."

"I was thinking we could leave the children here with Becky and the train."

"Yes. Yes, yes." She'd sounded too enthusiastic, she knew. But, by God, she wasn't having them interrupt her again, not if there was even the slightest chance that he would finally kiss her. And if he *didn't* kiss her, she had half a mind to kiss *him*. Soundly.

❧ 25 ❧

H E WAS WAITING for her when she climbed down from the wagon the next morning. The storm had blown itself out, and the sky was crystal clear. The morning star shone in the east, and everything sparkled with raindrops. There was a rind of pale pink and purple light just curving over the horizon.

Georgiana admired the view as she swung down from the wagon. She thought she was alone and squealed in shock when Matt stepped in front of her. "You scared me," she said breathlessly.

He must have been waiting for her to emerge, because he was fully dressed and had Wishes and Pablo saddled and ready to go. "I've already packed us some food and fetched Becky back to watch the children. I thought you might want to watch the sun come up with me. The morning after a storm is always mighty pretty."

He must have been up terribly early to have all that done already. Or perhaps, like her, he hadn't been able to sleep . . .

He'd shaved, she noticed. He'd also done something to his hair. It was neat. It was never neat. And what was he wearing? Since when did he wear a nice shirt to go scouting?

"You want to tell the little 'uns where you're going? You might want to tell them you'll be gone awhile."

She might? Oh my. What was he up to? He was smiling in a way she'd never seen him smile before. It was bashful and sweet and . . . kind of mischievous. Oh my, oh my. Georgiana looked down at her stained travel clothes.

"Have I got time to change?"

"Of course, sweetheart."

Sweetheart! Who *was* this man?

Don't ask questions! *Move.* Before this one disappears and grumpy, distant Matt comes back.

She scurried into the wagon and then realized her trunk was in the tent. She was blushing when she scurried back out, babbling an explanation as she dashed to the tent. He was still smiling that stomach-turning smile.

Because they were riding, she couldn't wear a dress. The best she could manage was her least stained riding culottes and a fresh shirt. Her waistcoat was filthy, so she left it behind. It was too warm for so many layers anyway. What on earth could she do with her hair? It was a nightmare. She tried to brush it, but the curls were so tangled that it would take her hours to get it neat. So she bundled it up and crammed on a hat.

It was silly to be going to so much effort just to go scouting, but look at *him*, all clean and combed like that.

By the time she emerged, the children had tumbled out of the wagon, and Becky was yawning and asking them what they wanted for breakfast. They barely even looked at Georgiana as she said good-bye.

"You look nice," Matt said as she took Wishes' reins off him. "C'mon or we'll miss the sunrise."

He swung onto Pablo's back and led her into the grasses. There were bent and broken stalks from the storm, but most of the grassland was supple in the breeze, waving and bobbing, glimmering with moisture. He led her to where the grassland ended, right by the banks of the river, which churned with the night's rainfall.

"See that?" He pointed.

The sun had broken over the horizon, a pale gold sliver, sending streamers of color into the indigo sky; petal pinks and lavenders, shades of mauve and deep rose spreading like spilled paint. It was stunning. She held her breath as the color bled until the entire sky was streaked with gauzy shades. The raindrops on the grasses glittered like jewels, and the river glinted with gold light.

"Ain't that the prettiest thing you ever saw?" He was grinning like he'd shown her one of the wonders of the world.

Was he *courting* her?

The realization pierced her like an arrow. He was. He was courting her! Matt Slater, her pretend fiancé, was *courting her*. He pointed out landmarks on their ride to the springs, cheerfully told her Indian legends about the creation of the land around them, and at one point he led her to a field of wildflowers and actually got down and picked her handfuls of the blue and purple blooms.

"Those ones there are prairie flax," he said, pulling a hunk of them out of the wet earth. He snapped off the muddy roots. "I reckon they're about as close as nature can get to the color of your eyes."

She took the clump of flowers graciously, trying not to laugh. He was the clumsiest suitor she'd ever seen. But maybe also the most charming—just by dint of how unpolished he was. She watched him, amused, as he kept up the awkward chatter until they reached a grove of willows. By then the sun was up and the sky was a breathtaking bright blue.

He self-consciously rushed to hand her down from her horse. She bit back a smile and let him help her, enjoying the feel of his hands on her waist. He made her feel like she was sixteen again. It was a giddy, hopeful feeling, like her whole life was ahead of her and all the mistakes had been erased.

"Are you hungry?" he asked awkwardly. "I forgot you didn't get breakfast."

Before she could answer, he'd already started unfurling a blanket under the willows. The fragrance of sweet water filled the shadowy grove.

"The spring's just over there, if you'd like a cupful while I unpack?"

The spring water bubbled up in the middle of the field of pillowy emerald grass. The smell of it was intoxicating. She took the offered cup and went to fill it. The grass was spongy under her feet. She dipped the cup into the icy cold water and took a drink, aware of him coming up behind her.

"It tastes so good after the horrid Platte," she sighed.

He was watching her mouth as she licked a stray drop off her lower lip.

"Georgiana?" His voice had that tight huskiness again, that barely repressed desire. It made her weak.

"Yes?" Was he finally going to kiss her? He hadn't kissed her since Independence. She swayed toward him slightly and tried to look inviting. *Yes. Keep going . . .*

"I've been thinking . . ." He took a deep breath and then just plunged in. "I don't reckon we should pretend anymore."

"What?" She straightened up. *What?* This had all been an attempt to sweeten her up so he could *abandon her to Wendell*? The giddy feeling evaporated.

"I don't reckon we should pretend anymore," he repeated. He put his hands on his hips and nodded. "I think we should do it for real."

Her mouth popped open. *What?*

"Hear me out," he said, holding up his hand. "I've done a lot of thinking. We've got a thing, you and me."

"A thing?" She felt a little light-headed.

"There's no cause to go denying it. Look at last night in the wagon." His hair flopped as he shook his head. "I don't know how much longer I can go without laying hands on you."

Oh my. Her gaze flew to his large hands, which were spread on his hip bones.

"That ain't all we got going for us neither. Your little 'uns seem to like me. And you don't seem to mind me either."

Mind him? She could barely think for wanting him. He was *perfect*.

"As you said last night, I ain't got a wife. I didn't give much thought to having one before I met you, but I ain't averse to the idea. At least not anymore. And I know for sure you're in the market for a husband."

He didn't say anything about love, she noticed. Somehow that made her even weaker at the knees. Leonard had proposed with flowery words and strings of bright promises. Matt's proposition was blunt and practical, sturdy and *honest*.

"I like you," he said, "and you like me. That seems as good a place to start as any."

"Yes," she whispered. It was about all she could say. Her brain seemed to have floated clear away.

"Yes?"

"Yes." *Yes, yes, yes, yes, yes, yes, yes, yes!* It was exactly what she'd wanted since the first time she'd seen him on the street in Independence. The big, rough brute.

"Yes?" He couldn't seem to believe it.

"Yes!"

His eyes grew wide. He didn't seem to know what to do next. "All right, then."

She gave a startled cry as he seized her by the arms and

yanked her to him. The mug went flying and her hat tumbled from her head as his mouth fell on hers. He kissed her hard. Hungrily. His hand plunged into her curls, easing her head back as his tongue parted her lips. He kissed her like he was dying of thirst and she was a fresh spring.

Georgiana melted into him, surrendering to the storm of feelings sweeping through her. It felt good to surrender, to give herself over. He held her up as her knees gave way, his kiss at once tender and demanding. The flick of his tongue caused shivers in the deepest parts of her, and the feel of his fingers against the back of her head sparked a wildfire in her blood.

The intensity of the kiss deepened until Georgiana lost all ability to think. When she finally resurfaced, his kiss had become a soft series of tongue strokes. The smell of him, the taste of him, was utterly intoxicating. He pulled away and she moaned in protest.

"Are you *crying*?" he asked, shocked.

She was. She was crying. She smiled witlessly at him and nodded.

"Why are you crying?"

She shrugged, still smiling as the tears rolled. "I don't know. I suppose I'm just happy."

He held her at arm's length, inspecting her. "I guess there's a lot I got to learn about women."

"I guess so."

"Can you make them stop?" He reached over and brushed the tear tracks away with his thumbs. "They make me feel like I did something wrong."

She laughed. "You did. You took *ages* to ask me to marry you."

"Technically, you asked me," he corrected her. "I was just the one to make it for real." He led her back to the picnic blanket, where they sat in the shade of the willows, unable to keep their eyes off each other.

"What made you change your mind?" she asked.

"This." He leaned over and kissed her.

And that was how they spent the rest of the day.

❧ 26 ❧

MATT HAD DEFINITE ideas on how they were getting married. He wasn't about to get hitched out here in the middle of nowhere. Mostly because the woman he was marrying was a proper sort of lady and he'd got it into his head that she deserved a proper sort of wedding.

"But there's a pastor in the train," Georgiana protested. "He could marry us tomorrow."

He'd almost been convinced, but that was only because she was kissing his neck and he could barely keep a train of thought.

"Stop that," he'd said eventually, putting her at arm's length.

"Don't you like it?"

That wicked look she had was almost his undoing. It was taking a superhuman strength of will not to give in when her hands wandered. He hadn't felt so lusty since he was a youth. He was hard all the time. Kissing her just made things worse. But it was a delicious kind of pain; he'd never felt so alive. It was like the world had taken on sharp edges and all the colors were brighter. Things smelled better.

And he was determined to wait until after the wedding. Because she was a lady. And he was . . . well, never mind what he was.

"No," he said firmly, "we're doing this properly." And properly meant no bedding before the wedding.

The next half-decent settlement was Fort Bridger, so that was where he planned for them to get hitched. It was slightly out of their way, since he'd planned to take Sublette's Cutoff, but he'd be damned if he'd wait till Fort Hall to marry her. The weeks until Fort Bridger were looking bad enough. And hell, he wasn't *actually* superhuman. His resolve would give out eventually. He figured no one would complain if they took a detour; they could pause the train for a couple of days, and everyone could rest and take advantage of the trading post. Until then, he'd just have to suffer permanent arousal.

Once he'd decided to marry her, he'd felt the most immense relief. It felt *right*. And now the decision was made, he didn't know why he'd ever hemmed and hawed about it. He congratulated himself on making the right choice. And took every opportunity he could to spend time with her, to touch her, to kiss that plump, smiling mouth. He had to do it when no one could see though, as they hadn't told Wendell of their plans yet. Matt figured there was no point in starting trouble before they had to. He'd tell Wendell in good time, but why upset the applecart early?

July was both sheer pleasure and sheer torture. The storms eased and then gave way entirely to long, hot days and starry nights. The multiple river crossings were accomplished with little fuss; they navigated the Laramie, the Horse, the Cottonwood and the La Bonte without incident, and crossed the Sweetwater nine times in quick succession as it wound toward Devil's Gate. His emigrants were seasoned travelers now and needed very little guidance from him, which meant he could spend less time babysitting them and more time with Georgiana. They reached Independence Rock in time to celebrate the Fourth of July, and Matt and Joe toasted their most successful train to date. They'd made it almost halfway without any serious injury or loss of life.

"Touch wood," Matt warned, knocking his knuckles against a wagon side.

"Yeah," Joe laughed, "especially considering the havoc those whores are playing. You owe me for that one. I thought for sure I woulda had a shooting or two by now, the way the men fight over them."

Matt saw how Georgiana glowered at the mention of the whores. He wrapped his arms around her once they were alone and tried to kiss her soundly. But she resisted, pushing him away. "Jealous?" he teased.

"I think anyone would be," she said stiffly.

"You got no call to be."

"Why? Because she's a whore?" Her expression went as

black as a thundercloud. "I don't want you touching anyone but me." And now she was tearing up again. He sure hated when she did that. It caused a sick feeling to settle in his stomach.

"I ain't like your last husband," he said huskily.

She jumped like she'd been bitten by a flea. "What do you mean?"

He shrugged. "Look, I never met the man, and I hate to speak ill of the dead, but he sounds like he had a silver tongue and a black heart. I ain't like that. My tongue is pure wood. I couldn't charm a grouse, let alone a bird out of a tree. I ain't going to lie to you, sweetheart. I ain't the lying type. Or the cheating type. It ain't the way I'm made."

Her tears were falling now.

"You do that a lot," he said, pulling her close.

"You'll get used to it," she sniffed. She pulled away again. "I know you saw that whore back in Independence." She held up a hand to silence him when he tried to speak. "Don't. I *know* you did. You were with her the night of the dance, that first night, when I wore my blue dress."

"You looked mighty pretty," he told her, dropping his head to rub his cheek against her curls. "You should wear that dress to our wedding."

"I wore it for *you*," she said sharply, "but you weren't there. You were with *her*."

He frowned. She was serious. Hell. "You got no call to be thinking that I've been with her."

"She came to see you at Mrs. Tilly's."

"To do business, sweetheart."

She was scowling again.

"Not *that* kind of business. Wagon train business."

She pursed her lips. "I know men have needs," she said.

He nodded. He could feel his needs every time she leaned against him.

"And I don't blame you for consorting with whores before we got engaged. Properly engaged," she amended, "not pretend engaged. But I just need you to know that now that we're getting married I can't, I *won't*, share you."

And there she went, crying again. That Leonard Blunt must have been a real horse's ass.

He sighed. He'd been hoping to put this off until the wedding night . . . but he sure hated to see her hurting like this when he could easily put her out of her misery. "Georgiana," he said carefully, "I need you to know that I never slept with that whore."

"It's fine," she sniffed, although it wasn't. "I understand." She clearly didn't. The thought of him sleeping with Seline was clearly cutting her up inside. He understood—he felt the same way when he thought about her sleeping with Leonard Blunt.

"No, you don't understand. Not at all." He tensed. Hell. How could he tell her? He'd look like . . . God only knew what he'd look like.

"I *do* understand," she wailed, and then she burst into proper crying.

He held her at arm's length. "I need you to listen to me, honey. Take a deep breath and try to stop crying for a minute. Just a minute. Once you've heard me out, you can cry all you want."

"I don't want the *details*!" She sounded outraged.

"I think you do." He squeezed her shoulders and sighed. "I never slept with that whore . . . or any whore."

She searched his face, looking suspicious. "You didn't?"

"No." He cleared his throat. "In fact . . . I ain't never slept with any woman."

"What?" She'd stopped crying completely now.

He closed his eyes and braced for ridicule. "That's right," he said, feeling time draw out interminably, "I'm . . . well, I'm a . . . virgin."

❋ 27 ❋

A VIRGIN.

Oh my. He was a *virgin*.

How was that even possible? He was so . . . well, virile. He was the manliest man Georgiana had ever encountered. He was an expert kisser. He was clearly aroused when he kissed her. So . . . how? *Why?*

"I don't know," he'd mumbled. He'd gone the shade of a beetroot when he'd told her. Wilby and the boys had interrupted them before she could pursue it further, and Matt had avoided her for ages afterward. When she finally managed to speak to him alone again, they were scouting South Pass, which wasn't so much a pass as a broad, grassy meadow. He kept riding ahead so she couldn't see his face, which was both touching and exasperating.

"I know it ain't normal," he said sullenly. "I know a man's expected to be more experienced than his bride."

"I don't see why," she retorted, pushing Wishes to catch up to Pablo. "Slow down so I can talk to you!"

"Do we have to talk about it?" He wouldn't meet her eye.

"I guess not."

He looked startled.

"I don't see that it changes anything." She smiled at him. "Except that it makes me very happy that you never touched that whore." She wheeled Wishes around so that she blocked his way. "Now, before we go on, I think you owe me something."

"An apology?" He didn't look pleased. "I don't know that I want to apologize for it."

"No, not an apology," she laughed, "a kiss."

Knowing he was a virgin made everything more intense,

she thought as he kissed her. The idea of his inexperience was highly arousing. No other woman would touch him the way she touched him. And when she did get to touch him properly on their wedding night, sliding her hands over every last warm inch of him, it would be with the knowledge that he'd never felt a touch like that before.

As she lay restless and wakeful through the hot July nights, she imagined all of the things she could introduce him to, the ways and places she could kiss him, the art of running her tongue down the length of him, of taking him into her mouth, of taking him into the aching wet depths of her.

Oh, but July had too many days in it, and the trail had too many steps until Fort Bridger.

BY THE END of July, they'd reached the Green River, which was at high water and was too treacherous to cross except by ferry. Georgiana watched proudly as Matt organized his train in the fields by the Mormon Ferry. They had to camp for a couple of days, as the ferry was congested with another party, this one headed for California. They paid their fares (an exorbitant sixteen dollars per wagon) and settled in to wait. It was hard to get a moment alone in the congested campground with the children at a loose end, and Georgiana was going mad with being so close to Matt but unable to touch him.

"You know what?" Matt finally suggested to the children when the day was waning and he and Georgiana were champing at the bit for some time alone. "Let's play hide-and-seek." He winked at Georgiana.

She flushed as she realized what he was up to. She was itching to touch him.

"I'll be it," he volunteered. "I'll count to fifty and then come and find you all." He ostentatiously closed his eyes and started counting. The children scattered. "Go to the bushes over past the ferry," he hissed at Georgiana between counting, "I'll come find you. We oughtta get a good ten minutes alone at least."

She skipped past the ferry and just about dove into the bushes and onto the pillowy grasses beneath.

"How long do you think it will take for them to realize no one's looking for them?" he asked breathlessly, when he tumbled in after her. He didn't wait for her to answer, falling straight into a kiss.

Their kisses had escalated over the month. Kissing just wasn't enough anymore. Today, as the children played hide-and-seek, Matt and Georgiana struggled to contain themselves. Their hands slid over each other hungrily. Matt was obsessed with the full curves of Georgiana's breasts, holding her through her shirt until she moaned. She'd taken to not wearing her stays, just so she could feel his touch more intimately. With only her thin shirt and a linen chemise between them, his hands drove her wild. His thumb rubbed over her swollen nipples, sending sparks through the heart of her. He covered her breasts with both hands, his tongue penetrating the heat of her mouth as he bent her backward, sliding between her legs until the friction of him against her sent her wild. She would have let him take her right there and then, if he'd been willing. But he held himself back, trembling with the effort it took. They writhed, cradled in the high cool grasses, pushed to the very edge of desire.

"Georgiana, stop," he moaned. "Stop or we won't . . . stop."

She couldn't stop. She didn't want to stop. She rolled him onto his back and straddled him. "There are things we can do," she whispered, leaning down to kiss him. He tried to protest, but she took his lower lip between hers and gave it a nip. His golden-brown gaze was drugged with lust.

Feeling powerful, she sat up, enjoying the grind of him against her aching center. Slowly, she unbuttoned her shirt. The weight of his gaze made her senseless with desire, and the friction of her chemise against her breasts was torturous and wonderful all at once. The shirt parted, revealing the sheer linen beneath. His hands were trembling as he reached up to ease her shirt wider. She heard his breath catch. The chemise was the sheerest whisper of fabric; the contours of her breasts were clearly visible, as were the pebble-hard thrusts of her dusky nipples.

"Georgiana . . . " He sounded like he was in pain. But there was something else there in the aching sound of his voice. She thought it might be wonder.

No one had ever looked at her like that before.

The sheer admiration in his eyes made her burn, made her

melt. Feeling like she was moving through the weight of water, slowly, languidly, she pulled the ribbon holding the neck
of her chemise together. She could feel the hard swell of him
between her legs. He was pulsing with wanting her. She
couldn't help herself from grinding gently against him. He
groaned and grabbed her hips to keep her still.

"Don't," he begged, "or I won't be able to . . ."

"I don't mind," she said, feeling wicked. The ribbon pulled
free, and the neck of her chemise gaped open, showing the
plump swell of her cleavage. His eyes were riveted. She lowered her hands and placed them over his, where they rested on
her hips. He was trembling like a leaf in a strong wind.

His inexperience was intoxicating. She'd never been so
wet, or so ready to be taken. The delay increased her desire to
an unbearable hungry pleasure.

"Touch me," she whispered. If possible, the hardness
against her grew harder still. She squeezed her thighs against
his hips as she guided his hands up her body until they were
resting on her rib cage, directly under her breasts, which were
swollen and aching. She arched her back.

"Touch me," she sighed again, arching and pressing down
hard against the iron length of him.

He groaned. His hands seemed frozen, clenching her ribs.

"If you won't," she threatened, "I will." Teasingly, she took
the edges of the chemise between her fingertips and eased it
open, revealing the swell of her breasts inch by inch. He
couldn't look away. His hands had tightened on her until it was
almost painful. Her breasts were sore with wanting him. Oh
God, she wanted him to touch her.

She felt cool air swirl against her skin as she peeled the
linen free, until she was completely exposed. As he watched,
eyes glazed, his bottom lip caught between his teeth, she ran
the tips of her fingers lightly over her exposed breasts. She had
large, high, round breasts, and now, aroused as she'd never
been aroused before, they were even larger, taut and heavy to
the touch. As her fingers passed over her hard nipples, she felt
lightning spike through her, all the way to her wet depths.

He moaned again. She trailed her hands down to his and
peeled him away from his death grip on her ribs. She twined
her fingers through his and brought his hands up to her breasts.

She pressed him to her, feeling his palms hot against her nipples. She let go of his hands as he cupped her, gently at first, and then squeezing as he felt the weight of her. It was the most delicious thing she'd felt in her entire life.

She tilted her head back and closed her eyes, and he clumsily felt his way. His inexpert fingers drove her wild. He traced her curves, rubbed her aching nipples, cupped her and squeezed her, stroked her and held her until she thought she might die of pleasure. Unconsciously, she rocked against him.

He sat up abruptly and she gasped, feeling the thrust of him against her as their angle of friction shifted.

"Oh God," she sighed as he pressed his face into her chest, his hands settling on her hips. His lips traced a path between her cleavage. "Matt . . ."

She was shivering, trembling, close to the edge, ready to come. The pleasure was a bright shimmering feeling, darting through her.

"Matt," she begged, as his lips led a hot trail to her nipple.

Just when she was mindless with want, her head back, surrendering to the promise of his mouth, a scream broke the spell.

"Mama! Mother! Motherrrrrrrrrrrr!"

It was Susannah.

Georgiana and Matt snapped apart. Georgiana felt like someone had thrown a bucket of cold water over her.

"Motherrrrr!" Susannah was screaming, endlessly, the single word rending the evening. And the terror in her voice changed Georgiana's world forever.

❋ 28 ❋

"WILBY!" THAT'S ALL Susannah could say. She was hysterical, her voice rising with every word. "Wilby! Wilby! Wilby! Wilbeeeeeeeeeee." She was pointing to the river.

Georgiana tore down the banks. Her hair flew behind her, her hastily buttoned shirt flapping. Oh God, please, let him be all right. Please, God. Please, please, please, *please*.

But she knew in her gut he wasn't. It was the terror in Susannah's voice; it was the silence of the camp; it was the fact that the twins were sobbing in panic as they thrashed about at the edge of the river. The twins *never* panicked. They never cried. They always seemed indestructible.

"He fell in!" They were white, their eyes rolling like spooked horses.

Time trapped Georgiana in a horrifying moment that seemed to last forever. As though from a great distance, she heard Matt's voice, barking questions, giving orders; she saw men fan out along the river; she felt the cool slap of the grass as she ran along the riverside. The smallest details leapt out at her with shocking clarity: the spangles on the surface of the rushing river, the barking of a dog, and above it all, there was a strange high-pitched noise. It went on and on, ringing in Georgiana's ears.

Distantly, she realized it was *her*. She was wailing. And like her daughter, her wails consisted of a single word . . . *Wilbeeeeeeeeeeeeeee.*

And then they found his wooden sword.

Tangled in storm debris, there it was. Wilby's chipped and well-loved wooden sword. The one he played knights with. The one he whacked his brothers with. The one he took with him everywhere he went . . .

She could hear screaming now. On some level she knew it was her screaming, but the sound seemed to come from outside of her. And there was no way she could ever stop it.

"I'VE SEDATED HER," Doc Barry said when Matt eventually returned to camp. It was close to dawn, and he'd only come back to eat and saddle Pablo. He needed to keep looking, and he'd searched as far as he could on foot. He'd need to be on horseback to cover the rest of the ground.

He knew at this point he was only looking for a body, but he couldn't leave the boy out there alone. The thought was almost his undoing. Wilby was barely more than a baby. He needed his mother. Even dead . . . Oh God, how could that be? Of anyone, why did it have to be Wilby . . . ?

"Is she . . . " Matt had to clear his throat. It had tightened up to the point he could barely speak.

"She's about as to be expected," Doc Barry told him. "I've given her laudanum so she can sleep. The boys are with Becky."

Matt grimly kept about his business. He didn't have the stomach for food, but he needed fuel if he was going to get through the hours ahead. The bread tasted like sawdust. He felt like gagging but choked it down.

"Matt," the doc said, stepping in front of him, "you need to rest."

"No." Matt shook his head. He needed to find Wilby.

"At least think of the children."

Matt looked up, startled.

"She's not capable right now," the doc told him, "and you're as good as their nearest kin. The little girl is sleeping with her mother, but those boys need you."

"You said they were with Becky." The bread was like a lump of clay in his mouth. He couldn't face those boys.

"They *are* with Becky." Doc Barry sighed and fixed him with a sad gaze. "But Becky's barely more than a child herself."

"I have to find him, Doc."

"I understand, but you can't help him. You *can* help those two." The doc nodded at the tent closest to Georgiana's lead wagon. The tent was glowing with lamplight, and Matt could see the shadowy figures hunched within. "I can only imagine the night they've spent."

Matt managed to swallow the bread. Barely. He tossed the rest of the crust aside.

"I assume we're not crossing the river today," Doc Barry said. "If it's all right with you, I'll send for the pastor to be with Mrs. Smith when she wakes." The doc gave Matt a gentle pat on the arm and went back to his tent, where Georgiana lay, drugged, shattered with grief.

Matt wished he could see her. Every fiber of his being wanted to wrap himself around her and keep her safe. To stroke away her pain.

But stroking her was what had caused all this pain in the first place, he thought bleakly. Wilby's death was on him.

He was the one who'd sent the children off to hide. And why? So he could roll around in the grass with their mother. He was the one who was ultimately responsible for Wilby falling into the river. He was light-headed with the horror of it. He had to hold on to the chuck wagon for a moment until it passed. His gaze drifted to the glowing tent. Hell. What good could he do those boys?

He wasn't good for people. The people he loved died. Just look at his past: his mother, his father.

It was hard to breathe. The feelings were hitting him hard and fast, feelings he'd worked a lifetime to avoid.

He wasn't like his brother. Luke took charge, made things better; Matt messed everything up. And look at today, Matt thought, feeling ill enough to vomit. Look at *today*. He'd been so focused on his own pleasure . . .

He'd been selfish.

And he was *still* being selfish. That family was suffering, and he was just standing here, obsessed with his own self. Just like always. He had the luxury of standing here, alive, blaming himself, while Wilby . . .

He felt tears swell. God, he hadn't cried since he was a kid. Matt pressed his face into his forearm. His throat hurt fit to split, and he was on the verge of collapsing into sobs. If *he* felt this way about Wilby, imagine how *she* felt. Imagine how those kids felt.

He didn't need to imagine. He knew. He remembered the

cold sucking terror of his parents' deaths, the black void that opened through the heart of him, the hopelessness that rushed in.

But he also remembered Luke. The great mass of his older brother at his side: the weight and steadiness of him. Luke had been like a tree, something for Matt and Tom to cling to, something to shelter them from the worst of the storm. Luke had been the one to move them on when they could barely rise from their bedrolls; Luke had been the one to plan and scout and feed them when they could barely eat. He'd been the one to remember birthdays and to keep them at what book learning he could. All Matt remembered from that time was the cold black-and-white awfulness of it: the nightmares and the ashy pit in his stomach.

He'd always assumed Luke had a quality he didn't, that his despair had been lesser or his courage greater. Matt wiped his face on his sleeve and tried to pull himself together. But what if he'd been wrong? What if Luke had stood alone like this all those years ago, in the darkness before dawn, feeling this toxic storm of guilt and shame, searing loneliness and fear? What if he'd wept in the dark where no one could see, and then pulled himself together, rounded them up and driven them on to Oregon? Because what else could he do? He was the eldest. There was no one else to do what needed doing.

Matt stared at the glowing tent.

There was no one else to do what needed doing.

His feet were heavy as he crossed the camp to the boys' tent. They were awake, as he'd known they would be. They sat up when he came in.

"Did you find him?"

They looked horrible. They were dark-eyed scarecrows.

Matt shook his head. "I was about to go out again. I thought you might want to come with me?"

They scrambled out of their bedrolls and had their boots on before Matt had finished speaking. In their haste, they'd each pulled on one black boot and one brown. Matt didn't bother to correct them. What did it matter?

"Come on," he said gruffly, settling his hands on the back of their necks as he led them to the horses. "We'll need to pack saddlebags. We'll be gone all day."

* * *

ACTION WAS THE only sane response to shock and grief, Matt thought as he watched the twins thrash through the grasses by the riverside. They stopped at every clump of bushes or reeds, combing through them until they were black with mud. They called Wilby's name until their voices were hoarse. Matt followed along after them, but by afternoon he no longer called out. He trailed them, watching over them, letting the action of searching for Wilby funnel their horror and rage and guilt. At midday he made them eat, even though they hadn't wanted to. He tossed them the water canteen regularly. They were both pale and tense and clumsy on their horses. Grief was a hard master.

By late afternoon, they'd traveled miles and hadn't found so much as a sign of their brother.

And they never would. Matt had resigned himself to Wilby's fate many hours ago. He wouldn't be able to bring his little body back to camp so his mother could have the thin relief of a Christian burial. Wilby had either been washed along the Green River, far beyond their reach, or he was caught at its bottom, tangled in the watery half-light. The thought was Matt's undoing. Like an avalanche, the sobs took him. After a while, he'd stopped fighting and had just given into the tears, weeping as he rode. The sight of the boys searching tirelessly, helplessly, made him cry harder. He cried for them and for their mother, whose pain he couldn't even begin to imagine. And he cried for Wilby, barely more than a baby, lost and alone. The thought of the boy out there, with no one to comfort him in death, had Matt crying until his head throbbed.

The sight of him unnerved the twins when he caught up to them at the end of the day. He'd kept back, making sure they were in sight, but far enough away so they wouldn't see his distress. When he finally rode up to call the day off, they were standing in the low afternoon light, caked with mud, their eyes dull with the realization that the search was ending. When they saw Matt's red eyes and wet face, they cracked.

Phin shook his head and backed away until he just about tumbled into the river. Matt was off his horse and pulling him back from the lip of the river before he could fall. He couldn't lose another one of these children.

"So, that's it?" Flip asked. His voice was thick with tears. "You're giving up?"

"No!" Phin thumped Matt with his fist. It hurt but Matt let him thump. "NO! We'll go out again tomorrow!"

"There's no point," Matt told him gently.

"Fuck you!" Phin launched himself at Matt, punching him hard.

Matt did the only thing he could think to do and yanked the boy into a bear hug, lifting him off the ground. Phin struggled in his arms. Matt let him struggle.

Flip started to cry. "It's all my fault," he said, sinking into the grass and burying his face in his hands.

Matt let him cry, much as he let his brother struggle. Eventually, Phin grew still, even though he was as rigid as a tent pole.

"What if he's out there?" he asked Matt fiercely.

"He *is* out there," Matt told him, "but not anywhere we'll ever find him." He lowered the boy to the ground but kept tight hold of him. "He's dead, Phin."

The boy glared at him. But Matt could see the shine of tears and the black gleam of despair behind the rage.

"There's nothing more we could have done," Matt said gently.

Flip cried harder behind them.

"It's not your fault," Phin growled at his brother.

"It is. I wasn't watching him properly." Flip was wretched with grief. He cried so hard he started to vomit.

Matt let Phin go and went to hold Flip's head as he threw up. He pulled the boy's hair out of the way and held him up.

"It isn't your fault," Phin raged at him. "It's *mine.*"

Matt looked up and saw the shame at work in Phin.

"He followed *me* into the rushes."

"It's not your fault," Matt told him. "Nor yours." He stroked Flip's hair. The kid was wringing himself inside out. "If it's anyone's fault, it's mine. I oughtta have been watching out for you all."

"Don't be stupid." The shine in Phin's eyes had materialized into angry tears, which tumbled freely. "You can't watch us every minute of the day."

"Wilby was my job," Flip whimpered. He'd stopped vomiting now and sagged back against Matt.

"It was his dumb dog's fault," Phin said, wiping his face, still angry. "If Woof hadn't jumped in the water, Wilby wouldn't have jumped in after him."

Something inside Matt shriveled up at that. He'd been the one to give Wilby the dog.

"It weren't your fault," he said sternly, "and I won't hear any more about it. You two might be big for your age and as impertinent as all get-out, but you're still kids. And kids ain't responsible for things like this. You let the adults take the blame for this one." He rubbed Flip's back. "You two got one job and one job only now, and that's to look after your womenfolk. Your ma will be suffering like you ain't seen suffering before." His heart twisted at the thought. "She needs you now. And your little sister will too."

He saw how Phin straightened. That was one raw nerve of a kid. Flip was gentler, more sensitive; Phin was brasher, more impulsive. He was more likely to run wild. Of the two of them, Matt was more worried about Phin. Flip would cry it out, but Phin would carry Wilby's death with him like a thorn in the heart.

Maybe a mission would help him.

"Phin, I'm going to put you in charge of taking care of your mother, you hear? She's going to need reminding to eat, for a start. Grief saps your will to live. I need you to help keep her alive until that will comes back."

Phin nodded. He latched onto the order like it was a lifeline. His jaw set stubbornly, and the shine of tears dried up.

"And you need to look out for Susannah," Matt told Flip. This twin's eyes were shimmering with misery.

He stood up, pulling Flip to his feet. "It's up to us now, boys. We need to keep this family safe until the storm passes."

"What if it doesn't pass?" Flip's hand was shaking as he wiped his face.

Matt rested a hand on his shoulder and looked him dead in the eye. "It will pass. All things pass. Just when you think it hurts so much you can't take it anymore, you find you can. And then it eases off, a little more every day, until it don't feel so bad." He took a shaky breath. "It will always hurt. But it won't always hurt this bad." He hoped that was true. "Now, clean yourself up."

"Wilby never even got to meet Leo," Phin said as they watched Flip wash his face and hands in the river. "He was born after they left."

Oh hell. Matt winced. That poor woman. He'd almost forgotten about her other lost son. She never spoke of him—he guessed the fear and worry made speaking of him too sharp. Jesus. Imagine the pain she was in, lying back there in that tent, grieving her last born and in mortal fear for her firstborn.

"Come on," he said tightly. "We'd best get back to your ma."

"Can we take a minute to say good-bye to Wilby?" Flip asked. He was still weeping.

"Of course." Matt joined the boys at the riverside. They watched the streaky sunset shine on the rushing waters, split into slivers of copper and gold. Matt could hear Flip sniffling. Phin picked up a stone and skipped it across the water. The water drops looked like liquid gold as they sprayed into the air.

"I'm taking one of these," Phin said gruffly, pocketing a stone, "to remember him by."

Mutely, Flip did the same.

Matt picked one up too, feeling its cool length fit neatly into his palm. He took one for Georgiana and one for Susannah as well. One day, when things weren't so sharp, he'd give them the stones so they could carry a piece of Wilby's resting place with them.

"It's going to take us half the night to get back," Flip sniffed as they mounted up. But they didn't rush. They kept the horses to a walk, taking in the shimmer of the river and the beaten bronze sky, keeping watch over the fading of the day. Tomorrow would bring a new day. One without Wilby in it.

IT WAS DEEP night when they returned to camp. The sky was a great arc of stars, moonless and cloudless. The men on watch gave them sympathetic looks and took the horses from them.

"We'll feed and water them," Earl Colicut assured Matt. "You go to your lady." He nodded his head toward the campfire.

Matt's heart squeezed at the sight of Georgiana. She had

Susannah cradled on her lap and a quilt over her shoulders as she stared sightlessly at the flames.

Matt led the sleepy boys toward her. She looked up at the sound of their approach. Ah hell. He hated the way hope flared in her eyes at the sight of them. Some part of her still thought they'd be bringing Wilby back to her, muddy and scratched up from his adventure . . . but alive.

Matt tasted bile as he shook his head at her. The hopeful spark fizzed out and her face crumpled. She seemed to collapse in on herself, her cries hoarse and hopeless.

Matt gave the boys a nudge. They looked up at him.

"Go to her," he told them in a low voice.

They did as he asked, rushing over, even though the sight of their mother's pain was clearly distressing for them. He watched as they huddled close, awkwardly putting their arms around her.

Phin looked over at Matt and gestured him closer. "You too," he mouthed.

Matt shook his head. It wasn't his place.

Phin glared at him.

He shook his head again. He felt agonizingly unsure. What if she didn't want him there? He didn't want to intrude.

Phin broke free and stomped back to Matt. He was looking mutinous. "You said she needs us," he hissed, "and that means you too." He grabbed Matt's sleeve and yanked him along.

"I don't want to get in the way."

"Don't be stupid."

When they reached Georgiana, she fixed Matt with a suffering gaze. There was such misery in her eyes. But also something else. A plea. He didn't know what she wanted, but she was mutely begging him for something. Something he wasn't sure he could give. He dropped to his knees beside her and clumsily put his arms around her and Flip. He felt Phin's arms lock around him, pressing him closer to Georgiana. Georgiana dropped her head and pressed her face into Matt's neck. He felt her shudder as she broke into earnest sobs. That woke Susannah, who whimpered and looked up from the center of the hug.

"It's all right, Sook," Flip said, his hand burrowing down to pat her dark curls, "we're here."

Matt felt their bodies lean into him. He braced, taking their
weight. Their tight knot shuddered with Georgiana's weeping.
He took the shock of it. Because there was no one else to do
what needed doing. And also because tonight, in the welter of
grief, there was nowhere else he could imagine being. This
was where he belonged. He lowered his head, resting his
cheek against Georgiana's curls, murmuring senseless sounds
of comfort.

T HEY HAD A funeral, even though there was no body to bury. Matt made the coffin himself, and they put Wilby's wooden sword in it. Georgiana had intended to put his quilt in there too but panicked at the last moment and took it out. She slept with it afterward, burrowing her face in the fabric to extract the last lingering scent of her baby. When she found his scent, she would weep. When she didn't, she wept even harder.

They held the funeral at sunup on their last day at the campsite. The grave was close to the river, in view of the Mormon Ferry, and people came from Josiah Sampson's train as well as from Matt's to watch them bury the empty coffin. Even the whores gathered at the back of the group, crying. Most of them knew what it was like to lose a child, and they stood in a tight knot, comforting one another as the tiny coffin was lowered into the earth.

The funeral was the one time Georgiana didn't cry. She was numb with the horror of it. Her mind kept snagging on awful thoughts. Like the fact that the coffin was empty, like the fact that she would never know where her baby was laid to rest, like the fact that he was all alone out there, at the mercy of the elements. He was exposed to the heat and the cold. Her baby was all alone. The thoughts made her limbs weak. Her stomach was hot and sour, and her head felt like it was caught in a vise. This couldn't be happening.

But it was. The pastor said his words. Georgiana couldn't focus on what he said; for all she knew, he might have been speaking a foreign tongue. All she heard was the scratchy quality of his voice and the sound of people sniffling behind her.

The morning seethed with the promise of coming heat; the

river rushed on, full of storm water heading to the sea; and the dirt was warm and loose in her hand, making a dry patter on the coffin as she dropped it into the grave. *Earth to earth . . .*

But he wasn't in there. He might not be in earth at all. He might be in water.

She clenched her jaw to stop the scream that was building. She was a Fairchild Bee, and Fairchild Bees didn't scream in public. Not even when the rasp of a shovel signaled the filling in of her baby's grave, not even when the earth was patted down and a wooden cross was spiked into the fresh earth. Not even when she saw his name burned into the cross: *William Bee Blunt.* She'd given up all pretense of the name Smith—no one had believed it anyway.

Oh God. She couldn't do this. She felt her knees shake. She was going to fall.

But she didn't fall, because Matt was there to hold her up. And he kept holding her up, all through those long days and weeks to Fort Hall.

There was no more talk of weddings. There was no more kissing. There was just the long trail and the beating sun of August. The day of the funeral, Matt had taken the reins of Georgiana's lead wagon, and he didn't let them go. He surrendered the scouting to his employees and stayed by her side. Georgiana sat next to him on the bench, Susannah close beside her, while the twins flanked the wagon on their horses. Wilby's nest behind the wagon seat was painfully empty, but none of them could bear to move the blankets, or the slate and chalk, or the small toys Wilby had left behind.

They crossed the river on the ferry, and when they reached the other side, Georgiana had to press the back of her hand to her mouth to stifle a scream. She couldn't leave him. *How could she leave him?* Matt reached over and took her free hand, which was clenched in her lap. She gripped his hand for dear life as he flicked the ox team and drove them away from the Green River and away from Wilby.

That first day was sheer hell. It took every ounce of strength she had not to go tearing back to the river. Half of her wanted to stay there forever in the land where her baby had died. But the other half of her was driven by a different grief . . .

Leo.

The need for her eldest son was so strong it was physical.
Her arms ached to hold him. It had been so long since she'd
seen him . . . she didn't even know what he looked like anymore. He'd be so much taller . . . Oh God, please let him be
safe. She couldn't bear it if something had happened to
him too.

Georgiana passed the first week in a daze. It took all of her
energy just to stay upright. Breathing was difficult. Her
thoughts swung madly between Wilby and Leo. She felt like
she'd been torn in two: half of her was on the riverbanks of the
Green River, and the other half was ahead of her in California.
And none of her was right here, right now. Somehow, she kept
breathing. And eating. She couldn't sleep, but she didn't expect to. She lay through the long reaches of the night, crammed
into the tent with the children, listening to them breathing, her
mind running over memories of Wilby and Leo, trying to fix
their faces in her mind.

She had no hope of being happy again. Her heart seemed
to have turned to stone in her chest. But she didn't need happiness for herself. All she needed was to get her son and to
keep her children safe. She had been a fool to think she could
find happiness with Matt. She'd forgotten that her first and
only goal was protecting her children . . .

HE'D INTENDED TO marry her here, Matt thought morosely as
they headed into Fort Bridger. Usually, he bypassed the trading post, preferring the shortcut along Sublette's Cutoff. But
the cutoff was brutal, a fifty-mile stretch without fresh water,
grass or relief from the heat, and Matt wanted to let his party
find a little ease first. They could buy fresh animals from Old
Gabe, restock their supplies and enjoy a very slight touch of
civilization before the long hell ahead. He wanted to get them
over the cutoff in a week at most, which meant pushing them
hard. He needed them fresh to handle a push like that.

Or more accurately, *he* needed to be fresh, and he wasn't.
He was wrung out after Wilby's death. Georgiana was still
deep in grief, and Matt found the children turning more and
more to him as their mother withdrew into herself. They
missed her. Matt knew how they felt. He missed her too. She
was silent these days, a tense white presence, like a ghost in

their midst. The boys were living up to their promise, making sure she ate and generally watching out for her welfare, and the women of the camp were godsends, cooking for the family, washing their clothes, making sure Matt and the children were coping. And they were coping. But miserably, watching Georgiana closely for signs of life.

As they rattled up to the palisaded log cabins that made up the modest settlement of Fort Bridger, Matt couldn't help but ruminate on better times. Those golden days back on the Sweetwater, when he'd kissed her at will; her glee when she'd said she'd marry him; the brightness of her prairie flax blue eyes; the ease of her smile . . .

He'd thought he'd be getting married here. *Him*, the most unmarrying man he knew. And now that he wasn't getting married, he was genuinely bereft. Instead of a celebration, their stop in Fort Bridger was a morose event. It was just a series of cheerless chores. Matt took the children with him to the blacksmith to get repairs made; he had them help him and Kipp and Wendell with the iron wagon tires, which already needed refitting; and they stocked up on water barrels, which they'd desperately need on the barren plain ahead.

"Thatta girl," Matt said, lifting Susannah down from the wagon, where she'd been helping secure the barrels. She kept hold of his hand. She'd grown quieter since Wilby's death and was prone to sucking her thumb, something Matt had never seen her do before. She also didn't want to be alone, ever, sticking close to either her mother or Matt at all times.

Oddly, Matt found he didn't mind her shadowing him. It was a damn sight better than being alone. The minute he was alone, his feelings bit him in the ass. The worst time was at night, when they were all in their tent, and everyone bar the lookouts was asleep. He'd roll up in his blankets by the damped-down fire, feeling like the last man on earth, even though he was surrounded by tents full of people. When he was alone, his thoughts got too big to handle.

It was the damnedest thing. He'd spent most of his life alone and never thought he minded it. He'd thought he *preferred* it. But here he was, staring up at the infinite sky, feeling a loneliness so bone-deep it made him ache. He longed for someone to come and slide into his bedroll with him. No, not someone. *Her.* He wanted her here with him, nestled in close. He wanted to stroke her hair and watch the stars with her, or to simply sit with her through the worst of her grief. He wanted more than anything to fix it for her, to take away the pain; but if he couldn't take away the pain, at least he could suffer it with her, so she wasn't so alone.

But she was so alone. And so out of reach that she might as well have been on another planet. Every night, when the stars got too much for him, with their merciless distance, he rolled over and stared at the pale bulb of her tent instead. He knew she wasn't sleeping. The twins had told him, but even if they hadn't, he would have known by the dark circles under her eyes. He stared at the canvas of her tent and wondered if she was missing him as much as he was missing her.

SUBLETTE'S CUTOFF WAS brutal. The tableland was a waterless wasteland, baking in the searing August sun. They lasted two days before Matt called a halt and changed the schedule so they'd travel at night, to avoid the worst of the heat. Everyone was sunburned and limp, and they were using more water traveling through the daylight hours than they would traveling at night. Worse, the animals were being depleted; even the fresh ones were suffering. Night traveling would help them all survive. Matt had the party spread out and travel side by side, rather than in a snaking train, as the alkali dust out here was thick and gritty and made traveling an utter misery. The wagons stretched abreast across the broad and desolate plain, their wide trail of dust silvery white in the moonlight. Matt arranged for the scouts, and as many of the boys as he could round up on horseback, to travel a few yards ahead with lanterns aloft, to lead the way.

The nights were eerie, dreamlike hours, as they shuddered in the wagons across a black and silver landscape, the sounds weirdly amplified by the darkness. The days they spent sweltering in their tents or under the wagons. It only took a few days before everyone realized that the ground beneath the wagons was the coolest place to be. They draped the canvas from their tents so it fringed the wagon trays all the way to the ground, until they'd made dark caves between the wagon wheels. They piled quilts and bedding on the horrid dusty ground and curled up in the low space to wait out the worst of the day's heat. Matt would have slunk off to join Seb under the chuck wagon if it weren't for the children. They begged him to join them under their lead wagon. All three were tense from the emotional labor of caring for their mother and were desperate for Matt to step in and take responsibility. Being alone with Georgiana under the wagon suffocated them. Matt could see Wendell scowling as Matt crawled under the canvas to join Georgiana. Wendell hadn't been happy to be shunted to the second wagon, or to see Matt grow closer to the children. The only comfort he could take was in Georgiana's coolness to Matt. But then, she was cool to everyone these days.

It was cramped under the wagon, but Matt preferred it to sleeping out alone. These reversed hours had one benefit: he now got to spend his sleeping hours with other people. It made a huge difference. For the first time since Wilby's death, he could actually sleep. The sound of the children's breathing, deep and slow in sleep, was soothing. Oddly, so was the sight of Georgiana's back across the way. Just being close to her helped ease the pressure in Matt's chest, and despite the close heat, he drifted off into deep and dreamless sleep.

He woke once, thinking he heard crying. He lay still, straining to hear, but there was nothing but the sound of breathing. The twins were sprawled on their backs, mouths open, and Susannah was curled up in a ball by the wagon wheel, like a cat. He heard the sound again. It was Georgiana. She was at the far end, between the front wheels, with her back to him. She had her face buried in Wilby's quilt. She was too far away for Matt to reach, and he couldn't get to her without climbing over the children. He lay still, listening to her cry for a few moments. The sound was like needles being pushed into his skin.

He wriggled out from under the wagon, emerging into searing afternoon light. The sun was glaring down on the camp, striking hard glints off the iron tires. The animals were sitting in the pasture between the circled wagons, looking utterly defeated. Jesus, he'd be glad to be out of this wasteland. It wasn't fit for man or beast.

He moved to the front of the wagon and lifted the canvas. He heard Georgiana make a muffled noise of surprise. When she lifted her face from the quilt, she was a red-eyed picture of misery.

"Ah, honey," he said quietly. Then he ducked under the canvas and crawled around her until he was between her and the children.

"What are you doing?" There was a spark of her old self in the question. A bit of zap and zest.

"What I should have done all along," he sighed, lying down on his side behind her and wrapping his arm over her. He pulled her up against him. It was too hot to be this close, but somehow, he didn't think either of them would care. "You mind if I share your pillow?" He didn't wait for her to answer, but put his head down behind hers. She was stiff against him, but she didn't ask him to leave. He ran his hand up and down her arm, slowly, the way he'd soothe a spooked horse. He heard her start weeping again. He didn't try to stop her—how could he? If anyone had cause to weep, it was her. He simply lay behind her, stroking her arm, until he felt her melt back into him.

"Hush, now," he murmured eventually. "I'm here. Sleep."

And, astonishingly, she did. She cried herself right to sleep, relaxing in his arms. In sleep, her face was soft, her lips puffy and downturned, her eyes swollen. He twined his fingers through hers and felt her unconsciously tighten her grip.

"Hush," he whispered again. "Hush, I'm here."

She gave a shuddery sigh and slipped deeper into sleep. He watched over her, murmuring when she grew restless, holding her to keep the loneliness at bay. His loneliness, as much as hers.

❧ 30 ❧

Deathrider had barely been back a week before Two Bears was hounding him about marriage.

"You need a wife," his adopted father told him.

"This is why I don't come home," Deathrider grumbled. "You're like an old woman." He hadn't been back for a couple of years, but nothing seemed to have changed. The summer village was pitched, the tepees spread in the usual order, the buffalo hunts planned, the children running underfoot with the dogs.

It was good to be home.

"Running Elk's daughter has come of age."

Deathrider groaned. "So that's what this is about."

"The Lakota are our allies." Two Bears was his usual implacable self. Not even a buffalo stampede could deter him when he was set on a path. "It would be good to strengthen our bonds."

"Running Elk won't want me." Deathrider didn't bother to hide his frustration. "You know this. You may have adopted me, but Running Elk sees only a white man."

Two Bears shrugged. "We won't know until we ask."

"Ask for yourself; you need a new wife."

Two Bears shook his head. "It is too soon for me."

"It will always be too soon for me," Deathrider said sourly.

"You should have been married years ago. You're becoming an old man."

Deathrider walked away. But Two Bears wouldn't let up.

"At least meet her," his father said a week later. "You might like her."

"I don't want a wife," Deathrider reminded him.

"Her name is White Buffalo." As though that should sway

him. Deathrider didn't care what her name was; he wasn't interested in marrying her.

"I'm not staying," he told his father, "so there's no point in marrying anyone. No woman wants to be left behind."

"If you had a wife, you would have a reason to stay."

There was just no arguing with him.

"If the treaty is so important to you, let Spotted Tail take her to wife." Spotted Tail was Two Bears's youngest son.

"He's promised elsewhere."

Deathrider snorted. "Then have your brother's son Stands Tall do it."

"I hear she is beautiful."

And then Two Bears played dirty and invited Deathrider on a buffalo hunt. Only when they were riding out did he casually mention they would be hunting with Running Elk's tribe and the feast would be held in their village.

"This is why I stay away for so long," Deathrider grumbled, "because of you and your damn matchmaking."

"You brought the white man, I see," Running Elk told Two Bears when they arrived in his village.

Deathrider gave his father an I-told-you-so look, but Two Bears was staring resolutely ahead.

People had gathered to gawp as Deathrider and Two Bears met with Running Elk. Deathrider's fame had spread even through the tribes of the plains.

"I am glad you're here, White Man," Running Elk said soberly.

Deathrider cringed. Oh hell. Did Running Elk actually *approve* of Two Bears's mad idea? If so, it was going to cause no end of trouble and offense when Deathrider turned the girl down.

"I did not know you were coming, but since you are here, I have something for you," Running Elk told him.

Two Bears almost smiled at that.

Hell, hell, hell. This was going to be unpleasant. Deathrider tried to head it off. "I'm not staying," he said shortly. "I have travels to make."

Two Bears shot him a poisonous look.

Running Elk nodded, satisfied. "That suits me."

Deathrider's stomach sank. What did that mean? That he

could leave the girl behind? Or that he was expected to take her with him? Because he wasn't about to do either.

"White Buffalo!" Running Elk called for his daughter.

Deathrider could have throttled his father, who looked far too self-satisfied for his own good.

Eventually, a girl appeared. She was too young for Death-rider's taste. She should have been called Shy Deer or Darting Rabbit, or anything but White Buffalo. She had none of the buffalo's strength and power, none of its bullish nature. She crept forward, eyes downcast, looking on the verge of tears.

Running Elk's face darkened at the sight of her timidity. "Where is it?" he snapped.

Deathrider frowned. Where was what?

The girl risked a glance at her father and blanched. "Please don't make me," she said softly. "I don't wish to disobey you in public."

Running Elk's expression was as angry as a thundercloud. "Then do not disobey me. Go and fetch it. The white man can have it. It is not our problem."

Ah, *there* was the reason she was named for the buffalo. She had gone rigidly stubborn and shook her head. "Don't ask me." Her eyes had filled with mutinous tears.

What the hell was going on here?

Running Elk made a noise of complete frustration. "I have lost patience with this whim of yours." He turned back to Two Bears and Deathrider. "Come. If she won't bring it to you, I shall take you to it."

The tribe studiously avoided their eyes, so as not to shame Running Elk as he overrode his disobedient daughter.

"Please don't," White Buffalo begged, trotting along after them. "He causes no harm!"

Deathrider and Two Bears exchanged looks. This was the strangest visit they'd ever experienced.

Running Elk led them to a tepee, which clearly belonged to his daughters. The younger girls scattered respectfully to make way for their father. Deathrider could hear the excited yipping of a puppy.

White Buffalo darted in front of her father. "No! He's mine! The river sent him to me."

"You will go in there and get him and give him to the white

man," Running Elk growled. "He doesn't belong here. He belongs with his own kind."

Deathrider tried not to take offense. He could feel his father bristling beside him. He caught Two Bears's eye and gave a small shake of his head to stop the old man from speaking. It helped no one to rehash the old arguments.

"If you don't go in there and get him, I will," Running Elk threatened.

Tears were spilling down White Buffalo's face. She was clearly on the verge of surrender and wasn't happy about it. Her big brown eyes shifted to Deathrider.

"You'll take care of him? You won't make him a slave? Or mistreat him?"

"White Buffalo!" Running Elk had passed into fury now. "It is not your place to question my guest!"

She didn't care. Even through the tears her gaze was firm. "He has nightmares," she told Deathrider, "and gets upset if you take his dog away from him. You have to let him keep the puppy."

"He doesn't *have* to do anything!"

"I have no idea what you're talking about," Deathrider said honestly, "so I can't promise anything."

Running Elk was out of patience. He pushed his daughter aside and plunged into the tepee. White Buffalo dashed in after him, and they could hear the manic barking of a pup.

"Perhaps she has a bear cub in there," Two Bears mused. "I once knew a woman who kept a bear. She was a powerful witch. Maybe White Buffalo is a witch." He paused. "If she is, you won't be marrying her."

"I won't be marrying her even if she isn't a witch."

They were interrupted by Running Elk emerging with an armful of writhing fur and flailing limbs. An Indian puppy was wriggling and yipping and licking Running Elk's chin. The chief tilted his head back to avoid the flicking pink tongue. But it wasn't the puppy that sent a shock through Deathrider, even though he recognized it. It was the boy. He dangled over Running Elk's other arm, cheerful despite the chaos, his dark curls corkscrewing in every direction, his blue eyes laughing.

"Wilby!" Deathrider felt like he'd been struck by lightning. What in hell was Georgiana's son doing in a Lakota village?

"There," Running Elk told his daughter smugly, "I told you the white man would help. They all know one another."

"Tom!" Wilby threw his arms out and launched himself at Deathrider. Deathrider caught him awkwardly. The boy hugged him fiercely. "Tom-Tom-Tom." He patted Deathrider on the back of the neck. "Where's Mama?"

"Tom?" Two Bears's eyebrows went up. "Since when have you been called Tom? Don't you have enough names already?"

Deathrider ignored him. "Wilby?" He held the boy at a distance. It was definitely Wilby. And the dog was definitely Woof. He wasn't imagining it. "What in hell are you doing here?"

"Playing hide-and-seek!"

"You what?"

"She found me!" Wilby pointed at White Buffalo. "Now you found me! Can we find Mama now?"

"Are all white people so careless with their children?" Running Elk asked Two Bears.

Two Bears sighed deeply. "This is why I can't let him choose his own wife. What if he chose a white woman? I don't want my grandchildren wandering lost."

Running Elk nodded sagely.

"I had thought . . . " Two Bears began.

"No!" Deathrider and Running Elk said simultaneously, cutting him off. They both knew marriage was on his mind.

"I have travels to make," Deathrider said shortly, tucking Wilby under his arm and starting for his horse. Woof followed along, yipping.

"You see," Running Elk told Two Bears, "white people are too erratic. He would be a terrible husband."

"I would!" Deathrider agreed, calling back over his shoulder.

Two Bears sighed again.

Running Elk gave him a sympathetic look. "I warned you when you took him in that he would bring you pain."

"You did." They watched Deathrider mount his horse and settle the white boy on the saddle in front of him. "You are wise not to keep the child," Two Bears said sadly. "It is hard to watch them go."

"That is the way of the white people," Running Elk grunted. "They are always moving, never happy. Even their children run away." He glanced at his daughter, who was weeping as she watched Wilby gallop off with Deathrider. "I don't understand the appeal."

He walked off, leaving Two Bears and White Buffalo watching until the last trace of Deathrider's dust had faded from the air.

❦ 31 ❦

TIME LOST ALL meaning in the Lava Lands. Forever after, Georgiana would equate the feeling of grief with the grotesquerie they found in the gray and bitterly hot stretch of land between Fort Bridger and Fort Hall. Despair would feel like dust and thirst and the baking heat of the closeted space under the wagon, and the deepest, blackest hopelessness would taste like the sulfuric springs and geysers that spat from the scorched earth. It was as close to Hell as any landscape was likely to get, Georgiana thought as they wound between the great rocky cones that rose from the ground. The springs around them ran hot and cold, and billowed steam; the waters were undrinkable, red and yellow and chalky in color, some with the metallic taste of hot blood, some the flavor of yeasty beer gone bad. On all sides, geysers vomited great explosions of stinking water into the sky.

This was the world of her grief.

As they hit the ravaged reaches of the Lava Lands, Matt had them traveling during daylight again. It was too dangerous to traverse the springs in darkness. Once they were back in their tents at night, and not cowering under the wagon through the worst of the day's heat, Matt no longer slept with them. He stayed close, unrolling his bedding just outside the door of the tent, but he was no longer at her back, one arm heavy across her, anchoring her. Once he'd gone, Georgiana felt like the last tethers keeping her tied to the ground had broken free, and she was adrift, lost in a half-light of grief. She spent the days in a trance, swaying next to Matt in the jolting wagon, holding Susannah's hand, not speaking. If she could have, she would have slept every moment of the day. Only in sleep was there any relief from the pain. Except when the dreams came . . .

In her dreams, Wilby was still alive. Night after night in her dreams she ran along the riverside, sweating, her heart racing, feeling an overwhelming sense of anxiety. And then Wilby would appear out of the cool emerald grasses, everything would grow quiet and still, and a sense of blessed peace would take her. In her dreams his face was crystal clear: the tiny pearly baby teeth when he smiled, the impish gleam in his blue eyes. The joy she felt at seeing him was overpowering: it was as though the world was a flower and was opening to her, revealing the majesty and mystery of being. She had Wilby. And that was all that mattered.

Then she'd wake up to the oppressive heat of the tent and to the stark horror of reality. She'd feel the crushing grief all over again, as fresh as the first day. It was wearing. But she would take the grief if it meant she could see Wilby again, even if it was only in her dreams.

"Oh, thank God," Matt sighed late one afternoon as they rattled and shuddered to the end of another wretched day. "We're almost there."

"There" was Steamboat Springs.

"Just you wait." He reached behind Georgiana and ruffled Susannah's hair. "We're nearly out of the woods. Boys," he called, sounding exuberant with relief, "go on and ride ahead until you see a big piece of water! That's where we'll be stopping." The twins whooped and rode off. "Be safe!" Matt yelled after them.

Georgiana noticed numbly that the ground was now spattered with grass. Eventually, they rolled onto a carpet of the stuff. It looked strange after so many miles of the grassless wasteland behind them. Strange and wonderful. There were hills, *green* hills, not just rocky upcroppings, and trees, *real trees*. Georgiana had forgotten how pretty trees could be. But prettiest of all was the large spring nestled among the grass and hills and trees.

"See all those bubbles?" Matt asked Susannah, pointing at the churning water. He'd given up trying to speak to Georgiana directly days ago. She knew she should be polite and speak when spoken to, but somehow, she couldn't. She felt trapped down deep in her own body, unable to do more than just sit here and let the world roll by. Just staying upright and breathing and blinking (and not screaming) was almost more than she could handle.

"You know what those bubbles mean?"

Susannah wrinkled her nose. "That it tastes as bad as the stuff Phin got me to drink?"

Matt laughed. "No, honey. Not this time. This is pure carbonated water. And you know what we're going to do with it when we camp for the night?"

Susannah shook her head.

"Make lemonade!"

Georgiana watched them as though from a great distance. She couldn't remember what it felt like to be happy, she realized suddenly. She couldn't even imagine it. The idea of smiling seemed immensely foreign. As did caring about a trivial thing like lemonade.

Before they'd even camped, there was a great gathering of people at the waterside. There was whooping and laughing and cheering. They were celebrating the end of the Lava Lands. Georgiana watched dully as they fell into an impromptu party, mixing great batches of lemonade (with liquor for those old enough to take it), singing and telling tales of their great journey through the wasteland. Georgiana didn't feel the slightest stirring of joy as she stared at the spring. She felt like she hadn't really left the Lava Lands behind, and perhaps she never would. Her world was as barren as it had been before. No cup of lemonade forced into her hand could change that.

She saw Matt's expression falter when she didn't drink from the cup. She should feel something. But she didn't. She drank the lemonade because it was expected of her, but it tasted no better or worse than the sulfur springs of days ago. No one expected her to join the party, and she didn't. As soon as the tent was pitched, she retired for the night, watching the shadows leap against the canvas and hearing the sound of music and voices from an immense distance, like hearing noises from the shore when you were miles out at sea.

THEY STAYED AT Steamboat Springs for a few days. The journeying had been hard and had taken its toll. People lolled by the water or went rambling, discovering smaller springs, some as cold and fresh as a cupful of heaven. Or so they said. Georgiana didn't go and see for herself.

"How long are we here?" she asked Matt after a couple of days.

He shrugged. He was giving her that look he gave her lately, the one that made her feel like she was a wild animal and he was working out how dangerous she was. Whether he should shoot her or run. "Until I feel everyone's ready to move on," he said carefully.

"I'm ready to move on."

He looked dubious.

"I have to get to my son."

Now he was giving her that other look he had. The one that was full of sympathy and pity and care and something else—something that looked an awful lot like love. Before Wilby's death that look would have meant something to her. But not now. Day by day her heart had grown as barren as a desert.

"We'll go as soon as we can," he said, his voice tender. The Georgiana from before would have melted to hear that tone in his voice. "Just as soon as the animals have recovered and the people are robust again."

"I need to get Leo."

"I know." His hand moved to touch her, but he hesitated at the last minute and then dropped it helplessly to his side. He frowned for a moment. "Would you take a walk with me?" he asked.

She shook her head. The thought of walking anywhere was too much. She was so tired.

"We need to talk," he said gently. "About the future."

What future? She had to get her son. That was the only future there was.

"Come on," he insisted. She was too weary to even bother resisting. It seemed easier to plod along beside him than to keep protesting. He led her away from the camp, around the edge of the spring, which made disconcerting bubbling noises.

The sound of birds was also disconcerting. There'd been no birdsong since Green River.

"We ain't far from Fort Hall now," Matt said gruffly, not looking at her.

Fort Hall. That was one step closer to California. From there, they would turn south, to the goldfields: to Leo.

Georgiana was so preoccupied that she didn't notice Matt's growing frustration.

"The trail splits at Fort Hall," he reminded her.

She nodded. She knew. She was hanging on by a thread just to get to California; she knew all too well what Fort Hall meant.

"Goddamn it," he said. He stopped walking and ran his hands through his hair as he turned to face the springs. He took a deep breath. "Goddamn it," he muttered again.

He didn't look like he was going to move again anytime soon, so Georgiana sat down on a fallen tree. From here she had a clear view over the springs to the campsite. Threads of smoke rose into the hot August sky.

She heard the rasp of Matt's whiskers against his palms as he rubbed his face.

"Look," he said, putting his hands on his hips and turning to face her, "I know that you're in no state to be making decisions right now. I know you near about got the heart ripped out of you. But we're just about to Fort Hall, and we don't have any more time."

She had no idea what he was talking about.

"Goddamn it," he said again. "The wedding," he explained. He clearly found it hard to get the words out.

"What wedding?" She still had no idea what he was talking about.

"*Our* wedding."

Georgiana stared at him, astonished. What on earth did he mean, *our* wedding? There wasn't going to be any wedding. Wilby was *dead*.

She felt a burn spreading through her. Her hands and feet prickled with heat. Her son was *dead*, and he was talking about *weddings*?

"I know getting married is the last thing on your mind," he sighed, "but I've done a lot of thinking on this, and it's best for everyone if we get this thing done."

"Best for everyone?" Somehow, he'd broken through her numbness. The world was no longer at a great distance. It came rushing in. "It's not best for *me*."

"I beg to differ," he said tersely. "You need me."

"I don't need anything but *my son*." Pain flashed through her at the words. Because the words made her think of Wilby more than of Leo. Oh God, she did need him. And she couldn't have him. Never, never, never, never again.

Matt blanched.

"I can't get married. I'm in mourning," she told him fiercely.

He nodded. "That's as may be. But things are different out here. We do what we must, and that means we don't always cater to fine sensibilities."

"It's not a sensibility," she cried. Her composure was cracking. "It's *common decency*."

"Common decency won't save Leo," he said grimly. "And I don't fancy you and those little ones waltzing into Moke-lumne Hill and putting yourselves at the mercy of Wendell and his boss. You'll find yourself pressured into marrying Wendell Todd before you're even there. Marrying me will mean that ain't a possibility no more. That's why you propositioned me in the first place, remember?"

She clenched her jaw. She wasn't so grief-stricken that she'd lost her reason. His words struck a nerve.

"Georgiana . . . " His eyes were soft with golden light. Pleading. "You *wanted* to marry me."

"That was before." There was a swelling in her throat. Like she had swallowed an apple whole.

"I know." He took a step toward her but stopped when she flinched. "I can't even imagine the pain you're in right now. If I could stop time right here, right now, I would. I'd give you a season by the springs to feel your hurt. To heal. But I cain't do that. Time's marching on, and once we start marching on with it along that trail, we're going to reach Fort Hall. And at Fort Hall, Joe's party turns to California, and mine . . . " He stumbled and had to clear his throat. "And mine . . . doesn't."

"I release you from our arrangement," she said numbly. Was that what he wanted? Was that what this was about?

"I don't want to be released, goddamn it!" He lost his temper at that and kicked at a tussock of grass.

Exhaustion rolled over Georgiana in a heavy wave. She al-most sank back down under the weight of it. "What do you want?" she asked. She just wanted to go back and curl up in her tent. She wanted the world to go away. She didn't want to see anything, hear anything or feel anything.

"I want *you*," he said helplessly. "I want to help you. I want to get your son back. I want to keep those children of yours safe. I want to sleep next to you at night and not be lying outside your door like a pet dog. I want us to do this *together*."

Georgiana let his words roll over her. She could barely take them in.

"Honey," Matt said, moving toward her and taking her hands. "I know you're lost right now, but trust me. Please. Let me help you. Trust that you'll come through this blackness, and I'll be there. *We'll* be there." His thumbs stroked the backs of her hands. She felt the urge to melt into him, to surrender to him. "I know it won't be the wedding you deserve. I know it won't be a happy day, and that ain't right. But marrying me at Fort Hall is your best option right now. We'll go with Joe. Seb can lead my party to Oregon City—he's done the trail plenty of times before, and he'll be fine. Please, Georgiana, let me come with you to California; let me help you get Leo back safe; let me protect the twins and Susannah. Let me be your husband."

He was so earnest. Georgiana found herself crying. Once she'd longed for a man to say those words. For *him* to say those words. He was everything she'd ever dreamed of. So why didn't she feel anything but sorry for him? Sorry for all of them.

"Ah, honey," he sighed. He lifted her hands to his mouth and kissed them. "You're going to have to trust that this will pass. I don't expect you to act happy or to be wifely. I won't exercise any marital rights or demand anything from you. And if, when all of this is over, you want to divorce me and kick me all the way home to Oregon, that's fine too." He tried to smile but couldn't quite manage it. "Right now all your energy is where it should be, focused on your little ones. And on Leo. I don't expect any different."

The feel of his hands on hers was calming. The low murmur of his voice was more calming still. It was like those days spent under the wagon back in the horror of Sublette's Cutoff, when he soothed her until she could sleep. She'd missed the anchor of his touch. When he touched her like this, murmured to her like this, she could stop holding on so tight. And when she did, the pain eased off a bit.

"Georgiana, I know this ain't a joy for you, but will you marry me when we get to Fort Hall?"

She squeezed his hands to steady herself. Then nodded. Yes, she would. If only because the thought of letting go of him made her feel . . . hopeless.

"Is that a yes?"

"Yes." God help her. God help *him*. He didn't seem to realize that her heart had been burned away. And that there would be no happy ending for them.

"Can I go back to the tent now?" she asked dully. There was a new ache in her chest, a new sense of loss. She thought back to those heady days of stealing kisses, to the hope that had sustained her: the hope for a new life in a new land, with Matt at her side.

She would have her new life, and he would stand by her side, but the Georgiana who could treasure those things no longer existed.

❧ 32 ❧

THIS WEDDING WAS nothing like her first one. The first one had been held in Trinity Church in New York, managed to perfection by her mother, who hadn't approved of the match, but who was far too proud to let anyone know. Vivian Bee had kept her haughty demeanor as the cream of New York gossiped behind their fans about the dashing little nobody her daughter had taken up with. The *fortune-hunting* dashing little nobody.

That wedding had been a gilded affair. In Georgiana's memory it shone: the light falling through the stained glass windows, the vast majesty of the organ serenading her walk down the aisle, the smell of incense and lilies, her own ridiculously misguided happiness . . .

There was no grand church this time. No organ, no whispering crowds, no mother to smile at her as she swept by in her French silk gown. No misguided happiness. And no fortune hunter.

As Georgiana stood before the pastor in the dim and dusty trading post, in well-worn traveling clothes that were still damp from being hastily washed in the river, she realized that the biggest difference between her last wedding and this one was the groom. At her first wedding, Leonard had been puffed up like a prize rooster, decked out in superfine, his dark hair pomaded and perfumed. He had regarded the congregation with pride and (Georgiana had to admit now) no small measure of pomposity. In contrast, Matt was in his usual buckskins and boots, his face deeply tanned from traveling, his hair curling around his collar. He didn't look puffed up or proud. He stood earnestly before the pastor, his gold-speckled eyes sober and a little sad.

Although perhaps the groom wasn't the biggest difference between the weddings . . . Perhaps the biggest difference was in the bride.

Leonard had married a blushing young debutante whose bank accounts had been plump with cash. Matt, in stark contrast, was marrying a penniless widow who came with children and a world of trouble. She wasn't young anymore. She wasn't a virgin. She wasn't wealthy. She came with a broken heart; her looks had been ravaged by grief. And yet, as she stood there, she realized Matt looked at her with more longing, more admiration and more care than Leonard ever had. Here he stood, pledging to protect and honor her for all the days of her life, when, as far as she could see, he had nothing to gain by doing so.

"Wait," she said abruptly, interrupting his vows. She held the wild sunflowers Susannah had picked for her in unsteady hands. They had thick, prickly stems. She was trembling from head to toe all of a sudden. Beneath the sandy desert of her heart, she felt enough care for him to call a halt to this farce. "I can't let you do this," she said.

Behind her, she heard the twins groan.

"I told you," Phin complained. "I told you she'd be difficult."

"Hey"—Matt flicked him a scolding look—"watch your manners."

"Is there a problem?" the pastor asked Georgiana. He peered over his spectacles at her.

Matt was watching her too. And so were the children. Along with the traders, who were leaning on their bench, chewing their tobacco. They'd let Matt use the trading post after closing hours for the ceremony, but they had no intention of missing the show themselves. Georgiana felt the weight of all their gazes.

"I can't let you do this," she told Matt. "I can't let you throw your life away like this."

"What on earth are you talking about?" He was frowning. The golden lights had gone from his eyes. "We talked about this. We agreed."

"I'm not marrying material," she said helplessly.

"Neither am I."

"That's settled, then," Phin interrupted. "Keep on with it, Pastor."

"No!" Georgiana felt a surge of panic. "I can't. It's not right. You deserve better than this. You deserve a proper wife. Someone strong and young, someone comely, someone who can bear you children, someone . . . who can love you." She stared deeply into his warm brown eyes. "The way you deserve to be loved."

"Which bit are you up to?" Flip asked the Pastor, peering over his arm at the open prayer book. "Can you skip ahead or is it all necessary?"

"Just say the 'you may kiss the bride' bit," Susannah suggested. "She likes it when he kisses her."

The priest looked taken aback.

"She's right," Phin agreed. "Just kiss her, Matt."

"No," Susannah protested, "the priest needs to tell him to do it first or it doesn't count."

"Georgiana," Matt said quietly, ignoring them, "I told you when we first met that I ain't the marrying kind. I got no interest in marrying for marrying's sake."

Her heart was pounding like she'd run a race. She was no good for him. She was a burden, a curse, an albatross around his neck. She didn't want to be a weight for him to carry.

Matt stepped closer to her. His eyes were hypnotic. The golden lights sparkled again, like the flare of candlelight in the window on a wintry night, calling her in from the cold. "I ain't looking for a wife," he told her, his voice husky. "Not a young wife, not a childless wife, not any kind of wife."

"Then why is he getting married?" Phin asked, outraged.

"Be quiet," Susannah hissed. "I think he's about to kiss her."

"I don't want a *wife*, Georgiana," Matt said, reaching out to brush a finger down her cheek. "I want *you*."

Georgiana felt the tears fall. She didn't know why she was crying. The feelings were too big and messy and knotted together for her to work out exactly what they were.

"Don't say no to this marriage on my account," he told her softly, catching one of her tears on his fingertips. "You've got no call to protect me from this. I want it."

"Say it now," Susannah hissed at the pastor. "Go on. '*You may kiss the bride*.'"

"It won't work," one of the traders called over to the children. "He has to say all the other guff first."

"Say it, then!" Phin ordered. "Quick, before she thinks of more reasons not to marry him."

"You seem very set on this marriage," the pastor observed.

"We want to keep him," Flip said.

"Shall I go on?" the pastor asked Georgiana gently.

Still crying, she nodded.

"I don't think brides are supposed to weep like that," Susannah said disapprovingly.

"Oh, trust me, they do," the pastor sighed, returning to the vows. "Repeat after me: I, Georgiana . . . "

Georgiana said her vows in a shaking voice, promising Matt her obedience, her loyalty and her body.

"Now," the pastor said, closing the book, "you may kiss the bride."

"About time!" Phin whooped as Matt dropped a chaste peck on Georgiana's salty wet lips.

"WE HAVE TO make it look as though the marriage was consummated," Matt apologized, as he closed the door behind them. He'd managed to get use of the back room of the trading post for their wedding night. Becky had taken the children to their tent. The wedding was being kept secret for the night so Wendell wouldn't have the opportunity to protest until the morning. Matt wasn't taking any chances. He knew Wendell would blow up when he found out, and he wasn't about to have their marriage overturned. There was less chance of interruption here than back at the camp. If they went back, Wendell was bound to sniff Georgiana out, and it wouldn't take more than a minute for him to notice the cheap wedding band on her ring finger.

Matt wished he'd had something better to slide onto her finger, but that was the best Fort Hall had to offer. One day he'd buy a nicer ring for her.

"We need to act like the marriage is real in every way," he said gently, "but it'll only be an act." He cleared his throat. He felt wretched enough about the situation as it was; she was in no condition to be consenting to anything, let alone something as momentous as marriage. But, as he'd said, he'd not stand between her and a divorce if she wanted one once they'd found Leo.

Which meant he was sleeping fully clothed and not touching her. It wasn't exactly how he'd pictured their wedding night. His mind drifted to the way she'd pulled the ribbon on her chemise back at Green River. Oh God. He'd never seen anything so magnificent. The memory of her heavy breasts and thrusting pink nipples made him rock-hard.

Which shouldn't have been a problem, given it was his wedding night, he thought wryly. But, as things stood, it was going to be a long night.

"You take the bed," he said. He watched as she sank onto the narrow camp bed. She looked beyond exhausted. The sunflowers hung limply in her hand. "Come on, honey. You're safe and sound. I ain't planning to touch you." He took the sunflowers out of her hand and dropped them on the stack of crates by the door. "Get some rest. I have a feeling we've got quite a day ahead dealing with Wendell." He sank to one knee and began unlacing her boots for her. They were caked in dust, and the soles were near about worn through. He made a note to resole them before they left Fort Hall.

"I'm sorry," she whispered as he pulled the blanket over her. She was welling up again.

"Don't be sorry, honey." Ah, it just about killed him looking at the mute misery in her gaze. "You're all right. Get some sleep. I'm here."

He settled himself on the floor, his back against one of the crates.

"Matt?"

"Yeah, honey?"

"Thank you." The tears were rolling now. He reached over and held her hand, which was curled limply near her cheek.

"Hush now. You got nothing to thank me for. Get some sleep." He kept hold of her hand, stroking her skin with his thumb until she drifted off to sleep. A faint frown marred her pretty face even in sleep.

He sighed and closed his eyes.

AS EXPECTED, WENDELL had a complete conniption when he discovered that they'd got themselves properly married.

Luckily, Matt had been prepared for it and managed to knock the gun out of Wendell's hand before he'd fully drawn it from its holster.

"Settle down," he growled, twisting Wendell's arm up behind his back to immobilize him. They were a fair distance from the camp by design, as Matt had assumed Wendell would act out.

"You lying cowpuncher," Wendell frothed, bucking and writhing against Matt's grip. "You woman-stealing two-faced son of a whore! You promised me you'd only *pretend* to marry her!"

"What?" Georgiana looked suitably confused.

"She was *mine*," Wendell fumed.

Georgiana gave Matt a startled look.

"No, she's *hers*," Matt disagreed, keeping tight hold of his arm. "Now, stop your tantrum and let us explain things to you."

"If you think I'm keeping quiet about that Indian now, you got another thing coming!"

"What Indian?" Georgiana was looking increasingly alarmed. Matt shook his head at her. He'd tell her later.

"It don't matter," Matt told Wendell. "Knowing him, I can't imagine he's keeping a low profile. Folks will know soon enough that he's back from the dead." Matt didn't doubt that was true. Deathrider stuck out like a sore thumb and was too contrary to stay dressed as a white man for long.

"Goddamn you, Slater, we had a deal!"

"And exactly what deal was that?" There was a certain snap to Georgiana's voice that Matt hadn't heard for a good long while.

"He was going to stop you marrying anyone else by pretending to be your fiancé," Wendell wailed as Matt twisted his arm, "so I could have a fair crack at you."

"I beg your pardon?"

Matt winced as Georgiana fixed him with an appalled blue stare.

"It ain't like it sounds," he assured her.

"Yes, it is," Wendell shouted.

"Well, yes, it is," Matt sighed, "but not exactly how it sounds. He was threatening to kill my . . . brother."

"Tom?"

"Yeah."

"He ain't his brother; he's that goddamn Indian!"

"You're making this harder than it needs to be," Matt told Wendell.

"I don't understand." Georgiana stared at him like she was trying to read his mind.

"Trust me, honey, you don't need to. It was a nasty mess that never should have happened. All you need to know is that I didn't mean you any harm."

He saw her nod.

"If you hadn't wanted me to pretend to be your fiancé, I never would have done it. It just seemed the easiest thing to do, when he wanted it and *you* wanted it and . . . Tom's . . . life was at risk."

"Don't you go acting like the nice guy," Wendell complained. "You're nothing but a lying son of a bitch."

"I didn't lie. I fulfilled my part of the bargain—you wanted until Fort Hall to woo her and you got it. She weren't wooed, so I married her."

"You were trying to woo me?" Georgiana couldn't keep the astonishment out of her voice. Matt tried not to laugh.

"Not lately," Wendell objected. "It didn't seem right after your boy."

She flinched.

"That didn't stop *you* though, did it?" Wendell sneered at Matt.

"I would *never* have married you," Georgiana told Wendell, her voice dripping with dislike, "no matter how hard you tried to 'woo' me. You kidnapped my son!"

"I figured that would convince you if the wooing didn't," Wendell admitted.

"Because nothing seduces a woman better than holding her child hostage," Matt said sarcastically.

"I was trying to marry her, not seduce her," Wendell snapped.

"I'm amazed it didn't work with charm like that."

"It didn't work because you were after her like she was a bitch in heat." Wendell gave a sudden yell as Matt pulled his arm upward.

"There's no point in this," Georgiana interrupted. She'd picked up Wendell's fallen gun. "We're married now, so there's no point in discussing it. Now, let's all try to get along until we get to Mokelumne Hill and meet your friend Hec Boehm."

Wendell gave her a poisonous look. "I only wanted you for your land," he spat, "so don't go thinking otherwise."

"Don't be an idiot," Matt told him. "We're willing to play nice, if you are."

Wendell gave a sour laugh. "You're an idiot if you think Hec will play nice with the likes of you. You'll be lucky if the boy is even half-alive by the time we get there."

Matt heard Georgiana gasp. Then he heard the click of the hammer being pulled back, and before he knew what was happening, she had the gun at Wendell's head.

"What did you say?" Her face was white, her eyes blazingly blue.

Wendell gave her a crafty look. "Shoot me and you'll never get the boy." He sized her up. "Or . . . you could put that gun down and we can make a deal of our own. Unlike Slater here, I can keep a bargain."

She didn't move. If looks could kill, Wendell would have been flat-out dead.

"If you sign that land over to me," Wendell said hastily, "I'll help you get your boy away from Hec. Alive."

Georgiana shook her head. "Why on earth would I sign away the very thing Hec Boehm wants?"

"Not *that* land," he sneered. "Not the gold claim. I ain't suicidal. Hec would skin me alive and roast my liver if I took his gold. I mean the plot on Main Street."

"That's all I have left," she protested. "I was going to open a store."

Wendell looked at her like she'd taken leave of her senses.

"You can't stay in town after you get Leo," Matt told her gently. "Even if he gets your land, that man ain't going to be safe for you or the kids to be around."

"Besides, you're married to *him* now," Wendell whined, "and everyone knows he's got more land than he can even use. According to Seb, those Slaters are lousy with land. It ain't fair not to leave any for the rest of us."

Matt resolved to talk to Seb about gossiping with the likes of Wendell Todd.

"He'll be packing you all off to Oregon," Wendell kept whining, "so what do you need with a plot in Moke Hill?"

But it was all she had left, Georgiana thought in panic.

"If she won't give you the land, will you take cash?" Matt asked abruptly.

It turned out Wendell would take anything, and once Matt had paid him off, he had no more interest in courting Georgiana than he had in courting Kipp. Matt paid him half before they left Fort Hall, and promised the other half once Leo was safely in their care.

TAKING LEAVE OF his train was harder than he'd expected. He'd grown quite attached to his people, and it was hard to leave them with Seb.

"Stop fussing," Seb complained, when Matt went over the route for at least the tenth time. "I've been doing this longer'n you have." Which was true. Seb had run the chuck wagon for Matt's brother Luke when Matt was still a youngster trapping his way through the Oregon hills.

"You give this to my brother when you get to Utopia," Matt told Doc Barry, handing him a crumpled note of introduction. "He'll be sure to look out for you. He's wanted a doctor in the town for years, so I'm sure you'll be well taken care of."

"You're like a mother hen," Seb grumbled.

"You'd best be too, if you want to get them there alive."

"Cluck, cluck." Seb patted him on the back.

"I might see you in Utopia by winter, if everything goes to plan."

"I'll be there. If the widow Hooks is still single and hoping to warm her bed for the winter." Seb winked at him.

Matt watched the train head out. Their road was still long and treacherous. He felt like he was abandoning them to their fate. But better them than Georgiana and the children. Resolutely, he returned to his new family, marveling at the twists and turns fate had in store for a man.

❧ 33 ❧

ALMOST AS SOON as they hit the fork where the Snake River split off to Oregon and the Raft River struck out for California, the whores were causing trouble. Or rather, the men caused the trouble and the whores set to protesting. Loudly.

"You tell 'em to keep their goddamn hands to themselves!" Seline's voice carried all the way up the line.

Matt didn't envy Joe, who bore a long-suffering look as he headed back to deal with the trouble. "This is your fault!" he called over his shoulder as he passed Matt's wagon.

"What did he mean, this is your fault?" Georgiana didn't sound pleased.

"What's a whore?" Susannah asked.

Matt was glad the children took up the issue of defining a whore at that point, as he didn't really want to discuss Seline with Georgiana.

"You're *all* wrong," Honey LeFoy called from where she trotted on her donkey, valiantly trying to keep up with the twins and their horses. Her golden curls flopped in her face with every jolt. She pushed them back. "A whore is like a wife only she gets paid."

"That's enough of that," Georgiana cut them off sharply. "Polite people don't speak of such things."

"How do wives get paid?" Matt heard Susannah whisper to Ginger, who was sitting close beside her on the bench.

Matt tried not to laugh. The LeFoy girls were good for the kids; they brought them back to acting like children again. Susannah and the twins had been subdued since Wilby's death; they watched their mother with anxious eyes and were too serious for children of their age. They hadn't spent much time with the LeFoy girls since Independence, as the LeFoys rode at the back with Joe's party, miles behind Matt's wagon train. But now they were all in the same train, and the LeFoy girls worked like a tonic on the children. They were loud and animated and filled with humor. Ginger and Susannah had become inseparable, even though Ginger was a good couple of years older. They were both prim, ladylike girls who liked to spend their time daydreaming together, sometimes up in the wagon with Matt and Georgiana and sometimes riding pillion on Princess. Flower and Honey were sturdier sorts than their sister and tended to muck in with the boys; particularly Honey, who was a tomboy through and through. LeFoy wouldn't let his girls ride his only horse, so Honey had spent the months on the trail, cap in hand, singing after supper, collecting coins from the wagoners until she could afford to buy an animal for herself. She had a lovely voice and a way of making people laugh, so she did fairly well. By Fort Hall she'd saved up enough to buy a swayback old donkey, which she promptly named Thunder, on account that it was an incredibly flatulent swayback old donkey.

"You tie that donkey up well away from the tents," Becky nagged every night. She had taken to acting like LeFoy's wife, mothering the girls whether they liked it or not. Most of the time they didn't.

No one had been happier about joining the California Trail than Becky. She'd inserted herself into LeFoy's daily life, trying to make herself indispensable. She volunteered to drive LeFoy's wagon, to cook for him and his daughters, and to do their wash.

A wife who didn't get paid, Matt thought dryly, as he watched her wrestling with LeFoy's ox team up ahead. Meanwhile, LeFoy's girls had decamped to Georgiana's wagon, spending their days with the Blunt children so as to avoid the young woman who was trying to marry their father.

This was his life now, he thought, resting his elbows on his knees as the wagon rattled alongside the rushing waters of the Raft. He didn't have to scout trails or manage disputes; he just had to roll along, watching the people around him, listening to the chattering of the children, talking aimlessly with his wife.

His wife. That word never failed to make his heart skip a beat.

"Hey, Matt, can we go fishing tonight?" Flip called over.

"Sure." He didn't have to think twice. He no longer had to do the rounds of the wagons, making sure everything was well and good; he didn't have to pore over his map or check on the rations. Once he'd pitched the tents and settled the animals, he had all the time in the world to go fishing.

"Can we take the rifle?"

"No."

"Come on," Phin protested, "it would be easier with the rifle!"

"It would be dumb," Matt said, stretching his legs out. "One shot and you'd scare off all the other fish."

"Matt!" Joe returned from the back of the line and fell into a trot beside the wagon. "Can I borrow you for a bit?"

Matt could see by Joe's expression that there was trouble. Real trouble. He sighed. He'd spoken too soon. The evening might not hold fishing after all.

"SOMEONE'S GOING TO get shot," Joe complained, as they rode down the line. "And I cain't say I blame her."

"Jesus." Matt was shocked at the sight of the whores. They were thin and worn, many sporting bruises. "What in hell happened?"

"I told 'em we were closed for business," Seline snapped, "that's what happened." She had a pistol in each hand and a box of ammunition next to her on the bench. She also had the angriest-looking black eye Matt had ever seen. It was bloodshot and surrounded by puffy purple flesh.

"They stopped turning tricks back in Fort Hall," Joe explained.

"They're animals," Seline elaborated, jerking her head at the cloud of dust ahead. They'd pulled to a stop beside the rushing river, to talk plain with Joe and Matt. "We cain't be working all night and traveling all day. Everyone's plumb wore out. And now Ella is pregnant and Dottie is feeling poorly. We'll never make it to California being used up like this."

"What's with the bruises?" Matt asked grimly.

"They didn't like being told 'no' by a pack of whores," Seline snapped. "Like we don't have the right to say no."

Matt swore.

"Damn straight," Joe agreed. "What should we do? There ain't no way we can hold that lot off 'em." His gaze was on the retreating train ahead.

Joe's party was predominantly gold hunters, rough men who gave Matt pause. They were bored and tired from travel, with drink and cards and whores their only entertainment. The few families scattered in were woefully outnumbered.

"To be honest, it's been a right struggle keeping it under control," Joe said. "They're like kids in a candy store."

"And we sure as shit ain't candy," Seline snapped. For all her bravado, Matt could see that she was more than a touch scared. And Joe was right: she was heavily armed and on a hair trigger; she was liable to shoot first and ask questions later.

Matt scratched his beard. Goddamn. Life could never just be easy, could it?

"You likely to want to turn any tricks between here and California?" he asked Seline.

"Hell, no. You think we want to do anything but sleep after a day spent in these hell wagons?"

Matt nodded. He and Joe exchanged a look. There was really only one thing for it. Unfortunately.

"All right, set up camp," he told the whores. "Wait here till I come and get you." He swung back up onto Pablo's back.

"Thanks," Joe told him as they rode back down the line.

Matt accepted his thanks without much grace. "You want to tell my wife for me?"

"Hell, no." Joe looked appalled.

"You think anyone else will join us?"

Joe didn't think so.

"WHAT DO YOU mean, we're traveling with the whores!"

Matt winced. He'd expected Georgiana to be mad, but he hadn't quite expected her to be *this* mad. It was the most lively he'd seen her since Wilby's death.

"Just let me tell you why," he strove to sound calm. "You might not yell at me after." Or she might. Maybe sympathy for whores wasn't in a proper lady's constitution.

She listened but only got madder when she found out that

they weren't breaking camp the next day, but were waiting for a couple of days so Joe's train could pull safely ahead. They didn't want any of the men to be able to ride back to the whores when the train stopped at night.

"What about Leo?" she asked him. "Are you really putting a pack of whores ahead of my son?"

Matt didn't know how to answer that. He couldn't see that two days would make a big difference. But also, yes, he guessed he kind of was. Because what else could he do? He wasn't about to let Seline and her girls suffer at the hands of those gold diggers. Leo might be in danger, but he'd been in danger for the best part of the year, and a day or two more wasn't going to change that, while Seline and her girls might not make it through another day without shooting someone, or getting shot.

"We'll all be safer with a couple of days between Joe's group and ours," he tried to explain, but she was already stomping off. She didn't speak to him for the next couple of days.

Their new party was small. The LeFoys opted to stay with them, as did two other families: the Tuckers and the Boyds. None of them were too pleased about traveling in close proximity to the whores, but they liked the drunken ways of the gold diggers even less. Matt had promised until his face was blue that the whores weren't trading on the trail anymore and that their husbands and sons were safe from sin. He asked Seline to have the girls button up so not an inch of extra flesh was on display, and she complied. Her girls were exhausted and more than happy to have relief from male attention. They settled cheerfully into small-train life, pitching in enthusiastically. Seline in particular turned out to have a knack for cooking and always made enough to share. She made fresh sourdough daily in her Dutch oven, with a starter she said she'd nursed since she was fourteen years old, and her gifts of hot bread slowly won people over. Gradually, people relaxed around them, although Matt noticed that the women never left their husbands unattended in the camp.

Matt and Georgiana's wagon was the new lead wagon, as Matt followed in Joe's wake. The train ahead left a clear enough trail to follow. They'd stay in their wake until they'd crossed the mountains, and then they'd break off to Mokelumne Hill, while Joe's party headed for American River. Matt hadn't told Georgiana yet that Seline was considering following them instead of rejoining Joe. The whore didn't fancy seeing any of Joe's party again. Ever.

Sometimes Matt had to saddle up and ride ahead, but he preferred to sit next to Georgiana on the wagon seat. As the days passed, she talked more and brooded less, and he learned a lot more about the woman who was his wife: about the queer ways of her childhood, with its servants and governesses, town houses and lake houses and beach houses; her proud mother and her distant father; and the lonely days she passed in all those grand places, without another child for company. At least until she was sent off to finishing school. Matt knew loneliness when he heard it—he should do; he'd felt it often enough.

And as he listened, the days passed. They traveled through the granite spires and cathedrals of the City of Rocks and down the South Fork of Junction Creek, following a dozen small streams until they reached the Humboldt River, which traced a crooked path across the Great Basin. When they reached the Basin, they near about groaned in despair. The arid desolation was far too reminiscent of the Lava Lands for comfort. Everyone got a grim, mulish look and was short of temper and out of sorts.

"I knew it was going to be a long way to California," Georgiana said glumly, regarding the blazing stretch of treeless plain ahead. "I just didn't know how hard it would be." The skin under her eyes was so dark it looked bruised. She still didn't sleep well, and grief had made her thin.

"If you don't start eating soon you'll waste right away," Seline told her one morning when she was ladling out bowls of her creamy porridge. She dominated the cook fire, whether people liked it or not. Becky was as black as a thundercloud because the LeFoy girls ate from Seline's pot rather than hers.

"I'm not hungry, thank you," Georgiana said politely.

Matt kept close watch on them from where he stood yoking the oxen, ready to step in if need be. He could see the stiffness in Georgiana's shoulders from here.

"Sure you are," Seline said, filling a bowl and leaving it on the ground next to her, "you just ain't realized it yet. Your body's screaming out for vittles, but your mind's too noisy to hear it."

Georgiana merely handed the bowl to Phin as soon as Seline moved off.

"You need to do something about that woman of yours," Seline told Matt a few days later. She'd found him by the river gutting fish. The twins were big on fishing but tended to disappear into thin air when it was time to scale and gut their catch.

"I don't recall asking your opinion." Matt didn't look up from the flick of his knife.

The whore snorted and flopped down by the riverside. A puff of dust rose into the air around her. She sneezed. "I surely miss grass," she complained. "When I get a place of my own, I'm having grass as far as the eye can see. And trees. The kind that turn all sorts of colors in the fall and just about shout with blossoms in the spring."

Matt kept on with his work.

She sighed again. "Look, Slater, I know it's none of my business, but you've been good to me, so I thought I could help you out."

"I didn't realize I needed help."

"Your dumber'n I thought, then." She tugged her boots off and rolled down her stockings so she could lower her bare legs into the cool water. "You keep going on the way you are, both you and the lady are going to have a miserable time of it all the way to California. That woman is sadder than that fish you're gutting."

"She lost her son, Seline," Matt said tightly. "Have some compassion."

The whore gave him a filthy look. "I ain't stupid. I'm well aware of her misfortune."

"I think she's got every right to be miserable."

"Maybe so. But maybe she needs someone to pull her out of it." Seline's tawny eyes narrowed. "She ain't the only woman ever to lose a child, you know. Life's a mean old drunk. And you can either get down in the gutter with it and keep pouring hooch down its throat, or you can pull yourself up and move along."

Matt shook his head. "That's the worst way of looking at it I ever heard."

"It ain't no way of looking at it; it's the *truth*. I lost my first baby when I was fifteen years old," she snapped at him, "and I've lost a damn sight more since then. Some stillborn, some gone before they had chance to even take root, some lasted a month or two, one a whole year."

Matt's filleting knife paused. He took in the fierce glitter in her eyes and the severe set of her shoulders.

"And I bet you most of the women in this camp could add to that list, those respectable married sorts as well as my whores." She kicked her heels in the water. "Grief is a hard and bitter thing . . . but it ends. You *make it end.*"

Not for the first time, Matt wondered where Seline hailed from and what in hell had brought her to whoredom. She was powerful clever, one of the sharpest women he'd ever met; she was still young and had her looks; and she was as enterprising as all hell. Put her in a respectable dress and get the henna out of her hair, and she wouldn't look any different from the decent women Matt knew. Except for the hardness in her gaze. She had a flinty stare and a directness that was more like a man than a woman. There was no softness in her manner. And no wonder, he thought, after so many losses. And God knew how many black eyes and bruises.

"Your woman needs to be reminded that she's still alive," Seline told him. "And that she's got three healthy kids left."

Four, Matt amended silently. If Leo was still alive.

"And she's got *you.*" Seline looked vaguely annoyed as she said it. "She was making calf-eyes at you from the moment she saw you, and now she's got you." The fury faded from Seline's voice. "She's a lucky woman, and she needs to remember that. She could be like *me*, or like Ella back there, knocked up by one of those gold-hungry animals. Ella would *kill* to have a man like you to watch out for her. Hell, who even knows if her baby will make it out of the womb safe, the way we're traveling? You want to talk misery, Ella's the one who should be miserable."

"She'll come through," Matt said.

"Who? Ella or your woman?"

"Both."

Seline snorted. "Easy enough for you to say."

"Are you here just to harangue me?" Matt tossed the fish guts into the river.

"No. I'm here to tell you to do your husbandly duty. Nothing brings a person back to life like a bit of—"

"That's enough!" Matt cut her off. Goddamn it, he was blushing.

"It's the most natural urge there is," Seline kept on, ignoring his bashfulness. "Nothing reminds you that you're alive like skin on skin. When it's someone you actually like," she added. "And she sure likes you."

He should have lit out of there before she continued, but he didn't. Part of him wanted to hear what she had to say. Because, truth be told, he was out of his depth with his wife.

"Look, Slater, I know you've lived half your life in the woods with the bears and the badgers, and you don't have even half an idea of what a woman needs at a time like this. Or ever. So I'm here to tell you. What she needs is *you*."

Matt shook his head. She didn't need him. He'd done nothing but fail her.

"Yes, she damn well does," Seline argued.

"You don't know that."

"Ha! Do you know how many idiot husbands have come crawling up my skirts instead of going to bed with their grieving wives? Too damn many. The longer you let this go on, the worse it'll be. Grief is a lonely hell. Get in there with her and fuck her through it."

"Jesus, Seline." He got to his feet. "Do you have to be so crude?"

Seline gave a shrug. "What do you expect? I'm a whore. And not even a fancy one." She kicked her feet back and forth in the water and sighed, looking older than her years. "Sex is a powerful thing. Most of the idiots I see don't even know it. They go at it like they're tossing back a glass of cheap hooch. It's just an itch to scratch for them. But it can be a powerful weapon, or a moment of grace. I've been raped and I've been used, but I've also been made love to." Her eyes were sad. "And those moments of love were the best moments of my entire life. They reached places in me I thought had been destroyed. You've got the power to reach her, Slater. To show her that things ain't over. That it's just the season before things grow again."

Matt stared at the bloody knife. "What if she says no?"

Seline shrugged. "Then she says no and you stop. But you ain't going to know what she'll say unless you try it. She *married* you, didn't she? She must want you. But she's an eastern lady, and they have some queer ideas about what's proper. I don't imagine she'd be starting things."

Matt had a disturbing thought. "How did you know that we haven't . . . ?"

Seline laughed. "Fucking's my business. You got that pent-up look."

"I don't want to take advantage of her."

"Hell and damnation, honey, you won't. If you were the type to take advantage of her, you would have done it by now."

He turned that over in his mind as he finished filleting the fish.

Seline let out a moony sigh. "Your brother was just the same. Your momma sure made some fine men."

He made a noise of disgust. He didn't want to hear about Seline and his brother.

She took the hint and fell silent, although he heard her give a few more moony sighs, so he was under no illusion what she was thinking about.

"Hey," Seline called when he was done and moving off, "are there any more like you at home?"

"Yeah," he called over his shoulder, "Tom. Only he don't stay home much."

"Well, you tell him to come calling at my place if he ever passes through California."

Matt snorted. It wasn't likely. Tom was even more uncomfortable with women than he was.

❧ 34 ❧

GOD HELP HIM, he was going to do it. He was going to seduce her. At least, he was going to try.

Matt could barely think, he was so nervous. He was so unsteady he cut himself shaving and had to ask Seline to finish the job. He was scared he might slit his own throat; it was much safer to let her handle the blade and swipe away his whiskers. While she had him, she also forced him to sit still so she could cut his hair. Although she seemed less interested in his hair than whether he'd done everything she'd told him to do.

"You pitched the tent already?" she asked. "Somewhere nice and private? Somewhere pretty?" He nodded and she shrieked. "Don't move or I'll cut your ear off!"

He froze.

"And you sent those little 'uns to pick flowers, like I told you?"

He'd learned his lesson about nodding and merely grunted an assent.

"Maybe it's a good thing it took you so long to get your nerve up," she said as the scissors rasped, sending his dark hair tumbling into his lap. "If you'd decided to do this back in the desert, there wouldn't be so much as a grass stalk to pick, let alone any flowers."

After the Basin, they'd faced the Forty Mile Desert, another merciless stretch of land that just about desiccated them. But there were certainly plenty of flowers now that they were in the lower reaches of the Sierra Nevadas. Susannah and Ginger had taken his instructions to heart and had strung long chains of wildflowers every which way around the tent.

"It's your *honeymoon*," Susannah told him impatiently

when he commented that they might be overdoing it. "That's what you told us."

"Do they have this many flowers on honeymoons back east?" he'd asked. It seemed a bit much, in his opinion.

"More," Susannah told him, outraged. "When Felicity duBonnet's brother got married, they had seven hundred lilies. That's what Felicity said."

"I thought lilies were for death?" Ginger wrinkled her nose.

"These are different lilies than those ones. Big, trumpety ones. They smell a lot. We had them in the greenhouse."

Females and flowers, Matt thought in bewilderment. He was glad he'd asked the girls to help, or he would have been sure to botch it.

"You look very nice," Susannah whispered to him, when he slunk back from getting his hair cut. "It's good to see you washed your shirt too."

"Thanks," he whispered back.

"You shaved," Georgiana blurted when she saw him. She was far enough out of her grief that her gaze lingered on his haircut and dropped to the unbuttoned collar of his shirt. Maybe Seline was right, Matt thought. Maybe she was ready to make their marriage a real one . . . His stomach gave an unsteady jolt.

He saw the children hovering by the wagon, watching them closely. Thank God they had no idea what people really got up to on honeymoons or he might have died of embarrassment. It was bad enough that he caught the LeFoy girls smirking at one another. And he had no beard to hide his blush anymore.

"Yeah, I shaved," he said stupidly. "I thought we might go for a walk?"

"At this time of day?" She frowned at him. The brilliant sunset was in full bloom, and the camp was buzzing with evening activity. This was one of her busiest times of day.

"Yeah." God, he seemed to have swallowed his tongue. "Seline said she could feed the kids."

"Did she?" One dark eyebrow rose archly. She still didn't like Seline, and she certainly didn't approve of Matt speaking to her. Which was also a good sign, wasn't it? If she was jealous, it meant she cared.

"Yeah." Hell. Was that all he could say? *Yeah.* He sounded like an idiot.

Idiot or not, she took off her apron and came with him. She looked tired, which made him feel guilty as hell. He couldn't shake the feeling that he was taking advantage of her. She should be left alone to grieve.

Only . . .

Seline was right: the loneliness of her grief was wearing Georgiana away. He could see it in the tiredness around her eyes and the brittle way that she moved, like an old woman. He led her gently through the grassland, crossing the stream where the twins had rolled boulders in to use as stepping stones. She didn't notice the setup until they were almost right on top of it.

"What's this?" she gasped.

They'd reached the rolling hill where he'd pitched the tent. She stopped dead at the sight of it. They'd done a good job of it, if he did say so himself. The tent glowed pale against the stands of pine and ash, facing the easy slope of grass leading down to the stream. A lantern burned on the picnic rug, ready for the evening to fall. The girls had garlanded the entrance of the tent with wild roses, larkspur and late-flowering yarrow, and there was a bunch of wallflowers propped in a water pitcher in the middle of the rug.

Georgiana looked stupefied. There was a hint of her old self in those summer blue eyes. It gave Matt a lick of courage.

"I thought you deserved a break," he said honestly. "I've got supper waiting for us." A supper cooked by Seline, but he wasn't dumb enough to tell her that.

Gingerly, she sank to the blanket. "There's enough food here for ten people."

"Yeah." That was the twins' doing. He'd tried telling them that Georgiana's appetite wasn't as large as theirs, but they didn't believe it. They'd even harassed Seline into baking a pie. Maybe so they could eat the leftover stewed fruit. When he'd left the camp, they'd been sitting with huge bowls of the stuff, their mouths smeared with sugary syrup.

"She likes sweet things," Flip insisted innocently.

"You don't want her too full," Seline had warned Matt.

"Too full for what?"

She gave him a significant look.

Matt had turned bright red and taken himself off at that point.

"Is that wine?" Georgiana sounded astonished. Astonished was better than tired, at least.

"Blackberry wine." He'd never had it before. Seline had donated that too.

Georgiana had gone all still now. She knew what was up; that was clear. How could she not? The tent wasn't just pitched, it was lit with low lamplight, so it glowed like a firefly in the lavender dusk; through the open flaps, she could see the strands of wildflowers and the thick pile of quilts. The scene screamed seduction.

As did his extreme awkwardness.

He busied himself pouring the wine, the scent of the rich fruit rising to join the smell of river water and forest and flowers.

"It's good," she said quietly once she'd tasted it.

He didn't know what to say next, so he didn't say anything. He busied himself making them plates of food. They ate in silence, the tension getting thicker by the moment. The lavender dusk became a deep purple evening. Cicada song rose from the forest behind them, and the fresh perfume of pine and roses and water intensified. They ate the food and drank the wine and sank into their silence. A full yellow moon broke over the horizon, heavy in the summer night and seeming close enough to touch.

She made a hopeless little noise when she saw it. "Did you arrange that as well?"

It wasn't a *good* hopeless little noise. She sounded panicked.

Matt put his plate down. This wasn't right. It should have been as romantic as all hell, but instead it just felt . . . wrong. He'd ambushed her. And she wasn't exactly swooning.

"Ah hell," he said, "I cain't do this."

She was staring at him like she was a baby rabbit about to be clubbed. He sighed.

"I'm sorry," he apologized. "It seemed like a good idea at the time. I just thought . . . you look so lonely, and so sad. I thought this might cheer you up. But it was dumb. You don't need to be cheered up. You just need to be left alone. I got no right foisting myself on you like this, especially after what I promised you before our wedding." He poured himself another glass of wine. "Why don't we just have dinner and forget the damn tent is even there. Whenever you want, I'll walk you back to the camp."

They were close enough to the camp that he could hear the faint sound of the LeFoy girls singing as they washed their dishes. Even that distant song should have been romantic, he thought glumly. But of course it wasn't. The woman had just lost her son.

"Sorry," he mumbled again. He'd lost his appetite. He was so stupid. This whole thing was stupid. It was an insult to Wilby's memory.

"It's fine," she said, but her voice was trembling. Her eyes had filled with tears.

"No, it's not. It wasn't fair. You're in no state to be . . ." He couldn't finish the sentence and drained his wine instead.

"Thank you," she said. She didn't seem to have much appetite either, judging by the way she pushed her food around the plate.

"Just enjoy the peace," he suggested gruffly. "You deserve a night with no chores."

And that's what he gave her. They drank the wine and ate the pie, and then lay back on the rug, cushioned by soft grass, staring up at the huge sky, the stars clearer than ever in the mountain air. Matt relaxed now that he wasn't aiming for seduction. The night unfolded gently, a slow and beautiful late summer evening. He could smell her beside him, that scent he couldn't name that was uniquely Georgiana. He heard her breathe a deep, contented sigh and he smiled. He closed his eyes and soaked it in. This was the best he'd felt for weeks. He got so relaxed that he drifted off to sleep, listening to the wind in the pines and the soft sound of her breathing beside him.

GEORGIANA FELT LIKE she'd stepped through a magic veil into another world. The night closed in, lusciously purple, humming with the sounds of summer insects and thick with herbal scents. It was like something from a dream.

Every breath she took was a tonic. She could taste the night on her tongue. A playful mountain breeze dashed over their small field and soughed through the pines.

She felt like she'd been buried deep in the earth and had only just emerged, pebbles of dank soil falling from her as she faced the wild and breathing night. It was the first time since Wilby's death that she'd been away from the camp, away from the wagon, away from the tomb of her tent and away from the scrutiny of people.

The thought of Wilby wasn't a fresh-cut pain tonight. It was a deeper ache, arthritic and dull. She didn't feel the need to keep him in the forefront of her thoughts. There was something about being out here in the wild, in the dark, that let her release her tight grip on his memory.

The majesty of the mountains hulking behind the pines and the vast spread of the sky, along with the slow rise of the moon, which went from parchment yellow to bone white as it rose, and the infinite scattering of stars winking at her: all of it made her feel small. And in her smallness, she felt her grief diminish. Who was *she*? Only one creature among many. She could hear the scurry of creatures through the grass, the hooting of owls, the splashing of something in the river: so many creatures crawling on the earth, each of them with their own grief and pain.

She turned her head to where Matt was sprawled beside her. He had his pains as much as she had hers. On the trail through the desert he had told her about the loss of his parents. And about the nights he had sat up, alone, in the cabin he and his brothers had built, the only human for miles around. About how they'd left him to go wandering and how he'd been scared of the dark and the unexplained noises. About how he took to sitting up, rifle in hand, feeding the fire. So many long hours, alone, an orphaned boy in the wilderness.

And yet here he was, a man. No longer feeding the fire to keep the dark at bay. Able to smile, able to move through the world without pain and fear.

And one day she would be able to do the same.

She watched him sleep. The faintest of frowns marred his brow, but otherwise, he was peaceful. His eyelashes were thick fans, dark as sable, and his dimples were shallow grooves in his clean-shaven cheeks. She felt a pang. He'd gone to so much

trouble. He'd even cut his hair and worn his nicest shirt. And
then there was this feast and all these flowers . . . She stole a
glance at the inside of the tent, where the lantern still flickered, picking out the colors of the wildflowers: pink here, lacy
white there. The nest of quilts looked inviting, but not inviting
enough to tempt her away from the night outside. She was
tired of being closeted away.

As quietly as possible, she cleared their supper off the rug,
moving the great bunch of blue flowers in the pitcher, and then
she pulled a quilt from the tent and tucked it around Matt. The
night breezes had a cool edge. He opened his eyes a crack.

"Walk you back," he mumbled.

"No," she said quickly, "I like it here. Sleep." She brushed
a lock of hair off his forehead. Still mostly asleep, he turned
his head to press his cheek against her hand. She ran her fingers gently through his hair and he sighed. "Sleep," she said
again.

"You?" His voice was thick. He was barely awake.

"Soon."

He sighed and surrendered to sleep. She tucked the quilt
around him. Then she extinguished the lanterns. There was no
real need for them as the full moon cast a bright silvery light.
She turned her face to the sky, bathing in it.

She didn't know how long she sat there. It felt eternal. The
peace sank into her bones. She drank the rest of the blackberry
wine and listened to the symphony of the forest. The faint
sounds of their small wagon train had faded away as the night
aged and people drifted off to sleep, until Georgiana might have
been the only person left in the world . . . save for Matt, who
was breathing softly beside her.

She took off her boots and stockings, enjoying the feel of
the cool grass against her toes. As she wriggled them in the
silky grass, she picked at the leftover pie, pulling syrupy apple
pieces loose and eating them with her fingers. It was magical,
being so alone in such majesty. But perhaps it was only magical because Matt was here, she thought, licking apple syrup
from her fingers. She might have been afraid if he wasn't here
beside her: afraid of the darkness and the forest and the unknown. But with him here, relaxed, she was relaxed too.

She was sticky now from pie and wine. Not just pie and

wine, she amended, pulling a face. It had been a long time since she'd bathed properly. She must smell awfully ripe. It was amazing that he'd wanted to seduce her at all. She had a sudden urge to get clean, and she'd had just enough wine to consider going for a swim. There was a stream running through the field; it wasn't a big one and would prove no risk to swim in. She doubted if it would even come up to her neck. The water was crystal clear in the moonlight, so clear she could make out the individual stones on the bottom when she reached the edge of it. She'd dragged a quilt from the tent with her to wrap around herself afterward. She dumped it on the banks and, feeling wicked, began peeling her clothes off. She darted a couple of quick looks at Matt, just to check that he was still sleeping—he was—and let her filthy traveling clothes fall away.

She'd never been naked outdoors before. It felt deliciously sinful. The breeze slid over her bare skin like a caress, and she was intimately aware of every last inch of herself. The moonlight shattered and rippled on the water as she crept in. The water was cold, but wonderful all the same. It made her feel alive. The stones pressed into her feet, and the gentle current sliding by sent shivers through her.

Her instinct had been right. The water only reached her waist. She sank into it and pulled her knees up to her chest. Oh, it was fresh. Icy fresh. It made her skin sing. She pulled her hairpins out, not caring if they were lost, and dunked her head under. Working her fingers through her tangled curls, she savored the feeling of getting clean. As the grime washed away, she felt renewed.

She swam in the little stream until the moon was lowering toward the mountains. She might have stayed in all night if she hadn't been afraid that moonset would plunge her into darkness and leave her stranded, not knowing where the tent was. She should have brought the lantern with her, she thought as she stepped out of the stream and back into the night air. Now *that* felt fresh.

There was something wickedly delicious about the feeling. Her nipples were hard and aching from the cold. She ran a hand over her chest and felt a spark ignite inside her. Her gaze wandered to the pale smudge of the tent at the edge of the field. He'd planned to seduce her in there. Desire came so suddenly it took her breath away. She gathered up the quilt and wrapped it around her shivering body. The chill of the stream had made her tingle, but it seemed her body couldn't tell the difference between cold tingles and lust tingles. Or maybe she was feeling real and genuine lust . . .

He meant to make love to me tonight.

The tent, the lamplight, the flowers, the wine, the nest of quilts . . . Oh my. She was besieged with visions of how his seduction might have played out. Kisses. Oh, she remembered how his kisses felt . . . Her mouth tingled. Her breasts grew heavier, her nipples harder, the aching more intense as she entertained the visions. The memory of his tongue flicking against hers . . . She slid a hand inside the quilt and touched her own damp skin lightly. She shivered as a firebolt shot through her. As her fingertips brushed over the firm plumpness of her own cleavage, she remembered the look in his eye when she'd revealed herself to him that time by the river. She took her nipple between her fingers and felt the firebolt shoot again. Her belly tightened. She felt herself grow slippery wet.

She bit her lip and circled her nipple with her fingers, enjoying the sparks cascading through her. He was sprawled on the rug right over there . . . There was no reason she couldn't go back . . . She could tell him she'd changed her mind . . .

Yes. That was all she had to say. *Yes, Matt. Yes. Yes, yes, yes.*

She wasn't just wet now, she was throbbing. She ran her hand down her body, over her shivering stomach and between her legs. The pleasure was so intense it was almost pain. Oh God, she wanted him. She'd wanted him since the first moment she'd seen him. She remembered the sight of him in the bath back at the hotel in Independence: skin golden and shining wet in the lamplight, the hard slash of his hip, the musculature of his belly, the long, thick thrust of his cock. Her finger slid into the hot squeeze of her own body, imagining it was him. She'd had so many fantasies since that night she'd seen him in the bath, fantasies about helping him to wash that hard, wet body. Running her hands over the long muscles, taking his swollen cock in her hot, soapy hand and rubbing it . . . up . . . and down . . . squeezing . . . teasing . . .

She wasn't even thinking as she crossed the field back to their campsite. She was elemental: her most basic self. It felt wonderful. Powerful. Right.

He'd kicked the quilt off and was spread out on the ground, his face turned away from her. She drank in the sight of him. Even fully clothed, he was magnificent.

Georgiana kept the quilt around her as she sank to the rug beside him. She wanted to touch him. Desperately. Tentatively, she reached out and touched her fingertip to his cheek. It was raspy with new stubble. He grew a beard just about as fast as he could shave. He stirred but didn't wake at her touch, and so, emboldened, she ran her finger along his jaw, tracing the hard angle of it. He was so incredibly beautiful. Her fingers trailed to his dimple, grazing the shallow groove.

His eyelashes fluttered, but still, he didn't wake. Her gaze drifted to the open neck of his shirt and the swirl of dark hair against his golden skin, and then it drifted lower. One long leg was bent, thigh muscles bulging. And that wasn't all that was bulging . . .

She was so full of lust she was just about crawling out of her skin. She couldn't for the life of her think why she hadn't accepted his tentative advances earlier. After all, why shouldn't they have a honeymoon? They were married. She'd been too mired in misery to feel much of anything at their wedding, but she didn't feel quite so mired anymore. What good did her perpetual misery do anyone? It certainly didn't bring Wilby back. And Matt had been . . . well, perfect, these last few weeks. As numb as she'd been, she hadn't missed his kindness to Susannah and the twins. He'd stepped in and parented them when they'd most needed parenting, when their mother had been lost to them almost as surely as their brother had . . .

She hadn't missed his attentions toward her either. He'd made sure that she ate, that her tent was pitched and her bedding laid out; he drove her wagon and fed her animals; he managed Wendell and Kipp so she never had to speak to them. And during her lowest nights, he'd been there with her in the darkness, his arms around her, soothing her as she wept, stilling her after vicious nightmares wracked her sleep.

He'd never once pressed her or taken advantage of her, even though there had been plenty of opportunities for him to do so.

It seemed to matter to him that she be not only willing, but also eager.

Well, she was certainly eager now.

She leaned in close until her lips were near his ear. "Matt," she said huskily, calling him back from sleep.

"S'all right," he slurred sleepily, reaching out. His hand found her leg and gave it a clumsily reassuring pat. "Go sleep. I'm here."

"I don't want to sleep," she whispered against his ear.

"Sleep," he agreed. And then he sighed and was off into slumber again. His hand dropped from her leg.

Oh no, that wouldn't do at all. Georgiana sat back up, disgruntled. The *last* thing in the world she felt like doing was sleeping. She felt *alive* again. She let the stuffy quilt fall to her waist, enjoying the caress of the lowland mountain breezes. Her breasts were heavy, aching to be touched. Georgiana slid her hands over Matt's collarbone, lightly slipping her palms over his shoulders and down his arms. He sighed happily. Carefully, she brushed her hands back up his arms, and then over the planes of his chest. His hard, warm chest . . . She felt his nipples pebble through the much-washed material of his shirt. She let her hands linger there. Featherlight, she rubbed her fingertips over their hard peaks. She heard his breath catch, and he arched ever so slightly into her touch. She smiled. She bet he was having pleasant dreams.

As she played with his nipples through his shirt, she bent close again, this time aiming for his lips. His beautiful, sharply bowed lips. They were slightly parted, and his breath was uneven, sweet as apple pie and hot against her skin. She kissed him. Her kiss was so gentle their lips were barely touching, and yet she felt it pass through her like a wave. She kissed him again, remembering with a shock the power of his kiss. Memory hadn't done it justice. It was the most intense pleasure she'd ever felt in her life. His lips were full and soft, his stubble scratching at her skin, his mouth hot. He moaned beneath her.

He was definitely awake now. He'd gone very still. He shivered. And then his mouth opened for her, his tongue rising to meet hers, exploring gently, questioningly. She took his nipples between her fingers and pinched softly as she plunged her tongue into his mouth. He made a helpless noise and gripped her shoulders until they hurt. One hand plunged into her wet hair, and he gave her lower lip a long suck.

Then he seemed to realize she was naked. She felt the hand on her shoulder pause in its caress, and then tentatively explore the expanse of her warm, naked back.

"Georgiana," he moaned as he pulled away. She sat up, knowing the sight of her naked body would be his undoing.

It was.

His gaze locked on her chest. Her arms were pushing her breasts together, making them seem even bigger than they already were. Her large pink nipples were fully erect, begging to be touched . . . pinched . . . kissed . . . sucked . . .

It was only as he lay there, totally frozen, that she remembered that he was a virgin. His gaze was full of wonder, but also wariness. He didn't look able to move. She took his hands in hers and, guiding him, placed his wide palms on her chest. She heard him swallow hard. His palms were hot and damp against her skin. It felt magnificent. She arched her back, pressing harder into his palms. Shooting stars ran from her nipples to the wet heat between her legs.

Clumsily, he touched her, exploring her round curves, tracing the swell of her breasts, then dipping to run along their lush undersides. She put her hands on her feet behind her and arched further, tilting her head back. She heard him sit up, his breathing labored. His fingers brushed from her collarbones to her rib cage, flicking over her begging nipples. Oh God, the lightness of his touch was exquisite torture. She closed her eyes and gave over to pure sensation. He seemed intent on touching every last inch of her breasts. They were so swollen they almost hurt. And then he settled his attention fully on her nipples, running his thumbs around her aureoles, pinching the nubs, the way she'd pinched his. She moaned.

"That feels so good," she told him, her voice catching in her throat.

Georgiana's experience of sex had been limited to the short times her husband had visited home. While she'd enjoyed sex with Leonard, it had never felt remotely like this. Leonard was enthusiastic but efficient: making love didn't take long. Matt was the opposite. He savored every last second, and the seconds drew out into minutes, until Georgiana was wild. And he was still only playing with her breasts.

When he finally lowered his head and pressed a kiss into the valley of her cleavage, she just about jumped out of her skin.

"No?" he asked huskily.

"Yes!" she insisted. "Please, God, *yes*."

He dipped his head again, his hands sliding around her back, pulling her closer. He pressed a faint line of kisses down the valley of her cleavage, tracing the landscape of her body intricately, gently. Then he kissed his way across to her left nipple. She was so weak with pleasure by that point that she was glad of his hands on her waist, holding her up. The hot tip of his tongue flicked across her nipple and she cried out. It felt so good. He tasted her in quick strokes, then long, wet rasps, and then he took her nipple in his mouth and gave her a hard, slow suck.

She was wetter than she'd ever been, but he wasn't near done with her yet. He gave the other breast an equal amount of attention, his hands sliding up and down the hollow of her back, finally dipping below the quilt and finding the upper curves of her behind. He traced her buttocks as he sucked on her breasts. She was a storm of sensation, lost, unable to think. She felt shudders coming like an earthquake.

"Stop," she begged, "I don't want to come yet."

He stopped, pulling away, his hands tracing a regretful retreat over the wide curves of her hips.

"My turn," she said, pushing him back. She didn't want the night to end. She wanted to draw it out and to stay in this heavenly maelstrom of feeling, where there was no tiredness or grief, where there was only skin and sensation, and his glistening, hungry eyes fixed on her.

She kept her hand in the center of his chest and pushed him down until he was flat on his back. She could see the bulge of his cock through his pants. There was time enough for that, she thought, giving him an impish smile.

Teasingly, she unwound the quilt from her waist, revealing the flare of her hips, the gentle curve of her stomach, the white flesh of her thighs and the triangle of dark curls where they met.

He made a low animal noise as she tossed the quilt aside. He sounded like he was in pain.

"Patience," she whispered. Her fingers were trembling as she unbuttoned his shirt. Inch by inch she revealed the delicious line of hair that speared down his hard torso, circling his navel, before thickening and disappearing below his waistband. She brushed her hands over his warm skin as she parted the shirt. He made that low noise again and arched into her touch as she rubbed her palms over his nipples.

"I told you it was your turn," she told him, lowering her head and mirroring his treatment of her, kiss for kiss. His chest hair was silky-scratchy against her lips and tongue. His nipples were small and thrusting, salty to the taste. She sucked on them until he whimpered. Her arm was resting across his hips and she could feel his cock pulsing, hard and hot and ready.

She licked her way down his chest, trailing her tongue around the ridges of muscle and along the lines of his hip bones. His hips rose off the ground to meet her.

"Honey, I'm close," he warned in a worried gasp.

She lifted her head. She didn't want this to end, so it was best to slow the torture. She rose and reached for his belt buckle. She was clumsy with desire and fumbled trying to undo it. Then she ran her fingers lightly over the bulging cloth beneath. She could make out the shape of him, the length and the swollen head of his cock. She unbuttoned his fly. The cords in his neck stood out as he fought to restrain himself. As the cloth parted, she saw a bed of dark curls, and then the thick length of him. She sighed and traced her fingertips down his shaft, circling his throbbing, dusky head when she reached it.

"Georgiana," he barely got the words out through his gritted teeth.

Next time, she promised herself. Next time she'd be able to linger, following her fingertips with her tongue. The thought made her melt. To think he'd never felt anyone's touch there, let alone anyone's tongue . . .

But one lick would tip him over the edge right now, and she didn't want that. She wanted him inside her when he came.

He lifted his hips as she pulled his trousers down. His swollen cock sprang free. He still had his boots on, but she was too impatient to remove them, so she left his pants bunched around his knees and climbed astride him.

He moaned.

"Don't come yet," she ordered. Then she positioned herself and slid onto him, slow as syrup.

He made a noise low in his throat, his head tilting back and his eyes closing. Oh my. Imagine how it felt, doing that for the first time. His hands grabbed at her hips.

He felt magnificent inside her. He was so hard that she felt him throb and pulse. She was slick with wanting him and slid easily as she lifted herself. He gripped her hips and his eyes flew open, fixing on where their bodies joined. She rose until only his tip remained inside her, and then she lowered herself, inch by magical inch. She was trembling, so close to giving in to pleasure. His hands dug in as he struggled to hold on.

Oh God. The look on his face was her undoing. The sheer intensity of his lust sent a cascade of sparks spiraling through her. She gasped and would have faltered, only he'd taken over, his hands firm on her hips, guiding her rhythm, up and down, up and down until the sparks became an explosion. She heard her moans become cries as she came. And she came hard. As she locked around him, he came too. He gave a guttural cry and thrust into her with one last violent movement. She felt his convulsions deep inside of her and moaned as her explosion continued in a shower of sparkles.

Afterward, she collapsed onto him, her breasts pressing into the warm scratch of his chest hair, her cheek over his thundering heartbeat.

"Oh *my*," she exhaled. "We should do that again."

She heard him laugh. And then she shrieked as he locked his arms around her and rolled her over onto her back. He kissed her fiercely.

"Yes," he said. "*Yes.*"

❧ 35 ❧

DEATHRIDER HAD SPENT better weeks in his life. In fact, *all* of them had been better than the last few. Riding with Wilby was like riding with a demented ferret. He squirmed and wriggled and yapped and almost killed himself at least a dozen times a day. When they eventually found some trees again, Deathrider happily lopped them down to fashion a travois, just so he wouldn't have to ride with the boy in front of him anymore. His arms were killing him from holding the kid. Or rather, *trying* to hold the kid. It was no mean feat keeping the boy in the saddle. Once the travois was hitched to his horse, Deathrider spread it with buffalo skins and tossed Wilby on top of it. He wasn't likely to hurt himself badly if he fell off the low travois, unlike if he fell from the horse. It was far more comfortable for all involved.

Wilby quickly learned the trick of jumping on and off the travois, so he could run with the dogs some of the time and sit in his nest of blankets the rest of the time, watching the world go by. The best bit was that Deathrider could be alone on his horse, without a half-mad human ferret flopping this way and that.

But Deathrider didn't get more than a day or two of enjoying the freedom before they hit the Lava Lands. Riding through that hell with Wilby almost ruined his nerves for good. As they crossed the hellscape, the kid almost drowned, poisoned himself on rank spring water, got blasted by steaming-hot geysers, fell in a sinkhole and cut his head open on a sharp rock. And that was just on the first day.

By the time they made it through, Deathrider felt like he'd aged a decade.

And then things really got bad. They fell in with a bunch

of stragglers at the back of a train. They were all dour white
people from somewhere far away, none of them spoke English,
and each and every one of them was suffering from a severe
case of influenza. Which they promptly gave to Deathrider.
Wilby, on the other hand, seemed utterly immune. If babysitting a human ferret had been hard when he was well, it was
damn near impossible now he was laid low.

Even worse, he seemed to terrify the whites; they didn't so
much as offer to share a pot of coffee with him. They watched
him carefully and muttered to themselves, and Deathrider had
the distinct feeling that they thought he'd kidnapped the boy.
He was glad when they straggled their way out of the Lava
Lands and back to grass and trees and drinkable water. He
didn't plan to stay with the dour whites with their fever-sweats
and suspicious glares. Not when there were so many other
whites to glare at him.

There were people crammed three wagon trains deep at
Steamboat Springs. It took him and Wilby the best part of a
day to comb their way through the crowd, Deathrider sneezing
and shivering with fever all the while.

"They're not here," Wilby said, squinting up at him.

No. They weren't here. There was no sign of Matt, no sign
of Seb, no sign of Joe Sampson and no sign of Wilby's mother.

He didn't want to go to California, Deathrider thought
grumpily. He was drenched with cold sweat, and the world was
shimmering around him. He didn't want to do much more than
pitch camp and sleep this foul sickness away.

But that wasn't an option either. Because the dour white
people took it upon themselves to talk to all these other white
folks, and before night had fallen, Deathrider found himself
accused of kidnapping a white boy.

Then he compounded matters by *actually* kidnapping the
white boy and getting the hell out of there before they could
string him up from a tree. The whole affair was a bit hazy, as
he was running a high fever, but it came back to him in bits and
pieces: gunshots, the pounding of hooves and the barking of
dogs as a posse charged after them, and the sound of Wilby
squawking in his ear as they tore through the moonless night,
Dog and Woof racing alongside them. Deathrider could imagine a year or so from now there would be an account of the

whole thing in one of those cursed dime novels. It would probably claim he'd ridden into a camp of honest emigrants, like a ghoul risen from the grave, stealing children in the night; he'd probably vanish into the desolation of the Lava Lands, where he kept a lair. Which was rubbish. He actually ended up bouncing around off-trail, delirious, for days before they found any kind of "lair" to hole up in. And even then, it wasn't his.

THEY STUMBLED ACROSS the campsite on their fifth day. Deathrider was struggling to stay in the saddle by that point and had lost track of where they were. He'd kept well away from Fort Hall, knowing that was the first place the posse would look for him, but he'd lost consciousness a few times, and things had become rather hazy. Now he didn't know quite where he was. He wasn't sure if the river he was looking at was the Snake or the Humboldt. That was when he realized how sick he was. He should have been able to tell them apart in a heartbeat, but all he saw was a smear of water in his blurred vision.

"We need to stop," he slurred. Not only did he have no idea if this was the Snake or the Humboldt, he had no idea if these people in the camp were friend or foe. Had the posse come here before them?

It was a sad-looking campsite, with a stained tent pitched next to a rickety farm wagon. There were two nags tethered close by, and the campfire was a desultory-looking affair. Whoever they were, they didn't look like they were having a good time of it.

"Stop," he slurred again. He could barely keep his seat.

Wilby somehow yanked at the reins until the horse pulled up. He'd insisted on riding in front of Deathrider again, and sometime in the last couple of days the boy had quit wriggling and had started helping.

Deathrider fumbled for his gun. You could never be too careful.

"Well, my goodness, you look a touch under the weather."

Deathrider was so fevered he just about fell out of the saddle as he turned to find the owner of the voice. It was an easterner, looking absurdly out of place as he emerged from the brush. He was dressed like a town-dweller, in dusty-hemmed

dark trousers and a broad-brimmed black hat. Deathrider
squinted, trying to make the man clearer. The easterner held
an empty trap in his hand and had a calculating look on his
face. Deathrider took an immediate dislike to him.

"Tom's sick," Wilby said.

"So I see." The man's gaze flicked to the gun. "If you put
that away, I can have my woman, Ruth, take a look at you."

Cautiously, Deathrider let the man lead them to the fire.
With Wilby's not terribly helpful assistance he tethered the
horse and sank to the ground. Wilby sat next to him, patting
his leg reassuringly. Dog and Woof piled in too, crowding
close. Dog didn't seem to trust the easterner either, judging by
the way he followed the man's every move.

Deathrider wouldn't normally have stopped if he didn't like
the look of a man, but he'd reached his limit. If he didn't stop,
he was liable to fall headfirst off his horse. And then what
would happen to Wilby?

"Ruth," the man called over to the tent, "I've told this trav-
eler you'll help him. Get out here." He told his guest, "She's
good with herbs."

Ruth wasn't too pleased, Deathrider noted, when she
emerged from the tent to help. She was enormously pregnant
and suffering in the heat.

"She's useless now that the baby's coming," the man confided, as though the woman wasn't there. "It's her first baby,
and you'd think she was the only woman who'd ever carried a
child before."

Deathrider disliked the man even more. He kept one hand
on his gun.

"I guess I'll be doing supper again," the man grumbled,
"while she gets you fixed up. We only have beans to share," he
warned as he went to the river to fill the cook pot with water.
"I'm not having much luck with the traps now Ruth is abed."

The woman was Indian, Deathrider saw, but she dressed
like a white.

"Who are your people?" he asked, while the man was gone.

"No people," she said, as she rummaged through a shape-
less leather bag. "They're all dead. Tell me what sickness you
have."

He told her about the dour white people and their influenza, about his fevers and headaches and the feeling that the world was slipping away, like he was sinking under water. He trusted this woman more than he did the man. She had a clear, direct gaze. She was young, but her calm was reassuring.

"Here," she said, pulling a pouch free. "Bear root." Abruptly, she squeezed her eyes shut and held her breath.

He might have been sick, but Deathrider didn't miss the import of her pause. "Your baby is coming," he said.

She nodded. "It's early still. That's why we camped here." Her expression blackened when she saw the man returning. "Why I *made* him camp here."

"You don't have any meat on you, do you?" the man asked Deathrider, as he set the pot by the fire and went about trying to liven up the flames.

The woman rolled her eyes and stole some of his water to make Deathrider the bear root tea.

"No meat," Deathrider said shortly. Now that he was sitting down he felt steadier, but his head was pounding like it might burst.

"Does your boy like sweets?" the woman asked.

"Yes!" Wilby answered for himself, his eyes lighting up.

The woman smiled and took a small paper packet from her bag. She opened it and gave Wilby two boiled sweets. "They came all the way from California," she told him.

"We're going to California!"

"You are?"

"I got lost," Wilby told the woman matter-of-factly. "Tom found me." He patted Deathrider again.

"Your mother must be very worried," the woman clucked. She poured the steeped tea into a tin mug for Deathrider. "I got lost too when I was a child, but I never got found again."

The tea was familiar to Deathrider, but his people called it osha, not bear root. "This is good," he told the woman approvingly. It should stop the pounding in his head and ease his chills.

"I told you she was good with herbs," the man said, as he sprinkled a stingy handful of dried beans into his cook pot. "And she doesn't charge much. It will only be a dollar. Or we'll take it in food if you have it . . . provided you don't offer beans."

The woman gave the man another black look. He ignored it.

"If you don't have a dollar or any food, I'll take it in ammunition." He eyed Wilby, who was sucking intently on a boiled sweet. "Consider the sweets a gift."

Deathrider heard the woman mutter something. He didn't know the language.

"You called him Tom?" the man asked Wilby, gesturing with the wooden spoon at Deathrider. Wilby nodded. The man's gaze flicked to Deathrider. "You're an Indian." It wasn't a question.

Violent shivers hit Deathrider. He didn't deign to answer. He could tell all too well what the stranger thought of Indians by the tone of his voice. Ruth covered Deathrider with a blanket and gave him another mug of bear root tea.

"I can't say that I like to leave a white boy with an Indian," the man said, as he stirred his pot.

"Will!" Ruth gave him a filthy look.

He ignored her again and focused on Wilby, the only other white person at the fire. So far as he knew. "What's your name, boy?"

"Williambeeblunt." It all came out as one word.

"What?"

Wilby spat his sweet into his palm and wiped his mouth on his sleeve. "Williambeeblunt." It still all came out as one word.

Which was why they called him Wilby, Deathrider guessed. Because that's how he said his name: *Wilbeeblunt*.

The man blinked, startled by the stream of words. He probably couldn't make heads or tails of it. "What's your mother's name?" He tried another tack.

"Mama."

Deathrider heard Ruth laugh.

"No. Her *name*."

"Her name is Georgiana Bee Blunt," Deathrider sighed. There was no point in pussyfooting around. Maybe this man Will and his woman, Ruth, had seen the wagon train on its way to California. The sooner he got Wilby back to his mother, the better. "Sometimes she goes by the surname Smith," he added.

Will had turned to stare at Wilby. Deathrider didn't like the way he was looking at the kid. He was probably wondering if there was a reward. He seemed like the mercenary sort.

Ruth gave a low moan, and Deathrider turned in her direction. She was bent over, her face screwed up in pain.

"It's just the baby," Will said dismissively, still more interested in Wilby than in his woman, who was clearly in agony. "The boy's mother is in California?"

"Do you need help?" Deathrider asked Ruth as he made to rise.

"No!" The woman waved him back down. "You'll give the baby the sickness. Stay back."

"If you're going to have that thing, go do it in the tent," the easterner snapped at her. "Even if you are a native, it's not decent to have it out here in public."

Even Wilby gave him a look at that one.

"Aren't you going to help her?" Deathrider asked sourly as Ruth disappeared into the tent.

"God, no. What do I look like: a savage? Birth is no business for a man."

As the night went on, Deathrider liked the man less and less. He carried on like Ruth wasn't screaming on the other side of the canvas. He ladled out watery beans and ignored her completely. He gave Wilby a bowl first, making a comment about him being a growing boy, but it was clear that what he really meant was that Wilby was a *white* growing boy. Deathrider ranked somewhere closer to the dogs.

Deathrider wanted to get out of there, even though he was still shaking with fever, but he couldn't bring himself to leave until he knew Ruth was safe. Vaguely, he listened to the easterner ask Wilby why he'd been heading to California with his mother, but he couldn't concentrate over Ruth's cries. Eventually, he had to say something.

"She might need water," he interrupted the easterner, who, unsurprisingly, was trying to find out if there was a reward posted for Wilby's return.

"Be my guest," the easterner said, not rising from where he was mopping up bean-flavored gruel with a hunk of rock-hard bread.

"I can't. I'll make the baby sick."

The easterner flicked his hand like he was waving away a fly.

It was a long night. Wilby curled up with the dogs in front

of the fire and went to sleep. Will sat back and watched Deathrider carefully. Deathrider was in no mind to go to sleep; he
didn't trust the man one bit. Dog clearly didn't trust him either,
sleeping so lightly that whenever Will moved, his eyes
snapped open. Deathrider dozed uneasily, his fever dreams
tangling with the reality of the camp. Deep in the night, long
past moonset, he heard the wailing of a baby. He saw the easterner disappear into the tent and heard low voices, which carried clearly through the still night.

"It's alive, then."

"You have a son."

"Another one. They're coming out of the woodwork." The
easterner sounded amused.

"What shall we name him?" Ruth's voice was cold with
dislike. Deathrider wondered how the two of them had become entangled. They barely seemed to tolerate each other.

"I don't care. Just pick something white. It's bad enough
having a half-breed for a son without him having a savage's
name." The canvas parted, and the easterner emerged. "And
get packing," he said over his shoulder. "We're heading off to
California tomorrow."

"I thought we were running away from California."

"Things have changed."

Deathrider watched through slitted eyes as the easterner
paused to gaze down at Wilby, who was sleeping with both
arms wrapped around Woof. Deathrider didn't like the calculating look on the easterner's face or the smug little smirk that
lingered as he went back to his bedroll.

He had a bad feeling about this.

❊ 36 ❊

MOKELUMNE HILL WAS nothing like Georgiana had expected. Although, to be honest, she wasn't sure what she'd expected. Nothing this big, or this busy, that was for sure. After months on the empty trail it was overwhelming. They'd seen nothing bigger than a trading post since Independence, and the bustle and noise and sheer number of *people* they saw as they rode into town was startling. New buildings were being thrown up on every dusty street, the smell of sawdust was heavy in the air and the sound of hammers beat out a constant drumbeat. They heard a dozen different languages before they'd even reached the main street: there were Chinese men and Frenchmen, men from Germany and Spain and Mexico, men from all corners of the globe, come to find gold. The place was a veritable Babel of men.

But no women. At least none that Georgiana could see.

As they rattled toward the center of town, the men of Mokelumne Hill stopped to watch them pass, their gazes lingering on Georgiana. She squirmed under their close examinations. There seemed to be an unending line of them, staring like they were dying of thirst and she was a pail of water. She knew when their gazes lit upon the whores at the back of the train, because a wave of cheers went up. The catcalls followed them through the town. Matt and Georgiana exchanged a wry look. This reaction was exactly what Seline had hoped for, and exactly why she'd had the girls wear their "best" and display themselves, standing tall, holding on to the wagon frames for balance, ready to wave and blow kisses and generally advertise for business. This was also why Matt had told them to ride several lengths behind the rest of the train.

Seline had seceded from Joe's wagon train, which had

plunged northeast toward American River. She planned to pitch camp in Moke Hill and do a little business before moving on. "Unless things are too good to leave," she'd said with a shrug. "I'm not fussy. I don't care where the girls work, so long as long as there's lots of work for them to do."

The flat, businesslike tone of her voice had made Georgiana shudder. She didn't know how Seline and her girls did it. The thought of these men touching her made her skin crawl.

"Beggars can't be choosers," Seline had told her, clearly reading her mind. "We all do what we must."

Yes. We do, Georgiana thought, steeling herself for the ordeal ahead. She kept a sharp eye on the streets, looking for a glimpse of her son. Not that she expected him to be walking around unfettered. But she couldn't help looking . . .

No matter how many times she and Matt and Wendell had discussed their plan, she remained uneasy. As they'd crossed the vast Sierra Nevadas, hauling the wagons up inclines so steep they were almost vertical, the ropes burning their hands, she'd grown increasingly anxious. A ball of dread grew in her belly. *What if Leo was dead?* The horrid, slimy black thought wriggled through her mind like an eel. What if she was too late? What if she'd failed him, just as she'd failed Wilby . . . ?

"I don't like this place," Susannah whispered as they passed the clumps of staring men. She held tight to Georgiana's arm.

"Me neither," Georgiana whispered back.

Hearing them, Matt put his arm around Georgiana and rested his hand on Susannah's shoulder. His touch stilled them both. Georgiana didn't think she could have faced the trial ahead without him.

Mokelumne Hill made Independence look positively civilized. The buildings were roughly thrown up, many of them out of kilter, and the streets were nothing but churned-up dirt and manure. Tree stumps littered the town. The trees had been hacked down for their lumber, but no one had bothered to remove the stumps. They blocked streets and stairways and jutted in alleyways, giving the whole place a careless look. There was even one right in the middle of the street that they had to maneuver around.

She didn't see a church or a schoolhouse or a barber, or any sign of decent life. What she did see were saloons and opium dens and gambling houses. Finally, she spotted some women. But they weren't the kind of women she wanted to see. Draped in doorways and on balconies were an assortment of saloon girls and whores, wearing precious little more than their underclothes. Each and every one of them had a somnolent, weary look. Some were clearly drunk. She couldn't imagine why she'd thought she could settle in a gold town, where men lay in the gutter, sodden with booze, and whores plied their trade right in the open street. This was no place for women and children.

She couldn't believe that her boy, her gentle son, had to live in this filth, among these degenerates. Her heart squeezed in her chest as she imagined Leo here. Darling Leo. The most sensitive of all her children. What had he endured in the years they'd been apart?

"Nearly there," Matt murmured, feeling her tension. He gave her a sympathetic smile. "Nearly there, honey. We'll get him."

Yes. They would. When Matt said it, she felt no doubt at all. He was like a mountain on the seat beside her. She blinked the tears back and faced the town head-on.

Leonard's letters had described a clean and open country, with pine trees and rushing rivers, and gold lying around for the taking. He'd written of a new settlement, with great swathes of land to build on; he'd told her about the riches and the possibilities, the home he was building and the wholesome life they'd lead.

He'd never once mentioned that every second building was a saloon.

He'd said he'd built them a whitewashed house with a wraparound porch, she thought sourly. Where? Right here on the main street, where that man was vomiting up his night's liquor? Or over there, by the alley, where that whore was pressing her hand into a man's crotch?

There was no whitewashed house that Georgiana could see. There was just a series of raw timber storefronts, the clutter of mining equipment and the stench of sawdust and booze.

"There it is," Matt said softly, "the hotel. And there's Kipp."

Kipp had ridden on ahead. That had been the first thing to

go wrong with their plan. It wasn't a good sign, Georgiana thought superstitiously. They'd meant for Wendell to ride into Mokelumne Hill and to tell Hec Boehm Georgiana was on her way. He'd been supposed to set up a meeting. They'd planned it carefully. They'd meet on their terms, in a place of their choosing.

But they hadn't counted on Kipp.

"I ain't driving this crapbox while you go moseying on into Moke Hill like you did it all on your ownsome," he'd snarled at Wendell. "I'm coming with you."

"You can't, you dolt. Someone's got to stay with her," Wendell had argued. "That's the whole point of us traveling with her. To make sure she don't get up to any nonsense. One of us has to stay."

"Well, it ain't going to be me. You think Hec's going to be pleased that she went and got herself married? I ain't sitting here while you go laying the blame on me."

They were such immoral little rodents that they didn't even trust each other. And Kipp's instincts were good: he was right not to trust Wendell; Wendell *was* betraying him. Just not quite in the way he thought. It wasn't much of a betrayal, since Hec still got the gold claim, but Wendell certainly wasn't being honest with his companion. He was going to make himself a little money on the side.

Let them betray each other and lie to each other. So long as her son was delivered to her in one piece she didn't care . . .

Don't think about it. Those kinds of fears only sapped her courage, and she needed every last ounce of courage for the day ahead.

Kipp was waiting for them on the rough porch of the Golden Nugget Hotel, where he'd booked them rooms. The hotel was so new it still smelled like lumber and paint. The sign out the front was enormous, done in bright colors, with a chunky gold nugget in place of the O in "Golden."

"Imaginative name," Matt said. He was trying to lighten the mood, but Georgiana's mood couldn't be lightened. She felt all wound up, like a tin toy.

Kipp was watching them through slitted eyes as they pulled up.

"I know you like things fancy, so I got you the biggest room they had," he said bluntly in greeting. "And I ordered you a bath so you can wash the stink off. Hec'll meet you at seven. Over there."

She followed his pointing finger to the saloon just across the way. It was the biggest building on the street, also raw timber, the brand-new nailheads shining in the sun. It didn't have a name; the sign just said "Saloon." The rough-hewn wooden sign swung on its hinges, squeaking. Georgiana glimpsed movement on the second floor and looked up to see a man standing at the open window, lifting a cigar to his mouth. He was a slab of a man, square faced, with small features and even smaller eyes. Hec Boehm. It had to be. He was watching her the way a hawk would watch a mouse, head to the side, ready to swoop.

Her dread intensified. This wasn't the plan. They'd meant to set the meeting themselves, to organize a private room, to be there waiting for him: they were supposed to take control. She'd planned to bathe and to dress in her very best. By the time Boehm saw her, she was supposed to look every inch a soft eastern lady. That was what they'd planned.

"I don't see what my appearance has to do with anything," she'd protested originally, when Matt and Wendell had hashed out the timeline.

"You look more gullible in your finery," Matt had told her gently. "Easier to manage. We want to look as unthreatening as possible."

"What about you?"

"I'll play simple backwoodsman," he said with a grin.

Georgiana didn't think Matt could play simple to save his life. He was too capable. Too canny. And the sheer size of him was enough to threaten anyone, simple or not.

"Hec ain't used to ladies," Wendell said. "I reckon it'll gentle him a bit if you come dressed like one."

"A lady is a lady no matter what she wears," Georgiana said primly.

Wendell snorted. "I reckon if you was dressed like *them*, you wouldn't be such a lady," he told her, nodding at the whores, who'd been trying on clothes to wear into Moke Hill the next day.

"Humph," was all Georgiana could manage in response.

"Hec fancies himself a bit of a gentleman," Wendell said. "He likes to give himself airs. You might be able to use that to your advantage. Act like you and he are civilized and the rest of us are savages. He'd like that."

"Is he a gentleman?" Georgiana asked.

Wendell shrugged. "He wears a suit."

He did wear a suit. Georgiana had seen it with her own eyes now. She doubted it made him a gentleman though, if he was in the business of holding young boys for ransom.

"Why is he meeting her over there?" Wendell asked, joining Kipp on the porch of the Golden Nugget. "I ain't ever known him to set foot in Barker's place before. It don't make no sense."

Kipp shrugged. "It ain't my job to question him. He's organized dinner for the lady in the private room upstairs." Kipp didn't make "lady" sound like a compliment. "He wanted to meet there, so he's meeting there."

"It gave him a pretty clear view of you arriving," Matt murmured to Georgiana. "He can watch our every move from there. He can see us unloading, monitor how we interact and have a good view of us walking over to meet him. He's about as prepared as he can be."

Wendell and Kipp were too busy sniping at each other to hear what Matt said. Kipp was ordering Wendell over to see his boss. Wendell was kicking back.

"You tell him she's gone and got married?" Wendell asked.

Kipp smirked. "No. I thought you could tell him that one yourself."

"Why tell him at all?" Matt asked quickly.

Georgiana's heart sank. No. No, no, no, no. She could only cope with the thought of this meeting because Matt was going to be there with her.

"Is there any point in antagonizing him?" Matt suggested. "Why not simply have Georgiana sign the papers over and let her and her boy go? She doesn't care a fig for that land; she ain't going to put up a fight."

Kipp gave a bitter laugh. "Nice try, Slater. I told Hec all about you, and you know as well as I do that you're the one who owns the mine now. Her signature ain't worth shit. You got ownership of that mine the minute you said, 'I do,' and no wife can go signing away her husband's property." Kipp gave him a look so venomous it curdled Georgiana's blood.

"I don't want it," Matt said calmly. "I ain't planning to stay in California one minute longer'n I have to."

"That's all well and good, but you'd best put your signature on that deed before you leave. Hec's got the judge coming up to witness it. All legal and civilized like, over dinner, like the lady is used to back east."

The lady was used to nothing of the sort. Doing business at the dinner table was the least civilized thing she could think of.

"Where's my son?" she asked tightly.

"Safe." Kipp's gaze was oily. "For now."

"I want to see him."

"Tonight. You wanted to look decent, and Hec's being kind enough to give you the afternoon to pretty yourself up. So go make yourself pretty." His gaze slid over to Wendell. "You come with me. You can be the one to tell him that she got married, and I'm going to watch while you do."

Wendell had gone the shade of chalk. "You all right looking after the animals on your own?" he asked Matt.

"They're *his* animals," Kipp snapped. "He can damn well look after them by himself. We're done acting like your hired hands, Slater." Kipp spat at Matt's feet.

"I don't think he enjoyed traveling with us," Matt said dryly.

They watched the two of them march off over the road. Georgiana looked back up at the open window, but the man— Hec Boehm—was gone.

"You all right?" Matt asked softly.

Georgiana was shaking but she nodded. She straightened her back and lifted her chin. She'd be damned if she'd show any fear.

The whores bid them farewell and trundled off to find a campsite. Now they were in town, Seline was all brusque business. She was also heavily armed, Georgiana saw.

Georgiana was surprised to feel a pang as Seline and her girls rolled away. They'd been oddly pleasant traveling companions. Seline gave her a wave as they passed.

"Good luck, missus," the whore called. "And good work on bagging one of those Slater boys. Send the other one my way when you see him!" She winked.

Georgiana wished she had even an ounce of Seline's grit.

When she turned back from watching the whores roll away, she found Becky waiting to ask her a favor.

"Would it be all right if the LeFoy girls stay with us for the afternoon while Pierre tries to find them lodgings?" Becky asked anxiously. She was teary at the thought of parting from LeFoy. "The hotel is full, and they need somewhere to stay."

Georgiana had been surprised when LeFoy had followed them to Mokelumne Hill instead of striking out with Joe. Becky seemed to have hopes that he'd stayed with them because of her, but Georgiana suspected he was merely tired of traveling. It was no small thing to drag three children over the mountains the way he had. Why keep going when there was a gold town closer than American River? One gold town was as good as another. And his endgame was to get to San Francisco anyway, after he'd turned a few coins among the miners. American River meant nothing to him except it was where Joe's train had been headed.

"They won't be any trouble," Becky assured her. "I promise. And I'll watch your little 'uns too while you go out to your meeting."

Of course Georgiana agreed. She felt for the girl. Becky was so lovelorn it was painful to watch. She let Becky take Susannah and the LeFoy girls up to the room while she helped Matt and the twins take care of the animals and the wagons. Labor had become second nature to her and she barely thought about it. The old Georgiana would have expected to go rest in her room while someone else did the lifting and carrying. These days it didn't even cross her mind to do anything but roll up her sleeves and get to work.

There was a heavy brocade curtain to divide their room, with a brass bed on one side and four camp beds on the other. A bath had been set up next to the brass bed on the far side, behind the partially closed curtain. Steam rose enticingly from the surface of the water.

"Your mother goes first," Matt told the children. "She's got an appointment to keep. Once she's bathed, Becky will dump you all in one by one. You're filthy, the lot of you."

"Look who's talking," Phin scoffed. "You look like you rolled in a pigsty."

"You smell like it too," his brother agreed.

"Get on with you." He rounded them all up to go downstairs to eat. "I'll get them all fed," he told Georgiana. "You clean up and I'll come up soon to make myself decent. We've got about two hours."

Two hours. Georgiana felt a wave of nausea. In two hours she'd see her son . . . If he was alive . . .

Stop.

She focused her attention on each little task, so she wouldn't let the eely thoughts in. God knew they tried to slither in the moment she fell idle.

She had to look like a lady. She pulled a face as she looked in the mirror. The dirt was caked on her skin three layers deep. Her clothes were stiff with it, and her hair was matted. She looked thin and tired. There wasn't so much as a trace of the pretty, plump widow who had left New York. She looked like a frontierswoman, through and through.

The Sierra Nevadas had been hard on her. And yet they had also been her salvation, she thought. No. *Matt* had been her salvation. Matt and the children and the days of toil. Being *necessary* had brought her back. They all needed her.

Something had washed away from her in the river that night, something heavy and suffocating. And then Matt . . .

He had saved her, she thought as she searched for a dress in her trunk. His kisses, his touches, his tenderness, the ecstasy of the nights in his arms: he'd brought her back to life. Her hand brushed over a dress as she went through her trunk. The blue gown. The one she'd worn to the dance that night in Independence. She tugged it free, remembering how she'd come out of mourning and dressed to catch his attention. Perhaps it was time to come out of mourning again.

She could see the strength in her body now as she undressed; her thighs had become lengths of muscle; her stomach was firm, her arms strong. She was remade into a steelier version of herself, not better, but more indestructible. Harder.

And that hardness would be a good thing when she met
Hec Boehm.

Georgiana went through a whole bar of soap trying to get
the dirt off. It was one of the small cache of fancy soaps she'd
brought from home, not the liquid potash she'd stocked up on
in Independence. She'd been saving the bars for special occa-
sions, but she thought the meeting with Hec Boehm was probably a good time to smell as fancy as she looked. The fragrance
in the bars had been blended by her personal perfumer back in
New York. It seemed like something from another world now,
the idea of a perfumer. It *had* been another world, a world she
would probably never see again. The fragrance of rose and
lemon and frankincense flooded the room and transported her
momentarily home. It smelled like the New York town house,
like youth, like evenings by the lake with her mother, nights
at the theater and dancing in the Astors' ballroom. It made her
remember how it felt to sleep on fresh linen sheets, how it felt
to pull the bell cord and summon one of the maids to fetch for
her. She would have liked to be able to summon a maid to
comb the knots from her hair, she thought now as she struggled to pull the comb through the tangle.

Then she heard the key in the lock.

"I've given Becky permission to let them eat as much dessert as they want," Matt called as he closed the door. "That
should keep them down there for a good long while."

"Are they safe?" she called back, feeling a sudden burst of
anxiety now that he wasn't with them.

"LeFoy is there now. He's armed. It's a private room, so he
can watch the only entrance, so they should be safe enough."
He pulled back the curtain.

She saw his gaze drop. Her body was clear beneath the
soapy water. As always, the breath was pulled from her lungs
by the way he looked at her. His hunger for her was never satisfied. She hoped it never would be.

"Brush my hair?" she asked huskily, holding out the comb.
"I can't get the tangles out."

His golden-brown eyes smoldered while they lingered on
the swell of her breasts as they broke the water. Without tearing his gaze from her breasts, he pulled a chair up behind the
tub and took the comb from her fingers. He was clumsy but

gentle as he pulled the teeth of the comb through her hope-lessly knotted curls.

"How are you feeling?" he asked. She could tell when the sight of her breasts bobbing in the water distracted him, be-cause the comb would pause for a moment. And his voice had that tight sound it got when he was feeling lusty.

"Better now," she sighed, closing her eyes. She always felt better when he was near.

"You need help washing your back?" he asked, when he'd finished her hair.

She gave him a regretful look. "I don't think we have time." They both knew what it would lead to. His hands would curve up her back and over her shoulders, they'd slide down along her ribs and around to her breasts; they'd slip under the water to follow the line of her hips . . .

The water sloshed as she twisted to face him. "Tomorrow," she promised, rising from the water to kiss him. He couldn't quite stop himself from reaching out to cup her breast as they kissed. His palm slid against her wet skin. "Tomorrow," she sighed, "when all of this is over, *I'll* bathe *you.*"

He groaned at that.

Maybe tomorrow she'd tell him about the time she'd watched him bathe in the lean-to of Mrs. Bulfinch's hotel, about how she'd lusted after him as she watched the water run-ning down his long, hard body . . .

"It's going to be a long night," he sighed.

Yes. In more ways than one.

❧ 37 ❧

"LOOKS LIKE THESE are your last days in Moke Hill, eh, boy?" Hec said as he clipped the end off a fresh cigar.

As usual, the boy didn't answer him. And, as always, it annoyed Hec. He'd be glad to get rid of the kid. Not because he'd been trouble, because in fact he'd been quite the opposite: unnaturally obedient. He moved through the place as silent as an Indian, doing everything he was told. But it didn't matter how obedient he seemed; Hec always felt like the boy was mocking him. He didn't trust the little bastard. He was too clever by half; he grasped things long before any of these other idiots did. Not that being smarter than this lot was hard. Hec gave the Koerner brothers and Wendell a disgusted look. They were the most woolly-headed backcountry louts he'd ever met.

Hec himself was from Königsberg in Prussia, which in his opinion was the seat of civilization. His was the bloodline of the Teutonic Knights, and he'd always had a sense of his own destiny. It was destiny that had brought him to the frontier, and it was destiny that had made him all but lord of Moke Hill. These weak-blooded Americans were no match for a Teuton. One day he'd go back to Prussia like a conquering hero, his pockets stuffed with gold. He'd show those sniffers back home who never thought he'd amount to anything. He'd show the old man in particular. Hec surveyed his dusty kingdom through the open window. His old man had never presided over anything like this, he thought smugly. He had no idea of the fortune his son was amassing here on the frontier. Once Hec added Blunt's claim to his collection, he'd be richer than Midas. Then he could go home, with the shine of gold lighting his way. Hec certainly had no intention of staying here with these cowhands for the rest of his days, in this godforsaken dirt bowl. These idiots didn't even know where Prussia was. He'd asked Kipp once, and the dunce had hazarded a guess it was somewhere just northeast of Kansas. *That* was what he was dealing with.

"Wendell, why don't you tell the kid the good news?" Hec said, lighting his cigar and giving it a strong suck. He savored that first fragrant draw and watched the kid carefully. He hoped the news upset the little bastard. He was too composed for a kid his age; he deserved a kick or two in the guts. "Go on. You tell him who else he's going to see when his momma comes for supper."

Was it his imagination or did he see a ripple of unease? It was hard to tell. The boy had none of his father's looseness of manner. Leonard Blunt was as transparent as a sheet of glass. He liked to think of himself as a smooth operator, but he was nothing but a cheap charlatan. Anyone with half a brain knew it the minute they met him. His own son, this silent kid, had known. Hec had seen the way the kid winced when his father spoke, and he'd seen the banked rage when Leonard had given the kid over as security. *You've got to know I'll be back for my own son*, the slippery eel had said as he slid out the door. Hec hadn't known any such thing. And never would now, as the eel had gone and died within days of sliding out the door. The useless waste of a man made things difficult even in death. His magnificent lode of gold was now the property of his distant widow, thanks to that dead idiot, and the judge was ferocious in refusing to let Hec have the boy here act as her intermediary and sign it over.

That goddamn crazy old judge. Hec had tried to have the old bastard killed a dozen times, but he was proving to be indestructible. Speaking of the old buzzard, he should be here any moment. Hec checked his fob. It was nearly time for the show to begin. Hec was looking forward to it. Life could be monotonous here in Moke Hill, and a man took his entertainment where he could.

"Go on, Wendell. Tell the boy," he barked. "We don't have all night." To his satisfaction, Wendell jumped to obey.

"Your ma has gone and got you a new pa," Wendell told the kid.

Aha. Now that got a reaction. The kid's head whipped

around, and his bright blue eyes fixed on Wendell. He was tall
for a kid, almost Wendell's height, and he seemed even taller
as he stared into Wendell's eyes. He was a haughty boy, full of
that eastern breeding Blunt liked to brag about. He might have
been a blood prince, the way he carried himself. Hec smirked
to see Wendell's discomfort.

"What are you talking about?" the kid said. His accent
grew even colder and more clipped than usual.

Hec puffed on his cigar. He *knew* it. The kid was up to
something. Hec could tell by the tension in the kid's body and
by the sharpness of his gaze. This was more than a kick in the
guts. Something was ticking away up there in the kid's fancy
mind. He could tell.

Hec didn't trust quiet people. They were always trying to
screw you. And it wasn't hard to work out how this kid might
screw him. Leonard Blunt had one of the richest gold claims
in Moke Hill. If Hec had been in the kid's position, he wouldn't
have been signing away the rights to it without a fight. It didn't
take a genius to know he must have been scheming all these
months, trying to find a way to keep hold of the gold. Which
was exactly why Hec had no intention of letting the little weasel anywhere near his mother until the deal was done. He
wasn't about to let the kid convince the woman to keep the
land. It was *Hec's* land and *Hec's* gold.

He was concerned enough about this new husband acting
up without having the kid involved too.

"Your mother remarried," he said bluntly, still watching
the kid's reaction.

"What do you mean?" The kid's face had drained of blood.

Of course it had. Now he had to reckon with a stepfather
taking his gold too. And a brute of a stepfather, by the look of
it. Hec smirked. *Now you know how it feels, you little bastard,
to have people putting their grabby hands on your property.*

"She can't have!" the kid cried. "She *wouldn't* have."

"Show him the paper," Hec ordered Wendell.

Wendell handed the boy a ragged news page. "She advertised for one. And she got one."

"Because these idiots lost her between New York and Independence," Hec growled, "and she had a chance to get ideas
into her head."

"Slater don't want the gold," Wendell said quickly. "He's got land of his own in Oregon. He says he'll sign the papers and they'll be on their way."

Hec laughed. "You're more of an idiot than I thought," he said, "if you think he's signing away a claim as big as this as easily as all that."

The boy was staring at the ad in the newspaper, growing as white as milk. Hec felt a savage satisfaction. *Think you can take my gold, you little bastard? Looks like you've got more than just me to reckon with now. Looks like you've got some inbred backwoodsman as legal owner of your claim now. Shove that up your superior eastern ass.*

Hec couldn't have put into words the rage he felt at the boy's composure, at his patrician manners and fine accent. Leo moved through the world like he belonged in it, like he *owned* it, while Hec had always had to fight for a seat at the table. It made a man bitter.

"They just want the boy back," Wendell was wittering.

"And they'll get him." Hec met the boy's gaze. He looked shaken. As well he should. "Provided everyone behaves themselves."

There was a brisk knock at the door.

"That'll be the judge. Let him in, boy."

Obedient as ever, the boy did as he was bid, the newspaper dangling limply from his hand.

"Ah, Leo," the judge said as he came in, "I'm glad you're here."

"Of course he's here," Hec growled. "He's the whole reason we're here."

The judge ignored him. "I want you to go down and see if Barker can get Peanut one of those pickled sow's ears." Peanut was the judge's ridiculous Mexican dog. It looked like a hairless rat.

"He's not going anywhere," Hec snapped. "Get it yourself."

The judge's snapping little eyes fixed on Hec. He was the picture of a mean old turtle. "I'm too old to be up and down those stairs again."

Hec scowled at him and reached over to yank the raw hemp rope that hung in the corner. Barker had pretentions but no actual class. This place was like a parody of a dining room. It was all kind of there, but in raw form. The walls were un-painted timber, complete with knotholes, the furniture was so unfinished it gave you splinters, and the bell pull was just a hemp rope dangling in the corner. Yanking it set off an unholy clattering in the hall below.

"Dinner ain't ready yet," Barker yelled up the stairs. "You said seven!"

Hec snapped his fingers at Leo.

"The judge wants one of those sow's ears for Peanut," the kid called down.

They heard Barker grunt.

"You're a good lad," the judge said, lowering himself into the chair at the head of the table.

"Get," Hec ordered him. "That's my chair."

"Not now it isn't."

He was as mean as a whore with the clap. "It's my meet-ing," Hec told the judge. Then he reached over and grabbed the table, yanking it sideways, so the judge was now sitting at the side of the table and not the head. Chairs went flying.

"You're a small man, Hec Boehm," the judge told him, his beaky little mouth forming a sneer. Peanut yapped, its bulgy black eyes looking like they'd pop right out of its rodent little head.

"I'm bigger'n you, so watch your mouth."

"Leo," the judge called the boy over. "Hold Peanut while I work." He thrust the little rat into the boy's arms.

"He ain't staying," Hec warned. "Kipp 'n Carter are taking him next door."

"Peanut can go with him. He likes Leo." The judge had a folder, which he laid on the table. Then he fussed with his ink well and quill. "But if anything happens to my dog, I'll disem-bowel the lot of you."

"We'll take care of him, judge," Carter promised. The idiot made the mistake of trying to pet the rat and got bit.

"Don't touch him!" the judge ordered. "You know he only likes Leo."

They didn't have fools like these in Prussia, Hec fumed. Look at the men he was surrounded with. The Blunt woman was going to come in and see a bunch of idiots bleeding and sniping, and then she was going to sit down on a splintery

chair at a crooked table and have to make conversation with a
mean old turtle, while this hairless rat barked in the next
room. It didn't fit Hec's vision of the night at all. She was supposed to come in and be impressed. Intimidated.

As Carter stanched the bleeding and the judge polished his
spectacles, Wendell and Kipp tried to put the chairs back in
order. Hec stood at the head of the table. The new head of the
table. Which now conveniently faced the door.

"I've written up the contract." The judge handed it to him.

"You'll have to rewrite it," Hec snapped. "The woman went
and got herself married."

The judge peered over his spectacles. "Did she now? Well,
that changes things."

"No," Hec corrected him, "it doesn't. It doesn't change
anything at all."

"The fellow might not want to sell."

"Carter," Hec snapped at the elder Koerner brother.

Carter took his gun out of his holster and pointed it at
the boy.

"He'll sell," Hec said grimly. "As soon as he sees that."

"If you accidentally shoot my dog, I'll have you strung up
from the nearest tree," the judge said calmly. Then he cocked
his head. "You know, the new husband might not care if he
loses a stepson. He's less of a bargaining chip than he was."

"Then I'll have Kipp point a gun at *her*."

The kid flinched at that. Interesting. He was a mother's boy,
was he? Hec filed that away. It might be useful.

The judge looked disdainful. "He can always get another
wife. He can't get another claim like this one."

"From what Wendell says, he's fond of the woman."

The judge's small black eyes glinted. "He's not too bright,
then? That will help."

"Change the contract."

The judge dipped his nib into the ink. "What's the fellow's
name?"

"Slater," Wendell supplied. "Matthew Slater."

The nib drew a harsh line through Georgiana's name and
replaced it with Matt's.

❧ 38 ❧

THEY WERE AN incongruous pair as they crossed the dusty street, she in her fine blue satin gown, with its ridiculously wide skirts, and he in his fringed buckskins.

"You look exactly like the kind of man I advertised for," Georgiana told him as they stood in the shadow of the saloon.

He smiled tightly. "Let's hope I can be exactly the kind of man who gets us all out of here in one piece." He held the swinging doors open for her.

She took a deep breath and stepped through.

The room fell quiet. Mokelumne Hill had never seen a lady like her, judging by the expressions on these men's faces. The proprietor just about tripped over himself escorting them upstairs.

"Hec's secured the finest private room in our establishment for your dining pleasure," he said, tripping over both his words and his feet. "Just this way."

It took all of Georgiana's courage to keep her spine straight and her knees from knocking as the door was flung open and she came face-to-face with the monster who had her son.

He was exactly what she'd expected. A bullish, none-too-bright-looking beast, crammed into a suit that was several years out of date and a size or two too small. The room was cramped and stank of cigar smoke, sawdust and boiled meat.

"Welcome," the bull said, gesturing for them to enter. His features were too small for his big, square head, and were crammed into the middle of his face in a manner that disconcerted Georgiana. She felt Matt take her hand. She held on to it for dear life. She couldn't see her son anywhere in the room.

"We're glad you could join us," Boehm told them. There

was a low kind of animal intelligence in his small eyes. "I thought we'd eat before we did business, like civilized people."

There was nothing civilized about this farce. The bareness of the room reflected the bareness of the pretense. There wasn't so much as a tablecloth, and the cutlery was made of speckled tin, but Boehm acted like he was presiding over a grand affair.

Georgiana relied on her years of social training to act like she was indeed at a grand dinner. And, somehow, they got through the farce.

"It's been a pleasure taking care of your boy," Boehm told her as he sawed through the great slab of gray meat on his plate. This was the first mention of why they were really there.

Georgiana flinched at the mention of Leo. From the corner of her eye, she saw Matt go still. He hulked at the table, mountainous as ever, silently trying to pass as a simple backwoodsman. She saw Boehm watching him closely, gauging his temperament. The judge was also watchful, but he seemed to treat it all like a night at the theater. He gummed at his food, his black eyes snapping with malice and mirth as they flicked back and forth between the players. Georgiana couldn't wait to get away from these malignant people.

"Leo?" Georgiana's voice cracked. She cleared her throat. "He's well? I was hoping he'd be here . . . "

Boehm smiled. He might have meant it to be reassuring, but actually, he just looked like he wanted to eat her. "Come now, Mrs. Bl . . . Slater," he corrected himself. "This is no place for a boy. He's eating in the kitchen with the Koerners."

"But he's well?" Her voice cracked again.

She revised her earlier impression of him. He didn't look like a bull at all. He looked like an alligator. The more he smiled, the stronger the resemblance grew.

"You won't recognize him," the horrid man said, his tongue swiping gravy from his lip. "The frontier air agrees with him. He gets bigger every day. But, of course, he does miss his mother."

"I miss him," Georgiana said, a touch desperately. "I would so like to see him . . . "

"Of course." His knife screeched against the tin plate.

Georgiana's stomach turned. She didn't know how she

managed to force the food down. Under the table, Matt's foot found hers. He kept his eyes fixed on his plate, as his boot rubbed reassuringly against her ankle. It kept her calm.

And she needed to stay calm, because Hec Boehm was in the mood to prolong her torture. After the foul boiled meat came dessert. It was a sludgy trifle, complete with yellowing cream that had dried into a cracking crust. He tried to get her to eat two helpings as he and the judge regaled them with stories about the growth of Moke Hill. A lot of the stories seemed to involve people getting shot.

Just when she thought she might start screaming, Wendell cleared all the plates away, dumping them unceremoniously in a pail and hauling them downstairs, and Hec decided he was in a mood for business.

"You don't talk much, do you, Mr. Slater?" Hec said, suddenly turning his attention to Matt.

"Not if I don't have anything to say," Matt replied. He radiated calm and practicality, and looked every inch a woodsman. Which, she supposed, he was.

"What has your lovely wife told you about this meeting?"

Matt met his gaze. "She told me you've got her son."

Georgiana tensed. She had no idea how this was going to go. Hec struck her as a mistrustful man.

"Someone had to care for the boy when his father died."

Matt nodded. "I reckon we're grateful to you, then."

Hec tilted his head on the side. "He's almost like a son to me now."

The judge snorted, and Georgiana almost jumped out of her skin.

"Enough of this nonsense," the old judge said. "I ain't sitting here all night, and Peanut will be needing a walk. You've had your fun, now let's get this document signed and get on with things."

Hec shot him an evil look, then readjusted his expression and turned back to Matt. "You must understand how fond I am of the boy. We've spent a long time together."

"I'm sure the boy is fond of you too."

How he managed to say that with a straight face, Georgiana never knew.

"It's been my pleasure to care for him until his momma

came, Mr. Slater," Hec said. His face didn't seem to quite be cooperating with his voice. He couldn't seem to help the smug little quirking of his lips.

"And, as my husband says, we are very grateful," Georgiana told him. "More than I can ever say." She almost choked on the words.

"I've also been more than happy to protect your assets here in Moke Hill, Mrs. Slater." Hec tried, and failed, to look humble.

She bet he had. She bet he'd hauled a good amount of gold out of her land as well.

"For the love of God, Hec, you do waffle on." The judge slapped his folder and ink pot down on the table. "He's buying the land off you. There don't seem to be any disagreement about that. The documents are right here, ready for signing."

"Buying?" Hec's voice turned poisonous. "We ain't talked none about 'buying.'"

"Slip of the tongue," the judge said dryly. "I forgot the matter of the 'reward.'" He grinned at Georgiana. "It is kind of you to recognize his protection of your son in such a generous way."

"We're generous people," Matt said, equally dryly.

That was the moment Hec realized Matt wasn't simple. Georgiana saw it happen. He suddenly seemed a whole lot less friendly. If such a thing was possible.

"Do you read?" the judge asked Matt.

"Yes." Matt took the document in his big hand. He read it and then looked up at Hec. "We don't want any trouble, mister," he said frankly. "And we got no interest in any gold. My wife wants her son and then we're out of your town and off for Oregon."

Hec sat back in his chair. He was suspicious. Suspicious and disbelieving.

"You're an idiot, son," the judge told Matt as he passed him the quill. "You ain't got any idea what you're losing."

"No," Matt said, his gaze meeting Georgiana's across the table, "you don't have any idea what I'm gaining."

She almost cried at that. She'd never expected when she'd advertised for a husband that she would find a man like Matt Slater. He had all of the qualities she'd wanted in a man, and so many she never thought existed. He'd taken care of her through the darkest days of her life. And it didn't even cross his mind to keep the gold he'd taken rightful ownership of when he married her. The gold meant nothing to him. He looked at *her* like she was the treasure.

"Wait!" she said. "You can't sign until we see Leo. I need to know he's well. That he's alive . . . "

Hec stood, the chair scraping on the floorboards, and she jumped. "He's fine," Hec snapped. "If you're trying to stall . . ."

"Please," she said. "Matt's right. We don't want your gold. But we're not signing until you give me my son."

"Get the boy, Wendell," the judge ordered.

"You ain't in charge here!"

"Sure I am. I'm the judge." The old man picked something from his teeth, not even bothering to look in Hec's direction. "Off you go, Wendell."

Wendell stole a glance at Hec, who nodded tersely.

"You'd best watch your back, old man," Hec warned.

"I already do." The judge cackled. The sound made Georgiana's hair stand on end.

"You see the boy, you sign, and then you leave town," Hec told Matt. All pretense of civility was gone now. Hec was fixed on that gold claim, like a dog fixed on a bone.

"Sounds good to me." Matt dipped the quill in the ink. Hec's gaze was riveted on the nib. "You want us to leave tonight or wait until morning?"

"You leave straight after you sign."

Georgiana would be glad to. Her heart was in her throat as she heard footsteps on the stairs. She turned and stood. She was shaking so hard she had to hold the back of the chair to steady herself.

And then, there he was. Her boy.

She gave a broken sob. *Leo*. It was *Leo*. He was half a foot taller, much taller than she was now, but it was *Leo*. The same big, serious blue eyes; the same dark curls; the same long face.

"Mother." He said it numbly, like he didn't quite believe she was there.

She lurched toward him.

"Not so fast!" Hec reached out and grabbed her arm.

Matt was on his feet in a second, his chair flying across the room. "Let go of my wife!"

Suddenly, there were guns drawn. One of them was held right to Leo's head.

"I just wanted to touch him," she said weakly.

"After Slater has signed." Hec was squeezing the blood right out of her arm.

"After you let go of her," Matt said fiercely. All placidity was gone. There was nothing simple about him now. He was an enormous, blazing mass of fury. "And get those guns back in their holsters."

Hec nodded at the Koerners, who put their weapons away. "You've seen the boy," he told the Slaters. "You see he's well. Now, sign that contract."

Leo was in one piece, but he didn't look well. He was underfed and desperately pale. There were dark circles under his haunted eyes. She couldn't wait to get out him out of here, to feed him and care for him. Every fiber of her body called out to touch him.

"All right, Boehm," Matt said calmly, bending over the document. He touched the nib to the paper. "You let my wife go to her boy as I sign."

"It ain't official until I sign it and stamp it," the judge sniffed.

"She can have the boy when the judge is done," Hec said.

"Fine. Get those goons out of the doorway, so we can leave."

The rest of it happened so quickly Georgiana's head spun. There was the flick of the quill, then the smack of a stamp, and then Leo was in her arms and Matt was ushering them out of the room and down to the street. "Enjoy your gold, Boehm."

"Oh, I will. Don't have any accidents on the way out of town," he called after them. Then he laughed.

"Move," Matt instructed Georgiana and Leo. "I don't trust him."

Georgiana wouldn't let Leo out of her sight as they dashed across the street.

"Leo!" The twins were impossible to contain when Georgiana and Matt burst into the hotel room with Leo. They launched themselves at their brother and had to be dragged off him by Matt.

"There's time enough for that later," he snapped. "We need to get out of here. I'll take the lead wagon, you take the second," Matt said to Georgiana. "Can you fire a weapon?" he asked Leo.

Leo nodded, and Matt passed him a pistol and two boxes of ammunition.

"How come *he* gets a gun?" Phin asked, outraged.

"He's going to protect your mother while she drives." Matt grabbed him and swung him up into the back of the lead wagon. "You lot are coming with me. Your ma and Leo have a lot to talk about."

"Give us the rifle, and we'll protect you while you drive," Flip suggested.

Matt snorted. "I can drive *and* shoot."

Matt passed LeFoy an envelope to give to Wendell. "Tell him it's what I owe him, plus a bit extra."

"Becky!" Georgiana called to the girl, who was standing on the porch with the LeFoys.

"I'm going to stay," the girl called back.

"Are you sure?"

She nodded vigorously.

Georgiana reached down and gave her a hug. "Good luck, Becky."

The girl smiled. She looked surprised she was getting her way.

"I need to stop and see Seline as we leave town," Georgiana told Matt as she took the reins. "I have some land she might like to buy."

The LeFoy girls chased alongside the wagons as they rolled down the street, waving them off. They weren't the only ones who said farewell. Hec Boehm gave Georgiana a jaunty wave as she passed under his window. Then he flicked the ashes from his cigar onto the street below and laughed. Oh God, she'd be glad to never see him again as long as she lived.

They found the whores camped on the outskirts of town. It was impossible to miss them. Their campsite looked like a fairground: the lanterns were lit, there was music playing, and Seline stood on the back of a wagon, advertising the assets of her girls. She saw the Slaters pull up and gave them a wave. She looked flabbergasted when Georgiana gestured her over.

"Is this your boy?" Seline asked breathlessly, when she finally managed to push through the crowd to Georgiana's wagon. "He's a handsome lad."

Georgiana was glad to see Leo look at Seline with no small measure of distaste. Although she also noticed his eyes couldn't help but drop to the whore's all-too-exposed breasts.

"We're leaving town," she told the whore.

"So I see. And I can see why. These men are animals!" She pulled a face as she surveyed the debauchery of her camp. "Still, a girl can make a pretty penny out of animals like these."

"I have land on the main street that I won't be needing," Georgiana said. She had the deed ready. "It strikes me that the location would be a handy place to build a whorehouse."

Seline's eyebrows shot up, and she gave a startled laugh. "I thought you didn't approve of whorehouses?"

"This seems like the kind of town that would suit one," Georgiana said dryly. She didn't mean it as a compliment.

Seline grinned. "What kind of price are you thinking?"

Georgiana named her price.

Seline laughed. Then she realized Georgiana wasn't joking.

"We've got a long journey ahead," Georgiana told her, "and we had to leave town before we restocked. You can have the land in exchange for all the foodstuffs you have on hand. Any barrels of water you have too."

And so they left town fully provisioned for the journey ahead. And Seline was the happy new owner of a prime location in the richest little gold town between here and San Francisco.

Georgiana felt her spirits lift as they struck out from Moke Hill. She savored the look of admiration Matt gave her as he loaded Seline's supplies into their wagons. She'd *done* it. She'd set out from New York all those months ago, afraid and alone, green as a new leaf. It had been a hard and horrid year. The loss of Wilby would leave a scar that would never heal. But she had survived, and she would continue to survive. And she had *Leo*! The twins and Susannah hung over the backboard of Luke's wagon, grinning like monkeys and waving at them as they rattled along. The twins pulled ugly faces at their brother. Georgiana laughed. She had her children. And she had Matt. They were *free*. And they were together.

She didn't think she'd ever felt such soaring joy in all her life. She turned to grin at her eldest son, reaching out to tousle his hair.

He didn't grin back.　·

"Oh, honey," she said, unable to stop the waterfall of happy tears. "It's going to be all right." She pressed a kiss against his cheek. It seemed magical that he was here beside her and that she could touch him whenever she wanted to.

But he wriggled away from her.

"Mother," he said, his expression grave, "you didn't really marry that man, did you?"

Her heart went out to him. "I know it's a shock, but he's a wonderful man. The others adore him, and he's been so good to us . . ."

"You *can't* marry him."

She squeezed his arm. "Oh, darling, I know it must be a surprise."

"No, you don't understand. You can't marry him!"

"I already have."

He closed his eyes and groaned. "No."

"Yes. Back at Fort Hall, months ago."

"You don't understand." His voice was deeper than it had been the last time she'd seen him, and he seemed far more adult. He opened his eyes and fixed her with a firm stare. "You can't marry him, because you're *already married*." It was his turn to give *her* arm a squeeze. "You can't marry him . . . because Father is *still alive*."

❧ 39 ❧

IT WAS A nightmare. It had to be a nightmare. Georgiana felt like throwing up. Her ears were ringing, and the world was too bright and too sharp. It *had* to be a nightmare.

"What do you mean, he's still alive?"

The story Leo told was sickeningly believable.

Of course Leonard had abandoned his son and faked his death to save his own hide. Goddamn him for a useless coward.

"He said to meet him in San Jose after you got me back from Boehm," Leo said.

"How did he know I *would* get you back?"

They question hung between them, an unanswerable horror. He couldn't have known. That was the God's honest truth. He'd had absolutely no way of knowing that Georgiana would get to Leo safely. New York was a hell of a long way from Mokelumne Hill. What if Boehm couldn't be bothered to send word to Georgiana? What if he'd simply killed Leo and bribed the judge and taken the land? What if he'd abused the boy, in any number of ways Georgiana couldn't bear to think about? There were far too many "what ifs." The fact was that Leonard had abandoned his son.

And he was *alive*. The goddamn son of a bitch was *alive*.

"Do you think he'll even *be* in San Jose?" Georgiana asked.

Leo shrugged. He had a cynical look that didn't belong on a boy of his age. It made her heart ache.

Alive. Oh God. The horror of it. Georgiana circled the idea, her stomach lurching. If he was alive . . . then she was a bigamist.

The world seemed to fall out from beneath her. Oh God. She was still married to Leonard.

"Mother? You're not going to faint, are you?" Leo took the reins out of her hands. "Where are your smelling salts?"

Georgiana laughed. It was a jagged, hopeless sound. Smelling salts. She was no longer the type of woman who carried smelling salts. She'd hauled this wagon over boulders the size of small houses, had traversed deserts and had forged across raging rivers. She wasn't one to faint. Certainly not over Leonard bloody Blunt.

But Matt . . .

His wagon rumbled along ahead of them, raising a cloud of dust that was silvered by moonlight. She couldn't see him, but she could picture him, sitting with his legs splayed, with his elbows resting on his knees. She'd seen him drive so many endless hours in exactly that position, his expression serene as the children chattered at him.

Oh God.

Grief hit her like a flash flood. It roiled through her, as dark and devastating as it had been when Wilby was taken by the river.

No. *Don't think about it.* Not yet. It had been more than a year since Leonard had left Leo in Mokelumne Hill. Anything might have happened in a year. He might *actually* be dead.

She winced. Oh God, now she was wishing the father of her children dead. What kind of person was she becoming?

Damn you, Leonard Blunt. This is all your fault.

"You need to tell him," Leo said, bringing her sharply back to the moment. He held the reins loosely, confidently, looking much older than his years.

"Tell who?" But she knew what he was talking about.

"Him." Leo nodded at the wagon in front of him.

"Not yet," Georgiana said, a touch desperately. "We'll get to San Jose first. We'll see . . ."

"See what?" Leo sounded exasperated. "It doesn't matter if he's there or not; he's alive and he's your husband. Which means *he* can't be."

It was like having a knife plunged between her ribs and into her heart. She put her hand to her mouth to stop the noise that was rising up her throat.

No, she thought fiercely. It wasn't fair! She'd come all this way . . . she'd walked through hell . . . and all she wanted, all she *needed*, was Matt.

She loved him, she realized, as the knife lodged permanently in her heart, causing a pain that would never leave her.

So this was what love was. It was nothing like the frothy feeling she'd had for Leonard in her youth. There was nothing light and airy about this. It was as solid as the earth beneath her feet, as natural as breathing, as monumental as the mountains. It was a part of her, something so essential that living without it felt like a kind of death.

The only thing Georgiana knew was that *Matt* was her husband. The only husband she ever wanted.

"We'll wait," she told Leo firmly.

"But—"

"No!" She cut him off. "I'm your mother. You'll do as I ask in this. I will tell him, but not yet. I need time to think."

"There's nothing to think about. You can't change the facts."

The knife twisted in her heart.

"Just give me until San Jose," she said. Maybe by then, she could find a way to work a miracle . . .

SHE HAD A stay of execution for five and a half days. Leo watched her interacting with Matt disapprovingly, and out of respect, Georgiana no longer shared a tent with him. How could she? She was married to someone else.

"Leo will take a while to get used to this," she lied to Matt. "Let's give him time."

He didn't like her sleeping in the tent with the children, but as always, he respected her wishes. "It makes sense you wouldn't want to let him out of your sight for a while," was all he'd said. It was a shame, because Georgiana would have crumbled at the first protest from him. He knew she was hiding something, and he didn't like it, but he didn't press her.

Because he *trusted* her, she thought miserably.

"Why San Jose?" he'd asked, thoroughly bewildered when she'd asked him to turn around and head south again.

And God help her, she couldn't think of a lie. "Can I tell you when we get there?" she asked lamely.

"It's the opposite direction to Oregon, honey."

"But we need to resupply properly," she said, feeling sick about the lies, "Seline's supplies won't last us long. And we could all use a rest."

"We don't have time to rest," he told her gently. "We don't want to be caught on the trail when winter hits."

No. Of course not. But she might not be going on the trail at all, if Leonard was in San Jose . . .

But then one night, as she lay in the tent, staring at the rippling canvas, it came to her with the force of a lightning bolt. *Divorce!* She'd get a divorce! She'd never met anyone who'd been divorced before . . . It was scandalous. But who cared about scandal out here on the frontier? Whores stood out on the open street, for heaven's sake. And if she got divorced, that meant she could marry Matt!

It was so simple! How had she not thought of it earlier?

You're still a bigamist, a little voice whispered in her ear. *You slept with a man who wasn't your husband. You'd* still *be sleeping with him, if you could get away with it.*

Yes. And she didn't regret it for a moment, she thought savagely. She would do it all again in a heartbeat. Matt was the best thing that had ever happened to her and her children. He was a blessing, not a curse. If anyone was a curse, it was Leonard.

Although, he *was* the father of her children . . .

In the cold light of day, divorce took on a sharper edge. She watched the children ride their ponies as she drove the wagon. Leo was riding Wishes, and the twins were harassing him mercilessly. He seemed bewildered by them. Susannah rode shyly behind them. She barely remembered her big brother and was more than a little awestruck by him.

If Leonard was alive, what right did she have to keep the children from him? To take them all the way to Oregon? To replace him with a stepfather? Leonard had been an absent, neglectful father, but he *was* their father.

A new thought struck her, one that splashed over her like a bucket of icy water. What if she didn't get to keep the children? When people divorced, the children were taken away from their mother . . . Oh God. The thought was untenable. She would never let herself be separated from them.

"Are you going to tell me what's going on?" Matt asked her on their final night. The children had gone to bed, and she and Matt were sitting up by the fire. He'd thrown another log on the crackling flames and had moved to sit beside her. He put his arm around her and hauled her closer, reaching for a blanket to drape over them. The nights were getting cool, and his body was soothingly warm.

"Nothing's going on."

Matt sighed. "You're a terrible liar."

"I'll tell you tomorrow. I promise," she said miserably. "Can't we just enjoy tonight?"

"You look like you're enjoying it about as much as you'd enjoy a funeral."

She pulled a face.

"I know how to make it more enjoyable," he whispered in her ear, his warm breath making her shiver. He pressed a kiss on her neck.

Oh yes. It had been so long . . . *Days.*

His warm mouth kissed a trail down the slope of her neck.

Oh no. No. She wasn't supposed to be doing this. "We shouldn't," she protested. "The children . . . "

"They're asleep." His tongue flicked against the hollow at the base of her neck, and she ceased being able to speak.

It felt so good to be in his arms again. It felt *right.* And who knew what tomorrow would bring . . . if she'd ever be in his arms again . . .

Stop it. Don't think about it.

This was a sin. She had a husband. She shouldn't be doing this.

But then he lifted his head and kissed her, his mouth covering hers, his tongue plunging into her, and she threw aside any thoughts of sin. The only word in her head was "yes."

She let herself fall into the bliss of kissing him, wrapping herself around him, trying to fit every last inch of herself against his body. She didn't protest when he hauled her across his lap and fumbled hastily with the buttons on her shirt. She ran her fingers through his hair as he pulled her shirt free of her waistband and yanked it open. He was more impatient than she'd ever seen him. Her breasts were visible through the gauze of her chemise, and he squeezed them with his big hands, looking up at her, his eyes hot with lust.

"Wait," she protested, before he could go further. She took his hand and led him to his tent, so they could have privacy. As soon as the canvas closed behind them, he was on her, hungry, his mouth everywhere his hands weren't.

"Wait," she gasped again. She was wearing her riding culottes, and they were hopeless for this kind of thing. She
pushed him off her and wriggled out of them. He moaned as
her long legs slid free, her skin pale in the darkness. He joined
her, peeling off his buckskins as she tossed her shirt aside.

"Leave it," he said roughly, when she went to remove her
chemise. "I like it."

She could see that. He was fully erect, thrusting toward
her, the tip of his cock slick. He couldn't take his eyes off her.

She was naked except for the flimsy thing, which ended at
her waist. Her breasts strained at the gauze, her nipples dark
and pushing at the thin material. The frill around the waist
skimmed her navel and made her seem even more naked below. His gaze was fixed hungrily on the darkness between her
legs. She was lying on the rug as he knelt over her. Teasingly,
she parted her legs, feeling the night air swirl against the secret heat of her.

He moaned softly again and crept between her legs, his
hands pressing against her knees, widening her legs until she
was fully open to him. She reached out and slid her thumb
across his slick tip.

"Uh-uh," he protested. "Hands to yourself this time."

She made a small noise of protest that quickly turned into
a mewl as his fingers trailed up her legs and found her aching
wet center. She loved the way he took his time. Tonight he ran
his fingers over every wet inch of her, and then followed with
his mouth, tracing each swollen curve with his tongue, dipping
into her until she was mindless with pleasure.

"You," she gasped, "please. *You.*"

He grinned and braced himself on both arms over her
body. She lifted her hips. The head of his cock brushed against
her.

"Now," she begged.

And, as always, he complied.

"THERE'S SOMETHING I have to tell you."

She'd waited until the last possible moment. They'd found
a quiet Spanish-style inn on the outskirts of San Jose. It was a
sprawling single-story building, with grapevines turning purple leaved over the eaves, and orange chickens running loose

in the courtyard. San Jose was a real town, the first truly civilized place they'd seen since leaving the east. It wasn't large, but it was peaceful, with orderly streets and buildings that were decades old. If only they were riding in under better circumstances, Georgiana thought glumly. How nice it would have been to finally rest after such a brutal journey. The inn looked pleasant and comfortable, calm and clean and shady: a haven. Matt had booked them two rooms, one for the children and one for the two of them, and Leo had finally put his foot down.

"You tell him or I will."

Leo resisted every effort Matt made to get to know him. He refused to speak to the man who had "married" his mother and barely even acknowledged his existence. Georgiana was consumed with guilt when she saw how patiently Matt treated the boy. He thought Leo was just taking time to adjust.

"It's *wrong*," her son told her.

It was. It was all completely wrong. Utterly wrong. Everything was upside down and backward. But of course that wasn't what he meant.

"I'll tell him now," she promised as she ushered him and the others into their room. "You help the little ones get themselves cleaned up, while I speak to him." She managed to close the door on him before he could give her another disapproving look. Then she stood in the hall for a good few minutes, trying to gather the courage to do what she needed to do.

Matt was sprawled on the bed when she finally entered the room. She felt ill. She didn't want to have this conversation at all.

"I could sleep for a week," he sighed, not opening his eyes, as he patted the bed beside him. "Come and join me."

"There's something I have to tell you." She didn't join him on the bed, but clung to the door.

"I was wondering when you'd get around to it," he said, propping himself up on his elbows.

She made a right mess of it, stumbling and stuttering, but eventually she got it out. By the time she did, he was on his feet.

"What in hell are you talking about?" He looked like a brute again, a big, glowering wall of manhood. "He's *dead*."

Georgiana shook her head miserably. "Leo says not."

They hadn't discussed Leonard much, but Matt knew enough to know she hadn't grieved too hard when she'd heard of his death. Even so, she saw fear mixing with rage in his expression and, beneath it, a heartrending vulnerability.

"Matt," she said softly, finally creeping away from the door, "there's something else I need to tell you."

He looked up, his brow furrowed. "When you said you had something to tell me . . . I thought you were going to tell me you were pregnant," he said softly. He seemed tentative. "I thought that's why you'd been so lost in your own thoughts." The vulnerability on his face was heartbreaking. "Is that what you're going to tell me now?"

She felt her stomach drop. She hadn't even thought of that. Oh my. *Pregnant.* Given her past fertility, she felt like a fool for not thinking of it. But why should she have fretted? She'd thought they were *married.* A child would have been welcome. But now . . . Oh Lord, she could be married to one man and pregnant to another . . .

"No," she said shakily, "I'm not pregnant. At least not as far as I know."

"Is he here? Is he in San Jose?" Matt's hands had settled on his hips. His jaw was clenching and unclenching.

"I don't know," she said. A great distance seemed to have yawned between them. He seemed like a stranger. "Leo said he would be."

Matt nodded. He was staring into space. "I guess we should see if we can find him, then," he said tersely.

It was only later, when he'd closed the door behind her, that she realized she'd never told him the other thing she wanted to say.

She'd been going to tell him that she loved him.

❧ 40 ❧

LEONARD BLUNT LIKED to make an impression. When he and little William got to San Jose, he checked them into the finest hotel, and then they went shopping. He could hardly see his wife again looking like this, could he? And William was wearing some kind of buckskin shirt with quills on it. He looked like a little savage.

At least he didn't have that mutt yapping after him anymore. That was something to be grateful for.

They bought clothes, had haircuts and purchased gifts for Georgiana and the other children. Leonard didn't blink as the bills piled up. After all, Georgiana was here now, and her pockets were bottomless. Those Bees had more money than was good for them. He did them a favor by spreading it out a little.

"Send the account to the hotel," he told people. They trusted him, as people always did, because he had breeding. Leonard was a firm believer in breeding. And in money.

"Where's Tom?" William asked, for the thousandth time. "You said Tom was going to be here with Woof."

"Children don't speak unless they're spoken to," Leonard reminded him. He couldn't wait to hand the child over to the nanny. That Indian had given the boy some truly appalling manners.

Just look at the god-awful mess the boy made in the washroom. He'd clearly not had much experience with bathing. Leonard was glad the hotel had a dedicated bathroom, because William splashed filthy water over every last inch of the walls and floor.

"I can't do buttons," the boy said, after he'd inexpertly dried himself off and struggled into his clothes.

"Don't be ridiculous," Leonard told him, without breaking from his toilette. "Do up your buttons or I'll get the strap."

The boy did his buttons up just fine after that. You only had to strap a child once, hard, for them to learn their lesson. The same had proved true for Leo. One good strapping and a boy would be obedient until the end.

He was glad Leo had come through his ordeal in Mokelumne Hill in one piece. It showed a certain character. Leonard had been quietly tracking his family for a couple of days, watching them from a distance, asking after them as he made his purchases. Last night he'd had his closest look at them yet, as their trail guide led them into a dining room. It seemed Leo's little adventure might even have done him good. He was taller and broader and less spindly looking than he'd been when Leonard had taken him from New York. His wife had always spoiled the boy; she'd made him soft. A son needed his father, Leonard thought, conveniently ignoring the fact that he'd spent half his life avoiding his children.

Georgiana was looking well too. She stood out in this provincial backwater in a gown that must have cost a small fortune. She'd always had style. And she was still a beautiful woman, although she was a bit mature for his tastes now. And she had marks from her pregnancies, he thought, wrinkling his nose at the memory of the last time they'd slept together. Children did so ruin a woman's body.

Look at Ruth. She'd been a lithe young thing, all perky little breasts and muscular thighs, and then she'd gone and got fat with child, and the next thing you knew those perky breasts were all distended, with red squiggly stretch marks making a horrid mess of them. She'd looked even worse after she'd dropped the child, her belly all slack, her face droopy with exhaustion. It seemed not even the savages were immune from the ravages of childbearing.

Leonard pivoted to check himself in the mirror. He looked a thousand times better than he had when they'd dragged in from the trail. He'd clipped his whiskers and waxed his mustache. He'd bought the most charming suit, which showed off his lean figure to full advantage, and the leather shoes were spit shined until they gleamed.

Yes. Now he was ready. "Come, William, let's find your mother."

"Wil*by*," the impertinent lad corrected him.

Leonard picked up his old belt, which he'd left in a heap with his dirty clothes. He held it up in front of William's face. The boy flinched.

Good. He was learning.

"Your name is William Bee Blunt," his father told him firmly, "of the New York Bees and the Boston Blunts." The Bees had the money, and the Blunts had the breeding. Well, the Bees had the breeding too, probably more than the Blunts had, to be honest. But the Blunts had *cunning*, and the Bees were ripe for the plucking. Leonard grinned. It was time for some fresh plucking. His coffers were bare.

He was a handsome lad, Leonard thought, as he straightened William's collar. He took after his father.

"Where's Mama?" That mulish look though he got from his mother. Georgiana had always been prone to a stubborn set of the jaw. She was a docile sort, but there was an edge to her, like she was thinking things she'd never say. Ruth had been the same.

The next one would be properly docile, he resolved. Her eyes would match her manner, and not shoot secret sparks at him.

"I want Mama."

That mulishness would have to be beaten out of him. But not right now. Leonard would crease his new suit if he took the strap to the boy now.

"And I'm sure your mama wants you too," Leonard told him. "Put your shoes on and we'll go find her."

He knew exactly where she was. Leonard had planned every inch of their reunion for maximum effect. It was Sunday, and Georgiana was going to church. She'd been both Sundays since she'd arrived in town, to say a prayer for her dead child, they said. He'd overheard people talking when he was at the barber's. People were fascinated by his fancy wife and loved to gossip about her. Leonard's grin widened. That was another good thing about Georgiana: she made a delightful accessory.

He drew his own share of admiring glances as he paraded

toward the church. He'd bought himself a rather extravagant silver-headed cane, which he swung to maximum effect as they promenaded.

Like a good Protestant girl, Georgiana bypassed Our Lady of Guadalupe for the Presbyterian service, which was being held in the courthouse until a church could be built. Leonard made sure to be tardy, as he didn't want to ruin the effect of his surprise by accidentally running into them on the street. He and William lingered under the shade trees for a while, listening to the hymns, and then he asked the boy if he remembered what he had to do.

"Find Mama," the boy said.

"You wait until they're filing out," Leonard instructed. "I'll be standing right here, under this tree, watching."

He stage-managed it to perfection, he thought later. It was a scene the people of San Jose would be talking about for generations. It must have brought a tear to the eye of those with even the hardest hearts. Leonard only managed to bring a tear to his own eye by scratching it with his fingernail. It was a trick he'd learned a long time ago. Tears could win people over fast.

The last hymn ended, the lovely sound hanging in the air for a moment as the doors to the courthouse opened and people streamed out. And there she was, a vision in palest blue.

"Now," Leonard hissed, giving William a shove with his cane. "There she is, go now. Just like I showed you."

And for all his mulishness, the boy played his part to perfection. Perhaps because he wasn't playing at all, but was genuinely overjoyed to see her.

"Mama!" William yelled, his voice splitting the morning air. And then he was pelting across the street and hurling himself at Georgiana. He might have knocked her sideways if that brute of a trail guide hadn't been there to hold her up.

The crowd parted, muttering.

And then there was a desperate cry as Georgiana realized who was hugging her. "Wilby? *Wilbeeeeeeeeeeee!*"

Leonard watched, satisfied, as she dropped to her knees in the dust, hugging the life out of the boy, rocking and weeping and generally making a spectacle of herself.

Leonard let her get the hysterics out of her system, and only then, when she'd calmed enough to pull back and look up, did he step out of the shadows.

"Hello, darling," he said, modulating his voice so it sounded husky, as though he was suffused with emotion. He'd flicked his nail into his eye before he'd stepped forward, and he blinked, to let a tear roll down his cheek. "God must have been watching over us"—he paused for effect—"because I rescued this boy in the wilderness . . . and it turned out to be our son."

She looked up at him, astonished.

And then she began to cry in earnest.

❧ 41 ❧

THE SISKIYOU TRAIL stretched six hundred miles ahead of him, into the vast and lonely wilderness between San Jose and home. He traveled light and he traveled alone. Now and then he passed a wagon train headed south to the goldfields of California.

"Hey, mister, you're going the wrong way!"

He nodded and smiled tightly each time he heard it, giving a tired wave, although the joke had worn thin fast. He didn't have much of a sense of humor these days, and maybe he never would again.

"You got gold in those saddlebags, mister?"

"How'd California treat you, mister? You going home a rich man?"

He moved Pablo off the trail to let yet another band of hopeful gold hunters pass him by. No, he thought, as he watched them rumble away; he wasn't going home a rich man. In fact, he'd *come* to California a rich man, richer than he'd ever believed possible. And he was leaving impoverished.

Matt resumed his long trudge north home to the Willamette Valley, his thoughts a thousand miles away. He remembered meeting Georgiana in Independence: her freshness, her intelligence, her beauty and her sadness. She'd taught him what real wealth was. Real wealth was *her*. For all the sadness of losing Wilby, those months on the trail had been the richest and most meaningful of his entire life.

Wilby. The thought of the boy sent a blazing pain through him. It was all he could do to keep breathing, the pain got so strong.

He'd failed them all. It was his fault that Wilby had been lost, and his fault Wilby hadn't been found. Georgiana had suffered needlessly for all of those months because of his failure.

And it had been Leonard . . . her *husband* . . . who had restored her son and her joy.

Ah, that hurt like hell. The memory of Wilby running headlong into Georgiana outside the courthouse-come-church hurt so much it was hard to breathe. The astonishment, and then the joy of it . . . For that first moment or two, Matt had believed in miracles. It was really, truly Wilby. He was taller and less babyish, and he looked different with all his hair shorn, but it was *Wilby*.

And then Blunt had stepped forward.

Matt kicked Pablo into a trot, as though he could outrun the feelings that threatened to run him down. No matter how hard he tried to leave them behind, the memories tracked him, every minute of every day, and he lived with a constant ache in his chest.

Blunt was everything Matt was not. He was slender and elegant, finely dressed and softly spoken. He treated Georgiana with extreme courtesy and gentility. And—this hurt, but it was true—he looked like he *belonged* with her. They were a matched pair. Where Georgiana always made Matt feel oversized and clumsy as he towered over her, Blunt was in proportion. As they stood in the middle of their brood, staring into each other's eyes, Matt had felt his heart stop in his chest. They looked *good* together. They looked *right*.

Georgiana had turned to look at him, her eyes red and swollen from crying. His instinct was to step forward and pull her into his arms, but what right did he have? Her husband was right there beside her. It was *his* privilege to comfort her.

Matt felt a jealousy so sharp it cut to the bone. It only worsened when Blunt bent down to speak to Susannah and he saw their resemblance. This was *his* family, not Matt's.

Matt was suddenly and irrevocably an outsider.

The next day or so after that had been sheer hell. He'd watched Blunt lead his family away from the courthouse, and Matt hadn't quite known what to do with himself; he followed behind for a few steps and then stopped. He had the repulsive feeling that he was intruding. He felt like a stray dog skulking

behind them, in hopes of picking up scraps. It didn't help that
Blunt treated him like some kind of servant.

"Can you arrange for their belongings to be brought to my
hotel?" the man called back to Matt. "Many thanks!"

Georgiana had looked at him helplessly. She had Wilby in
her arms, her cheek pressed against his head. What could she
say? There was *too much* to say, and a public street wasn't the
place to say it.

Right then, at that exact moment, Matt had known it was
over. Maybe not consciously, but certainly deep down in the
pit of his stomach. Even if Georgiana told Blunt about Matt,
what did it change? She was Blunt's wife, not Matt's. The children were Blunt's children, not Matt's. Her future was with
Blunt, and not with Matt.

And where did that leave him?

Alone in their room at the inn, that's where it left him. The
room was screamingly empty, loud with her absence.

Matt had numbly packed their belongings, but he couldn't
bring himself to carry them across town and deliver them like
a servant. He didn't want to come face-to-face with Blunt
again. He didn't want to be witness to their family reunion. It
hurt bad enough to know it was happening without having to
witness every last detail of it. So he'd paid some of the locals
to deliver their things.

He needed time. And Georgiana knew where to find him.
What was going on over there was her business, not his. She'd
come and speak to him when she was ready.

And he was afraid of what she was going to say.

"LET'S RUN AWAY!"

He'd opened the door to find her crying. She'd reverted to
the woman he'd met in Independence: beautiful, nervous,
weeping.

She burrowed her face against his chest and gave in to sobs
of pure despair. "Please," she begged, "let's pack up and go. You
can take us to your home in Oregon, like we planned."

That was when Matt got angry. At her, at Blunt, at the
whole damn world. Because she didn't mean it. The way she
was crying told him that she didn't mean it.

Which meant he had to be the one to say it, and it was the

one thing he didn't want to say. Every single part of him wanted to grab her and those kids and run home.

"You don't mean that," he said, taking her by the arms and prying her off his chest.

"I do!"

It took every ounce of his self-control not to lose his temper. "No, you don't. If you meant it, you wouldn't be crying. You'd have your bags packed and the kids here, and we'd be loading those wagons. You'd be kissing me, instead of getting my shirt all wet."

She cried harder at that, her shoulders hunching over and her head hanging so low her chin was practically touching her chest.

He was so mad he could have shaken her. *Fight*, he wanted to rail. *Fight, Goddamn it.* Fight for *me*, for *us*. For all that we are and all that we could be.

Matt loved her with every last inch of himself. He'd *die* for her.

He loved her so goddamn much he'd even work against himself. He'd do the thing she was finding so hard to do. He'd say their good-byes.

But he wouldn't make it easy for her. He wasn't *that* noble.

"Here, have a glass of water. You're crying yourself dry." Hurt made him sound cold. He moved away from her and poured her a cupful from the pitcher. He wished she'd stop staring at him like that, with such mute misery.

She drank the water and drew a couple of shuddery breaths.

"Tell me how he found Wilby," Matt said flatly. He kept his distance from her. He'd only be able to get through this if she didn't get too close. If he got too close, he might start kissing her, and then he'd be lost.

"Some Indians had him." Georgiana's voice was shaky. "Leonard didn't even know who he was when he rescued him."

Matt winced as Georgiana said her husband's name. It sounded so familiar to her, so intimate as it fell from her lips.

"It was the first time he'd ever seen him." Georgiana gave a slightly hysterical laugh. "He and Leo left before I even knew I was pregnant."

Matt nodded and clenched his teeth. That was the final nail

in the coffin, right there. "He deserves a chance to know his father and his brother."

Georgiana pressed her lips together and nodded, sending fat, slow tears sliding down her cheeks.

He sighed, his anger warring with jealousy and hurt, and the urge to comfort her.

"I love you," she whispered.

"Don't."

"I do. I love you. That's what I was going to tell you the other day, when . . ."

"Please," he said harshly. "Please, don't." He closed his eyes. He heard her weeping softly. "Let's not draw this out."

"Matt . . ."

"No." He opened his eyes. "*Don't.*" His voice was raw with pain. She heard it and fell silent.

She swallowed hard. "What will you do?"

He laughed. It was a hard, bitter sound. "I'll go home. What else would I do?"

He saw the flash of pain in her eyes. But what in hell did she *think* he'd do? *Stay?* Watch her play happy family with her husband?

"When?"

"As soon as I can." There was no point in dragging this out. It wasn't going to get easier. And Matt had a sudden longing for home. He wanted to ride up the valley and see his people. He could practically see the house at the fringe of the foothills, surrounded by blazing autumn trees; his brother out working his horses; Alex in her vegetable garden; his nieces running in the yard. He felt homesick at the vision. He'd been gone for a long time. It was time to go home.

He'd wanted to go with Georgiana. To ride proudly up to the house and to introduce his brother to his wife, to see the look of happy shock on Luke's face . . .

Stop. Those thoughts just intensified the pain.

"Are you going to say good-bye to the children?"

Matt clenched his teeth so hard it was a surprise they didn't crack. He knew he had to say good-bye. It wasn't fair to them to disappear without a trace . . . But God, he couldn't think of anything more painful.

But he was wrong. Saying good-bye to the children was

bad, but there was something worse. And that was saying good-bye to Georgiana.

On the day he was riding out, they came to see him off. They stood by the inn's stable in a solemn clump as he cinched his saddlebags and tied Fernando's lead to Pablo's saddle. He had to work hard to keep his composure. They were upset enough, without his emotions upsetting them further. The twins had been resentful and bratty; Susannah had cried; Wilby had thrown a tantrum, yelling senselessly about Tom and Dog and Woof and now Matt. Leo had watched it all from a distance.

"I'll take care of them," he'd told Matt quietly, before leading the little ones away so Matt and Georgiana could have some privacy.

This is the last time you'll ever see her.

Neither of them could find the words to say good-bye. Matt drank her in, trying to commit each detail to memory. Those prairie flax blue eyes, the way her dark curls tangled at her temples, that perfect mouth. He reached out and pressed his palm to her cheek.

As he stared into those blue, blue eyes, his anger fell away, subsumed by the deepest sadness he'd ever known.

"You were the best thing that ever happened to me," he said huskily. And he meant it. He wouldn't give up a single moment, not even to save them this pain.

He rubbed his thumb against her soft skin. "Be safe, sweetheart."

And then he couldn't take anymore. He swung himself up into the saddle and rode out, before he lost his nerve and kidnapped the lot of them.

THE MILES HAD never been so desolate. And for all his experience with being alone, he'd never felt *this* alone before. He pushed himself, barely sleeping, determined to reach home before winter blocked his way.

Even though he knew he couldn't have stayed, he couldn't shake the feeling that he'd made a mistake. That there should have been something he could have done.

"Hey, mister, you're going the wrong way!" The cry followed him all the way up the trail.

Hey, mister, you're going the wrong way . . .

LEONARD LIKED SAN JOSE. He decided they should stay, at least for a while. One day he led Georgiana and the children to a house in the older part of town. It was a low Spanish building, with terra-cotta tiles and a shady veranda.

"It's ours!" he declared, expecting them all to be thrilled.

Georgiana tried to act thrilled, she really did. But she didn't feel thrilled at all. She felt even less thrilled a couple of weeks after they moved in, when the creditors started coming to the door. Her stomach sank to her knees. *Not again.*

She hadn't really thought Leonard would change. But everything had happened so fast: Wilby's return, Matt leaving . . . it hadn't given her much space to think about the future with Leonard.

Truth be told, she didn't think about much else than Matt Slater . . .

Sometimes on the street she thought she saw him and her heart would leap. But of course it wasn't him. He'd be a hundred miles away by now.

The first night in the hotel, Leonard had tried to kiss her, and she'd pushed him away, muttering a weak excuse about shock and nervous exhaustion. After a week or two, he was getting impatient with her, but the thought of letting him touch her filled Georgiana with dread. She didn't care what the law said; she felt married to *Matt*, not Leonard. Being with Leonard felt like a betrayal. So she offered excuse after excuse. It was that time of the month, she had a headache, she was poorly, she was tired . . . Eventually, he got so irritated he reverted to a version of himself she hadn't seen for a very long time. A *mean* version of himself.

"Ah, who wants to sleep with you anyway," he'd sneered,

when she'd rejected him yet again. "Your tits are sagging after all those brats."

She'd flinched at his crudity. She'd forgotten his cruelty. She was relieved when he'd pulled his boots on and slammed out of the house. He'd probably gone to a whorehouse, she realized sickly.

"Mama?" Susannah had appeared in the doorway. She was sucking her thumb again.

"It's all right, darling. Daddy just had a bad moment."

Daddy had a lot more bad moments. Especially after the creditors came and he and Georgiana had their first real fight about money.

"Just pay them!" he'd ordered her.

"With what?" she'd asked in astonishment. And that's when he found out her money was gone. At which he'd thrown a monumental tantrum.

"It's *your fault* it's gone," she'd said coldly. "And it's *your fault* we don't even have the gold claim anymore."

Things went from bad to worse after that. Georgiana found they hadn't been paying rent when the landlord posted an eviction notice. After that, she started taking in laundry to pay the bills. It wasn't nearly enough. She begged the landlord for more time, and he gave it to her, but only another week, and only because he felt sorry for her. And then he dared to suggest that there were other ways she could pay the debt. His eyes ran over her body as he said it, and she shuddered.

And then there was that horrific day when she walked in on Leonard whipping Phin with his belt. Hard. He strapped him with all his strength. Hard enough to break the skin.

"Get off him!" Georgiana shrieked, pulling him away. He pushed her, and she went flying into the table. She got straight back up and launched at him again. "If you touch him again, *I'll kill you*," she promised. And she meant it.

The house was a brooding place, seething with unhappiness. The children were subdued and resentful. Georgiana lay awake at night while Leonard was out (doing whatever it was that he did), feeling tangled and bleak, worrying endlessly about money and how to pay the rent and put food on the table. In the depths of the night, her mind turned north to Oregon and Matt. She heard his voice in her head, describing his

home. The fall colors would be turning the trees orange and
red and gold by now. The valley would be preparing for winter. His family would be laying in supplies and splitting wood.
Smoke would be curling from the chimney. In her mind, the
Slater property was an idyll. She wished she were there with
all her might.

But when she woke, she was still in the small house in San
Jose, with Leonard snoring drunkenly beside her.

He was snoring exactly like that on the morning destiny
came calling. She could hear him from the yard, where she
was breaking her back over a cauldron of laundry, and had
been since before dawn. She stabbed at the boiling linens,
imagining she was stabbing Leonard. She was working her
fingers to the bone while he did nothing. Well, nothing except
rack up debt, stay out all night and whip their son. Phin hadn't
forgiven his father for the strapping, and neither had Georgiana. After that, she made sure the children were never alone
with him.

She was so busy stabbing things that she didn't hear their
guests arrive, not until she heard the yapping, followed by
Wilby squealing with joy.

"Woof!" he was screeching. "Woof! Woof!"

She looked up to see Wilby and Woof wrestling joyfully in
the yard.

"Where did he come from?" she asked, shocked.

"He's with me," a familiar voice drawled.

"Tom!" She faltered as she caught sight of him. "Tom?" she
said, a little more uncertainly. It *was* Tom. But he was dressed
like an Indian. *Rides With Death*, she thought with a shiver,
remembering Matt's story: the gunslingers hunting them, the
shooting, faking Deathrider's death.

Deathrider clearly didn't want to stay dead. His hair was
decorated with a single black-tipped eagle feather. He was in
full Indian garb, and he even had an Indian woman with him.
A woman and a baby.

"You got married?" she said in shock.

"No." His eerily pale eyes flicked around the yard, looking
for someone. "But I hear *you* did." The pale eyes flicked back
to her. "A couple of times."

"Matt's not here," she blurted.

"So I hear. But I'm not looking for Matt. I'm looking for the other one."

"The other one?"

"Your other husband."

"Tom brought Woof!" Wilby crowed. He threw his arms around Tom's legs and grinned up at him.

Deathrider lifted the boy off his legs and handed him to Georgiana. "Keep the kids out here, hmm?" he said. "I assume that noise is your husband. Or do you have a sick pig in there?"

Georgiana watched, nonplussed, as he strode into the house.

"Ruth," Wilby called, squirming out of his mother's grip.

"You're Will's wife?" the woman asked, stepping into Georgiana's yard.

"I beg your pardon?" Georgiana frowned. "Who's Will?"

"Daddy!" Wilby told her.

The screen door to the house flew open, and Georgiana screeched as Leonard came tumbling down the steps.

"Stand up and fight, you son of a bitch," Deathrider snarled.

Leonard didn't, of course. Fighting wasn't his style. Running was. But Deathrider wouldn't let him run.

"Wait!" Georgiana yelled, stepping between them. "Tell me what's going on."

"This son of a bitch turned us over to a posse," Deathrider spat. "He told them we kidnapped Wilby. We woke up one morning and Wilby was gone, and next thing we knew we were surrounded by maniacs trying to lynch us."

"Us?"

"You can't trust him. He's nothing but a savage!" Leonard spat. He struggled to his feet. "I saved our son from these savages."

Deathrider's lip curled. "And you gave your other son over to the lynch mob."

"Other son?" Georgiana's head was starting to hurt.

The baby gave a squall. Georgiana's blood went cold. *Other son?* She turned to see Ruth giving Leonard a cold glare. Oh. Oh *my.*

"Wilby," Georgiana called him to her. "Who saved you?"

"The lady."

"This lady?"

He shook his head.

"He was found at Green River by a Lakota woman named White Buffalo," Deathrider told her. "The Lakota chief summoned me to take him, because I . . . because I am known to the whites. This *filth* stole the boy off me when I was delirious with fever and his woman had just given birth."

His woman.

"Is that your child?" Georgiana asked Leonard bluntly.

In typical Leonard style, he went on full offense. "I'm not a monk," he blustered, "and you have no right to expect me to be!"

"Did you give your child over to a lynch mob?" She didn't need to hear the answer. She *knew.*

The boys had gathered on the porch. Georgiana took in their pinched expressions. She didn't remember the last time she'd had to discipline the twins, she realized. They hadn't accidentally shot stones through the windows or spooked the horses or harassed her to use the hunting rifle . . . And when was the last time she'd seen them do backflips or try to juggle knives? When had they laughed or teased their sister?

And Susannah . . . There she was, at the window staring out. She was quieter than ever and prone to sucking her thumb. She carried her doll with her everywhere, something she hadn't done since she was little. Her father never remembered her name. He called her *Susan.* Susannah had started out correcting him, but after a while she'd just given up, and now she even answered to "Susan."

Georgiana met Leo's gaze. Leonard had made him hard and cynical. If the twins didn't laugh, Leo didn't so much as *smile.*

Georgiana drew herself up to her full height of not much at all and gathered all her courage. She was about to do the bravest, most sensible, most scandalous thing she'd ever done in her life.

"Leonard," she said, pinning him with an icily haughty stare. "I want a divorce."

❧ 43 ❧

AN EARLY SNOWSTORM caught Matt out. He straggled into the closest trading post and resigned himself to spending the winter there. This made two winters in a row that he was sleeping rough. At least there were no gunslingers this year. And Hank Larson, who ran the place, was a decent enough fellow. There were a few old trappers who joined them for the winter as well, sitting around the fire and shooting the breeze for hours on end.

Matt helped Hank fix the place up, and then he took himself off trapping when he got bored. He preferred to be alone. It suited his melancholy.

"It's got to be a woman," old Perry told the others one afternoon when they were stuck inside due to the snow flurries that were battering the windows. "I'll bet you a silver dollar it's a woman that makes him look like that."

Matt was sitting by the window, fixing a bear trap, trying to ignore their gossiping.

"That's not a fair bet," Roland said, spitting a stream of tobacco into an old pail. It made a *thunk*. "It's *definitely* a woman."

As the flurries picked up, they fell into talking about women they'd known. The stories grew more ribald as the day darkened and the flurries turned into a more serious snowstorm. Matt ignored them as best he could.

The next morning, he went out trapping, to avoid more talk of women and love and heartbreak. He didn't want to think about women anymore. Or rather, one woman.

The forest was thick with new snow, the pine boughs lacy. Matt stopped at the crest of the hill, his breath coming in plumes. The snow muffled all sound, but something made him turn. He frowned. There was something at the bottom of the hill. And he thought he heard voices, faint and smothered by the snow. Concerned, he slogged down the hill, glad he'd worn his snow shoes. It wasn't uncommon for travelers to get caught out on the trail in this weather. Whoever it was must have had a brutally cold time of it last night.

A dog bounded up the hill, barking happily. A puppy came close behind it, tripping and falling face-first in the snow. Matt stopped dead. It couldn't be . . .

But it was.

At the bottom of the hill sat two familiar wagons and a very familiar Indian, digging the wheels free of snow.

"Deathrider?"

His friend looked up. "Are you just going to stand there, or are you going to help?"

"Matt!"

A snowball sailed through the air and hit him full in the face. There was a storm of laughter.

He wiped the snow off, disbelieving.

Another snowball came flying, but he managed to duck this one.

"Matt!" Wilby yelled. He was standing precariously on the wagon seat, waving madly. A hand snapped out of the wagon and grabbed his shirt to stop him falling.

Matt's heart clenched. He knew that hand.

He'd heard that men hallucinated when they froze to death. They grew warm and peaceful and had dreams so vivid they seemed real. That's what had happened to him, he decided, as he saw Georgiana emerge from the wagon. She was wearing her traveling clothes, including that vest that drove him wild. Her cheeks were pink from the cold, and her blue eyes were sparkling.

He was dying. This was a hallucination. He was sitting in the snow, lost in the forest, freezing to death. It made sense that he'd dream of her as he died. She was all he ever dreamed about.

Thwack. Another snowball hit him full in the face.

Hell. This was *real.*

"YOU'RE HERE," HE said stupidly, as soon as they were alone. They were in the stable with the animals. Everyone else was in the trading post, warming up by the fire.

"I am," she agreed. She looked very pleased with herself. "But . . . Leonard . . ."

"Yes." She bit her lip. "There's still Leonard."

"He's your husband," he reminded her.

"Oh no," she disagreed. "We had a *wedding*, but we never had a marriage. He is not, and has never been, my husband. He's just a man I married."

Matt frowned, lost.

She pressed her palms against his chest. It was hard to think when she touched him like that. "*You're* the only husband I've ever had," she told him earnestly. "You looked after me when I couldn't look after myself; you showed my sons what it's like to be a man, my daughter how a man should treat her; you fed us and watched over us, grieved with us and comforted us."

Her words flowed over him like warm water.

"Matt, I never felt for Leonard the way I feel for you." Her blue eyes held him captive. "You're all I want, and all I will ever want. *I love you*."

The months of pain and loneliness seemed to blow away, like snowflakes in the wind.

"But . . . *Leonard*," he said. "There's still the matter of Leonard."

"Yes. He's like a bad smell," she said, pulling a face. "He just doesn't go away." Her hands slid up his chest until they looped around his neck. "But . . . this is the frontier, after all . . ."

"What are you suggesting?" he asked, suspiciously.

"I'm not *suggesting* anything." She swayed closer. "I'm *saying* I'd rather live in sin with you than in sanctified hell with him."

"What do you mean?" he said, huskily, distracted by the way her fingers played with the hair at the nape of his neck and the way her body felt as she pressed against him.

"I haven't kissed anyone but you, touched anyone but you, or loved anyone but you since we said our vows. I consider myself married to you. And this is the frontier. And the whole point of the frontier is that we get to be free. We get to start again. We get to reinvent ourselves. Well, I'm reinventing myself as *your wife*."

She stretched on tiptoe and pressed a kiss against his lips.

He didn't know how to feel. When she said she loved him, his heart soared. But he didn't want to share her.

"I don't like that you're still married to him," he said gruffly.

"Me neither." She'd moved on to kissing his neck. It was hard to think when her tongue swirled against his skin. "Don't worry," she breathed between kisses, "I'm getting a divorce."

He grabbed her arms and pulled her away so he could see her face. "You what?"

"I'm getting a divorce."

Joy shot through him, a pure bolt of it, straight through his heart. "Why didn't you say that in the first place?"

She pulled another face. "Well, it's going to take a while. By the time I write to lawyers and we have it approved, it may be a couple of years."

"He's going along with it?"

Georgiana gave him a wicked smile. "Deathrider helped convince him." She laughed. "Not that he needed much convincing. He *hates* being married, especially when it's to a woman without money. And the only thing he hates more than being married is children." She sighed. "Let's just say, living with him was a disaster. It wasn't good for any of us." Her gaze turned serious. "And I was hopelessly in love with someone else."

"I love you too," he told her quietly. He touched her face in wonder, not quite able to believe she was here.

"Matthew Slater, will you marry me? In a year or two . . . and live with me in sin until then? Because I am *not* waiting two years to make love to you again. Not when we already got married."

"Yes, Georgiana Slater, I will marry you in a year or two. And I will most definitely live with you in sin until then." He laughed. "And this time we can have a wedding you can actually enjoy."

"And a wedding night!"

"Yes," he told her, kissing her thoroughly. "Yes, yes, yes."

She squealed as he swept her off her feet and carried her up to the hayloft.

"Unbutton that vest, woman," he ordered, tossing her into the straw. "It's been a lonely winter."

She giggled and hurried to comply. Soon they were naked and kissing hungrily. They were both so desperate, they came quickly the first time. The second time was slightly less rushed. And by the third, they were hitting their stride.

"Give me another shot," he whispered against her neck after she'd come the third time. "Fourth time's a charm."

"Oh *yes.*"

Late in the day, they were dozing, warm and damp with sweat, when they heard the children come looking for them.

"Matt!" Susannah called.

"Matt!" Flip yelled. "Can you tell Susannah she's full of hot air?"

Matt poked his head over the edge of the loft. "What do you want? We're having our honeymoon."

"You already had your honeymoon," Phin said scornfully. "I know because I got Seline to make the pie."

"Seline made the pie?" Georgiana gasped.

Matt winced.

"I should have got the recipe," she said, running her hand over his naked buttocks. "It was delicious."

"Honeymoons happen every month," he lied to the children, "so you better get used to it. Now, what do you want? I'll answer one question, and then you can go away and leave us to our honeymoon. Tell Hank I said you can have some rock candy. Just add it to my account."

"Quick, ask him the question, Sook, before he changes his mind about the candy."

"Do you have magic horses in Oregon?" Susannah shouted up the ladder.

"Nah." Matt shook his head and sighed with exaggerated regret. "They don't get along with the magic bears."

Georgiana pressed her cheek into the hard muscle of Matt's naked back and smiled. She could see this living-in-sin business was going to suit them all very well.

AUTHOR'S NOTE

The westerns I've always loved are larger-than-life affairs, from Larry McMurtry's novels, to old movies like *Seven Brides for Seven Brothers*, *Oklahoma!*, *The Searchers* and *High Noon*, to the revisionist gritty beauty of *Unforgiven* and *Dances with Wolves*, to the Shakespearean magnificence of *Deadwood*. While I base my westerns in history, it's a heightened Technicolor kind of history, with some liberties taken for the sake of the story.

The biggest historical liberty I have taken in *Bound for Sin* concerns the dime novels that make Deathrider's life a misery. In my novel, dime novels exist from the 1840s, when in actual fact they weren't in publication until 1860. The very first dime novel was published in 1860 in the *Beadle's Dime Novels* series (they coined the term). It was a work by Ann S. Stephens, called *Malaeska: The Indian Wife of the White Hunter*, which was actually a reprint of a story that she had serialized for the *Ladies' Companion* journal in 1839.

These stories *were* out there being published in journals at the time my characters were heading west (the 1840s and 1850s), but dime novels were not. But the "western" has a series of tropes that we are all familiar with, and dime novels are one of them. It's much easier to use the term "dime novel" than to clumsily explain serialized stories in journals. My fiction is more fiction than history, but this is one stretching of the truth I wanted to acknowledge.

Especially since Ava Archer will continue to play havoc with the Plague of the West . . .

Turn the page for a sneak peek of

BOUND FOR TEMPTATION

Coming soon from Jove

Moke Hill, California, 1850

SHE WAS RICH. Standing in her fancy office over the saloon, Seline watched as the lawyer's fountain pen scratched at the ledger, forming a beautiful little billow of zeros. She had to pinch herself. In less than a year, the Heart of Gold had made her wealthier than she'd ever dreamed of being. And this wasn't even all of it. She still had two other businesses to cash in. Once she'd sold the other whorehouses in Angels Camp and Mariposa, she'd almost be as rich as Midas himself.

She watched as the prissy eastern lawyer transposed all of those lovely zeros onto the contract, her heart a tight little ball in her chest. Each zero he added was another nail in the coffin of her current life. Goodbye, Seline. Goodbye, mining town. Goodbye, *men*. That money meant a nice little house in San Francisco, maybe even one with a view of the bay. It meant finishing her days when the sun was setting, rather than working through the night. No more hitting her pillow as dawn was breaking. It meant sitting on her lonesome, drinking her first coffee of the day in peace, without having to settle accounts and shoo out the last malingerers filling up her beds. It meant hammering out no more quarrels and mopping up no more tears and helping no more damn fool girls. Once she'd collected the last of her money, Seline planned never to see the inside of another whorehouse in her life.

"You're buying one hell of a business," she told Justine, who was equally transfixed by the ink flowing from the nib of the lawyer's fancy fountain pen.

"Don't I know it," Jussy said. She looked a little green at how much it was costing her. But she was no fool. She was getting the whorehouse at a cut price; if it weren't for Hec Boehm running Seline out of town, the place would have gone for more. But with a man like Hec snapping at her skirts, Seline was just happy to grab what she could and get gone. Luckily, what she could grab was eye wateringly wonderful.

Mr. Teague put the gold dust in neatly folded brown squares of paper and lined up the rows of bank notes, using the beautiful little gold nuggets to weigh the stacks down.

"You'd best be depositing all of that in the bank, quick smart," Mr. Teague told her, peering up over his crooked spectacles. "Moke Hill is no place for a . . . ahem . . . lady . . . to be carrying around a fortune like that."

Seline ignored him. Even if she planned to stay in town—which she didn't—she didn't believe in banks. Especially not the one in Mokelumne Hill, which was run by Wilbur Stroud, a man who liked to be tied naked to a chair while Seline's girls dressed up like nuns and told him that he was a very naughty boy. Sometimes, when business was especially stressful at the bank, he'd even ask the nuns to take a strap to him.

No. Seline would look after her own money, thank you very much.

"Would you like me to read you the documents?" Teague asked.

Seline snatched them off him. Honestly. These men were all alike. They thought being a whore meant you were stupid. How did he think she could run her businesses without *reading*? She went through the contract first, and then the deeds to the building and the business. Justine peered over her shoulder. They each found a couple of errors, which Teague swiftly corrected and initialed, looking sour.

Seline's hands were sweaty as she took the corrected documents back from him and checked them one last time. There, in a thicket of fancy legal words, was her freedom. From Hec Boehm and Moke Hill, and, best of all, from whoredom. And right at the bottom of the contract was a space for her to write her name. Her *real* name. The one she hadn't used for nigh on twelve years . . .

"You sign first," she told Justine, her voice a little unsteady. Hell. It was the thought of that name, she supposed. It was like seeing a ghost . . . a ghost that brought with it an ugly mudslide of memories. The weight on her. The pain. The smell of his rank corn liquor sweat. The feel of a hand clamped over her mouth and nose.

She exhaled. She hadn't been quick enough to get out of the way, that was all. Not then, and not now. Usually, she could jump aside before the memories hit. And there were more memories than she cared to count. The sludge of her past was a relentless tide, an avalanche of shame and fear, prone to sucking her down and drowning her alive.

But they were just memories, she told herself fiercely, as she watched Justine bend over the documents, pen in hand. They were the *past*. And this, right here, right now, was the beginning of her *future*.

And her future was going to be a gold-plated beautiful thing.

Justine finished her signature with a flourish and handed the pen to Seline. "All yours, boss."

"No, honey," Seline said, shaking off her sludgy past and the whipped little creature she'd been, and adopting her fancy welcome-to-the-whorehouse drawl, "it's all *yours* now. *Boss.*"

And as she signed the deed, her black signature an energetic slash on the page, she signed it with her real name. With the name of the girl who had been left back in Tennessee all those years ago, scared and alone, and with no other option than to let men buy her body by the hour.

Emma Jane Palmer.

She was free.

OR, ALMOST FREE. First, she had to get out of town without Hec Boehm or any of his greasy henchmen seeing her.

"He's got those Koerners parked downstairs waiting for you, and that Dutch thug is watching the back door," Justine told her. The newly promoted madam was eager to get Emma out of her whorehouse as quickly as possible. She didn't fancy her expensive business being the target of Hec's violence—not when she'd just paid her life savings for it.

"Don't fret. Teague's going to tell Hec I've sold up. He's headed there now." Emma swept her fortune into the saddle-bags she had waiting on the floor. The bags were deliciously heavy. She was glad the office had a connecting door to her room, so she didn't have to go out on the landing to get there, dragging her fortune with her. She knew Kipp Koerner would be watching the office door, probably without blinking. That man was like a tick on a dog when it came to doing Hec's business. His brother, Carter, on the other hand, was just as liable to be liquored up and counting his coins to do the nasty with JoBeth or Mona. He favored the young-looking ones.

"'Don't fret,' she says," Justine parroted, following her into the bedroom. "It don't matter a lick if he knows you sold, so long as you're *here*."

Didn't Emma know it. She dropped the saddlebags and yanked her carpetbag out from under the bed. "Teague's also going to tell Mr. Boehm that I'll receive him tomorrow, at nine P.M. sharp, to give him my decision." Justine didn't look reassured. "Teague will also pass on that my answer will, of course, be *yes*," Emma told her, as though that solved everything.

Jussy looked less convinced than ever. "And why would you sell this place if you were planning on staying in Moke Hill?"

Emma fluttered her eyelashes. "To devote my full attentions to his pleasure." She snorted. "Or so Teague will tell him—along with how much it will cost him to have me. He did say he wanted me exclusively. And that sure as hell can't happen if I'm busy running this joint every night." It would also flatter his vanity, the thought of having her completely to himself. He'd already offered to set her up in a little place of her own, right on the main street across from the Heart of Gold. She'd be like his personal canary, hung right where everyone could see him, strutting in and out of her gilded cage. He wanted everyone to know that he'd conquered the unconquerable whore. And he wanted to reinforce that she was, when all was said and done, still just a whore.

She'd made the price absolutely ridiculous. She didn't think Hec would believe any less, considering how much of a stink she'd kicked up over the whole business. Unconsciously, she touched her fingers to her neck. The bruises were just about gone now, but the memory of his hands around her throat was too fresh for comfort.

There was a sharp knock, and she and Justine both jumped.

Hell. Was that him now? She'd been *sure* he'd wait until to-morrow. He was enjoying the theater of her defeat too much to cut it short. Little did the fat pig know, she wasn't defeated at all. She'd be halfway to Mariposa before he worked out that she wasn't here.

"Boss?" Virgil's voice was muffled through the closed door.

"Yes?" Both Emma and Justine answered. Whoops. It was going to take a while to remember that she wasn't the boss anymore—Justine was. She gave Justine an apologetic look.

"You still want to open at the usual time?" Virge asked through the door.

"God, yes!" Despite her best intentions, Emma couldn't help responding. Nothing would tip Hec off faster than if the Heart of Gold was shuttered up past opening time. She needed him to think that she was still here. Still here and weeping into her pillow that the mighty Hec Boehm had bested her.

Emma hadn't turned a trick since she'd stopped her wagons in Moke Hill more than a year ago. She'd been well and truly done letting men paw at her. She'd spent too many years flat on her back for the profit of others; it was *her* turn to make the money. And she was a *good* madam. She paid her girls fair and helped them move on as fast as they could. Very few girls liked whoring. It was something a girl did when she was out of options. Emma made sure that they could do it safely and save their money to start over. She watched them light out after a couple of months, cashed up and free of the trade, and she couldn't wait to follow in their footsteps. But she was in it to make more than just a *handful* of cash; the Heart of Gold was her ticket to freedom *forever*. It took time to build that kind of nest egg; she'd been patient, and now her time had come, and she was glad to say that, since coming to Moke Hill, she'd bought her ticket out of here without letting a single man poke his stick into her. Her body was hers again, and hers alone, and she planned to keep it that way. No matter how much gold the mud-splattered miners offered her, she turned them down. Emma was bright as a peacock, strutting the bar downstairs, teasing and laughing and making sure they all had a good time—but that good time wasn't going to be with her. Her girls were as fancy as she could make them: scrubbed and scented and dressed to the nines. And the miners were happy enough when she turned them aside, so long as it was into the arms of one of her girls.

But not Hec Boehm. That man had taken one look at Emma and decided that *he* was going to be the man to knock her flat on her back and keep her there. He was the kind of man who had to play with other people's toys, Emma thought sourly, a selfish, spoiled brat of a man. And he had all of Moke Hill in his sweaty fist.

"Will you be down soon?" Virgil asked through the door. "We're opening up and we need you to play hostess."

"*I'll* be down," Justine told Virgil firmly. "It's my place now."

Emma took the unsubtle hint and left Justine to deal with Virgil. She turned her attention to packing. So long as the place opened as usual, she was happy. She dusted off her carpetbag. It was pitifully small, but she had to travel light. It was such a shame to leave all her pretty dresses behind though, she thought with a sigh. Still, she couldn't very well wear screaming pink satin now that she wasn't running a whorehouse. She ran her fingers regretfully over her favorite dress, which was heaped on the chair where she'd left it the night before. No more frills and furbelows for her . . . let alone her peacock feather headdress, which sat in pride of place on her dresser. She felt a pang about leaving it—but what use were peacock feathers now? She was hardly going to wear them baking bread or tending her kitchen garden, was she? She'd have to get herself some nice, simple clothes. Something dowdy and respectable. Gingham, maybe. Hell. Not gingham. She'd rather be dead than wear gingham. If Hec Boehm hadn't been such a hasty old hog, she would have had time to prepare properly, she thought grumpily, and there would have been no question of resorting to gingham.

"I have to get ready," Justine said once Virge had gone, "so you'd best stop telling me not to fret and start working out how to deal with Hec Boehm and his boys."

"You worry too much." Emma sounded more confident than she felt. "As usual. I've already got a plan."

Justine rolled her eyes. Emma's plans were notorious. "What plan?"

Emma threw open the big wardrobe opposite her bed and

rifled through it. There was a screech of hangers on the metal rod. The wardrobe was stuffed full. This was where she kept the girls' best gear, as well as her own. She yanked out gowns, tossing them on the bed. Oh, it hurt to leave them behind. Maybe she could just take one . . .

"*What* plan?" Justine demanded.

"*This* one." Emma found what she was looking for and brandished the coat hanger high in triumph. Well, as high as she could. The damn thing weighed a ton. It was like holding up a sack of potatoes. "I'm going to be a nun!"

"You're not serious."

"Of course I'm serious! It's a *great* plan." She turned the heavy black habit around and gave it a quick once-over. It was an ugly thing, made of many layers of coarsely woven wool, and it was as heavy as sin. It was like a big, old, black tent. No one would make out her shape under it, and the wimple would hide her blazing red hair perfectly. If she wiped the paint off her face, she was sure no one would recognize her. She looked totally different without the rouge and the kohl. More like a hick straight off a farm than a fancy lady.

"It's the daftest thing you've suggested yet." Justine sat on the bed and put her face in her hands. "What did I do? Hec's going to torch this place and *you're* dressing up like a nun. I've just bought a pile of ashes."

"Don't be like that." Emma wrestled with the habit, trying to get it off the hanger. There were so many bits to it. How in hell did you put it on? No wonder Wilbur never got the girls naked. He wouldn't have been able to afford the time it took.

"Don't you think they'll find it odd to see a nun leaving a whorehouse?" Justine asked, exasperated. "Especially when they didn't see her *enter* it?"

Trust Justine to go throwing logic at her.

"It ain't my fault Hec got all het up and impatient," Emma told her. "I'm doing the best with what I've got." She tossed the loose bits of the habit over her dressing chair, where the black cloth looked even coarser and uglier against her pink dress. She turned her attention to the biggest, sackiest bit of it, trying to work out which end was the head.

Her instincts told her the nun getup would work, and Emma had learned to trust her instincts. They'd kept her alive this far.

People were *nice* to nuns. Respectful. She wasn't likely to be accosted travelling to Mariposa in this getup. It was the safest way to go—especially carrying a fortune in her saddlebags.

"You've got to stop looking for problems," she told Justine as she wedged the habit under her arm and hunted through the bottom of the wardrobe for her old black boots, "and start thinking in terms of solutions."

"This ain't a solution! It's just plain crazy."

"Hush." Emma crawled backward out of the wardrobe, boots in hand. "What's crazy is nagging me when it ain't my fault. You want to go nagging someone, go nag old Hec. He's the reason for all this fuss and bother." She dropped the boots on the floor by the chair and turned her back to Justine. "Unbutton me, will you?" She heard Jussy sigh as she got to her feet. "You worry too much," Emma said kindly as Justine started on the little buttons running down the back of the purple taffeta gown. Emma played with the precious little scalloped frill on her sleeve. How was she going to leave this behind? She loved this dress. It had a double layer of fancy flouncing near the hem that had taken her forever to sew. And it looked so nice with those peacock feathers.

Justine ignored her and kept on with the buttons.

They were totally unprepared when the door burst open.

Justine shrieked and Emma leapt for the chair, coming half out of her purple dress in the process. Her gun was somewhere under the pink satin gown, where she'd left it the night before. Stupid. She should have kept it close.

She snatched up the Colt, turning it on the intruder.

"Goddamn it, Calla!" she swore when she saw who had burst in. "I mighta shot you!"

Calla was staring wide-eyed at the pistol, which was still pointed at her chest. "Why in hell are you wanting to shoot me?"

"Didn't anyone ever tell you to knock?"

The Mexican girl pulled a face. "No one ever told me I'd be *shot* for not knocking."

"Well, I'm telling you now." Emma's hand was shaking as she lowered the pistol. "Now close that door, can't you see I ain't entirely decent?"

"I've got a letter for you," Calla said as she closed the door. She was mighty calm for someone who'd almost been shot. But then, in Moke Hill, almost getting shot happened on a weekly basis. "Virge said to bring it straight up. It's from Hec Boehm."

Justine snatched it out of her hand. "You can go now," she said shortly.

Emma snatched the note off Justine. "You can go too," she suggested.

"No." Justine and Calla spoke in unison, equally annoyed.

Emma kept hold of the pistol as she read the note. She was shaking something fierce now. She turned her back on the girls so they couldn't see. The letters swam before her eyes as she struggled to read Hec's crabbed handwriting.

"It's a love letter," she said, feeling weak with relief. Oh thank God. The idiot had believed her when she'd said she would think about becoming his mistress. And he'd clearly believed Teague that she was looking to say yes.

"A love letter?" Justine sounded disbelieving. "From Hec Boehm?"

"Well, a love letter of sorts." It was more of a detailed map of what he was going to do to her. That was about as loving as a man like Hec Boehm was likely to get. He seemed to think she'd enjoy his—what did he call it?—*manly persuasion.* She thrust the note at Justine and wriggled out of her purple taffeta dress. It rustled as it fell to the floor. Emma jumped over the skirts and snatched up the tenty bit of the nun's habit. She could feel the phantom press of Hec's hands around her throat. The sooner she was out of here, the better.

"Oh Lord." Justine sounded ill. "This is worse than I thought. He's a lot more than keen on you; he's *besotted.* What's he going to do when he finds you've gone? He'll kill *me.*"

Emma had worried about that. But she had a plan. "I'll leave him a note."

"A note?"

Emma was glad Justine wasn't the one with the gun. She was looking a little murderous. "Listen before you judge," she cautioned. Why didn't people ever trust her? Hadn't she shown herself to be a sensible woman? Hadn't she brought a couple of wagonloads of whores two thousand miles from Missouri,

across those horrid plains, without losing a single one to disease or disaster? Hadn't she built a thriving business? In fact,
not one thriving business, but *three*? But people still treated
her like she didn't know what she was doing.

"How do you put this thing on?" she asked, confounded by
the habit. No matter which way she turned, she couldn't make
heads or tails of it.

"Put the shift on first," Calla told her, stepping up to help.
She'd been raised on a mission and threw herself into the role
of Mother Superior with vigor when Wilbur came calling. As
she helped Emma into the sack-like shift and then lowered the
even-heavier full-body apron over the top, she didn't bother to
ask why her boss was dressing up as a nun. The Heart of Gold
was the kind of place where it was best not to ask too many
questions.

"How's a note going to help?"

Unless you were Justine. Justine never *stopped* asking
questions.

"It's not just about the note," Emma said, distracted by the
contraption Calla was trying to cram onto her head. "It'll be
the whole setup."

"You know, proper nuns would cut their hair off," Calla
said as she yanked the white coif down over Emma's ears.

"Good thing I ain't a proper nun." Although she *had* been
wondering how to get the henna out of her hair. Henna didn't
shift. Maybe cutting her hair wasn't such a bad idea. It could
be part of her whole fresh start, and when her hair grew back,
it would be her natural color. *Emma Jane Palmer's* natural
color. She didn't quite remember what that color was anymore.
Reddish. But probably darker, now that she was a grown
woman.

"*What* whole setup? You give me such a headache!" Justine
was whipping herself into a frenzy. She'd have to learn some
serenity if she wanted to survive running this place.

"You should try wearing this thing, if you want to talk
headaches." Emma tried to wedge her fingers between the coif
and her forehead. It was pinching off the blood supply to her
brain.

"*What whole set up?*" Justine was so angry her eyeballs
were just about bulging out of her head.

Emma took pity on her and put her out of her misery. "I'll tell him we're playing a little game, honey. He likes his games. At least, according to the girls. Most of the time I think he's more interested in playing than in poking."

"You can say that again," Calla agreed, hefting the stiff headdress over Emma's coif. "Sometimes he likes to play hide-and-seek. We leave clothes scattered about like clues and he has to come find us. We're supposed to be naked when he does, but often we cheat. He quite likes having a reason to get all angry and give us a spanking."

"It never ceases to amaze me how many men like spanking," Emma mused.

"I don't mind a spanking myself," Calla admitted. "It's better than being poked. I don't mind anything that keeps them busy, to be honest, so long as they poke less."

"Are you suggesting that you're going to play *hide-and-seek* with Hec Boehm?" Justine sounded appalled.

"Of course not. I'm just going to *tell* him I'm playing hide-and-seek. I've already written the note—it's over there by the peacock feathers."

Justine all but dove for it. Emma saw her nose wrinkle as she read it.

"Did I lay it on too thick?" Emma asked.

"This is insane," Justine muttered.

Emma watched Justine closely. Her gut told her the plan would work. But maybe her gut was an idiot.

Justine looked up. Her dark eyes were frightened. But not *as* frightened as they had been. "You're going to send him on a wild goose chase to Fiebre del Oro?"

"Clever, isn't it?" Emma couldn't keep the smugness out of her voice. It wasn't just clever; it was on the verge of genius. Everyone knew she'd funded Dottie to set up a whorehouse in the gold town up north. It made sense that she'd go there.

Her lusty little note to Hec should prove a successful bit of bait, anyway. He fancied himself a hunter, so she'd play the prey. She'd have the girls set up her room for Hec's arrival tomorrow. Candlelight, a hot bath, the good Spanish wine set out in the best glasses. Rose petals floating on the surface of the water, she thought in a fit of inspiration. Calla had done that once for the Judge and it had worked a treat. She'd have

Gina and JoBeth lead him upstairs, where they would prepare him for her. He'd like that. They could undress him and bathe him, and maybe give his little soldier a tug if that's what he was up for. They could feed him the wine until he was all hot and pink from it. Towel him down. Then Gina could read him Emma's note—Gina was the only one of the two of them who could read, so it would have to be her—while JoBeth acted out all the things Emma promised to do to Hec when he finally found her. That note (and JoBeth's close attentions) should get Hec into the game. Then he could light out the next morning for Dottie's place at Fiebre del Oro, where Dottie would have another room ready for him, with her homebrew instead of Spanish wine, and her German twins instead of Gina and Jo-Beth. Emma had sent Blossom's boy Henry on to Fiebre del Oro already, with a second note and instructions for Dottie. She'd paid generously for the German girls' time and included a nice extra chunk of cash for Dottie too. The twins could keep Hec happily entertained for the night, reading Emma's promises to him while they used their plump white bodies on him. The note would send him on to Sutter's Mill next, to a whorehouse named the Silver Tongue. A whorehouse that didn't actually exist, but it would take Hec a while to realize it. By the time he worked out she'd tricked him and had ridden all the way back to Moke Hill, she'd be safely through Angels Camp and Mariposa, where she'd sell off her shares in her other whorehouses. By the time old Hec reached Angels Camp, she'd be off to San Francisco to buy herself that nice little house with a view of the bay. And by then, she'd be a demure little nobody in gingham—hell, not gingham, surely muslin would be dowdy enough—and men like Hec Boehm wouldn't look twice at her. She'd be boring Miss Emma Palmer, with reddish hair and not-so-dowdy muslin gowns, tending her cabbage patch and growing freckled in the sun. Hec would be tearing up California looking for a woman who no longer existed.

It was genius.

"Clever!" Justine was shaking. "You think it's *clever?*"

Uh-oh. Justine was still mad.

"And what's he going to do to *me* when he gets back to Moke Hill?" Justine's face had gone a bit gray.

"That's the cleverest bit!" Emma beamed at her. "That's when you give him the *other* note!"

Justine's hand was starting to clench around the first note and Emma had to prize it out of her hand. She didn't fancy rewriting it; she was on a tight schedule. Calla followed her as she moved, jabbing the black nun's veil into place with hairpins.

"He'll shoot me before I can give him any more damn notes!" Justine shouted.

"Hush. You don't want the Koerners to hear you, do you?"

"Tilt your head back," Calla instructed Emma.

"There's more to this contraption?" Hell, no wonder nuns were celibate.

Calla laughed and wrapped the wimple around Emma's neck.

"What's the other note say?" Justine asked through clenched teeth.

"Just that he's not to shoot you because you're going to give him ten percent of the take from now on."

"I'm *what?*"

"It's perfect! That man would walk over hot coals to pick up a dropped dime. He ain't going to hurt you if it hurts business, and as we all know, business at the Heart of Gold is *good.*"

"That ten percent ain't yours to give away," Justine raged, "it's *mine!*"

"Fine, don't give it to him, then. But he might shoot you if'n you don't."

Justine cast about to see if there was a weapon handy. But the only one was in Emma's hot little hand.

"You selfish, two-faced . . ."

"Hush, Justine," Emma snapped, "stop talking before you say things you'll regret. I've been good to you, and you *know* I've been good to you. It hurts me that you don't trust me."

"Trust you! After this!"

Emma frowned. It didn't matter how nice you were to people; they always wanted to believe the worst of you. "You honestly think I'd treat you bad? After all we've been through together?"

"You just did," Justine said bitterly.

"No, honey, I just saved you from getting shot by Hec Boehm." Emma moved to the dresser and opened the top drawer. Buried in her tangle of unmentionables was a sheaf of papers. "If you think I'd steal from one of my girls, you don't know me at all." She held the papers out to Justine, who looked at them suspiciously.

"What's that?"

"My shares in Dottie's place in Fiebre del Oro. I had Teague put them in your name. It's a forty percent share. It'll more than compensate for the ten percent you'll lose to Hec from this place. It'll also give you wriggle room if he demands more. You can give him up to forty percent of here, without putting yourself out of pocket. Dottie's place is the biggest whorehouse in that hellhole; it's making more than here already. No one but us three here and Dottie need to know you own it. And Calla won't tell, will you?"

"Nope," Calla's voice was muffled. She had her head stuck in the wardrobe. Scavenging through Emma's gowns, probably, now she knew her ex-boss was leaving town.

Justine wilted. She read the documents, turning grayer by the minute. This time her color was leeched by flat-out shame.

"I'm sorry, Seline. I shoulda known you'd treat me fair."

Yes, she should have. Emma was surprised to find herself on the brink of tears. It shouldn't hurt to be thought ill of. But it did.

"My name ain't Seline, it's Emma," was all she could manage to say in reply.

Justine nodded and rolled the papers up. "*Sister* Emma," she corrected shakily, taking in the getup.

Emma looked down at herself. "You gotta admit, it's a good plan."

Justine nodded again, and when she spoke, her voice was tight. "I gotta admit . . . it's better than I gave you credit for." She looked like she was going to cry for a moment, but she pressed her lips together hard and pushed her emotions back down. That was something they were all good at. You didn't survive around here if you weren't. "You might need a belt," Justine observed.

"I got one!" Calla came crawling out of the wardrobe, wav-